A JENSEN FAMILY CHRISTMAS

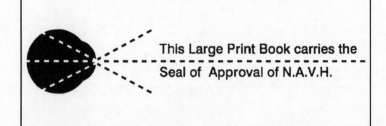

A JENSEN FAMILY CHRISTMAS

WILLIAM W. JOHNSTONE
WITH
J. A. JOHNSTONE

THORNDIKE PRESS
A part of Gale, a Cengage Company

GALE
A Cengage Company

Farmington Hills, Mich • San Francisco • New York • Waterville, Maine
Meriden, Conn • Mason, Ohio • Chicago

LIBRARY OF CONGRESS CIP DATA ON FILE.
CATALOGUING IN PUBLICATION FOR THIS BOOK
IS AVAILABLE FROM THE LIBRARY OF CONGRESS

ISBN-13: 978-1-4328-7147-5 (hardcover alk. paper)

Published in 2019 by arrangement with Kensington Books, an imprint
of Kensington Publishing Corp.

Printed in Mexico
1 2 3 4 5 6 7 23 22 21 20 19

A Jensen Family Christmas

THE SUGARLOAF RANCH, COLORADO, 1902

Nobody thought about Christmas on the hottest day of the year.

Denise Nicole Jensen wore a man's butternut shirt with the sleeves rolled up over tanned, smoothly muscled forearms. After reining her horse to a halt, she lifted her left hand and removed the brown Stetson she wore. Thick, curly blond hair that had been tucked up inside the hat tumbled free around her shoulders.

With her right arm, she sleeved beads of sweat from her face and said, "Well, hell."

If Sally Jensen had been here, she would have reminded her daughter that ladies didn't curse, but Denny's mother was miles away, at the headquarters of the vast Sugarloaf Ranch. And Denny was disgusted at the sight that met her eyes when she topped the rise, so she believed a little cussin' was justified.

She might do even more of it before she

7

was finished here.

She suspected the calf had wandered into the mudhole first and had got stuck, and then the mama cow had responded to her baby's bawls for help, had waded out there, and had got bogged down, too.

The calf was in the most danger of being sucked under, so Denny knew she needed to go after it first. She gathered up her hair with her right hand and stuffed it back under the hat. Then she unhooked the coil of rope from her saddle and started shaking out a loop as she nudged her mount down the slope.

Her mother wasn't particularly fond of Denny dressing like a man, riding the range, and working like one of the Sugarloaf's regular cowboys, either, but Denny had an argument in her favor that was hard for Sally to dispute: Sally had done much the same thing when she and her husband, Smoke, Denny's father, had established the ranch here in Colorado's high country a quarter of a century earlier.

Denny rode to the edge of the mudhole, which was about thirty feet across. Both the cow and the calf were still struggling and bawling. Those pathetic cries were what had attracted Denny's attention in the first place.

She swung the loop over her head a couple of times and then cast the rope at the calf. Over the years, Denny had spent a lot of time practicing with a lasso, even when she was staying with relatives in Europe. The loop sailed out and settled flawlessly over the calf's head.

Denny jerked it closed with a flick of her wrist, then took a dally around the saddle horn and started backing her horse. She couldn't pull too hard, because she didn't want to choke the calf. The extra support from the taut rope allowed the calf to get better footing and make some progress toward the edge of the mudhole. Denny continued backing her horse to keep any slack out of the rope.

A few minutes later, with a sucking sound, the calf broke free of the mud. The thick brown gunk coated the critter's legs, belly, and chest.

Denny dismounted and went over to take the rope off the calf's neck. She rubbed its nose and said, "There you go. Now I'll get your mama out of —"

Free again, the calf turned and lunged right back toward the mudhole, obviously intent on reaching its mother.

Denny's eyes widened in surprise. She exclaimed, "You little bast—" as she threw herself toward the calf and grabbed it around the neck to try to stop it from getting right back into trouble.

The calf was strong and jerked Denny off her feet. She managed to hang on for several seconds before her hands and arms slipped on the mud-slick hide. The calf had pulled her into the mudhole, so when she lost her grip and fell, she landed face-first in the smelly stuff.

Gagging and gasping, she pushed herself up before the mud filled her nose and mouth, although it covered her face and the front of her body. She wasn't far into the mudhole, so she was able to turn herself around, crawl out, and flop down on the grass next to it.

Meanwhile, the calf promptly got bogged down again and started complaining.

Denny lay there for several minutes, too disgusted by this turn of events even to move. Then she sat up, pawed mud away from her eyes, and started blistering the air with a blue streak of curses that would have shocked any of her father's ranch hands but made them proud of her inventiveness.

The sound of delighted laughter from the top of the rise behind her made her fall silent.

Denny remained seated on the grass but

half turned so she could look up the slope. The sight of her mud-masked face drew renewed gales of laughter from the three men on horseback who sat there looking at her.

"What the hell's so funny?" she demanded.

Her twin brother, Louis Arthur Jensen, wiped tears from his eyes and grinned as he said, "I was . . . I was just thinking that if all those dukes and counts who tried to romance you over in Europe could see you now, they wouldn't be so quick to try to seduce you!"

"You just shut up, Louis."

The two men with Louis were also twins, although the resemblance between them wasn't nearly as pronounced as it was between the younger siblings. William "Ace" Jensen was dark haired and broad shouldered, while Benjamin "Chance" Jensen was slender and had sandy hair. They were forty years old, almost two decades older than their cousins.

Ace studied the scene briefly with keen eyes and said, "What happened, Denny? You pulled that calf out, and then it ran right back in and pulled you with it?"

"That's right," Denny said. She struggled to her feet, a filthy, bedraggled figure now.

11

"Maybe I'll just shoot both brutes and be done with it."

"No you won't," Louis said. "You'd never harm a defenseless animal, and you know it."

Denny's eyes narrowed as she said, "Maybe I'll just shoot me a laughing hyena instead."

Ace heeled his horse into motion. "Come on, Chance," he said. "Let's drag those cows out of there."

Chance said, "Do I look like a cowboy to you?"

It was true. In his brown suit, white shirt, string tie, and cream-colored Stetson, he wasn't dressed for range work. Chance's natural habitat was saloons, where he excelled as a poker player. From time to time, he and Ace took jobs — usually something that involved guns and trouble — but it was mostly Chance's skill with the pasteboards that supported their drifting ways.

"All right, I'll take care of it," Ace said.

While Louis and Chance rode down and dismounted to stand with Denny on the mudhole's bank, Ace shook out a loop and dabbed it on the calf first. When he had pulled the calf to safety, he snubbed the rope shorter and dismounted, leaving his horse to stand and prevent the calf from returning to the mudhole.

Then he swung up into the saddle of Denny's mount and used her lasso, which was still wrapped around the saddle horn, to catch the mama cow's horns and gradually work her out of the mudhole. Ace could have been a top hand if he'd wanted to be, so it didn't really take him long to rescue the two animals.

He turned them loose and sent them trotting off, then started coiling the ropes.

"Don't feel bad, Denny," he told his young cousin. "You would have gotten them out."

"Sooner or later," Louis added, earning himself another glare from his sister. "You know, I believe there's almost as much mud on you as there is in that bog."

Chance picked up Denny's Stetson, which had fallen on the grass when the calf jerked her off her feet.

"Your hat's all right," he said. "I suppose that's something to be thankful for, anyway."

Denny snatched it away from him and hung it on her saddle horn.

"There's a swimming hole in the creek about half a mile from here," she said. "I'm going to go wash this mud off." The hot sun would dry her clothes and hair quickly enough, she thought. "Mother doesn't have to know about this . . . debacle."

"We'll come with you," Ace said.

"You most certainly will not!" Denny's face flushed warmly.

"We'll keep our backs turned," Louis said. "Nobody's interested in peeking at a scrawny little thing like you, anyway."

"We'll sort of stand guard while you clean up, in case some other riders come along," Ace said. "Just cousins helping each other out."

"All right. I suppose." Denny took hold of her horse's reins but didn't mount. She didn't want to get mud all over the saddle. Instead, she began walking, leading the horse.

Her brother and cousins came with her, leading their mounts, as well.

Rocks in the creek had formed a partial dam, creating a natural swimming hole. Trees on the bank shaded it, giving it a cool, appealing look even on a blistering hot day like this one. Louis, Ace, and Chance sat on a fallen log, with their backs to the swimming hole, as Denny waded into it and then dived under the surface. When she came up, she began taking off the soaked, muddy garments so she could wash them out.

"As filthy as Denny was, it may take a while for her to get clean," Louis said.

"We'll have to pass the time somehow. Have the two of you had any new adventures since you last visited the Sugarloaf?"

"Adventures? Us?" Chance scoffed. "You know things are always peaceful wherever we go."

Ace said, "Actually, we haven't run into any trouble for a while. Life's been downright tranquil."

"That's hard to believe," Louis said. "Trouble always seems to follow anyone named Jensen."

"We got that idea, even before we knew we were part of this family," Ace said."

Denny could hear them from where she was in the swimming hole, so as she scrubbed mud out of her shirt, she said, "That's right. The first few times you got mixed up with our father and Uncle Luke, you didn't know yet that you were related, did you?"

"No idea," Chance said. "We just thought we had the same last name."

"We started to get a mite suspicious, though," Ace said, "when Luke mentioned he'd known a woman with the same first name as our mother. And it wasn't a common name, either. Lettie."

Chance said, "I figured Ace was just thinking too much. He's got a habit of doing that.

15

Of course, in this case, it turned out he was right. Your uncle Luke really *was* our father."

"How did you finally find out?" Louis asked. "I don't think I've ever heard that story."

"Neither have I," Denny said. "I'd like to know."

"It's a long story," Ace warned. "It'll take a while to tell."

"We have the time," Louis said, "and nothing else to do while Denny tries to get all that mud off."

"I'm working on it!" Denny said defensively from the swimming hole behind them.

Ace thumbed back his black hat and said, "Well, this was more than fifteen years ago when it all got started, and the weather sure wasn't as hot as it is right now. In fact, Christmas was coming on, which means it was mighty cold here in this part of Colorado . . ."

CHAPTER 1
BIG ROCK, COLORADO

The blue sky was so clear, it almost glittered, but the sunshine didn't pack much warmth as a cold breeze swept along the streets of Big Rock, Colorado. Smoke Jensen's wife, Sally, had insisted on pulling the thick lap robe over his legs, too, as they rode in the buggy to town, and if Smoke was being honest about it, he didn't really mind. The robe felt good.

She had said that he ought to wear his gloves, too, but he wasn't willing to go that far. A man couldn't draw and fire a gun as quickly when he had a glove on. Even though Smoke wasn't expecting any trouble in the settlement, he knew better than to run unnecessary risks.

Being careless wasn't how he had survived all the dangers that had come his way during more than three eventful decades of living on the frontier.

"You must be about frozen," he said to

17

Sally as he drove toward the general store.

"Actually, I'm quite comfortable," she replied. She wore a fur hat with flaps that came down over her ears. A scarf was wound around her throat, leather gloves were on her hands, and the bulky fleece-lined coat she wore completely concealed the supple lines of her figure.

Despite all that, Smoke thought she was beautiful. He would always think she was the most beautiful woman he had ever seen.

"I still say Pearlie or Cal could have brought the buckboard in for those supplies you wanted."

"They have work to do," Sally said.

"And I don't?" Smoke asked with a snort. "I own the dang spread, after all. Well, *we* do."

"I'm glad you corrected yourself." Her voice was tart, but the smile she gave him took any sting out of it. "Anyway, I don't *know* exactly what I want. I have to think about it while I'm shopping to actually figure everything out. I need the makings for Christmas dinner, and even though we have decorations, we can always use more."

"I'm sure whatever you decide will be perfect."

"You're just saying that because you don't want to go shopping with me."

18

"No, I just have complete confidence in you," Smoke said with a smile.

Sally laughed and shook her head. She was still smiling when Smoke brought the buggy to a halt in front of Goldstein's Mercantile, where she would shop before visiting Foster and Matthews Grocery. He took the lap robe off of them, folded it, and placed it behind the seat. Then he jumped lithely to the ground and turned back to help her climb down from the vehicle.

Once Sally was on the ground, Smoke moved to tie the horse's reins to the hitchrack in front of the store. The horse was well trained and wouldn't bolt except in extreme conditions, but again, there was never any point in being careless.

"I'm going to say hello to Louis," Smoke told Sally, "but I should be back by the time you're finished at the grocery store. If I'm not, send somebody to find me."

Everyone in Big Rock knew Smoke Jensen. Although he would never get a swelled head about such a thing, he was the most famous citizen of the valley where the town and the Sugarloaf Ranch were located.

His fame extended well beyond those environs, too. Up in Idaho, for example, people still talked in awe about how he had killed more than two dozen gun-wolves in a bloody war against the men responsible for the deaths of his father, his first wife, and his unborn child.

There were plenty of other places where folks still remembered the man known variously as Kirby Jensen (his real name); Buck West, the wanted outlaw; and Smoke Jensen (the name most knew him by). For a short period of time after he and Sally had founded the Sugarloaf and settled down there, he had attempted to live anonymously, in the hope that he could put his reputation as maybe the fastest gun in the West behind him for good.

That hadn't worked, of course. Few men could deny their true nature for very long, and Smoke's nature was to battle against evil wherever he found it. So he hadn't tried to keep who he was a secret any longer, but he *had* made a determined effort to live his life as a peaceful, happily married rancher.

Sometimes that had worked. Sometimes it hadn't. And despite his best intentions, the legend of Smoke Jensen had grown.

The town itself was part of that legend. It had been founded as a result of Smoke's clash with a power-hungry man determined to rule this part of the state by blood and gun smoke and any other means necessary. But that man had long since gone under,

Smoke was still here, and Big Rock was thriving.

So it was no surprise that folks nodded and smiled at him as he left Sally at the store and walked along the street. Men shook his hand and slapped him on the back. Smoke had a grin and a friendly word for all of them.

At first glance, especially in the sheepskin coat he wore, he didn't seem that impressive a figure. He was just a man in the prime of life, with a face a little too rugged to be considered classically handsome, and ash blond hair under a brown Stetson.

A second look, though, revealed how wide his shoulders were, and when you watched him move, you could see the leashed power and easy grace of the man. He was like one of the big cats that could be found in the high mountains. He never seemed to rush, but he could be blindingly fast and deadly when he needed to be.

Today he was just bound for Longmont's, a combination saloon, restaurant, and gambling house run by his old friend Louis Longmont, where he intended to have a cup of coffee and invite Louis to come out to the Sugarloaf for Christmas the next week.

Louis stood at the bar in Longmont's, talking to the only bartender who was on

21

duty. No customers were bellied up to the hardwood, drinking, but a number of the cloth-covered tables were occupied by diners enjoying a belated breakfast from the kitchen.

"Good morning, Smoke," the dapper, dark-haired gambler and gunman greeted his old friend. "What brings you to Big Rock this morning?"

"Sally needed some things from the store," Smoke said.

"Ah, the best reason of all, making sure your beautiful wife is happy."

"I notice that you're not married," Smoke pointed out.

"Well . . . what's best for one man may not be for another." Louis changed the subject. "Would you like a drink?"

"No, but I'd take a cup of hot coffee. I could use a little warming up after the buggy ride into town."

The temperature was comfortable inside Longmont's, with fires burning in two potbellied stoves tucked into opposite corners, not to mention the heat that filtered out into the main room from the ovens in the kitchen. Despite that, Smoke was still a little chilled inside, but he knew the coffee would take care of that.

"I'll get it, boss," the bartender offered.

"Thanks, Wiley," Louis said. To Smoke, he went on, "Shall we sit down?"

"I've been sitting on the ride in. Feels good to stand for a while." Smoke paused. "You have any plans for celebrating Christmas?"

"I assume I'll be here. People who don't have families need somewhere to go on Christmas, so they won't be alone."

"Well, you *have* a family . . . Sally and me, and Pearlie and Cal and all the other folks on the Sugarloaf. You have folks working for you who can keep the place going just fine, so why don't you ride out and spend Christmas Day with us?"

"Why, Smoke, I'm touched," Louis said. "I wouldn't want to intrude —"

"I just told you, we consider you a member of the family."

Louis smiled and said, "In that case, I'd be glad to —"

The bartender, who was carrying the cup of coffee from the kitchen door to the bar, stopped short as he looked out the front window. He said, "What in blazes?"

That caught the attention of Smoke and Louis, who followed the bartender's gaze and saw several fancy carriages and a number of riders moving past in the street outside.

"Is it a parade?" Louis murmured.

"More like a caravan of some sort," Smoke said. He stepped over to the bartender and took the cup from the man, nodding his thanks, then said to Louis, "Let's go take a look."

He strode to the door and opened it, letting cold air gust in for a moment. He stepped out onto the boardwalk, and Louis followed quickly, closing the door behind him.

Because of the chilly day, steam curled thickly from the coffee as Smoke lifted the cup to his lips and sipped from it. The hot liquid was strong and bracing. He had unbuttoned his coat when he went into Longmont's, and he didn't bother fastening it again just yet.

Louis stuck his hands in his trouser pockets to keep them warm and said, "They appear to be strangers to Big Rock."

"I've never seen 'em before, that's for sure," Smoke said.

Four good-sized black carriages decorated with silver and brass trim were passing Longmont's. Each carriage was pulled by a team of four fine black horses. Their harnesses were also adorned with silver fittings. The drivers were Mexican and wore flat-crowned hats instead of the tall sombreros

24

common below the border. As Smoke and Louis watched, the last carriage in line pulled out of the procession and stopped in front of Goldstein's Mercantile, where Smoke had left Sally a short time earlier.

Smoke made a quick count and determined that twenty men on horseback accompanied the carriages. They were about evenly divided between Mexicans and Americans, but they all had a couple of things in common.

They were heavily armed, and their weapons and their hard-planed faces marked them as hired gunmen, a breed with which Smoke was all too familiar.

"To quote my bartender," Louis muttered as he stood beside Smoke on the boardwalk, "what in blazes?"

Several of the riders cast flinty glances toward the two men on the boardwalk as they rode past. Not looking for trouble, exactly, but checking to see if any signs of it were brewing. Smoke returned the looks steadily.

"Looks like they're headed for the sheriff's office," he commented.

It was true. The first carriage pulled up in front of the stone and log building that housed Sheriff Monte Carson's office as well as Big Rock's jail. The driver hopped down from the box and hurried to open the door on the side of the carriage next to the boardwalk.

A man in a thick fur coat and flat-crowned black hat stepped out of the vehicle. Just as his right foot touched the ground, the team lurched forward a step for some reason. That made the carriage jerk, and the man getting out of it lost his balance and almost fell. He would have if the driver hadn't reacted quickly and caught hold of his arm to steady him.

Despite that bit of assistance, the man in the fur coat yanked his arm free and pushed the driver back a step. The driver had a braided leather quirt dangling from its strap around his left wrist. The man in the fur coat ripped it away from him, strode forward, and started slashing at the horses in the team. One of the riders who had dismounted caught hold of the leaders' harness so the team wouldn't bolt as the man in the fur coat continued striking them with the quirt. Clouds of steam from the animals' hot breath filled the air around them as they whinnied in pain.

"Oh, no," Louis said softly as he looked over at Smoke.

"If you don't mind, Louis," Smoke said

tightly as he thrust the cup toward his friend, "hold my coffee for a minute."

CHAPTER 2

"I believe I'll take some of the red lace and the green lace, as well, Mr. Goldstein," Sally told the mercantile's proprietor. "I'll need about twenty feet of each. I can use it to trim that white linen I'm buying and make the new tablecloth for the dining room look even more festive."

"I'm sure it'll be beautiful, Mrs. Jensen," Goldstein said.

While he was cutting off the lengths that Sally wanted, the store's double front doors opened and several people entered. Sally felt the chilly wind sweep past her, even though she was standing at the counter in the rear of the store. Curious, she looked over her shoulder to see who had come in.

Two women had entered the store, one leading the way confidently, the other following in a more subservient manner. A pair of men trailed them inside, but they, too, hung back, as if they were just following

28

orders. One of them closed the doors.

The years Sally had spent with Smoke had taught her to check for threats whenever anything unusual or unexpected happened. She didn't recognize any of these four people, so she took a closer look, starting with the two men, because if there was going to be any trouble, likely it would come from them.

All Sally had to do was glance at them to recognize their type. She knew the lean, hard faces; the apparently casual stances, which actually masked a readiness to explode into action; the way they wore their guns so the weapons would be easy to draw. She had encountered too many hard cases not to know them when she saw them.

Both men were American, but the women were Spanish or Mexican. The one in the lead was young, probably in her mid-twenties, with clear, slightly olive-tinted skin and hair as black as midnight tightly coiled on her head. Her heart-shaped face was very pretty. Dark eyes flashed under finely plucked and shaped brows.

She wore a black quilted coat, which was partially open to reveal an expensive dark red traveling outfit. Black boots polished to a high gleam stuck out from under the long skirt. Rings glittered on her fingers, and a pearl brooch was at her throat.

There was a fine line between flashy and elegant, thought Sally, but this young woman managed to land on the elegant side of that line.

Her companion was much older and stouter, in a dark dress, coat, and shawl. The older woman's appearance and manner told Sally that she was the younger one's servant.

"Hello," the young woman greeted Sally and Goldstein as she came up to the counter. "Please don't let me interrupt what you're doing." Her English was flawless, but her voice had a faint accent to it.

"I'll be right with you, señorita," Goldstein said.

"Señora," she corrected him. "I am Doña Mariana Angelina Aguilar."

Goldstein nodded and said, "Of course."

Sally introduced herself to the newcomer, extending a gloved hand and saying, "I'm Sally Jensen. Welcome to Big Rock, Señora Aguilar. Are you just passing through?"

The young woman took Sally's hand. "No, I believe my husband, Don Juan Sebastian Aguilar, plans to remain here in the vicinity. He has a ranch and property nearby."

Sally couldn't help but frown at that statement. She said, "He does? I'm afraid I don't recall the name . . ."

"His claim is newly established."

Sally was more confused than before, but it was none of her business. She shrugged a little, smiled, and said, "Well, I hope you enjoy your new home. This is a wonderful area. The people are very friendly. The weather is nice most of the year —"

Doña Mariana shuddered. "It's so cold here," she declared. "Sometimes it is cold in Mexico, but not like this."

"It *is* pretty chilly out there today," Sally agreed.

Goldstein set the two coils of lace Sally wanted on the counter and asked, "Is there anything else I can get for you, Mrs. Jensen?"

"Let me think about it," Sally said. "Why don't you go ahead and see what Señora Aguilar needs?"

Goldstein nodded his agreement and turned toward Doña Mariana, but before he could say anything else, everyone in the store heard a sudden burst of loud, angry voices from outside, even with the doors closed.

The man in the fur coat was still venting his rage on the horses as Smoke approached. One of the riders noticed Smoke's determined stride and nudged his mount over to get in Smoke's way.

"Better move along, señor," the rider said. "This does not concern you."

Smoke barely glanced up at the man, noting his thin, drooping mustache, scarred chin, and cold-eyed gaze.

"I think it does," Smoke said flatly as he angled to the side to go around the rider.

The man moved his horse again and put his hand on the butt of his gun. "I told you —"

"And I'm telling you," Smoke said. "Make me pull my gun and I'll kill you."

The man cocked his head to the side, as if surprised, but he edged his horse back to give Smoke some room. However, as Smoke walked past, the man pulled his left foot free of the stirrup and drew back his lower leg, intent on kicking him in the back.

Smoke whirled. He'd expected the man to try something. The kick never had a chance of landing. Smoke caught hold of the man's boot in midair and heaved upward. With a startled yell, the man waved his arms wildly, toppled off the horse's other side, and crashed into the street.

Smoke turned around and started toward the carriage again.

The man holding the team had seen what

happened. His watchful eyes followed Smoke. The man in the fur coat was still caught up in his frenzy of rage against the horses, but he seemed to be tiring. He wasn't swinging the quirt as hard or as fast now.

But any vicious cruelty like that was too much for Smoke to tolerate. He stayed on his course.

A couple of the other riders acted like they were about to intercept him, but a gesture from the man holding the horses made them pause. He seemed to be telling them to let Smoke come ahead.

Or maybe he was just instructing them to let the first man handle the problem, because the man came around his horse and charged at Smoke from behind. His hat had fallen off when Smoke dumped him out of the saddle, and his black hair hung askew over his eyes. The morning sunlight flashed on the blade of the knife in his hand.

Again, the attack didn't take Smoke by surprise. He heard the rush of footsteps closing in on him and ducked under the knife as the man slashed at him. Smoke straightened, and his right fist shot out to land squarely on the man's jaw. The solid blow knocked the man back against his horse. He caught hold of the stirrup with his free hand to steady himself, then lunged at Smoke again.

"Carve him up, Pedro!" yelled one of the other riders. The rest of the men shouted encouragement, as well.

The man was fast, but Smoke's superb reflexes allowed him to dodge as the knife flickered toward him again and again. Then, as Smoke leaned aside from a thrust aimed at his throat, he caught hold of the man's wrist with his left hand. The muscles in Smoke's shoulders bunched as he squeezed. Bones ground together in the man's wrist as he cried out in pain and dropped the knife.

Smoke's right fist came around in a hook that smashed his attacker to the ground. He could tell by the way the man lay there whimpering that all the fight had been knocked out of him this time.

When Smoke turned back toward the carriage, he saw that the man in the fur coat had stopped beating the horses. Instead, he glared at Smoke with a furious expression on his lean, hawklike face. A pencil-line mustache adorned his upper lip. Childhood illness had pockmarked his cheeks. He was in his forties, Smoke judged, and held himself as if he were an aristocrat — or at least considered himself one.

Smoke came up to the team and looked at the man over the horses' backs. Seeing the bloody stripes on their hides from the quirt just angered him more.

But before he could say anything, the man in the fur coat demanded, "Who do you think you are, assaulting my man that way?"

"He attacked me," Smoke said. "I just stopped him from doing it. If you really care about him, mister, you ought to be thankful. I could have killed him."

"You reckon so, do you?" asked the man holding the team. "Pedro's pretty fast on the draw."

Smoke looked over at the man, who was tall and rangy, with a lantern jaw and a thatch of straw-like hair poking out from under his hat. His voice held an unmistakable Texas drawl.

"I think there's a pretty good chance he wouldn't have been fast enough," Smoke said, "but I guess when you get right down to it, you never know until the time comes, do you?"

"No, I reckon not," the Texan said, sounding a little amused.

"What do you want?" The question came from the man in the fur coat. "What right have you to interfere in my affairs?"

"I wanted you to stop beating these poor

horses," Smoke said. "You had no right to do that."

"They are mine to do with as I please! They failed to stand still when they stopped, as they have been trained to do. They could have caused me to fall and be injured!"

"Seems to me like you're mad because you're embarrassed about almost falling. Nobody thought a thing about it, mister, and it's sure no reason to hurt these animals."

The man raised the quirt, and the hand holding it shook a little from the depth of the anger he felt. He looked like he wanted to come around the horses and slash at Smoke himself, but his feet stayed on the ground, as if planted there.

"Hinton," he said through clenched teeth, "I want you to take out your gun and shoot two of these beasts."

The Texan frowned and said, "I don't know, Don Sebastian. They're pretty good horses, and they cost a pretty penny. Seems like sort of a waste —"

"I told you, take out your gun and kill two of them!"

Smoke looked over at the rawboned Texan, thought about what the man in the fur coat had called him, and said, "That wouldn't be Travis Hinton, would it? From Big

Spring?"

"Might be." Hinton's eyes narrowed. "Do we know each other?"

"We've never crossed trails," Smoke said, "but I've heard of you."

Hinton probed a tooth with his tongue for a second and then asked softly, "Have I heard of you before, amigo?"

"Maybe. The name's Smoke Jensen."

There might have been a little surprise in Hinton's pale gray eyes, just for a second, or there might not have been. Smoke couldn't really tell. But then the man's thin lips curved slightly in a smile and he said, "Yeah, I've heard of you, all right."

"Are you going to stand there and talk all day, or are you going to kill these horses like I told you to?" Spittle flew from the man's mouth as he practically screamed the words. "Or must I do it myself?"

He yanked open his fur coat and started to reach inside it.

CHAPTER 3

Smoke stiffened, knowing the man was going for a gun. At the same time, Hinton let go of the team's harness and moved back a half step to give him room to reach the revolver holstered on his hip. Smoke knew without looking that all the other gunwolves on horseback around him were ready to draw and fire, as well. All it would take for the shooting to start would be for him to pull his own iron. Given how outnumbered he was, they would probably kill him. . . .

But he would get lead in Don Sebastian first, and maybe Travis Hinton, too.

Before anyone could draw, a woman's voice cut through the frigid air, calling, "Sebastian, *mi amor*. What is wrong?"

The man stopped what he was doing before the gun came out from under his coat. He seemed to force himself to relax, and he put an unconvincing smile on his face as he turned to greet the woman who had called out to him.

"Mariana, dearest, I thought you stopped at the store."

"I did," the young woman said. She had come to a stop on the boardwalk. Smoke was a little surprised to see that Sally was with her, as well as an older Mexican woman. "But then I heard all the shouting, and it sounded like there might be trouble. I was worried about you, Sebastian."

From the corner of his eye, Smoke saw Travis Hinton make another conciliatory gesture to the men on horseback. Hinton had a reputation as a fast, ruthless gun for hire, but clearly, he didn't want a shoot-out on Big Rock's main street this morning. On that much, at least, Smoke agreed with him.

The feeling of impending violence in the air eased slightly.

"There is no reason for you to be concerned," the man in the fur coat told the young woman. "A minor disagreement, that is all."

"I don't reckon it was so minor to those horses," Smoke said. "They're the ones bleeding."

For a second, Don Sebastian's lips drew back from his teeth in a snarl. Then he controlled his anger and snapped at Hin-

39

ton, "See to it that the horses are well cared for. Spare no expense."

"Of course, Don Sebastian," Hinton said.

Sally asked, "Is everything all right, Smoke?"

He nodded and said, "Sure."

The young woman looked over at Sally and asked, "The two of you know each other?"

"I should say so. Doña Mariana, this is my husband, Smoke Jensen."

She smiled at Smoke. She was a very attractive young woman to start with, he noted, and the smile made her more so.

"Señor Jensen, your wife is charming."

"Yes, I know that better than anyone, I suppose." Even though all hell had been on the verge of breaking loose mere moments earlier, Smoke's natural politeness made him reach up — with his left hand — and remove his hat. "It's a pleasure to meet you, señora."

Sally said, "Smoke, this is Doña Mariana Aguilar."

Still smiling, the woman said, "I see you have already met my husband."

Smoke looked over the backs of the team again and said, "We haven't been formally introduced."

By now, Travis Hinton had climbed onto

the driver's box and taken up the reins. He got the team moving and drove the carriage out from between Smoke and the man in the fur coat. Standing there stiffly, the man gave Smoke a curt nod.

"I am Don Juan Sebastian Aguilar," he said. "Now we have been introduced, Señor Jensen."

Even though Smoke didn't like Aguilar and knew he never would, he supposed it wouldn't hurt anything for him to unbend a little. Often it took the bigger man to make the first move.

"What brings you to Big Rock, Señor Aguilar?" he asked.

"Business," the man replied, but his wife said, "We have come to take possession of our new home, Señor Jensen."

Smoke glanced at Sally, who gave him a tiny shrug to indicate that she didn't really know what was going on, either.

"You bought property around here?" he asked Aguilar.

"That was not necessary. It is mine by right."

Now Smoke was really confused. He said, "As far as I know, all the land around here has been bought and filed on properly. That wasn't the case when Sally and I got here. In fact, the whole valley was open range.

41

But that's not the way it is anymore, and I hadn't heard about anybody putting their place up for sale. Although . . . Wait, you said you didn't buy a spread."

"Mr. Jensen," Aguilar said, "have you ever heard of the Treaty of Guadalupe Hidalgo?"

The man's condescending tone put Smoke's teeth on edge again. He controlled that irritation and said calmly, "Of course I have."

"Part of the Treaty of Guadalupe Hidalgo specified that —"

"Talk, talk, talk!" Doña Mariana interrupted her husband. "Sebastian, it is *cold* out here. Can you and Mr. Jensen not discuss business inside, somewhere where it is warm?"

Aguilar jerked a hand toward Monte Carson's office and said, "I had hoped to speak with the sheriff, since he represents the authorities here in Big Rock."

"Monte doesn't appear to be here," Smoke said, "or you would have seen him before now. He would have shown up to see what all the yelling was about earlier. He's probably been called out of town on some law business." Once again, Smoke told himself to be the bigger man and extend an olive branch, despite his dislike for the man. "Why don't you come with me over to my friend's restaurant, and we'll have some coffee?"

Travis Hinton had driven the carriage along the street to Patterson's Livery Stable, where the horses would receive top-notch care. He came back, rubbing ungloved hands together, in time to hear Smoke's suggestion.

"That sounds like a good idea to me, Don Sebastian," the Texas gunman said. "I could use some warmin' up." He grinned at Smoke. "You think this friend of yours might have a bottle of whiskey to sweeten that coffee a mite?"

"Considering that Longmont's is as much a saloon as it is a restaurant, I think that's a pretty good bet," Smoke said.

"Longmont," Hinton repeated. He cocked an eyebrow. "Louis Longmont?"

"One and the same."

"Reckon I've heard of *him,* too."

"Very well," Aguilar said. "I will join you, Señor Jensen."

"Good," his wife said. She smiled at Sally. "And you and I will resume our shopping, Señora Jensen?"

"Might as well," Sally said. "I still need some things."

They turned and headed back down the boardwalk, trailed by the silent older woman in a black coat and dress, as well as by two of Aguilar's gunmen. Smoke figured their job was to watch over Doña Mariana.

Smoke held out a hand toward Longmont's and said, "Right this way, gentlemen."

Louis was still standing out in front of his place, holding Smoke's coffee cup in his left hand. Smoke noticed that Louis's coat was pushed back a little, so it would have been easier to reach his gun if a fight had broken out. Smoke had no doubt that his friend would have waded right in to back his play.

Twenty hired guns against Smoke Jensen and Louis Longmont? Those were still such overwhelming odds that both Smoke and Louis probably would have died.

But there would have been a large number of dead men on the other side, too, and any survivors would have then had to worry about Smoke's brothers, Luke and Matt, and the old mountain man called Preacher, not to mention Monte Carson, Pearlie and Cal, and all the friends Smoke had across the West who could handle a gun with speed and skill.

No, sir, it wouldn't have ended well for them, no matter whether they lived through today or not.

But, thankfully, that hadn't happened.

Now he could afford to be civil to Don Juan Sebastian Aguilar, and then the man could go on about his business. With any luck, Smoke wouldn't ever have to see him again.

"I'm afraid your coffee's gotten cold, Smoke," Louis said as Smoke and his two companions walked up. Behind them, the other carriages rolled on up the street toward Patterson's.

"You can have your cook warm it up with some more from the pot," Smoke said, "and pour fresh cups for these two fellows here. Louis, this is Don Juan Sebastian Aguilar."

"Señor Aguilar," Louis said as he nodded politely to the man. "I'm Louis Longmont."

Smoke noticed that his friend hadn't said that the meeting was a pleasure, as Louis nearly always would have, for the sake of politeness, if nothing else. After seeing the way Aguilar treated animals, though, being around him would *never* be a pleasure for Louis — or Smoke.

Aguilar returned the nod but just grunted. He had probably noticed the slight but wasn't going to do anything about it, at least not right now.

"And this is Travis Hinton," Smoke went on.

"We've met," Louis said.

Hinton tilted his head to the side and said,

"We have?"

"Briefly, about six years ago, down in San Antonio. At a saloon across from the Alamo. That was the night you shot and killed Hank Bedford."

"Old Hank . . . ," Hinton said with what looked like a nostalgic grin. "He was like the third or fourth fella who ever threw down on me. I've got to say, though, I don't recall meeting you that night, Mr. Longmont."

"Like I said, our acquaintance was brief. I was part of the game where the incident took place. I believe we'd played only one hand of poker before Bedford accused you of cheating."

Hinton's expression hardened as he said, "Yeah, I remember *that,* all right. I didn't take kindly to it." He paused. "You didn't happen to agree with him, did you?"

"No, I didn't. Hank Bedford was just a poor loser . . . and it cost him his life. That pretty much ended the game, though."

"Blood spilled all over the table has got a way of doin' that," Hinton said with the cocky grin back on his face. "Now, what's this I hear about some hot coffee?"

Louis led the way on inside, and a couple of minutes later, the four men were sitting at a table, with fresh cups of coffee. After

46

being in the cold air outside, they found the warmth inside the building almost oppressive.

"We were speaking of the Treaty of Guadalupe Hidalgo," Aguilar said. "One of its provisions was that it honored the validity of land ownership originally granted by the king of Spain to those who colonized this land."

"Wait a minute, Señor Aguilar," Louis said. "I believe that provision has been interpreted differently by the Mexican and American governments. There was no blanket validation of Spanish land grants in the treaty."

"That is the *American . . .* interpretation, as you phrase it, Señor Longmont."

Smoke said, "I've read some about this in the newspapers, too. Isn't the government in Washington leaving it up to the individual states and territories to figure out, taking the cases one at a time? Seems like I heard that some of the land grants down in Texas and New Mexico have been upheld."

"Indeed they have. And now it is time for Colorado to do the right thing, as well, and restore such land to its rightful owners." Aguilar sipped his coffee and went on, "It may not have seemed like it at the time, but actually, I am glad to have met you today,

47

Señor Jensen. I was going to be calling on you, anyway. In fact, I wanted to speak to the sheriff to ask where I might find you."

Smoke suddenly had a bad feeling in his gut. His eyes narrowed as he asked, "Why is that, Señor Aguilar?"

"Because this ranch you own . . . this so-called Sugarloaf . . . it sits right in the middle of the Aguilar Land Grant." The man smiled wolfishly. "*My* land grant."

CHAPTER 4
THE MACMURPHY
SANITARIUM, COLORADO

Sleet tapped like little fingers against the window behind Ennis "Doc" Monday, making the slender, gray-haired gambler glad he was inside, where it was warm, instead of out there in the weather on this cold December afternoon.

Doc had never been one for roughing it. Even in his younger, more adventurous days, he had much preferred the pleasant, comfortable environs of a saloon to being out on the trail somewhere. As far as he was concerned, the outdoors was a necessary evil to be endured while getting from one town to another.

Now that he was older and his health wasn't what it once was, he was doubly glad he had no need to venture out into the elements.

He had been a patient here at the sanitarium for several years, ever since the pain in his gut had gotten bad enough to force him to seek medical help. Dr. MacMurphy had examined him and declared that years and years spent mostly in saloons, breathing thick tobacco smoke, sipping whiskey, and playing cards, had taken a toll on Doc's innards, and the only real cure was rest, relaxation, and a carefully monitored diet.

That had sounded like a hellish prescription to Doc, but Ace and Chance Jensen, the two fine young men he had raised from infants after their mother passed away while giving birth to them, had convinced him to try staying at the sanitarium for a while.

To Doc's surprise, he'd found that he liked it here, and he could afford it — he'd had some very good runs at the poker tables over the years — so he had decided to give it a try. It had been a good decision, as his health had improved . . . for a while.

He looked down at the cards in his left hand and tightened his grip on the pasteboards as they began to shake slightly. The trembling that had cropped up more and more often over the past year wasn't as bad when he had something to hold on to and concentrated on that.

"I believe I'll take two cards," he said as he used his other hand to extricate the cards he wanted to get rid of. He tossed them facedown on the discard pile. The motion was smooth, without a quiver, which pleased him. The shaking came and went, seemingly at random, but plagued him often enough that he was glad when he was able to perform some old familiar task without it bothering him.

For Doc Monday, there was no task older or more familiar than playing poker.

Banjo Walsh, who had the deal at the moment, sent two more cards Doc's way. Banjo wasn't the most deft card handler, because the joints in the fingers of his liver-spotted hands were so stiff they didn't work right anymore. But this was just a friendly game, so if he fumbled a little and if shuffling and dealing took longer, nobody complained. It wasn't like he was using the clumsiness as a cover for cheating, as Doc had known some men to do in the past.

Despite that, Bill Williams, sitting across the table from Doc, often looked a little irritated and impatient when Banjo was dealing. But Williams was *always* grouchy about something, so Doc didn't pay much attention to it anymore.

In Doc's opinion, Williams didn't have that much to be annoyed about. He was one of the youngest patients at the sanitarium. His thick dark hair barely had any gray in it. He seemed to be in fairly good health, too. A little shortness of breath at times, and a tendency for a gray tinge to creep over his face when that happened, but other than that, he acted like he felt fine. Williams really shouldn't even be here, Doc had thought more than once, but it was none of his business who Dr. MacMurphy accepted as a patient.

Banjo, so called because he had played that instrument in music halls when he was younger and his fingers were more nimble, had dealt Doc a three and an eight, which didn't fill his full house but left him with two pairs, threes and sixes.

"It's a nickel to you, Doc," Banjo said.

"I'll see that and raise a nickel," Doc said as he pushed the two coins into the small pile in the middle of the table. The table was square, which just seemed *wrong* to Doc. He had spent so many thousands of hours playing poker at round tables. But in a situation like this, you took what you could get and were grateful for a pleasant way to pass the time.

Hubert Guinn, to Doc's left, saw the raise, as did Williams, and Banjo called. Doc's two pairs took the pot, if you could call it that when it added up to less than a dollar. But they were only playing for fun, Doc reminded himself yet again.

Sometimes it wasn't easy for him to remember that. Too many times in his life, hundreds or even thousands of dollars had been riding on the turn of a card, or a man's business, his entire livelihood. That had happened too many times for Doc to take the game less than seriously. . . .

"I've had about enough," Williams said. He put his hands on the edge of the table, clearly ready to push back his chair and stand up.

"But we can't play with only three," Banjo protested.

"That's not my lookout." Williams got to his feet and turned toward the other side of the big parlor, where flames danced and crackled merrily in the fireplace.

Hubert Guinn said, "I suppose we can go ahead and play, but it's not really the same with only three."

"Just doesn't feel right," Banjo complained.

"Maybe we can resume the game later," Doc suggested. "Perhaps Bill will feel like playing again then, or someone else will."

"But what'll we do between now and then?" Banjo asked plaintively. For the sick and elderly, filling the hours was a challenge.

Hubert said, "We could play checkers."

That made Banjo brighten. He sat up straighter and said, "Yeah, we could." Then he looked at Doc and added, "Unless you'd like to play, Doc . . ."

"No, no," Doc said. Waving his hand back and forth a little over the table, he added dryly, "That game's too exciting for me."

"I'll get the board," Hubert said. Doc began gathering up the cards, since they belonged to him. He put them into their box and slid it into an inside coat pocket.

Bill Williams stood near the fireplace, warming himself. Several of the sanitarium's residents sat in chairs they had pulled up close to the flames, in the hope that the heat would ease the chill time had settled into their bones.

Doc knew from experience it was a forlorn hope. Flesh and bone could be warmed, but the pall that impending mortality cast over a man's soul could not be lifted. Every man reached the point where he went to bed each night no longer able to avoid the knowledge that he was one day closer to the grave.

"My God, man, stop brooding," he muttered to himself. "Surely you can find something better to do."

He had a fairly recent novel in his room, he recalled, a tale of pirates or some such

54

by a man named Stevenson, so maybe he would start it. Reading about tropical islands might be just the thing on a cold, gloomy day like this, he thought as he got to his feet and left the parlor.

He was walking along the corridor where the patients' rooms were located when the door to one of them opened and a wizened face topped by fluffy white hair peered out at him.

"Oh, Dr. Monday," the woman said, "it's you. I'm so glad to see you."

"And, as always, I'm glad to see you, too, Mrs. Bennett," Doc said as he paused to greet the elderly woman. "But I've told you, I'm not a physician. 'Doc' is just what some people have called me over the years."

"I know that. I do. I just have trouble remembering sometimes . . ."

"We all do," Doc assured her. "How are you today?"

"Frightened," Mrs. Bennett said.

Doc frowned and asked, "What in the world are you frightened of?"

"When I heard footsteps out here in the hall, I thought it might be that horrible Mr. Williams."

"He's not the most pleasant company, I grant you —"

"I was afraid he might be coming to kill

me. He has a gun, you know."

Doc's frown deepened. He said, "No, I didn't know that. How do *you* know about it?"

"I saw it one day," Mrs. Bennett said. As if to check that no one was lurking nearby, she glanced up the hall toward the window at its end, then down the other way to where the corridor opened into the parlor. Then, satisfied that she and Doc were alone, she leaned forward and went on quietly, "I was walking past his room, and the door was open a little, and I looked inside . . . not prying, you know, just a glance, like people will do . . ."

"Of course," Doc murmured.

"Anyway, I saw him standing there holding it! It was a big ugly thing. He was turning something . . . the place where you put the bullets in, I think . . ."

"The cylinder."

"I suppose. And I could see there were bullets in it. He closed the part where he was looking, and then he opened one of the drawers and put the gun inside, and he *laughed*. I never heard such an evil laugh, Dr. Monday. I really haven't."

Doc didn't doubt that. But he didn't believe that Williams was plotting to kill Mrs. Bennett, either. As for the gun, Doc had one himself, a small pocket pistol, which currently was in his room. However, he didn't think it would be a good idea to mention that to Mrs. Bennett.

She went on, "Could you do something for me, Doctor?"

He didn't bother trying to correct her this time. Instead, he said, "I can certainly try. What is it you'd like for me to do?"

"Take that horrible gun out of Mr. Williams's room and get rid of it!"

Instantly, Doc regretted indulging the old woman's fantasies. He said, "I can't do that. I have no right to invade Mr. Williams's privacy and do anything with his personal property."

"But he's going to kill me!" she wailed. "I know he is. You see, when I was passing by his room and saw the gun, he . . . he looked up and caught me watching him. The expression on his face at that moment was murder, Doctor. Pure murder!"

CHAPTER 5

Doc reached out to pat the frightened old woman on the shoulder and try to reassure her. His hand trembled a little as he did so.

"Now, now, Mrs. Bennett, I'm sure it wasn't that bad. Mr. Williams was probably just surprised to see you standing there, that's all."

"He's a killer," insisted Mrs. Bennett. "A cold-blooded killer! I could see it in his eyes. That's why you have to get the gun away from him." She moaned. "If you let him keep it, he's going to slaughter us all in our beds!"

Doc saw now that he was going to have to have a talk with Dr. MacMurphy. Clearly, Mrs. Bennett needed more help than she was getting.

"I think you should probably go lie down for a bit —" he began.

"You won't help me?"

"I can't —"

"Then I'll do it myself! I'll get that gun and throw it out the window!"

With surprising speed and agility for such an elderly lady, the birdlike Mrs. Bennett darted past Doc. He reached for her arm to stop her, but she was already headed for Williams's room. Doc turned quickly to go after her.

Normally, he wouldn't have had any trouble catching up to her. But when he turned, the whole corridor suddenly seemed to spin around him, crazily out of control. This had happened to Doc before, usually when he bent over or turned too quickly, but in those cases, the sensation had lasted only a few seconds.

This time, the wild spinning continued, and it was made even worse when his muscles seemed to lock up for no reason and refuse to do what his brain was telling them to do. He wasn't able to stop the momentum of his turn, and before he was fully aware of what was happening, he was down, sprawled on hands and knees on the hallway floor.

He raised his head and saw Mrs. Bennett disappearing through the open door of Bill Williams's room.

Gritting his teeth, Doc forced himself up. He felt himself shaking inside and rested a hand on the wall to steady himself. While he believed that Mrs. Bennett was imagining things about their fellow patient's sinister plans, he knew that Williams would be angry if he came along and found the old woman in his room, rummaging among his belongings in search of a gun that might or might not exist.

As soon as Doc's spinning head and trembling muscles had settled down some, he made himself move again. Stumbling only slightly, he went along the hall to Williams's door and said, "Mrs. Bennett, please, you shouldn't be in —"

He stopped short when he saw her standing beside a chest of drawers with a big Colt .45 gripped in both hands. One of the drawers was open, so he assumed that was where she had gotten the gun.

"I told you it was here, Doctor," she said. "I told you!"

Doc grimaced and stepped into the room. Like all the others in the sanitarium, it was plainly, even spartanly, furnished with a bed, a single chair, a small table, and a chest of drawers.

The .45's barrel was pointed in Doc's general direction, close enough to make him nervous. The hammer wasn't cocked, but the weapon was a double-action, so all Mrs.

Bennett had to do to fire it was to pull the trigger. Doc didn't know if she was strong enough to do that, but he didn't want to find out.

"Please, Mrs. Bennett," he said as he started toward her, making calming motions with his hands, "put that gun down, or at least point it at the floor."

"I told you," she said again. "I told you, Dr. Monday! See!"

She shook the gun at him.

Doc felt like his heart had climbed all the way into his throat. He took a step to his left, to get out of the direct line of fire, but she just turned and kept the gun pointed at him. Evidently, holding the weapon had increased her terror, because she wailed, "What are we going to *do*?"

Doc eased closer. If his hands were shaking or if he was trembling inside, he didn't know it, because all his attention was focused on the muzzle of that Colt, which looked as big around as a cannon right now. He managed to keep his voice calm and steady as he said, "I'll take care of it, Mrs. Bennett. Just give the gun to me, and I'll take care of it."

He was close enough to her now that he thought taking the Colt directly from her would be safer than trying to get her to put

61

it down. He extended his right hand, hoping it would be as rock steady as it had once been.

Instead, it shook back and forth, no more than a half inch either way, but definitely visible.

"Oh, you're frightened, too! See how your hand is trembling?"

"It's all right," he assured her. "Nothing to worry about. Just . . . give me . . . the gun."

She turned the Colt and slipped it into his outstretched hand.

Relief flooded through Doc. He was no gunman, certainly nowhere nearly as skilled with an iron as Ace and Chance, but he had handled enough of them that he knew what he was doing. He opened the loading gate and shook the bullets from the cylinder into the palm of his other hand.

There were only five rounds in the gun, he noted. The hammer had been resting on an empty chamber. That told Doc that Bill Williams knew something about handling guns, too.

"All right, it's harmless now," he told Mrs. Bennett. "You can go back to your room and not worry about a thing."

"But he can put the bullets in it again, can't he? Throw it out the window, Doctor!

Throw it in the snow, where he can't find it!"

The ground outside had only a dusting of snow on it, so Doc didn't think that would do a very good job of concealing the gun. Anyway, it still wasn't his property.

"I can't do that, Mrs. Bennett, but I'll have a talk with Mr. Williams and let him know how frightened you are. Maybe he can sell it or send it to one of his relatives."

"But he'll know I was poking my nose in his business. He'll be mad."

Doc shook his head emphatically and said, "I'll take all the responsibility. I'll tell him that you're under my special protection."

"You'd do that for me?"

"Of course."

"Oh, thank you, Doctor." She came closer to him, rested the fingertips of one hand on his forearm, and then — *Lord help us!* Doc thought — she batted her eyelashes at him and gave him a coy, girlish smile.

Some things never changed, he supposed. And in some ways, that was good.

"Run along now, back to your room," he said.

"Will I see you at supper tonight?"

"Certainly. I look forward to it."

Still smiling, she left the room. Doc heaved a sigh of relief as he heard her door close a moment later.

But he was still standing there with Williams's gun in one hand and the bullets in the other, and he needed to do something with them. He turned toward the chest. If he reloaded the Colt and put it in that open drawer, Williams might notice that someone had disturbed it . . . probably *would* notice . . . but that was really the only thing Doc could do.

Quickly, he thumbed the cartridges back into the cylinder. As he did so, he couldn't help but notice that someone had scratched something into the gun's frame. *A word . . . no, a name,* he decided.

MALKIN.

The name meant nothing to him. He leaned closer to the drawer. There were several pairs of socks in it. He lifted some of them and started to slide the Colt underneath them. As he did, he saw that the socks also concealed a small bundle of envelopes tied together with string. The top one, the only one he could really see, had a name and an address in Laramie, Wyoming, written on it.

The name was William Malkin.

So maybe Bill Williams's name was really William Malkin. One thing about the frontier: A man could start over, make himself a whole new life with a new name, if he wanted to. Again, it was none of Doc's business.

He arranged the socks over the gun in what he hoped was at least a semblance of how they had been, and eased the drawer closed. Then he went to the door and looked out carefully.

No one was around. *Good.* He stepped out into the corridor, closed the door behind him, and, whistling softly to himself, went to his room to start reading that pirate novel.

At the end of the corridor where it entered the parlor, the man who called himself Bill Williams moved out from behind the bushy potted plant that had screened him from view. He had ducked behind it when he looked along the hall and saw that the door to his room was open. He had watched, waiting to see who came out of there.

He hadn't had to wait long. Less than a minute later, that damn gambler Doc Monday had peeked out, then emerged, closed the door behind him, and strolled on down the hall to his room.

Monday had no reason to be in his room, Williams thought as anger began to bubble up inside him. No reason at all. He strode along the corridor, jerked his door open, and went inside. At first glance, everything looked normal, because there really wasn't much in the room.

The important things were in one of the drawers. Williams yanked it open and saw right away that things weren't exactly as he had left them. He had gotten used to memorizing the layout and arrangement of everything, so he would know if somebody had come around snooping. He realized immediately that his gun had been moved, and he was pretty sure the little packet of letters had been, too.

Somebody messing with his gun was bad enough, but if Monday had seen the letters, that was worse. Williams should have thrown away those letters, and he knew it. He cursed himself for not doing it before now. But anybody could have a little streak of sentimentality left in him, no matter how much of his humanity life had stripped away.

He looked again at the letters, sighed, and pushed the drawer closed.

Then he said out loud to himself, "There's no getting around it. I have to kill the son of a bitch."

CHAPTER 6
DENVER

The hotel dining room was already busy,
even though it was a little early for supper.
Three-fourths of the tables with fine Irish
linen tablecloths on them were occupied,
including one in a back corner of the room,
where a man sat by himself.

He wasn't young, but that was about the
only thing he had in common with the other
diners. They were all dressed in expensive
clothing, because this was a fine hotel —
staid, dignified, almost pompous in its
luxuriousness. The people who stayed here,
who ate supper here, were wealthy and
didn't mind people knowing that. In fact,
they would have been disappointed if everyone else *didn't* know how rich they were.

The lone man at the rear table, however,
wore clothes that were clean and well cared
for but looked more like an outfit somebody
would wear to ride the range and chase
cows: boots, jeans, a light brown shirt, and

a darker brown vest. A dark brown hat with a round, medium-high crown rested on the table, next to a plate containing a rare steak and all the fixin's. As the man ate, he paused between bites to wash down the food with sips of strong black coffee from a cup on the other side of the plate.

He had asked the waiter to bring a pot of coffee and leave it so he could refill his own cup when he needed more to drink. The pot was in easy reach, sitting on a thick piece of leather.

It wasn't there just for drinking purposes, however. The hotel management frowned on guests packing iron in the dining room. So the man had made sure he got a table where he could see anybody who might come at him with trouble in mind. If that happened, he figured on throwing hot coffee in the fella's face and then using the heavy pot to stave the varmint's head in.

There were plenty of ways to kill an enemy other than with a gun, and the man called Preacher knew all of them.

Long decades of being exposed to the elements had browned his lean face permanently to the color of saddle leather. He was clean-shaven these days, but no matter how often he ran a razor over his face, it seemed like he always had a new crop of silvery stubble sprouting. His thick salt-and-pepper hair had thinned only a little from the days when it was a dark thatch. Because of his appearance and his air of unquenchable vitality, most people who looked at him probably took him for being in his sixties, when actually he was twenty years older than that.

Preacher sawed off another bite of steak and chewed it with teeth made strong by years of gnawing on jerky and pemmican. He took another sip of coffee and reminded himself to ask next time if the cook could brew it up a mite more potent. He liked his coffee strong enough to get up and strut around on its own hind legs.

He was well aware that some of the folks in the dining room were casting curious glances in his direction. A few of them even frowned in disapproval, as if they thought he wasn't fit to be in here.

Preacher had seen that same sort of look on the face of the clerk when he checked in earlier that day. Denver had become a mighty civilized place in recent years, and it wasn't often that a man walked into a fancy hotel lobby with saddlebags slung over his shoulder and a Winchester in one hand. The clerk had looked like he was ready to holler for one of those uniformed law dogs Denver had now to come and throw this mangy old saddle tramp out on his ear. He was new and hadn't been there for any of Preacher's previous stays at the hotel.

Then Preacher had plunked down a double eagle on the counter, and the sight of that gleaming twenty-dollar gold piece had changed everything. The clerk had yes-sirred and thank-you-sirred Preacher plenty after that.

He hadn't asked Preacher where the money came from, but as it happened, nearly twenty years earlier the old mountain man and Kirby Jensen, the youngster he had nicknamed Smoke, had found themselves a gold mine. It had made them both rich, although Preacher didn't give a hoot in hell about such things. Smoke had banked part of the profits in Preacher's name, though, and as such things sometimes happened, those funds had grown to the point that Preacher had more money than he would ever spend in the rest of his life.

He still didn't care about that and lived the way he always had, as a plain man who didn't need or want a bunch of fancy foofaraw around him. He liked to travel and see new places, or at least places he hadn't been to for a long time. With the adventur-ous, fiddle-footed life he'd led, Preacher sort of doubted there was anywhere west of the Mississippi where he *hadn't* set foot at one time or another.

At the moment, however, he wasn't drifting. He had an actual destination. He was on his way to the Sugarloaf, the successful ranch that Smoke owned these days. Sally, Smoke's beautiful wife, who was the best thing that had ever happened to him, had invited Preacher to spend Christmas with them. He did that every few years and was always glad to see Smoke and Sally again, as well as Smoke's brother, Luke and Smoke's adopted brother, Matt. The Jensens were his favorite people in the whole wide world. They might not be blood kin, but they were Preacher's family, anyway.

So Preacher didn't care if the other guests in the hotel thought he belonged here. The way he'd always figured it, he was at home wherever he was.

He had polished off his steak and trimmings and was waiting for the waiter to bring him a bowl of deep-dish apple pie when he noticed the woman coming across the dining room toward his table. She wore a dark brown traveling outfit and hat and had long brown hair lightly touched with gray here and there. Her gloved hands held a woven reticule. A nice pearl brooch was fastened on the jacket, just below her throat.

She didn't look like any sort of threat, but she could have a derringer in that little bag, thought Preacher. He sat up a little straighter in case he needed to dive for cover.

As the woman came closer, he realized there was something familiar about her. He had seen her before, but he couldn't say where or when, nor could he put a name with the face. He thought she might stop at one of the other tables as she crossed the room, but no, she was headed for his.

When she stopped on the other side of the table, his natural chivalry made him stand up. He greeted her with a polite nod and said, "Ma'am? Somethin' I can do for you?"

She smiled at him. She wasn't beautiful, but she was pretty, and the smile made her more so. She said, "You don't remember me, do you, Arthur?"

That was the clincher. He was acquainted with her, all right, even though he couldn't recall her name or where they might have met.

But she knew that his real name was Arthur. He had gone by Art as a boy, but he hadn't used the name for many, many years, ever since a run-in with some proddy Blackfeet as a young man had resulted in him being dubbed Preacher by his mountain-man friends. That handle had stuck, all this time.

"I reckon you have the advantage of me, as they say, ma'am. I know we've met, but dam . . . danged if I can call your name."

Her smile didn't waver. She said, "Some women might be offended to be found so forgettable."

"Oh, it ain't that. I'm old." Preacher tapped a finger against his temple. "Don't have much memory anymore."

That was an outright lie. His brain was as sharp as ever. But he had lived a hell of a long time and had met a hell of a lot of people, and it was only natural that he couldn't sort them all out.

"I'm Adelaide DuBois," she introduced herself.

All it took was for Preacher to hear the name, and then all the memories snapped back to him. His shaggy brows rose, and he exclaimed, "Polecat!"

The woman laughed and said, "Yes, that's what Pierre's fur-trapper friends called him, all right."

"Well, dadgummit, I should have knowed you right off. Is ol' Polecat here in Denver with you? I ain't seen that varmint in, Lord, must be twenty years or more."

Her smile went away and she shook her head, and when Preacher saw that, he cussed himself inside for blurting out the question.

"I'm afraid Pierre passed away a number of years ago, Arthur. When he got sick, he claimed it was from that arrow wound he suffered up in the Prophecy Mountains that time he and you were trapping together." She added hastily, "Not that he blamed you for it. He always said he would have died that day if it hadn't been for you."

"Maybe, maybe not," Preacher said with a half shrug. "It's pretty near impossible to know about such things for sure." He realized what he should have said and done before now and quickly went around the table to pull out a chair. "Please, sit down. We'll get the waiter to bring you somethin' to eat."

She lowered herself onto the chair and shook her head, then said, "I'm not really hungry, but I could do with a cup of that coffee if you can spare it."

"Sure, if you want, but it's a mite on the strong side, especially for a lady."

"I was married to a mountain man, remember. I don't think it will be too strong for me."

Preacher caught the waiter's eye, and

when the man came over, he asked him to bring a cup for Adelaide DuBois. Then he sat down across from her and said, "I'm sure sorry to hear about ol' Polecat . . . I mean, Pierre."

"Calling him that would just sound odd coming from you. You knew him as Polecat, and I have no objection to you calling him by that name. I suspect you'd be more comfortable if I called you Preacher instead of Arthur."

"Well, that's what I've gone by for a long time, but it don't really matter. Folks can call me 'most anything as long as it ain't late for dinner."

Adelaide laughed and shook her head. "You're as colorful as ever, I see. I didn't expect anything different, to be honest. You're as unchanging as those Rocky Mountains west of here."

"I reckon I've changed some. I'm a heap older than the last time you saw me."

"And I still say you haven't changed a bit." She reached across the table with her left hand, and before Preacher knew what she was doing, she'd clasped his right hand with it as she smiled at him.

What the hell?

A wild thought suddenly leaped into Preacher's head. According to what she had just told him, Adelaide didn't have a husband anymore.

Was it possible she was on the scout for another one?

With that worrying possibility nagging at him, Preacher was glad to see the waiter show up with that second coffee cup and saucer. The man poured for Adelaide and then withdrew, but the brief distraction gave Preacher an opportunity to gather his thoughts.

"Did you just happen to see me in here?" he asked. He hoped that would be the case. A chance encounter didn't have to mean anything.

"Not at all," she replied without hesitation. "I've been looking for you, Preacher. I wanted to see you again. So I wrote to Mrs. Sally Jensen at Big Rock. She's your daughter-in-law, isn't she?"

"Well, not really, but in a manner of speakin', maybe. You've been . . . lookin' for me?"

"That's right. I know about your connection with the famous Smoke Jensen, of course. You're mentioned in some of those dime novels they've written about him." Adelaide laughed. "Pierre was so tickled by that, reading about the exploits of someone he actually knew from the old days."

"Aw, most of them stories are just made-up tripe," Preacher said with a wave of his hand. "The crazy fellas who come up with 'em oughta be locked away somewheres in one of them asylums."

"Still, I knew I might be able to track you down through Mrs. Jensen. She wrote back and said that you would be coming to their ranch for Christmas, and I might be able to catch you in Denver on your way there. She told me you sometimes stay at this hotel. So I did, too."

"Just on the chance that I might come along?"

"That's right. You see, it's very important, Preacher. I need your help." Her hand tightened on his. "Someone is trying to kill me."

CHAPTER 7
THE PROPHECY MOUNTAINS, MANY YEARS EARLIER

Preacher peered over the barrel of his rifle, searching for a target. He knew the Blackfeet were out there, but they had good cover in the trees, and he couldn't spot any of them.

"Damn it," he muttered. "It's like the red devils up and vanished on us."

"You will see them again soon enough, I'll wager," Pierre DuBois said from behind the boulder where he crouched a few feet away. "When they are ready for us to see them."

"Yeah, you're right about that." Preacher eased down behind the slab of rock that provided protection for him. He knew from experience that you couldn't rush an Indian. They were notional critters who never attacked until they were good and ready.

He took off his broad-brimmed felt hat and dragged the right sleeve of his buckskin shirt across his forehead. The air held a hint of coolness, a foretaste of autumn to come, but it wasn't enough to counteract the heat of the sun. Or maybe it was the tension of waiting for a life-or-death fight to begin that caused beads of sweat to pop out on Preacher's forehead.

Either way, it was a gorgeous day in the high country. Much too pretty a day to die.

The scenery was beautiful, too. The cluster of boulders where Preacher and DuBois had taken cover after the war party jumped them was located on the rim of a deep canyon. A few yards behind them, the canyon wall dropped away in a sheer cliff to a swift-flowing river far below. On the far side of the canyon, steep, heavily wooded slopes climbed to a rugged, snowcapped peak that stood out sharply against the blue, crystal clear sky.

There was forest on this side of the canyon, too, and it came to within fifty yards of the gorge, leaving only that narrow open strip between the trees and the rimrock.

The open ground was the only thing that had saved Preacher and DuBois so far. The Blackfeet knew they would lose some warriors if they charged straight across it. Preacher believed they were sitting back there in the trees, trying to figure out if there was any way to flank the two white trappers.

As far as Preacher could see, there wasn't. He and "Polecat" DuBois had the cliff and the river at their back, but they had open ground in the other three directions and would be able to cut down some of the Blackfeet when they finally lost their patience and attacked.

Or maybe they would decide that killing two mountain men wasn't worth it, and would go away. Preacher didn't put much stock in that hope, but he knew it couldn't be discarded completely.

DuBois took off his coonskin cap and ran a hand over his long dark hair. A white streak went right down the middle of that hair, giving him the decidedly skunk-like appearance that had resulted in his nickname.

One night around their campfire, DuBois had told Preacher where he got that white streak. It had happened when he was a young soldier in the French army, during a battle with the English forces in some European fracas that Preacher didn't really understand or care about. A British officer had whacked DuBois in the head with a saber, but not before DuBois got him in the belly with a bayonet. DuBois had almost bled to death from the wound, but his friends had gotten him to a field hospital in time for a sawbones to shave off DuBois's hair and stitch up the gash. When the hair had grown back, covering up the ugly scar, it had come in white as snow.

From that point on, DuBois had had to get used to being called a skunk or some variation. It never seemed to bother him. He was a real ladies' man and didn't lack for self-confidence. And as he had told Preacher, some of those ladies seemed to find his distinctive appearance intriguing and attractive.

That white-streaked pelt might wind up dangling from some Blackfoot lodgepole before this was over, Preacher thought as he waited in the rocks with DuBois. They would give a good account of themselves and send some of their enemies to the spirit world before it reached that point, though.

"Do you know what I regret most about dying, Preacher?" DuBois asked abruptly.

"The 'not bein' alive' part?"

DuBois laughed and said, "It is true that life holds many pleasures I will miss, but my biggest regret is that I will never see my beautiful Adelaide again."

"Adelaide, Adelaide . . . ," Preacher repeated musingly. "Is she that yellow-haired dove who works at Red Mike's in Saint Looey, the sort of heavyset one with the big ol' —"

"Hold your tongue! I speak of Miss Adelaide Martinson, of the Philadelphia Martinsons. It is one of my most miserable failings that I never spoke to her of my true feelings, never revealed the great love for her I carry in my heart."

"Now hold on a minute," Preacher said. "I know good and well you cut a big swath through all the fancy gals in St. Louis, not to mention you got a squaw in almost ever' Injun village from here to the Milk River. And now you're tellin' me that you're — how would Audie put it? — that you're madly in love with this Adelaide girl?"

DuBois waved a hand dismissively and said, "Those other entanglements were affairs of the flesh. What I feel for Adelaide is an affair of the spirit! We are kindred souls, she and I, and if I made enough from this season of trapping, I intended to return to Philadelphia and beseech her for her hand in marriage."

"Huh. Well, don't give up on it yet, old son. There's still a chance them damn Blackfeet will decide not to —"

The angry screech that cut through the air told him he shouldn't have started to say such a thing or even thought it. Now he had gone and jinxed whatever chance they might've had of avoiding a fight.

The warriors burst out of the trees, not surprisingly attacking from three directions at once. Preacher aimed his rifle at the Indians coming from the right as he barked at DuBois, "Whittle down the ones on the left!"

The rifle boomed and bucked against his shoulder. One of the Blackfeet went over backward, as if swatted down by a giant fist. The heavy lead ball from Preacher's rifle had smashed into his chest and pulped his heart.

DuBois's rifle thundered, as well. Preacher didn't take the time to see if his partner had hit one of the attacking Indians. DuBois was a good shot and was coolheaded in times of danger, so Preacher assumed he had.

Preacher set the empty rifle down and yanked two flintlock pistols from behind his belt. Arrows cut through the air around him as he rose up, thrust the pistols straight out, eared back the hammers, and pulled the triggers. The double blast was deafening. Clouds of powder smoke rose around the rocks, stinging Preacher's eyes and obscuring his vision for a second.

As the smoke thinned, he caught a glimpse of several buckskin-clad shapes disappearing back into the shadows underneath the pines. Checking to his left, he saw that the other two groups were retreating, as well. Two more Blackfeet were down on that side, and a wounded man was being helped into the trees by his companions. That made half a dozen members of the war party out of the fight. He and Polecat might have a chance, after all, thought Preacher.

A gasp of pain dashed that hope. Preacher turned more and saw DuBois slumped against the boulder. An arrow's feathered shaft protruded from his chest, low on the right side.

"Son of a bitch! Polecat, you're hit."

DuBois lifted a face gone pale and haggard in a matter of seconds. He forced his lips into a grim smile and said, "Indeed. I am — how do you say it? — the goner."

"Now, hold on, hold on. It might not be that bad." Preacher was working swiftly to reload his rifle and pistols as he spoke. He wanted to check on DuBois, but first things had to come first. "I'll take a look here in just a minute."

"No need. I fear the arrow . . . nicked my lung. I will soon drown . . . in my own blood."

Preacher muttered a curse as he rammed home a ball and charge in the rifle. He primed the pan and then set the weapon aside. He had already reloaded the pistols, moving so quickly it would have been hard for inexperienced eyes to follow what he was doing. He placed them where they would be easy to grab, as well, and then knelt beside DuBois.

"Did the arrow go all the way through?" he asked as he felt around on his partner's back.

"*Non.* The head is buried within me."

That was going to complicate things, but it could still be dealt with . . . if they could manage to get out of here alive.

Problem was, Preacher didn't see any way they could do that. They were still outnumbered by the Blackfeet, and when the warriors charged again, Preacher wouldn't be able to hold them off by himself. Some of them would reach the rocks and overrun him and DuBois. There was no getting around it.

He glanced at the cliff. Maybe there was one way. . . .

DuBois saw where Preacher was looking and said, "Go, my friend. Help me load my guns . . . and I will slow them down . . . give you a better chance . . ."

"The hell with that," Preacher responded. "Either we both get out of here or neither of us does."

"But I cannot . . . possibly survive . . ."

"You don't know that. But one thing's for sure — we ain't either one of us gonna survive if we stay here."

DuBois reached up and squeezed Preacher's shoulder as he rasped, "My friend . . . *mon ami . . .*"

A war whoop split the air.

"Hang on," Preacher said. "Lemme kill a few more of them sons o' bitches 'fore we go anywhere."

He whirled back to his guns and snatched up the rifle. An arrow whipped past his ear as he drew a bead and drilled a lead ball through a warrior's head, shattering the man's skull like a dropped gourd. He pivoted the other way as he grabbed the pistols. The pair of shots crashed, and two more Blackfeet went down. Preacher rammed the pistols behind his belt, grabbed up the empty rifle, and turned to Pierre DuBois.

The Frenchman had already shoved himself to his feet. Preacher looped his free arm around DuBois's waist and held him up as both of them ran the few feet to the cliff. More arrows flew around them as they jumped. Preacher heard angry, disappointed shouts from the attacking warriors.

Then he couldn't hear anything except the air rushing past his ears and the involuntary yells that came from his and DuBois's throats as they plummeted toward the sun-sparkling river far below. . . .

Denver

Those vivid memories receded in Preacher's mind as he looked across the table at Adelaide DuBois. No need to go through the plunge, which had taken only seconds but had seemed to last hours, before he and Pierre DuBois struck the surface of the icy river. Pure luck, and the fact that the river was deep at that point, had kept both of them from being killed in the fall.

Preacher had lost his grip on DuBois and had to find him again in the fast-flowing river. Once he did, they rode its swift current for a mile or more before Preacher was able to get them to shore. He knew the Blackfeet might come after them, but they would have to go a long way around to do so. That gave Preacher time enough to find them a good place to hole up.

That place turned out to be a cave, where they spent the next two weeks, while Preacher nursed his friend back from the brink of death. In order to keep from doing even more damage, he had to push the arrow on through DuBois's body, break off the head, and then withdraw the bloody shaft. More than once, he thought that DuBois had slipped away, over the divide. But each time the Frenchman clung to life.

Six months later, the man Preacher delivered to Adelaide Martinson in Philadelphia was a thin, pale shadow of who he had been . . . but Adelaide welcomed him, anyway, sobbing as she took him into her arms and cradled him protectively.

Preacher didn't stay for the wedding. He hated big cities, and he felt the high country drawing him back. . . .

But he saw the two of them a few times after that. They moved to St. Louis, where DuBois worked for one of the fur-trapping companies and even went on a few more expeditions himself, once he had recovered enough. He was never again the man he had been before the ordeal, though.

"My goodness, Preacher, you look like you're a million miles away," Adelaide said.

"Not that far. Only a few hundred miles. And a bunch of years."

"Did you hear what I said?"

"About somebody wantin' to kill you? That don't hardly make sense. Who'd want to do somethin' terrible like that?"

"That's the worst of it," Adelaide said with a sigh. "It's my own grandson."

CHAPTER 8
AMITY, UTAH

Despite the name of the settlement, this didn't strike Luke Jensen as a very friendly place. As he rode in, icy gusts whipped through the single street, sweeping down from the snowcapped mountains to the west, but the wind wasn't any colder than the stares he got from the townspeople.

That didn't surprise him. As a bounty hunter, he was used to not exactly being welcome anywhere he went. Sometimes, people seemed to know his profession even before he told anyone about it. More than once, he had thought that he must have a scarlet letter sewn onto his coat that other people could see, even though he couldn't. A *B* for *bounty hunter* or *blood money*, instead of the *A* that Hester Prynne wore in Nathaniel Hawthorne's novel.

Making it even worse in this case was the fact that Amity was a Mormon town and Luke was a Gentile. How they could tell that by looking at him, he wasn't sure at first.

But as he rode slowly toward the squat stone building with a sign out front proclaiming it to be the marshal's office, he began to get an inkling. Everybody in town seemed to have the same sort of broad face topped by blond hair. It seemed far-fetched that the entire population might be related in some way, but he couldn't rule it out. They could sure spot an outsider in a hurry, no doubt about that.

Luke was dark, while the citizens of Amity were fair. That extended to his clothing, as well, since he dressed in black from head to foot. Even the sheepskin coat he wore was dyed black. The only things about him that stood out were the silver conchos that formed the band around his hat.

His craggy, weather-beaten face was darkly tanned. A narrow mustache adorned his upper lip. His eyes were deep-set and intense, and yet the lines around his eyes and mouth showed that he knew how to laugh, too. Still, about him hung the undefinable air of a solitary man, accustomed to riding lonely trails.

He pretended not to see the wary looks the townspeople gave him, and ignored the outright hostile ones, as well. When he reached the marshal's office, he reined his horse to a stop and swung down from the saddle.

The office door opened while Luke was still looping his reins around the hitch rail in front of the place. A man stepped out, rubbing bare hands together against the cold. He might have had blond hair like everybody else in town if he'd had any hair. His hat was thumbed back enough that Luke could see he was bald as an egg. His eyebrows were so pale and thin, they were barely there.

"Howdy," he greeted Luke. "Saw you through the window. New to Amity, aren't you?"

"That's right. I rode in right this minute." Luke nodded to the star the man wore pinned to the lapel of his coat. "You'd be the marshal?"

"That's right. Marshal Ed Rowan. Hope you won't take it unkindly if I ask you what your business is in our town."

"I was on my way to talk to you about that very subject," Luke said. "Why don't we do it inside, out of this wind?"

Marshal Rowan's friendly demeanor dropped away and his voice hardened as he said, "I don't recall invitin' you in, mister."

Luke looked at him for a second, then

nodded and said, "So that's the way it is."

"Just tell me what you're doin' here, mister."

"Jensen is the name. Luke Jensen."

"Didn't ask you that."

Luke suppressed the irritation he felt and said, "I'm looking for a man named Hank Trafford. He was headed in this direction."

Rowan stiffened.

"I know who Trafford is," he said. "He came from around here, a long time ago. But I haven't seen him and don't want to. The man's an outlaw. We're law-abidin' folks hereabouts. His kind ain't welcome." Rowan paused, then added, "Your kind ain't, either."

"I'm not an outlaw."

"You know what I mean," the marshal snapped. He cocked his head a little and went on, "Are you a federal man? Deputy U.S. marshal? We don't cotton much to federal men poking around. They ain't needed here."

Luke wasn't surprised to hear that. There was a long-standing history of hostility between the government in Washington and the Mormons. Quite a bit of blood had been shed on both sides.

He shook his head and said, "No. I don't carry a badge of any kind."

"You'd be a bounty hunter, then, after the price on Trafford's head. Well, you won't collect it here, so you might as well move on."

"Without even a hot meal?" Luke asked.

Rowan glared at him and said grudgingly, "We'll not turn away any man who's hungry, even a Gentile. Even a bounty hunter. But I say again, you're not welcome."

"I suppose I'll just have to live with that. What's the best place to eat around here?" Luke doubted there was actually more than one in a settlement of this size.

Wordlessly, Rowan pointed across the street. Luke turned and saw a sturdy-looking building made of thick, rough-hewn beams, topped with a wooden shingle roof. A sign that read simply CAFÉ was nailed to the wall beside the door.

Luke nodded to Rowan and said, "I'm obliged to you."

"Not necessary. Take your horse with you, so you can leave quicker once you're done eating."

Luke untied the reins and led his mount across the street. After tying the animal to the hitchrack there, he went into the café.

Inside, the air was warm and had the savory smell of stew hanging in it: beef, onions, spices. The hour was past midday, but the café still had several customers, some seated at tables, others at a counter along the right-hand wall. There were three empty stools at the near end of the counter. Luke took the one closest to the window, figuring the other customers would prefer that he keep his distance as much as possible.

He was a naturally polite man and didn't care for poking his nose in where it wasn't wanted, but that was something he had to do fairly often, and he didn't let it bother him, either. He didn't go out of his way to look for trouble, but he didn't back away from it.

Right now he wanted a bowl of that stew he smelled. He knew there was no point in asking for a cup of coffee in a Mormon town. He gave a polite nod to the woman who came up on the other side of the counter, but didn't smile at her. Mormons were touchy about outsiders coming in and being too friendly to their women.

This woman was young, probably in her early twenties, but thin faced and already careworn. Luke figured she was married to one of the local elders, with a bunch of sister wives and a gaggle of children in the house. He said, "I'd like to have some of the stew, if there's any left, please."

"Still plenty in the pot," she told him. She went through an open door into the kitchen and came back with the stew. As she set the bowl in front of him, he saw the quick worried glance she sent along the counter. Luke waited until she had walked down to the other end of the counter, then looked in the same direction the woman had.

The man sitting on the other side of the empty stools was glaring at him. He was fairly young, too, and had a short, curling blond beard. He was thickset, and his shoulders were massive, stretching the fabric of his cheap coat.

Luke gave him a curt nod and then dug into the stew.

It tasted as good as it smelled, but he had taken only a couple of bites when the man along the counter stood up from his stool and sauntered toward him.

The man didn't say anything, just stood there too close, scowling at him. Luke had another spoonful of stew and savored it for a moment before swallowing. Without looking at the young man, he said, "Something I can do for you, friend?"

"You're not anybody's friend," the man said. "Not in this town. You don't belong here."

"I think you're right about that."

The scowl on the young man's face turned into a frown of confusion. He said, "You do?"

"I don't have any desire to intrude on you folks. I'd just as soon conduct my business without any delays and leave you alone to go about your lives in peace."

"No Gentile ever felt like that about Mormons!"

"You might be surprised. Plenty of people just want to be left alone."

The curling beard jutted out on the man's defiant jaw as he asked, "What *is* your business here?"

"Your town marshal asked me the same thing. He wears a badge, so I thought it best to answer him, but I don't see one on you."

The man crossed his arms, which were almost as brawny as his shoulders, over his chest and said, "I'm used to getting an answer when I ask a question, mister."

The thin-faced woman on the other side of the counter had drifted up again while Luke and the young man were talking. She said, "You know your pa won't like it if you start a fight in here, Eli."

"My pa's at the ranch."

"Yes, but nothing happens in town that he doesn't know about."

The heavy shoulders went up and down

in a shrug. Eli said, "He can't stomach Gentiles any more than I can."

Luke had continued to eat, seemingly not paying much attention to the young man. In reality, though, all his senses were alert. If Eli actually tried to start anything, Luke would be ready.

Maybe trouble could still be headed off, though. He said, "You want me to get out of town, don't you?"

"You talking to me?" Eli demanded. "That's right. I want you to get out of town. We don't want you here."

"And I don't want to be here. So tell me what I need to know, and I can be gone that much sooner."

Eli looked confused again. Thinking didn't seem to be his strong suit. He said, "What is it you want to know?"

"Where can I find Hank Trafford?"

"What do you want with him?"

"That's between him and me," Luke said.

Eli stared at him for a couple of seconds, then said, "You're some kind of lawman. You think we'd betray one of our own to some Gentile star packer?"

"Eli . . . ," the woman said in a warning tone.

"Hush up, Ruth," he snapped. "You may be one of Pa's wives, but you don't tell me

97

what to do. You're not *my* mother."

Well, that clarified the relationship, anyway, thought Luke as he spooned up another mouthful of the stew.

Eli poked his shoulder as he was bringing the spoon to his mouth, jostling him enough that some of the stew spilled onto the counter.

"You didn't answer my question. Why are you looking for Hank Trafford?"

"He's wanted. I intend to take him in. I've been on his trail for a while, and he was reported to be headed in this direction. He grew up around here, so it's not surprising this is where he'd go to ground."

"And it never occurred to you that he might have friends here?"

"Friends?" Luke repeated. For the first time since riding into Amity, he allowed some of the anger bubbling under the surface to come out. "Do you know *why* Trafford is wanted by the law, Eli? Because he's an outlaw and a cold-blooded killer. He's held up stagecoaches and banks and gunned down four men who got in his way. And the last time . . ." Luke's voice was rising now. "The last time he hit a bank, he shot a woman and her four-year-old son on his way out of town. Murdered them both for no good reason except to slow down

98

pursuit." Luke turned on the stool and stared coldly at Eli. "Now, is that the sort of man you want to shield from justice simply because he once went to the same church you do? He probably hasn't set foot in a tabernacle in years!"

Ruth had gasped in horror when Luke recounted Hank Trafford's crimes, and for a second, he thought he had gotten through to Eli, as well.

But then the young man's features hardened, and he said, "Get out of Amity now and don't come back!"

Luke shook his head, not arguing, just expressing his disgust, and turned back to the bowl of stew.

Even so, from the corner of his eye, he saw Eli's thick shoulders bunch, and the next second, the young man's right fist rocketed toward Luke's head.

CHAPTER 9

The young man was undoubtedly strong, as evidenced by his heavily muscled arms and shoulders, but he wasn't very fast. Luke had plenty of time to twist around on the stool and lean away from the punch. Eli's fist missed entirely, and that caused him to stumble against the counter.

"Eli, stop it!" Ruth yelled.

He ignored her, pushed away from the counter, and charged Luke, who had slipped off the stool and now stood ready to meet the attack.

Eli swung a wild looping blow, which Luke ducked underneath easily. Stepping in, Luke hammered two short, powerful punches to the young man's ribs.

It was a little like hitting the thick wall of the café. Eli didn't seem to even feel the blows. He lurched toward Luke and tried to catch the older man in a bear hug. Luke darted out of reach. He knew that if Eli ever got those tree-trunk arms around him, their crushing grip would probably break his ribs.

Eli charged him again. At least none of the other men in the café were taking a hand in the fight, so far, anyway, so Luke had to worry about only one opponent. He stepped aside and snapped a punch to Eli's jaw. Luke had a little more luck with that one. It rocked Eli's head to the side.

Eli roared in anger and swung an arm in a backhanded blow. Luke couldn't avoid it entirely, but he took the brunt of it on his left shoulder. That arm went numb for a second and then didn't want to work very well.

But the right arm still worked fine, so Luke used that fist to pound two more punches against Eli's jaw. The young man's eyes were starting to get a little glassy now. He windmilled a couple of punches. Luke weaved between them and got close enough to land a hard jab on Eli's nose. Blood spurted hotly against his knuckles. Eli groaned and staggered.

One more punch would do it, Luke sensed. Eli tried to set himself and block it, but he was too slow. Luke's fist crashed against his jaw, and he went down, hitting the floor hard. He didn't get up but just lay there and groaned instead.

Luke stepped back and said in a voice loud enough to carry to everyone in the room, "I didn't want to do that. I'm sorry it came to blows."

"Eli's a stubborn kid who's too full of himself," said one of the men. "But that doesn't mean we want you around here, mister."

"I know that. But what I said to him goes for the rest of you, as well. Surely you don't want to protect a man like Hank Trafford. I promise you, he's not worth it."

Nothing but stony stares met those words.

Luke sighed. He still had some stew, but he had lost his appetite. He took a coin from his pocket and placed it on the counter.

"I'm sorry for the trouble," he told Ruth. "At least none of the furniture got busted up."

"You'd better leave, mister," she said. "Not just the café. You'd better get out of Amity."

"Not without what I came for."

"Then I reckon whatever happens is on your head."

Luke didn't like the sound of that. He recalled what Eli and Ruth had said about Eli's father. From the sound of it, the man was a wealthy rancher and quite possibly one of the local elders. He would have power and influence in this area, maybe a crew of tough cowboys he could send after the man who had whipped his son in a fight. Luke had run into problems like that before.

But he wasn't going to let that stop him, or the stone wall of hostility the citizens of Amity had put up, either. He would root out Hank Trafford no matter what it took.

He stepped around Eli's moaning, half-conscious figure and headed for the door. He wasn't quite sure of his next move as he stepped outside.

The blast of a gunshot and the wind-rip of a bullet passing close by his ear gave him a pretty good idea, though.

He turned toward the sound of the shot, and as he did, he dropped into a crouch and his hands flashed to the twin .44 Remingtons he wore in a cross-draw rig. Another shot roared as he drew the revolvers. This bullet chewed splinters from a boardwalk post right beside him.

Luke saw that second muzzle flash. It came from behind a wagon parked about forty feet up the street. He leaped off the boardwalk and lunged into the street, trying to get an angle on the bushwhacker hidden behind the wagon.

The gunman wasn't Eli, Luke knew that, because he had just left the young man mostly senseless in the café. He wasn't sure who else in Amity might want him dead, but there were several possibilities.

None of which mattered a damn right now, because staying alive was more important than the identity of the man trying to kill him.

Luke caught a glimpse of legs as the man darted around the wagon to keep the sturdy canvas-covered vehicle between him and his intended target. Luke snapped a shot with the right-hand Remington, trying to blow one of the bushwhacker's legs out from under him, but the slug kicked up dust between the man's hurrying feet. More shots sounded as the man fired over the wagon bed, through the canvas cover, in Luke's general direction. He heard the bullets whine past him and hoped they wouldn't hit anybody on the other side of the street.

If the citizens of Amity had any sense, all of them had scrambled for cover by now. It sounded like a small war had broken out in the street.

Luke took more careful aim and fired the left-hand Remington. This time, blood flew as the bullet nicked the ambusher's right calf. A pained shout came from the other side of the wagon. Luke heard boots thud on the boardwalk as the wounded gunman leaped up there.

Remingtons thrust out in front of him, ready to fire, Luke completed his circuit of the wagon in time to see the bushwhacker vanish through the front door of a general store, dragging his injured leg behind him. Frightened yells came from inside the building.

Luke ran to the boardwalk and pressed his back to the wall beside the door. He shouted, "Come on out of there, Trafford! You don't want any innocent people getting hurt!"

Luke was assuming that the gunman was Hank Trafford, the killer outlaw he'd been pursuing. Trafford had been hiding out here in Amity, just as Luke suspected, and someone had tipped him off that a bounty hunter was in town, looking for him.

Marshal Ed Rowan? Luke couldn't rule that out. Whoever had warned Trafford, it hadn't been difficult for him to spot the man who was after him. Nobody was going to mistake Luke for anybody else in this town.

"Trafford!" Luke called again. "Give yourself up! I'll take you in alive!"

"Go to hell!" came the response. "You want me, come in and get me!"

This much shooting would have rousted out most local lawmen by now. Rowan had to know what was going on, but there was no sign of him. He wasn't going to take a hand in this, Luke knew. It would probably be just fine with him if Trafford killed the bounty hunter. That would make things simpler.

Luke suddenly wheeled away from the wall and started to dash past the big window in the front of the store. Trafford must have been waiting for that. Bullets from inside shattered the glass and sprayed a million shards over Luke and the boardwalk. Luke's head was tilted down and to the side, so his hat brim protected his face. He kept going, unhit by any of the slugs, and when he reached the end of the boardwalk, he leaped from it into the mouth of the alley that ran alongside the general store.

That was where he stopped, just around the corner of the building. It was a tricky thing, putting yourself in the mind of the man you were trying to capture, but over the years, Luke had learned to do it. Many times, his life had depended on that ability.

He knew Trafford had seen him cross in front of the window. It made sense for the outlaw to believe that Luke was trying to reach the back of the store and get behind him. In that case, Trafford's best option was to reverse course and escape out the front of the store while Luke was going around the back. Trafford's horse was probably tied at one of the nearby hitchracks.

Once again, boots thudded heavily on the boardwalk. Luke wheeled around the corner, guns up, and saw the man limping across the planks. His hat had come off, revealing thin fair hair. A mustache of the same shade drooped over his mouth. Even in profile, Luke recognized the face from the wanted poster in his saddlebags.

"Trafford!" he called.

The outlaw jerked to a stop and tried to turn. The gun in his hand rose as he did so.

"Drop it!" Luke shouted, giving Trafford one last chance to surrender.

Trafford didn't take it. He squeezed the trigger but rushed the shot before his gun had come level. The bullet plowed into the boardwalk in front of the broken store window.

Luke didn't give him a chance to try again. He squeezed the triggers of both Remingtons. The .44 rounds sizzled through the air and punched into Trafford's chest only a few inches apart. The double impact knocked Trafford back. His feet got tangled with each other, and he fell. The gun slipped from his fingers and skittered away from him as he landed on his back.

Luke stepped up onto the boardwalk again and cautiously approached the fallen man, keeping him covered as he did so. Trafford's bloody chest rose and fell several times in a ragged pattern, then stopped just after he had pulled in a rasping breath.

That air went out of him in a long sigh as his chest slowly deflated. After that, it didn't move again.

As Luke came closer, he saw that Trafford's staring eyes were glassy and lifeless. The outlaw was dead, no doubt about it.

The street and both boardwalks were deserted. Anyone who had been out in the open had scurried for cover when the shooting started, just as Luke had hoped. He didn't see any other bodies lying anywhere and was grateful for that.

A few faces began to peek out doors and windows now that the gunfire seemed to have stopped. A couple of the more daring townspeople ventured out. Across the street, the door of the marshal's office opened. Ed Rowan strode out of the building with a shotgun in his hands.

Luke didn't holster his guns. He still suspected that Rowan was the one who'd warned Trafford. Lawman or not, if Rowan looked like he was about to cut loose with that Greener, Luke intended to stop him. That might lead to him having to shoot his way out of town, but he wasn't going to just stand there and let anybody fill him with buckshot.

Rowan kept the shotgun pointed at the ground in front of him, though. He stopped about twenty feet away and said, "Killed him, did you?"

"He didn't give me any choice," Luke said. "I would have been willing to take him in alive, but he wasn't having any of it."

"I'm not surprised," Rowan said, shaking his bald head. "He was always stubborn as a mule, and hotheaded, to boot. That's a bad combination."

"You've known him for a while, then?"

"Ever since he was a kid. We're second cousins."

Luke's eyes narrowed. He watched the shotgun, but even more he paid attention to Rowan's eyes. Those were usually the most reliable giveaway when a man was about to make a move.

"I know what you're thinkin'," Rowan went on. "I'm not gunnin' for you, Jensen. Yeah, I sent word to Hank that he needed to get out of town — you probably figured that out already — but that's as far as I'd go. He made up his own mind to break the law. He's got to pay the consequences for it."

"I'm sorry it had to happen in your town, Marshal."

Rowan shrugged and said, "At least this way we can see to it that he's buried proper. I'll sign any sort of affidavit you want so you can collect the bounty. You don't have to have the body, do you?"

Luke shook his head. "No, the affidavit will do, I suppose," he said. "I appreciate that, Marshal."

Rowan tucked the shotgun under his left arm, and Luke figured it was finally safe to pouch his irons. The marshal frowned and used his right hand to rub his chin.

"There's just one thing," he said. "Well, three things, when you get down to it. Bodie, Hannah, and Teddy."

Luke frowned and shook his head, then said, "I'm afraid I don't know what you're talking about."

"Not what, who. Those are Hank Trafford's kids. And since you just killed their pa, I reckon they're *your* responsibility now, Mr. Bounty Hunter."

CHAPTER 10
BIG ROCK

Smoke stared across the table in Longmont's at Don Juan Sebastian Aguilar.

A couple of seconds went by in silence after Aguilar's shocking declaration. Then Smoke said, "Are you trying to tell me that you think you own my ranch?"

"I am not *trying* to tell you anything, Señor Jensen. I *am* telling you that I *do* own your ranch. There is no question about the matter."

"Well, I'm sure as hell questioning it," Smoke said.

"I have a copy of the original land grant from the king of Spain," Aguilar said. "If you insist, I will allow you to examine it. You will see that it lays out the grant's boundaries in great detail."

Smoke shook his head and said, "I don't care about some paper drawn up by a Spaniard who's been dead for a hundred years."

"Your state authorities will feel differently. My attorneys are in Denver even as we speak, presenting my evidence to the officials there."

Smoke's eyes narrowed.

"Then you haven't actually gotten anybody to agree to this loco notion yet."

"It is only a matter of time," Aguilar said confidently.

"Well, I have attorneys, too," Smoke said, "and I plan on getting a wire off to them mighty damn quick like." He glanced at Travis Hinton. "Unless somebody plans to try to stop me."

"Take it easy, Jensen," Hinton responded with a cool smile. "Nobody's trying to start gun trouble here. My boys and I rode along with Don Sebastian just to make sure he didn't run into any unexpected problems. You know, like outlaws or redskins or some such. Like he said, he has lawyers to handle all the other things."

Smoke didn't believe that for a second. Hinton and the other gun-wolves hadn't signed with Aguilar simply to act as bodyguards. That job wouldn't pay enough for men such as that. They worked for fighting wages, and they didn't take jobs that didn't hold out a pretty good promise of gunplay — and a big payoff for those who survived.

Hired guns knew and accepted that they would probably die suddenly and unexpectedly . . . but until that day came, they would be well paid!

Louis leaned forward in his chair and said, "Gentlemen, I believe it might be best if you leave."

"Now?" Aguilar said, arching an eyebrow. "We have not finished our coffee."

"Nevertheless, this is my establishment . . . and I am particular about who I serve."

Hinton sat up a little straighter and said, "I'm not used to being kicked out of places, Longmont."

"You may have to become accustomed to it if you remain in Big Rock for very long. Smoke has many friends here."

"The don's just here on business, but if you want to make it personal . . ." Hinton nodded toward the door, where several of the men who had ridden into town with him and Aguilar were just now coming into Longmont's. "We can play it that way, too."

Smoke appreciated Louis coming to his defense, but a gun battle wouldn't solve anything, at least not right here and now. Aguilar had stated that he was fighting this by legal means, and Smoke figured he could do the same . . . for the time being, anyway.

But no matter what it took, he wasn't going to allow Aguilar — or anybody else — to take the Sugarloaf away from him. Not even if it *did* come down to gunplay.

"That's all right, Louis," he said. "You don't have to boot these two out on my account." He shoved back his chair. "I think I'm going to go see if Sally is finished with her shopping. I'd just as soon get home."

At the mention of the word *home,* Aguilar just smirked. Smoke resisted the temptation to knock the arrogant expression off the man's face, but it wasn't easy.

Instead, he stood up, nodded to Louis, and strode out of the place without looking back.

Sally had not failed to notice the tension between her husband and Don Juan Sebastian Aguilar. And because she'd been married to Smoke all these years, she had seen enough gunmen to recognize that breed in Travis Hinton and the other men.

Still, she couldn't blame Señor Aguilar for hiring competent men to accompany him and his wife in their travels. The West, while not as wild as it had been only a few years earlier, was still not exactly what anybody would call tame.

As she and Mariana browsed in Mr. Goldstein's store, Sally indulged her curiosity and asked the younger woman, "Where is this new home you mentioned, Doña Mariana?"

"I could not say, precisely. Sebastian says that I need not trouble myself with such details. He knows our destination, and he has the paper that tells where it is, besides. You know, the land grant from the king."

"The king of Spain?" Sally said.

"*Sí*. It gave the land to Sebastian's great-grandfather."

Sally thought about that and said slowly, "So that's why he was talking about the Treaty of Guadalupe Hidalgo."

"I know only a little about that, as well."

Sally knew, though. She was well educated, having believed that if she was going to be a teacher — her profession when she and Smoke first met — she should know as much as possible about everything she might be called on to teach to the children in her classes. She had studied quite a bit about the country's history and knew that the Treaty of Guadalupe Hidalgo had ended the war between the United States and Mexico and ceded a great deal of territory in the Southwest to the Americans.

Mariana just batted her eyelashes and smiled a pretty but empty smile. Sally ventured a guess and, hoping the younger woman wouldn't think the question was rude, said, "You're not the don's first wife, are you, Doña Mariana?"

The blunt query didn't seem to bother Mariana. She said, "No, Sebastian was married before, to a woman named Theresa Inez. She passed away several years ago, may she rest in peace."

"Amen," Sally murmured.

"Sebastian was lonely after that, so he got in touch with one of his friends in Mexico City . . . my father . . . and arranged for me to visit him with my duenna. Shortly after that, my father told me that Sebastian had asked for my hand in marriage."

"I see," Sally said. "Did you want to marry him?"

"My father told me it would be a good match. I am a respectful daughter and would not argue with my father."

So Mariana's father had, for all practical purposes, *sold* her to Don Juan Sebastian Aguilar, thought Sally. That really went against the grain for her. She never would have accepted such an arrangement.

Mariana, on the other hand, seemed to be all right with it. And she had spoken to Aguilar as if she genuinely cared for him, Sally recalled. She supposed that such things were possible, even though it never

116

would have worked with her.

"I am glad that we came here," Mariana said abruptly. "I feel that I have made a friend already."

Sally couldn't help but return the younger woman's smile. She reached out and clasped both of Mariana's hands with hers.

"Welcome to Big Rock," she said. "I hope you're very happy here."

Just as she voiced that, the store's front door opened and Smoke swept inside, along with the chilly wind. Sally glanced in his direction, then looked again. All it took was one glimpse of her husband's face for her to know that something was wrong.

Very wrong.

She let go of Mariana's hands and turned to him.

"Smoke, what is it?"

Instead of answering right away, Smoke nodded to Mariana and pinched the brim of his hat as he said, "Señora Aguilar."

"Señor Jensen," she responded. "Did you and my husband conclude your business?"

"Not really, but the matter's settled as far as I'm concerned," Smoke said tersely. Sally could tell that he was angry and that he was trying really hard not to let that overcome his natural politeness.

"I hope there was no trouble," Mariana

murmured.

"Not yet."

Sally was losing her patience. She said, "Smoke, you've got to tell me what's wrong."

Smoke nodded toward Mariana and said, "Señora Aguilar didn't tell you?"

"No. She said something about a land grant —"

It was rare for Smoke to interrupt Sally when she was talking, but he did so now. "It's an old Spanish land grant," he said, "and according to what Aguilar claims, it means this whole valley is his — including the Sugarloaf."

Sally drew in a sharp, surprised breath. She looked again at Mariana and asked, "Is this true?"

The young woman still wore that vacuous smile as she said, "I do not know the details. Sebastian handles all our affairs, including the land we own and where we shall live."

"He doesn't own the Sugarloaf, or anything else around here," Smoke snapped.

"That is for the authorities to decide, is it not?"

Sally saw Smoke bite back the sharp answer that almost escaped from him. Instead, he said, "I bear you no ill will, Doña Mariana, but I'm not going to let your

118

husband get away with this. You can tell him, if you want, that all of you would be better off going back where you came from."

She shook her head and said, "We cannot do this, Señor Jensen. Sebastian says this valley will be our home from now on."

"I'll have something to say about —"

Sally stopped her husband by putting her hand on his arm and saying, "Smoke, I think we should go."

He got control of himself again and asked, "Have you finished with your shopping?"

"Enough. Mr. Goldstein's clerks have already loaded some things on the buggy. Anything else I need, we can send Pearlie or Cal or one of the other men to get it in a day or two."

"All right." Smoke took her arm and nodded again to Mariana, but he didn't touch his hat brim this time. "Señora Aguilar."

"Señor Jensen." Mariana beamed sweetly. "And, Sally, if I may you call you that. I will see you again soon."

"I reckon you can count on that," Smoke said as he and Sally left the store.

CHAPTER 11
THE MACMURPHY SANITARIUM

Without being too obvious about it, Doc Monday kept an eye on Bill Williams — or William Malkin, if that was really his name — at supper and then during the evening, when some of the patients sat in the parlor. Many of them weren't healthy enough to come eat in the dining room or to visit with the other patients, of course.

Doc believed that his skill at reading other people, honed by countless hours of sitting at a poker table, allowed him to tell what they were thinking. Unless Williams was a better cardplayer than he had ever demonstrated during the games, he was his usual grumpy self, not bothered by anything in particular, just grouchy on general principles.

Mrs. Bennett stayed in her room and took her supper there, Doc noted. That was probably a good thing. She might not have been able to keep from staring at Williams in horror, and that would have just aggravated the situation.

As the patients settled down in the parlor, Doc allowed his curiosity to get the better of him. On a table in the corner was a big stack of newspapers that went back several months. Ever since he had seen those letters and the gun with the name Malkin on it, he'd had a nagging feeling in the back of his mind that something was familiar about it. As he walked toward the table, one of the nurses, a friendly young woman named Jessica, stopped him and asked, "Do you need anything, Mr. Monday?"

"No, I don't believe so," Doc said. Then a thought occurred to him. "Oh, wait. Perhaps you can confirm a recollection for me, my dear. How long has Mr. Williams been a patient here?"

"Mr. Williams?" Jessica frowned. She looked across the room to where Williams was sitting and talking with Hubert Guinn. "Let's see . . . this is the middle of December, and I believe he was admitted as a patient in August . . . so around four months, I'd say."

Doc nodded and said, "I was thinking the same thing, but I wasn't sure. Thank you, Nurse."

"Why do you ask?"

"Oh, it's nothing," he said easily. "Just a little game I play with myself. I try to remember how long everyone has been here. Sometimes I put them in order in my head. You know, just a silly thing to pass the time."

She smiled and said, "You've been here longer than I have, I know that."

"I've been here longer than most," Doc admitted with a rueful smile on his face. "I'm sure Dr. MacMurphy is surprised. He probably expected me to die a long time ago."

Jessica's eyes widened, and she exclaimed, "Goodness, don't say things like that, Mr. Monday!"

"Don't worry. I plan to be around for a while yet."

Still giving him a bit of a worried look, she moved on, and he continued to the table where the newspapers were stacked. Williams had been here at the sanitarium for four months, and the papers were cleared out usually every five or six months. Actually, Doc couldn't recall the last time any of them had been thrown away. So it was possible that if there was anything in one of them about a man named William Malkin, it was still here.

Of course, his memory could be playing

tricks on him. These days, he no longer trusted it as completely as he once had. . . .

He got a handful of papers from the bottom of the stack and was about to sit down in a comfortable armchair with them when Banjo bustled up to him and asked, "Are you up for another game of cards, Doc?"

Doc hated to disappoint his friend, but he shook his head.

"Not tonight, I don't think, Banjo," he said. "I'm afraid I'm rather tired. I thought I'd look at these old papers for a bit and then turn in."

Banjo's face fell. He said, "All right, if you say so."

"We'll play again tomorrow. I give you my word on that."

"Sure." Banjo summoned up a smile. "Don't you go dyin' in the middle of the night, before we have a chance to win some of our nickels and dimes back from you."

Doc chuckled and said, "That's definitely not my plan."

Banjo wandered off. Doc sat down and checked the dates on the newspapers. He had several from August in the stack and started with them.

He went through their pages story by story, looking for any mention of someone named Malkin. Earlier, he had tried to figure out why the name seemed familiar to him, and the question had vexed him so much, he'd had trouble concentrating on his pirate book, which was called *Treasure Island*. Stevenson, the author, was a vivid, exciting writer, but Doc had just been too distracted to enjoy the yarn the man had spun.

Not finding anything in the newspapers, he set them aside and pulled another handful from the stack. They had been pawed through so many times, they weren't in any real order. He didn't find any issues from August in this bunch.

I'll just have to dig deeper, he told himself.

Finally, after half an hour or so, in an early August issue of the *Rocky Mountain News,* something caught his eye. It was the name Malkin, just as he had thought he might find. He spotted it first in a headline.

What he saw in that headline made Doc sit up straighter and tighten his jaw.

TRAIN ROBBERY NETS MALKIN GANG
$50,000.

As he sat there reading the story, Doc recalled seeing it before, when the newspaper first arrived at the sanitarium. He didn't remember any of the details, but they

124

came back to him as his eyes followed the densely packed lines of type.

The holdup had taken place on the night of August 1. Seven desperadoes, led by the notorious outlaw Bill Malkin, had taken over an isolated flag-stop station in western Kansas. They had pistol-whipped and knocked unconscious the station's night manager, who was the only one there on that rainy evening. Then one of the bandits had donned the stationman's uniform and raised the flag to stop the westbound that was due through shortly.

That train had fifty thousand dollars in the safe in its express car, and it was thought that the Malkin gang had an inside man who worked for either the railroad or the express company, otherwise they wouldn't have known about the money shipment. Under the circumstances, the engineer shouldn't have stopped, since it was rather suspicious that the flag would be up on a night like that, out in the middle of nowhere.

But the presence of a man who apparently was the station manager on the platform must have lulled any suspicions, because he *did* stop. The fake stationmaster and another of the outlaws stormed into the cab and held their guns on the engineer and the fireman, while the other five concentrated their efforts on getting into the express car. A stick of dynamite blew the door open. The express messenger put up a fight, loosing both barrels of his shotgun at the outlaws, but even though a couple of them suffered minor wounds, the lead that the gang poured into the car riddled the unfortunate messenger until his corpse barely looked human.

After that, the outlaws opened the safe somehow, without blowing the door off and risking the destruction of the cash the safe held. One of them, a man named Lane Thackery, was known to be an expert safecracker, so the assumption was that he was able to open the door. They took the money, piled onto their horses, which were tied nearby, and vanished into the rainy night.

The stationmaster died from the blows to his head, but not before regaining consciousness long enough to identify Bill Malkin and his gang as the perpetrators of the robbery and killings.

Doc's heart was beating faster by the time he finished reading the story. Was it possible that "Bill Williams" was really Bill Malkin, the outlaw? Who would ever think to look for a train robber in a sanitarium?

Sensing that there was still more to the

story, Doc returned to the newspapers and searched through them until he found an issue from several days after the one that had the story of the train holdup.

That one contained a story about how a posse of railroad detectives and deputy U.S. marshals had caught up to the Malkin gang at a road ranch frequented by owlhoots just over the border in eastern Colorado. A fierce gun battle between the two groups had left five of the outlaws dead. The other two, the leader Bill Malkin and his subordinate Lane Thackery, had gotten away.

The posse had failed to recover the stolen fifty thousand dollars.

Doc thought furiously. Had anyone else become a patient at the sanitarium about the same time as Williams? Was it possible that the outlaw Thackery was hiding out here, too?

After a moment of searching his memory, Doc knew that wasn't the case. No one else had shown up around that time. And as far as Doc could recall, the only patients admitted since Williams had all been women. Wherever Lane Thackery was, it wasn't the MacMurphy Sanitarium.

But that still left "Bill Williams." Poor Mrs. Bennett, no matter how frightened she was, had no idea just how close she might have come to death. If Williams was Malkin, and if Malkin suspected that his masquerade had been compromised, there was no telling what he might do in order to conceal his secret. He had a hangman's noose waiting for him if he was caught, so probably there were no lengths he wouldn't go to.

Thank goodness, thought Doc, that Malkin had no idea he had been in his room and had seen the gun and the letters.

Doc spent a while pondering his next move. He couldn't very well march up to Williams and demand to know if he was really Bill Malkin, the outlaw and murderer. And if he told Dr. MacMurphy what he suspected, there was a good chance the doctor would believe the whole thing was just some flight of fancy. MacMurphy was a good man, kind and caring to his patients, but he was stolid and almost completely lacking in imagination, bless his heart.

No, thought Doc, his best course of action might be to write a letter to the railroad. They had detectives to investigate such cases, and if they showed up here and started poking into Bill Williams's past, Doc was confident they would uncover the truth. Best of all, he could write that letter without arousing any suspicion on Williams's part. Williams wouldn't even know about it.

During the evening, Williams played checkers with Banjo and Hubert, the three of them alternating, with one man sitting out each game. Williams seemed to be in a pretty good mood, for him. It boggled Doc's mind that the man sitting on the other side of the parlor, playing checkers with those two old men, was really a train robber and murderer.

And yet, looking at Williams's hard-featured face and his deep-set eyes, Doc had no trouble believing it. . . .

Tiredness crept up on Doc, as it always did. When he tried to stand up from the armchair so he could return to his room and go to bed, he had to push hard with both arms to lift himself to his feet. His legs just didn't want to support him very well. The muscles were too stiff. When he finally made it upright and turned his head, something in his neck crackled loudly. It sounded loud to him, anyway.

No one had ever said that getting old was easy, he reminded himself.

Back in his room, he put on his nightshirt and considered trying to read some more of Mr. Stevenson's book. With everything he had discovered this evening, though, he knew he would be even less able to concentrate on fiction. Figuring he might as well try to go to sleep, he blew out the lamp and crawled into bed.

He dozed off surprisingly easily. Weariness won out over racing thoughts for a change. As he lay there in the dark, he slipped deeper into sleep.

So he never heard the faint click as his door opened, had no idea anyone was in his room until big, strong hands closed hard around his neck, a heavy weight leaned over and into him, and a voice rasped in a harsh whisper, "You should've kept your nose outta my business, you damned old fool. Now you've got to die."

CHAPTER 12
DENVER

Preacher's mind could hardly credit what Adelaide DuBois had just told him. Surely he hadn't heard her correctly. He asked her, "Did you just say that your own grandson is tryin' to kill you?"

Adelaide nodded and said, "That's right." A tiny tear trickled from the corner of her eye and trickled down her weathered cheek.

"I didn't know you and ol' Polecat had any young'uns, let alone grandkids."

"We had two children," she said. "A boy and a girl. The girl, I'm sad to say, didn't survive childhood. She died of a fever when she was six years old."

"Sorry," Preacher murmured.

"The boy grew to be a fine young man, though. His name was Phillip. He married and had a son of his own. They named him George. Then Phillip and his wife both passed away at a fairly young age, too, so Pierre and I were left to raise George for a

131

few years, until he was grown. I always believed that he . . . he was devoted to us, as he was to his own parents." Adelaide sighed. "But money has a way of changing things, doesn't it?"

"Money?" Preacher repeated.

"Pierre did well working for the fur company, and then later, when that business was no longer successful, he was involved in several other ventures that proved lucrative. He left me . . . financially comfortable . . . when he died."

"Well, I'm glad to hear that, I guess. This grandson of yours, George, I reckon he's got his eye on that money?"

Adelaide lowered her eyes to the table, as if embarrassed, and said, "After he left our home, I'm afraid he forgot everything we tried to teach him. He began drinking and gambling and associating with all sorts of unsavory people. Pierre passed away during this time, as well. I've always suspected that he worried himself to death over George. I . . . I think if he had still been alive, he could have taken George in hand and straightened him out. I tried, Lord knows I tried my best, but I just never seemed able to get through to him."

"I could have a good long talk with the youngster," Preacher offered.

Adelaide shook her head and said, "I'm afraid it's gone too far for that. George came to me a few months ago and asked for money. He didn't even make any pretense about intending to pay it back. He wanted me to just give it to him outright. He said he needs it very badly. And then he said . . . he said he intends to get it, one way or another."

She closed her eyes as a shudder ran through her.

"Why, that dang young scoundrel!" Preacher said. "I'll do more'n have a talk with him. I'll give him a good hard kick in the hindquarters, and if that don't do the trick —"

Adelaide caught hold of Preacher's hand and squeezed it again.

"No, no, I don't want him hurt," she said quickly. "No matter what else happens, he's still my grandson."

Preacher reined in the anger he felt and asked her, "What was that about him tryin' to kill you?"

"After that conversation when it seemed like he was trying to threaten me, I made him leave the house."

"Dang right. You still live in St. Louis?"

"Yes. Not in the little cabin where you visited us all those years ago. I doubt if it's

133

even still standing. We moved to a better place while Pierre was still working for the fur company." Adelaide took a deep breath and then went on, "I was upset by that confrontation — of course, anyone would have been — but I didn't really believe that George would ever try to harm me. The idea of the threat being real just . . . just never occurred to me. But then, a few days later, as I was walking along the street, a wagon team nearly ran over me. I barely got out of the way in time."

Preacher stared at her.

"You ain't sayin' the fella drivin' the wagon was your grandson, George?"

"No," Adelaide replied with a shake of her head. "At least I don't believe so. To be honest, I never really got a good look at the man. He just whipped the team and kept going. He never even slowed down."

Preacher rubbed the bristles on his chin and frowned in thought for a moment, then said, "You know, some fellas drive like a bat outta hell. That's just the way they are."

"That's what I thought, too . . . at first. But then there was another close call . . . I was shopping when a heavy crate fell from a second-story window and nearly landed on me as I passed by . . . Just another accident, one might call it. And then . . . and then . . ."

She had to take another deep, shuddery breath. "Someone took a shot at me. I was inside the house, near a window, and the glass shattered suddenly and I *felt* something go past my head. It struck the wall opposite the window. The constable came and dug it out and said that it was a rifle ball."

Preacher knew all too well what it felt like to have a shot go right past his head. He had experienced that sensation many, many times over the years. And once somebody did, they never forgot what it was like.

"It sure sounds like somebody's out to get you, all right," he said. "I'm sorry for havin' to ask this, but is there anybody else who might want to hurt you? Any enemies you or Polecat — I mean, Pierre — made over the years?"

"I can't think of who it might be," she said solemnly. "Once Pierre stopped going to the mountains, we lived a very peaceful life."

"George is gonna inherit your money, I reckon?"

"Of course."

"And he knows that?"

"Yes."

"Well, then, maybe what you oughta do is take him outta your will and make sure he knows about *that,* too. If he ain't gonna profit by somethin' happenin' to you, then there's no reason for him to hurt you."

"But I couldn't do that," Adelaide said. "He's the only relative I have left. There's no one else to leave the money to."

"Hell, leave it to charity if you have to!" Preacher burst out. Then he went on quickly, "I'm sorry about the language, Adelaide. I'm just a mite worked up, because I don't like to hear about you bein' treated in such a no-good fashion."

She smiled and said, "I knew you'd feel that way, Arthur. That's why I came out here to Denver to try to find you. I thought you might be willing to protect me."

"Durned right I am!"

"You see, I believe, I really believe, that in time George will come to his senses. It's just a matter of making sure that he doesn't do anything . . . unforgivable . . . until then."

Unforgivable — like murdering his own grandma, thought Preacher.

"You want me to keep you alive," he said, more of a statement than a question.

"That's right. I'm not just worried about George himself. I think he's capable of hiring someone to try to harm me, like that wagon driver, if it *wasn't* him at the reins. And if he's sunk to the level of trying to have me assassinated by gunfire, by promising part of the profits to whoever performs the foul deed . . ."

"You need somebody lookin' after you, all right. Ain't no doubt about that." An idea occurred to Preacher. "And I'm right glad you came to me about it."

"You are?" For the first time since she'd sat down at the table, Adelaide DuBois looked a little hopeful.

"That's right," Preacher said. "It just so happens, I'm on my way to a place where you'd be safer than just about anywhere else east or west of the Mississippi. Did you have any plans for Christmas?"

"Christmas?" Adelaide repeated, apparently confused. "No, not at all, since I'm alone. And to be honest, with everything that's been going on, I . . . I haven't really felt much like celebrating."

"I understand that. But I'm on my way to the Sugarloaf, a ranch not all that far from here, to spend Christmas with some folks who are the closest thing to family *I've* got. You mentioned 'em yourself a few minutes ago. Smoke and Sally Jensen." Preacher squeezed her hand for a change. "I want you to come along with me."

She was shaking her head almost before the words were out of his mouth.

"Oh, no, I couldn't. I wouldn't want to

intrude —"

"Smoke and Sally wouldn't think of it as intrudin', I can puredee guarantee that. They'll tell you their own selves, any friend of mine is a friend of theirs."

"It just doesn't seem like it would be proper."

"Well, I don't know about you, Adelaide, but I'm so gosh-darned old, I don't much give a buffalo's hind end what folks think is or ain't proper no more."

She laughed and said, "I suppose we *are* past the age where respectability is the first consideration."

"Yep, that's the way I look at it."

A concerned expression came over her face again. She said, "But if George really has sent . . . well, hired killers . . . after me, it could easily be dangerous for me to visit your friends' home. There's no telling what trouble might break out."

"That's just what I'm gettin' at!" Preacher said. "Smoke's brother Luke is supposed to be comin' for the holidays, too, and maybe his adopted brother, Matt. So there's gonna be a whole family of Jensens there, and it don't matter how many gun-wolves that no-good grandson o' yours sends after you. With that many Jensens around, they're gonna be outnumbered!"

Despite that assurance, Adelaide still hesitated, but only for a moment. Then she smiled, reached over with her other hand so she could clasp both of Preacher's, and said, "I accept your very kind invitation, Arthur. And I hope that . . . well, that everything I've told you is just the maundering imagination of an old woman and there won't really be any trouble."

"Don't you worry about that," Preacher told her. "Shoot, I don't reckon Smoke and the others would feel like it was really Christmas if there wasn't some kind of Hades breakin' loose!"

CHAPTER 13
AMITY, UTAH

Luke Jensen had shot it out with countless outlaws over the years. He had been betrayed, gunned down, and left for dead in the closing days of the Civil War. He had endured torture at the hands of evil men.

Despite that, he had still felt a shiver go through him when he heard Marshal Ed Rowan's words.

Maybe that was because in addition to listing the names of Hank Trafford's three children, the lawman had also used the phrase "your responsibility now."

As a bounty hunter, Luke had spent nearly two decades drifting from place to place, never settling down or feeling any desire to do so. After Smoke had discovered that his older brother, long thought dead, was actually still alive, he had made it plain that Luke was welcome on the Sugarloaf anytime, even if he wanted to make the visit permanent and consider the ranch his home.

As much as Luke enjoyed spending time with Smoke and Sally, he had never even considered taking them up on that offer. He just wasn't cut out for putting down roots.

Because of that, he hadn't had any real responsibility for years, other than keeping himself alive. That was the way he liked it.

"Wait just a minute, Marshal," he said. "You can't pawn that off on me. I didn't even know Trafford had any kids."

"Don't matter whether you knew or not," Rowan snapped. "You're the one who just made them orphans. That means you've got to step up and do the right thing."

"No, I . . . Wait. You said orphans?"

"Yup," the lawman said, nodding solemnly.

"Their mother's dead, too?"

"Died six months ago. Her name was Alice." Rowan's lips pursed in disapproval. "From the way she looked and talked sometimes, most folks around here figured she must've been a soiled dove that Hank took out of a house somewhere. She wasn't any saint, that's for sure."

It took Luke a second to realize what the marshal meant. When he did, he said, "She wasn't a Mormon?"

"No, she wasn't, and Hank never should've brought her here. But they had those kids . . ." Rowan shrugged. "And I reckon she didn't have anyplace else to go. Probably didn't feel like she could ever go back to her own home, havin' lived such a shameful life."

By now, a number of Amity's citizens were clustered around Hank Trafford's body, and some hostile glances were being sent in Luke's direction. Rowan must have noticed that, because he said, "Go across the street there and wait in my office. I'll clear off the crowd and get our undertaker up here to deal with Hank's body. Best you're not just standing around out in the open while that's goin' on."

Luke understood what he meant. Rowan didn't want the resentment that the townspeople felt toward Luke to boil up into more trouble.

"All right," he said. "I'll wait there."

Luke crossed the street, while Rowan moved toward the crowd and started waving his arms and telling the townspeople to move on.

Inside, the marshal's office looked like scores of others Luke had seen over the years. The furnishings included a scarred wooden desk with a straight-backed chair behind it, a potbellied stove in one corner, a dusty sofa, a hat tree, a gun cabinet with rifles and shotguns racked in it, and a wooden cabinet with doors on it that was used for some sort of storage, more than likely. A door in the back wall led to a cell-block, Luke supposed, but he didn't open it to make sure of that.

One thing was different: No pot of coffee simmered on the stove, as it had in practically every other lawman's office Luke had ever set foot in. He didn't see how these folks survived without it, but that was their own business, he supposed. He craved a cup now but knew he would have to wait until he was on the trail again to brew some for himself.

Through the front window, Luke watched what was going on in the street. Rowan had succeeded in dispersing part of the crowd, anyway, although a few people were still standing around, watching to see what was going to happen.

A fat man with a jolly grin on his face pulled up in a wagon, and he and a couple of the remaining bystanders loaded Hank Trafford's body in the back of the wagon. Once the wagon had turned around and gone back down the street, the remainder of the crowd finally drifted away.

Luke expected the marshal to join him in the office, but instead, Rowan turned, headed along the street, and was soon out of sight. Luke didn't like that much. He wasn't sure what Rowan was doing, but he was suspicious enough that he considered getting on his horse and riding out of Amity right now.

But if he did that, it would mean giving up the reward for Trafford. He didn't have either the outlaw's body or the affidavit Marshal Rowan had promised to give him. Without one of those things, he couldn't collect.

He waited, with a frown on his face, still wishing he had a cup of coffee.

A quarter of an hour dragged by. Then he spotted Rowan coming back along the street toward the office, herding three small children in front of him like they were sheep.

Luke cursed through gritted teeth. If he stalked out of here, went to his horse, and rode out of town, it would look like he was running away, and that would stick in his craw.

Actually, it would more than *look* like he was running away, he told himself. He would be . . . and he couldn't bring himself to do that.

So he was still there when the marshal opened the door and ushered the youngsters inside the office. He closed the door behind him, looked at Luke, and grunted.

"Halfway figured you'd have lit a shuck outta here before now," he said. "You must really want that reward money."

"We don't have to talk about that now," Luke said with a tiny nod toward the three children.

"Oh, they already know you killed their pa."

Luke grimaced at Rowan's casual tone of voice.

The lawman went on, "It ain't like they ever saw that much of him. Hank was always gone, off robbing banks and such, and left their ma to raise 'em. He never stayed put any longer than he had to."

Luke looked down at the children. All three of them regarded him solemnly, their expressions so serious, it seemed unlikely that they ever smiled. If that was true, thought Luke, it was mighty sad.

They all had curly blond hair, a few light, widely scattered freckles, and snub noses. The oldest boy — Bodie, Luke recalled Marshal Rowan calling him — was about eight years old. The girl, Hannah, was maybe six, and then the littlest one, Teddy, was four or five.

Bodie and Teddy wore canvas trousers and homespun shirts. Hannah's dress looked

145

like it had been made out of a feed sack. The clothes were well worn and sported patches here and there, but the garments appeared to be clean. The children had decent shoes on their feet.

"You said it's been six months since . . . ," Luke began, but then his voice trailed off.

"Since their ma died?" Clearly, it didn't bother Rowan to talk about it. Why should it? She had been a Gentile, after all. "That's right. Some of the women here in town have been lookin' after them since then, sort of passin' 'em around. We're not monsters here, you know, Jensen. We're not gonna stand by and let kids go hungry or do without clothes and a roof over their heads. But there's a limit to how much we'll do for them, and now that you're here, we've reached it."

"Well, I'm not going to adopt them!"

The harsh words came out of Luke's mouth without him really thinking about what he was saying. As the expressions on the youngsters' face grew even more dour, he regretted that emphatic statement. He had only told the truth, though. He didn't need or want a ready-made family.

"That's all right, mister," Bodie said. "We don't want anybody to take care of us who don't really want to."

146

"Now, hold on," Luke told the boy. "I never said I wouldn't . . . Well, I don't really know what I can do . . ."

He had to bite back another curse of frustration.

"I don't really care what you do with 'em, as long as you get them out of Amity," Rowan said. "They don't belong here."

The little girl, Hannah, turned her head to look up at the marshal and asked, "Where do we belong?"

Rowan had the decency to look a little uncomfortable, at least, as he said, "I don't know. I reckon that'll be up to Mr. Jensen here."

Luke closed his eyes for a second and sighed. He didn't see any way out of this. He couldn't ride off and leave these three youngsters here, where they weren't wanted. He wouldn't abandon any kid to that fate.

Maybe he could find some place that knew how to deal with orphans. . . .

That thought was going through his mind when he suddenly caught his breath. He *did* know of a place like that, he realized, and as luck would have it, he had planned to head in that direction as soon as he finished with the chore of tracking down Hank Trafford and dealing with the outlaw.

A while back he had gotten a letter from

his sister-in-law Sally, asking him to come to the Sugarloaf and spend Christmas with her and Smoke. She was sending similar invitations to other members of the family, she had said in the letter, but she didn't know who else was going to be there.

And it didn't really matter, Luke told himself. What was important at the moment was that in the town of Big Rock, not far from Smoke's Sugarloaf Ranch, an orphanage had been established. The Holy Spirit Orphanage, that was what it was called, he remembered. And Sally had a lot of pull with the folks who ran it.

If anybody could find a good home for these three sad-faced youngsters staring up at him, it was Sally Jensen. She had done just that sort of thing before.

"All right," Luke said. "I'll take them with me. What about their belongings?"

Marshal Rowan looked relieved. He said, "The lady who's been takin' care of them lately said she'd pack it all up. You can go by there and get it on your way out of town."

"Speaking of that, I'm going to need a wagon and a team. I can't have all three of them hanging on me while we're riding horseback."

"Levi Anderson will give you a good deal,"

Rowan said. "You'll need some supplies, too."

"Yeah, I know." Luke sighed. "I don't suppose there's a bank here in town?"

Rowan shook his head and said, "Nope. Closest one is up in Fillmore, a day's ride north of here. You'll be able to collect that bounty there, I reckon. You got cash to pay for what you'll need here?"

Luke nodded. He had the money, all right, but paying for a wagon, a team, and supplies would leave him pretty low on funds. Still, he thought as he looked at the three children, it had to be done.

"Get that affidavit written out, Marshal," he said. "I don't suppose the townspeople would like it if I stayed here overnight and the kids and I got a fresh start in the morning?"

"Be best if you didn't," Rowan said.

That was the answer Luke was expecting. He said, "All right, kids, we'll pick up what we need, get your gear, and then we'll be on our way to the Sugarloaf." He glanced at Rowan. "It's a better place than this, anyway. You'll like it there."

"I don't know," eight-year-old Bodie said. "Ain't that what they say when you die? That you're goin' to a better place?"

"Nobody's dying where we're going,"

Luke said.

Then, as he remembered some of the violent Christmases he had shared with his family in the past, he fervently hoped that was true this time.

"Wait a minute," Denny said as she finished buttoning up her shirt, which had dried quickly in the thin air and hot sun. Her cousins Ace and Chance, along with her brother Louis, still sat on the log, with their backs to her. "This was supposed to be the story of how the two of you found out that Uncle Luke is really your father, and the only time either of you even mentioned yourselves, it was just in passing."

Ace and Chance had been trading back and forth as they told the story, although as usual, Chance was actually doing most of the talking and the more taciturn Ace just spoke up now and then to clarify some point or rein in Chance's exaggerations.

"All these other people are important to what happened later," Ace said. "You have to understand what brought them all together."

"We know what brought them together," Denny insisted. "They came to the Sugarloaf to celebrate Christmas."

"Yes, but they brought trouble with them," Chance said.

"As usual," Ace added.

Louis said, "That's another thing . . . How could the two of you possibly know all this that you've told us?"

"Dramatic license," Chance replied with a smile.

"And they told us about it later," Ace said.

"Now," Chance said, "do you want to hear the rest of the story or not?"

Denny said, "I want to know where the two of you were. After all, you're supposed to be the main part of it, remember?"

"When the Jensens get together, everybody has a part to play," Chance said.

"But for the record," Ace put in, "we were down in New Mexico . . ."

CHAPTER 14
RATON, NEW MEXICO

The Sangre de Cristo Mountains loomed north of the settlement. From a distance, they appeared to be an impassable barrier to anyone who wanted to continue traveling into Colorado. But as they rode closer, Ace and Chance Jensen were able to see the place where the rocky, thickly wooded heights folded back on themselves to form the fabled Raton Pass, one of the most important landmarks on the original Santa Fe Trail.

"Looks like quite a climb up there," Chance commented as their horses ambled along the trail, which up ahead turned into the main street of the town that took its name from the pass. The ground had a dusting of snow on it, and some of the powdery white stuff had collected on the branches of the pine trees they passed, too.

"Yeah, but from what I've heard, people on horseback don't have any trouble making it," Ace said. "With a strong enough team, you can even take a wagon over Raton Pass. Plenty of folks have done it. The trail is hardly ever closed, even in the winter like this."

Chance shivered and said, "I'll bet it's even colder up there at the summit. It's chilly enough down here! We need to find a nice saloon and warm our old bones a little."

Ace smiled. Their bones weren't exactly "old," since both of them were in their early twenties. They were the same age, technically, since they were twins, although Ace had been born a few minutes earlier than Chance.

They were fraternal twins, not identical, so while they bore a strong resemblance to each other, there were obvious differences, as well. Those differences extended beyond the physical. Ace knew good and well his brother had more in mind than warming up when he said he wanted to find a saloon. If some good whiskey, a pretty saloon girl or two, and maybe a card game were involved as well, Chance would be happy.

"It's late enough in the day that we probably ought to spend the night," Ace said. "We still have plenty of time to make it to the Sugarloaf before Christmas."

"That sounds good to me," Chance

agreed. "I don't recall where the next good-sized settlement is, north of the pass."

"I wouldn't want to get to the ranch late, though," Ace mused. "It was mighty nice of Miss Sally to invite us."

Chance grinned and said, "Hey, we're Jensens, too, aren't we?"

"Not blood relations. We just have the same name. Although I've been wondering about that ever since we were at the Sugarloaf last time and I heard Luke talking about how he used to know a woman named Lettie . . ."

"Yeah, yeah, I know, and that was our ma's name, according to what Doc told us." Chance laughed. "At least you've started coming up with crazy ideas about *Luke* being our father, instead of Smoke. When we first met him, you got it in your head that *he* was our pa."

"Not really. You can't blame me for wanting to know the truth, though."

"The truth of the past is still the past," Chance said. "We can't change it, and it doesn't have anything to do with the present unless we let it. So I don't see any point in worrying about it. Just be glad we have a place to go for Christmas and look forward to all the good food Miss Sally will have on hand. I know I'm looking forward to it!"

His brother had a point there, thought Ace. They would be surrounded by friends and warmth and plenty to eat. They were lucky. Beyond lucky, Ace thought.

"Afterward, though, we're still going to ride on up to the sanitarium and visit with Doc, right?" he said.

Chance nodded and said, "Sure. It's been a while since we've seen him. I'd like to know how he's doing."

While the Jensen brothers were growing up, Ennis "Doc" Monday had been the only father they had known. They had been aware from an early age that he wasn't actually their father, but he had raised them their whole lives, after their mother died shortly after giving birth to them. Ace didn't think their real father, whoever he was, could have been any closer to them. It had been hard, going out on their own, but Doc's health had gotten bad, and he had gone into the sanitarium and had insisted that Ace and Chance not feel tied down. Blood relation or not, the boys had the same sort of restless nature Doc did, so they had agreed, although reluctantly.

Since then, Ace and Chance had drifted, but they tried to make it to the MacMurphy Sanitarium once or twice a year to check on Doc. At the start, it had been their hope that eventually he would improve to the point that he could leave the sanitarium and rejoin them in roaming the West. But that hadn't happened, and Ace had come to realize that Doc actually liked it at the sanitarium and didn't want to leave. It had become a home, of sorts, to a man who had never really had one.

First things first, though, Ace told himself as he and Chance rode along Raton's main street. If it were up to him, that would have been finding a hotel room for the night, but he knew Chance was searching for a likely-looking saloon.

Chance spotted one and pointed it out to his brother, saying, "Look there. The Lady Luck Saloon. That's got to be an omen, doesn't it?"

"Maybe. If you believe in omens."

Chance grinned again and said, "What gambler doesn't? Come on, Ace."

He turned his horse toward the saloon, which had a big sign proclaiming its name attached to the railing along the balcony that ran across the second floor. The Lady Luck looked like it might be the biggest and best saloon in Raton. Chance had a positive genius for sniffing out such places.

As they drew rein in front of this one, though, something unexpected happened.

With the temperature as low as it was, and thick gray clouds overhead and a chilly breeze blowing, the batwings that normally would be swinging in the saloon's entrance were tied back, and the regular doors, which had pebbled glass in their upper panels, were closed to keep the cold air out.

They burst open suddenly, and a small figure raced out of the saloon. Boots clomping heavily, a man lunged onto the boardwalk after him and yelled, "Come back here, you little redskin bastard!"

The Indian boy leaped off the boardwalk, ducked under the hitch rail, and started into the street.

"Stop him!" the man giving chase shouted at Ace and Chance. "He's a thief!"

Chance took his left foot out of the stirrup and stuck his leg out. The boy tried to dart around it, but he was going too fast. His momentum carried him into Chance's leg. His own legs continued churning, but the upper half of his body went backward. He landed hard on his back and let out a stunned *"Ooof!"*

Instantly, a look of regret passed over Chance's face. He had reacted instinctively, Ace knew, and now he was wondering if he had done the right thing. The Jensen brothers tended to side with underdogs, and this scrawny Indian youth, in ragged clothes that couldn't be doing much to block that cold wind, certainly looked like he fell into that category.

The man who strode out into the street after him, on the other hand, appeared to be well fed and warm in a long, thick sheepskin coat. He wore a black hat with a round brim and crown and an eagle feather sticking up from a snakeskin band. The coat hung open, revealing that he was a two-gun man, with a pair of revolvers riding in holsters attached to crisscrossing cartridge belts. His face was ruddy from drink or the cold or both.

The Indian boy was having trouble catching his breath after the fall had knocked the air out of his lungs. Gasping, he tried to scoot away as the man reached down to grab him. He got hold of the boy's shirt collar with his left hand, hauled him to his feet, and drew back his right hand.

"A good beatin' will teach you not to steal from your betters," he said.

Now Chance looked downright angry. Ace felt the same way. He spoke up, saying sharply, "Hold it, mister. No matter what he did, you've got no call to hit that boy."

The man looked up in obvious surprise and demanded, "What are you talkin' about? He's an Indian *and* a thief. I've got every right in the world to wallop him. Hell, in some places, they cut off your hands if you steal something. I used to be a sailor, so I know. He'll be gettin' off lucky with a beatin'."

Having said that, the man ignored the Jensen brothers and got ready again to strike the boy.

This time it was the metallic sound of gun hammers being cocked that stopped him.

His head jerked around toward the two young men on horseback. He saw that Ace and Chance had both drawn their guns and were holding them low, close by their holsters, but leveled in his general direction. He was so surprised he let go of the boy's shirt. The youngster was still panting a little, but he was able to dart away, race to the mouth of a nearby alley, duck into it, and disappear.

"What in blazes?" the man muttered. "You're throwin' down on *me*? Because of an Indian kid?"

"It doesn't matter who he is," Ace said. "You don't need to be whaling away on a youngster who's a fraction of your size."

"But he stole!" The man's face flushed even more. He looked like he was about to pop a blood vessel. "I set my poke on the

159

bar just for a second, and the filthy little bastard grabbed it and took off!" He rubbed his angular jaw. "He shouldn't have been in there to start with. Redskins don't need to be around liquor. Everybody knows that!"

"So he got away with your money?" Ace asked.

"Yeah — because of you two!"

Chance said, "We're sorry about that. But you should have just taken it back from him instead of trying to beat him."

The man's eyes narrowed as he glared angrily at the brothers. He said, "By all rights, you ought to pay me back what I lost. I mean, I yelled first thing that he was a thief. You knew he had stolen something, and you still let him get away."

Ace frowned. The man had a point, he supposed. He and his brother had reacted to the sight of a much larger man about to hurt a boy and hadn't thought everything through. The way the situation was shaping up, nobody had really done the right thing here.

"We're sorry, mister —"

"Starkey," the man broke in, introducing himself. "Clint Starkey."

"We're sorry, Mr. Starkey. It seems to me we're all sort of to blame for this."

"Not me," snapped Starkey. "I didn't do

anything wrong."

"Other than threaten a kid," Chance said, his voice equally sharp.

"Oh, the hell with it!" Starkey said as he made an abrupt, dismissive gesture. "There wasn't more than twenty dollars in that poke, and I've got more." He jabbed a finger at Ace and Chance. "But you two steer clear of me! The next time I see you, I might not be so forgivin'."

With that, he turned and stalked back into the Lady Luck Saloon, then slammed the door behind him.

Chance sighed and said, "Well, so much for going in there to warm up, get a drink, and maybe rustle up a poker game."

He slipped his gun, a .38 caliber Smith & Wesson Model 2 revolver, back into the cross-draw rig under his coat.

Ace pouched his iron, a Colt .45, as well. He said, "There are bound to be other saloons in this town. We'll find one, or maybe this really *was* an omen and we ought to forget about that and hunt up a hotel instead."

"Time enough for that later," Chance responded without hesitation. He turned his horse away from the hitch rail. They had never tied their mounts or even swung down from their saddles.

Ace followed suit. They rode past the alley where the Indian boy had disappeared. Ace glanced along the passage but saw no sign of him.

That was because the boy was waiting at the next corner for them, Ace realized as he saw the youngster step out and raise a hand in a tentative signal for them to stop.

"What do you want?" Chance asked in an annoyed voice. "Do you speak English?"

The boy's head bobbed up and down. He said, "I speak English good. Learned at mission school."

"You'd better run on home," Ace told him. "You don't want to be around here, in case Starkey comes around again."

"That Clint Starkey bad man," the boy said solemnly.

"Then why did you steal from him?" Chance asked.

"Very hungry. Little sisters very hungry." The boy hung his head. "But it is a sin to steal. Learned that at mission school, too."

"Maybe you ought to give Starkey his money back," Ace suggested.

"Or give it to us, and we'll see that he gets it," Chance said. "You might not want to go around him again. He warned us not to."

The boy started edging away, clearly uncomfortable with the idea of giving back the money he had stolen. He said, "I stopped you to warn you, too."

"What about?" Ace asked.

"Starkey. Do not believe anything he says. He won't forget you pulled guns on him. He will get even. He will kill you!"

With that, the boy whirled and raced away, back toward the alley. He ducked to the left at the far end and disappeared around the building's back corner.

"Do you think he's right?" Ace asked his brother. "Have we just ridden straight into trouble again?"

Chance laughed and said, "We wouldn't be Jensens if we didn't, would we?"

CHAPTER 15
THE MACMURPHY SANITARIUM

The survival instinct welled up inside Doc and made him thrash around on the bed as Bill Williams — or Malkin or whatever his name was! — tried to choke him to death. Doc arched his back and attempted to throw his assailant off him, while at the same time punching Williams in the head.

Doc would have been the first one to admit, though, that he was a lover, not a fighter. The blows he landed were awkward and didn't pack much power. They didn't seem to bother Williams at all. His hands just clamped tighter around Doc's throat.

Doc's madly whirling thoughts settled down a little. A certain sense of calm came over him. Was that the realization of impending death? Fear still filled his brain, but he remembered something else that he should have thought of before now.

He writhed enough on the bed to slide his hand underneath his pillow. His fingers closed around the butt of the little pistol he had put there earlier, as was his habit, and he yanked the gun out and slashed at Williams's face with it.

Doc still didn't have much strength, but the gun made a difference. Williams grunted in pain and then cursed. His grip loosened for a second. Doc hit him a second blow, this time smacking the gun against the side of his head. When Doc bucked up from the mattress again, Williams toppled to the side, slid off the bed, and thudded to the floor beside it.

Gasping for air, Doc rolled the other way as fast as he could. He came off the bed, and his feet hit the floor. He stumbled but caught himself with his left hand on the small bedside table. Turning, he lifted the gun in his right.

Williams was just pulling himself to his feet on the other side of the bed. In the shadowy room, he was a dark, bulky shape, but Doc heard his harsh breathing. All he had to do was aim at that sound and start pulling the trigger, Doc told himself. At this range, he couldn't miss, and even the small-caliber bullets would do considerable damage.

He didn't fire, though, and when he thought about it, he knew why.

Williams laughed.

"Can't pull the trigger, can you?" he said. "You're not a killer, Doc. You never have been. Me, on the other hand —"

"You're an outlaw and a murderer," Doc snapped. "I know who you are — *Malkin!*"

Well, that was a stupid thing to say, Doc told himself. He had just confirmed that he'd discovered this man's true identity.

But Malkin had come into his room to kill him, anyway, Doc reminded himself. What he had just said didn't really matter that much. Malkin already wanted him dead.

"Yeah, I figured when I saw you come out of my room that you knew more than you should," Malkin said. "I was sure of it when I saw you'd moved my gun and my letters. What made you suspicious of me to start with? That old biddy Bennett tell you she spotted me with the gun one day?"

"I don't have any idea what you're talking about," Doc said stiffly. He wasn't going to get Mrs. Bennett into trouble, too. "I've never been in your room, Bill."

Malkin laughed again and said, "That's not going to work. You just called me by my real name, remember?"

Doc cursed himself mentally. All right, that *had* been a mistake, after all. It was

166

just so hard to think straight with his heart pounding so frantically and his throat hurting where Malkin had choked him; and now, just to make things worse, the hand with the gun in it was starting to shake. The trembling was bad enough he wasn't sure he could hit Malkin anymore, even at such close range. . . .

"Come on, Monday," the outlaw continued. "Tell me who else knows and I'll make it easy on you."

"You mean you won't kill me?"

"No, I'll still kill you, but you can lay down in bed again and I'll use a pillow on you instead of my hands. It won't hurt as bad. It'll be just like going to sleep. That's what I should have done to start with. I reckon I'm just used to more direct methods. I like to be able to feel it when the life goes out of somebody I'm killing."

A shudder went through Doc that didn't have anything to do with the condition that made his hands shake at times. He knew he was facing a monster across this bed.

"I'm going to start shouting for help," he said. "You're going to stand there until someone comes, and then the law will be summoned."

"I don't think so."

A match rasped into sudden life. Doc

squinted and flinched against the glare and almost pulled the trigger, but he held off on the pressure. The shot likely would have gone wild, anyway.

And what would be wrong with that? He didn't have to shout for help, he realized. He could just fire a couple of shots, and that would bring people running. He was about to do so when Malkin held up the burning lucifer so that its light spread through the room and washed over his leering face, which was bleeding a little on one cheek, where the sight on Doc's gun had opened a cut.

"I know what you're thinking," the outlaw said. "You're thinking you'll shoot and get help that way. But that won't do you any good, Doc. The night orderly will come in, and I'll tell him you came to my room and pointed a gun at me and forced me to come in here. You were talking crazy about me being some sort of train robber and killer. The orderly won't know what to make of it, so he'll go get Dr. MacMurphy. And MacMurphy won't believe you any more than the orderly will."

"But that's a pack of lies," Doc protested. "And when they search your room, they'll find the gun and the letters with Bill Malkin's name on them . . ."

His voice trailed off as Malkin stood there, shaking his head confidently.

"They won't find anything," Malkin said. "There won't be anything to prove that I'm not Bill Williams, who used to own a hardware store in Hays City until my heart started giving me trouble. You're the one who'll be waving a gun around and spinning some wild yarn."

"The . . . the doctor can contact the authorities . . . The railroad will start an investigation . . ."

Smiling in the match light, Malkin said, "All that takes time. And while you're waiting, you think there won't be a chance for me to get you alone again, Doc? Sometime when you don't know that I'm around and won't see me coming?"

The flame had almost reached Malkin's fingers. He let go of the match. It spiraled to the floor, going out as it fell. And the darkness that suddenly filled the room suddenly seemed darker than ever, which was just what Malkin intended, Doc realized.

He heard the bedsprings squeak and knew that the killer was coming across the bed. Coming for him.

He jerked the trigger.

The pistol was a small caliber, and when it went off, the report wasn't much louder than a hard handclap. The spurt of flame from the muzzle was small and quick and lit up the darkness in the room for only a split second.

That was enough for Doc to see Bill Malkin leaping off the bed at him. He didn't know if his shot had hit the outlaw or not, but if it had, it wasn't slowing him down.

Doc tried to twist aside and get out of the way of Malkin's charge, but the man's shoulder rammed into him and spun him back against the wall. He felt Malkin's hands grabbing at him and jerked away. The outlaw was cursing bitterly and relentlessly under his breath. His rage at his will being thwarted had made him insane, at least temporarily.

Doc thrust the pistol out in front of him, hoping to ram it into Malkin's body and pull the trigger. The barrel didn't encounter any resistance, but Doc fired, anyway. A second later, a blow swung wildly in the dark clipped him on the side of the head. The world spun crazily. He was about to pass out.

If he did, he was a dead man. He wasn't sure how Malkin would explain killing him. Probably, Malkin would claim self-defense and insist that Doc had attacked him. No one would be able to prove otherwise. And if Malkin had gotten rid of everything that could be used as evidence against him . . .

Doc felt the wall at his back and sagged against it as he tried to steady himself. He heard Malkin's curses and harsh breathing, but he couldn't seem to tell where they were coming from. They filled the whole room, along with the thudding cacophony of Doc's own heartbeat. He slid along the wall, not knowing where to shoot or even where he was anymore.

Then the curtains over the window brushed against him, and he knew where he was. He caught hold of them with his free hand and held himself up, but only for a second before a heavy weight slammed into him and drove him backward. His head and shoulders struck the glass, and it shattered under the impact, flying outward. The window's flimsy wooden frame splintered, as well. Doc felt the fiery sting of broken glass on his hands and face, and then he was outside, falling through the air toward the ground.

He was lucky his room was on the sanitarium's first floor.

But unlucky that the man who wanted to kill him had plunged through the broken window with him.

They hit the ground hard but not together.

Malkin didn't land on him, which was another stroke of luck for Doc. Doc rolled and felt snow puff up around him in a fine white cloud. The stuff was falling thickly now. The flakes landed on his face like tiny kisses. He could see the ones that caught on his eyelashes. Oil lamps burned here and there on the outside of the sanitarium. When he looked at them, he saw the snow falling through the nimbus of light they cast.

A few yards away, Malkin sounded like a bellows as he breathed. He was trying to get up. Doc pushed himself to a sitting position and scooted farther away. Malkin had made it to a knee but didn't seem to be able to get any farther than that. He rested a hand on the snowy ground and glared at Doc in the faint light that filtered onto the sanitarium grounds from those lamps.

Doc knew the look on the man's face. One of Malkin's spells had him in its grip. He couldn't breathe, could only struggle to draw in air against the pain.

But somehow Malkin managed to let out a broken laugh. He said, "You . . . you think I'm gonna die . . . don't you, Doc? You think . . . that'll solve your problem . . . for you. But I'm not. I'm gonna make it. And then . . . I'll be coming for you . . . when you least expect it . . ."

Doc knew it was true. The specter of death still hovered over him. No one would believe him, and if he went back in that building, he would die.

With that thought clamoring through his brain, he scrambled onto all fours and then came up on his feet. He broke into a stumbling run toward the brick wall that surrounded the sanitarium grounds.

"You . . . you bastard!" Malkin gasped behind him. "Come back here!"

Go back to the man who wanted to kill him? Who would do that except a lunatic?

And this wasn't *that* kind of sanitarium.

Or maybe it was, Doc thought a few minutes later, after he had pulled himself over the wall and dropped onto the road that ran toward the nearby town. He was fleeing through a cold, snowy night in only his pajamas, with nothing but the little gun he had managed to hang on to somehow. His feet were bare, and his toes were already starting to go numb, which was probably a good thing, because he couldn't feel what the road was doing to his unprotected flesh. Looking at the situation logically and objectively, the only reasonable conclusion was that he had gone insane.

But he kept moving, anyway, and soon the darkness swallowed him up.

CHAPTER 16
THE SUGARLOAF

When Smoke walked into the kitchen of the big ranch house the next day after the encounter with Don Juan Sebastian Aguilar, Sally looked up from the piecrust she was forming into a pan and said, "You didn't have any luck, did you?"

"You can tell that just by looking at me?"

"Considering that you look like you could bite a nail in two right now, yes. I think anyone could see that."

Smoke forced his angrily clenched jaw to relax and let out a chuckle. "I thought I might calm down on the ride back out here from town, but I reckon that wasn't the case. The whole thing is still eating on me."

Early that morning, he had ridden into Big Rock to visit with Dan Norton, the local attorney who handled some of his legal matters, and Pete Perkins, who ran the land office. He had also sent off several wires to legal firms in Denver and San Francisco that represented him.

Sally trimmed off the excess dough from the crust and set it aside. She would spread it out on a pan and bake it later, too. Calvin Woods, the young cowboy who had started out as a regular ranch hand and worked himself up to a position of responsibility second only to that of Wes "Pearlie" Fontaine, Smoke's foreman, loved to eat that extra crust, especially if he had some honey or jam to dip it into. Cal's sweet tooth knew no limits.

"What did Dan and Pete have to say?" Sally asked. She knew about the errands that had taken Smoke to town. There were very few secrets between the two of them.

"Pete assured me that all the claims we made on rangeland here in the valley were filed properly. He's going to get in touch with Don Pratt, the county clerk over in Red Cliff, and ask him to confirm that. And Dan says that Aguilar doesn't have a leg to stand on, that no Colorado court is going to side with somebody claiming an old Spanish land grant."

"Then it sounds as if we don't have anything to worry about."

Smoke grimaced slightly and said, "Yeah, but the thing is, Dan had to admit he doesn't really have any experience in inter-

175

national law, and that's what this boils down to. He may believe there's no chance a court ruling would go against us, but he can't guarantee that it won't."

"When it comes to the courts, can anything ever be guaranteed?" Sally wanted to know. "The law still relies on human beings to interpret it and enforce it."

"And human beings are unpredictable critters." Smoke nodded. "I can't argue with that. Anyway, I sent wires off to our other lawyers, too, and got them started looking into the problem. It'll probably be several days before they have any answers, though."

Sally smiled and said, "So in the meantime, we might as well not worry about it, right? We have a holiday to get ready for."

"That reminds me," Smoke said. "While I was in town, I picked up the mail, and there was a letter from Matt. He won't be able to make it this year."

"Oh, that's a shame!" Sally responded with a disappointed look. "Did he say why?"

"He's down in South Texas, mixed up in something. He didn't go into any details, but I got the feeling it was some sort of trouble he felt obliged to help out with."

"A Jensen getting mixed up in some sort of trouble?" Sally imitated a flighty Southern belle as she went on, "Why, I never heard of such a thing!"

That got a laugh from Smoke. He said, "Yeah, we're all such peaceable sorts."

Sally was brisk and businesslike again as she went on, "All right, I need a tree to put up in the parlor and decorate, so why don't you and Pearlie and Cal go find one for me? You might as well be spending your time doing something useful."

"Running the ranch isn't useful?"

"You know good and well you have everything set up so efficiently that the ranch practically runs itself, especially at this time of year."

She had a point there. All the stock had been moved to winter grazing a couple of months earlier. The snow they'd had so far wasn't enough to be a problem. It wouldn't be unless there was a blizzard or a hard freeze.

Either of which was possible at this time of year, but neither seemed to be looming. Pearlie claimed that his joints could predict the weather better than the almanac, and according to them, nothing major was going to happen until later in the winter.

"All right, I reckon I can go look for a tree," Smoke said, "but Pearlie can't come with me. He left early this morning to take some supplies up to Bob Bellem at the

Calder Peak line shack. Cal should be around somewhere, though, and he and I can handle the tree-finding chore."

"Do you think you'll be back by lunchtime?"

"Reckon you'd better fix us up some sandwiches out of that leftover roast beef," Smoke said with a smile, "and put in some bear sign, or else Cal might refuse to go."

Sally laughed and said, "As if Cal would ever refuse to do anything you asked him to do, Smoke. But I'll put in the bear sign, anyway."

She was right about Cal. During his time on the Sugarloaf, he had grown from a wild youngster, on the verge of a life filled with trouble, into a fine young man who would probably be a successful rancher himself someday. There was no one in the world he looked up to more than Smoke.

Smoke found Cal in the barn, mending a harness. He said, "You want to come with me and help me find and cut down a Christmas tree for Sally to decorate? She's putting up a lunch for us to take along."

A hopeful look appeared on the young cowboy's face. Smoke didn't even let him ask the question.

"Yeah, she's putting in some bear sign,

along with roast beef sandwiches. We'll eat good."

"Then count me in!" Cal said as he put aside the harness he'd been working on and stood up.

"Get a couple of good axes from the tool-shed. I'll fetch the lunch."

By the time Smoke got back to the barn, carrying a wicker basket, Cal had saddled a horse for himself and had lashed a couple of axes behind the saddle. He was putting a rig on another mount for Smoke.

"Didn't figure you'd want to take the same horse you rode into town this morning," Cal commented.

"No, I didn't. That was good thinking."

When Smoke's mount was ready to ride, he tied the lunch basket behind the saddle and swung up. Cal was already on his horse.

"Where did you plan on looking for a tree?" Cal asked as they rode out of the barn.

"I figure we can probably find a good one up on Catamount Ridge."

They headed north from the ranch head-quarters, into the higher country on that side of the valley.

"What did you find out in town this morning?" Cal asked as they moved along at a comfortable pace. Smoke hadn't told the whole crew about what had happened in Big Rock the day before, but since Pearlie and Cal were his most trusted confidants among the hands, he had filled them in on the situation.

"Nothing that really made my mind rest any easier," he said. "Dan Norton and Pete Perkins don't seem to think I have anything to worry about, but I'm not convinced of that."

Cal nodded and said, "Seems like some of those big-city lawyers who work for you would be better to ask about something like this."

"Yeah, I thought so, too, and that's why I sent off wires to them. Eddie at the Western Union office said he'd ride out here right away when the replies come in."

A couple of minutes of companionable silence went by, and then Cal asked, "What if the lawyers say this Señor Aguilar hombre is in the right?"

"He can't be," Smoke answered vehemently, without any hesitation. "The Sugarloaf is mine, legal and aboveboard. I don't intend to let anybody take it away from me."

"It's yours according to American law. Mexican law's a heap different, from what I've heard."

"And this isn't Mexico, so that doesn't

matter," Smoke said, with conviction filling his voice.

"I hope you're right, Smoke. But if things get messed up somehow and it comes down to a fight . . . I reckon you know you can count on me and Pearlie and all the other fellas to back your play, whatever it is."

"No doubt of that ever even crossed my mind."

They rode for about an hour, with the terrain getting rougher most of that time, before coming out atop a long, wide ridge with stretches of pine, juniper, spruce, and fir growing along it. The thickly wooded ridge, with clumps of snow nestled in the evergreen branches and the backdrop of spectacular mountain scenery, was beautiful.

Cal pointed at a young juniper and said, "I think that'd make a good Yule tree, Smoke. It's got a good shape to it for decorating, and it's not too big for us to get it in the house. A lot of these other trees would never fit."

"That's just what I was thinking," Smoke said. He and Cal rode over to the juniper and dismounted. They took off their coats and hung them over the saddles. Even though the temperature wasn't much above freezing, once they started chopping down the tree, they would get overheated fairly quickly if they wore their coats. Their flannel shirts would keep them warm enough while they were working.

Soon the ringing sounds of ax blades biting into wood filled the air. In this thin high-country atmosphere, such sounds carried a long way. Anybody who heard them would know that somebody was chopping down a tree.

Other sounds traveled, too, and during a brief pause when Smoke rested the head of his ax on the ground to catch his breath, he heard something that made him stand up straighter. Cal was still swinging his ax. Smoke held up a hand to stop him.

"Wait a minute, Cal," he said. "Listen."

Both of them listened, and the hoofbeats coming from somewhere nearby were even clearer. There was no mistaking them now.

"Horses," Cal said. "Somebody's coming."

Right on the heels of his words, half a dozen men on horseback appeared, emerging from a thick stand of pine about a hundred yards away. They rode toward Smoke and Cal, not getting in any hurry about it.

"You know them, Smoke?" Cal asked.

"Not right offhand, no," Smoke answered.

"But judging by the outfits they're wearing, including those sombreros, I can make a pretty good guess who they are."

It looked like some of Don Juan Sebastian Aguilar's vaqueros had ventured onto the Sugarloaf . . . where they had no business being!

Chapter 17

Smoke's keen eyes searched among the approaching riders. He didn't see Aguilar or Travis Hinton, the Texas gun-wolf.

But as they came closer, he did recognize one of the horsemen: The gunman with the scarred chin and the thin mustache who had been the first one to confront him on Big Rock's main street the day before — and who had gotten dumped roughly off his horse for his trouble. His jaw carried a bruise where Smoke had knocked him down after the man pulled a knife. His name was Pedro, Smoke recalled.

Pedro was the only one of the half dozen who appeared to be a hired gun, though. The others had the look of regular vaqueros, men who normally handled livestock instead of shooting irons. One of them pushed out ahead of the others, taking the lead.

This man was big. That much was obvious about him, even on horseback. His shoulders bulked in the lightweight jacket he wore, and his head sat like a solid block of stone on those impressive shoulders.

None of the men were really dressed appropriately for this weather, Smoke mused as he watched them. He supposed that coming from south of the border, as they did, they weren't accustomed to or prepared for the cold, unless they came from a mountainous region — which they didn't appear to.

The big vaquero reined in and signaled for the others to do likewise. Pedro started to crowd past him, but the man turned his head and spoke in soft, rapid Spanish. Whatever he said made Pedro halt his advance, but as he tried to control his skittish mount, he directed a hate-filled glare toward Smoke.

Smoke ignored the gunman, other than keeping half an eye on him. If Pedro tried to make a play, Smoke would be ready to draw and fire in less than the blink of an eye.

Instead, he nodded to the big vaquero and said in a cool but civil tone, "Howdy. What brings you fellas out here to the Sugarloaf?"

"Don Sebastian sent us," the man replied. "He told us to take a look around the place. You know, señor, get an idea of how good the range is and what will need to be done."

"I'd say that's not any of the don's business," Smoke snapped. "I make the decisions around here. It's my ranch."

The vaquero's heavy shoulders rose and fell. He said, "I only follow orders, Señor Jensen."

"You know who I am, then."

"You just said as much, did you not?"

The man's accent was fairly thick, but he spoke good English. Childhood illness had left deep pockmarks in his dark, broad face. A mustache drooped over his upper lip, and his jaw jutted out like a slab of rock. Despite his rather brutish appearance, he was soft spoken and seemed to be an intelligent man.

"I know you're doing what your boss told you to do, but I want you off my range," Smoke said. "There won't be any trouble if you turn those horses around and head back to Big Rock. I assume that's where Aguilar is staying?"

"Don Sebastian has taken a floor in the hotel. The rest of us are here and there, some in the hotel, some in boardinghouses, some camping."

"Mighty cold weather for that. You boys would be more comfortable if you headed back to Mexico."

Ponderously, the big vaquero shook his head.

"We cannot do that, señor. Not unless Don Sebastian says that is the way it will be."

Smoke regarded the man for a moment, then asked, "What's your name, amigo?"

"I am called Berto, señor."

Smoke was still leaning on the ax handle with his left hand. He swung it up now and said, "Well, I think maybe I like you, Berto, but you and your friends need to clear out, and don't come back unless you're invited. I know your boss thinks this is his land, but that hasn't been settled yet. And when it is, he's going to be out of luck. So right now . . . you're trespassing."

Sneering, Pedro edged his horse forward again.

"Let me kill him, Berto," he urged. "We can be done with this today."

"He is supposed to be very fast with a gun," Berto rumbled.

Pedro's lips pulled back from his teeth in a snarl. He said, "People say that only because of gossip and because it has been written about him. Nobody gossips or writes about me, but my speed is a fact, anyway. I am as fast as Jensen. Faster!"

Berto's voice hardened as he said, "Not today, Pedro. The don would not like it."

"Yes! Today!"

Pedro kneed his horse forward. Berto reached out, as if to grab his arm and stop him, but the gesture was too slow and missed. Pedro pushed out in front of the others and uncoiled lithely from the saddle.

"We settle this now, Jensen!" he said as he turned sideways and curled himself into a human question mark, with his hand poised over the grip of his holstered revolver.

Smoke glanced at Berto again. The man spread his hands and shrugged, as if to say that he didn't like what was happening, but what could he do? Smoke was pretty sure from Berto's commanding attitude that the vaquero was Aguilar's foreman or at least his *segundo* . . . but Berto probably didn't have any real authority over the crew of hired guns. Travis Hinton was the ramrod of that bunch.

"Hold on just a second," Smoke said. He lifted the ax in his left hand, and with what appeared to be no more than a flick of his wrist, he sent it spinning through the air. With a solid thunk, the ax-head buried itself in the trunk of the juniper he and Cal had been cutting down.

Smoke added, "Cal, keep an eye on those other fellas."

"Sure, Smoke," the young cowboy said, apparently quite confident in his ability to handle that assignment. Several of the vaqueros had rifles sticking up from saddle scabbards, but none of them were packing handguns, at least not that Smoke could see. Cal was no gunfighter, but he could get the Colt on his hip unlimbered pretty quickly when he needed to, and he was a good shot and was cool under fire.

As Smoke faced Pedro, Berto moved his horse to the side and jerked his head at the other men to indicate that they should do likewise and put themselves out of the line of fire. They did so, hurriedly.

"We don't have to do this," Smoke said to Pedro. "You can get back on your horse and ride back to town with your friends."

"Those men?" Pedro sneered. "They know nothing except how to eat dust and breathe in the stink of cows. They are not my amigos."

"Well, then," said Smoke, "maybe they won't be too broken up about it when you're dead."

Pedro's lean, scarred face twisted with rage. His hand flashed toward the gun on his hip. He'd been right about one thing: He might not have a big reputation and nobody had ever written a dime novel about him, but he *was* fast.

Not as fast as Smoke Jensen, though.

Pedro cleared leather and started to tip his gun up just as Smoke's Colt came level and geysered fire. The bullet smashed into Pedro's chest and knocked him backward. His arm kept coming up, and his finger spasmed and involuntarily jerked the trigger, but the shot sailed harmlessly into the sky. Pedro's other hand lifted toward his chest, where a little blood welled from the hole above his heart.

Before he could press his hand to the wound — not that that would have done any good — his feet got tangled up with each other and he went down in a twisting fall that ended with him curled on his side. He managed to draw in two desperate, gasping breaths before air rattled in his throat and he lay still.

With his gun still leveled, Smoke looked over at Berto and the other vaqueros. The men were coldly expressionless and sat very still in their saddles. Berto just shook his head and said, "I tried to stop him, señor."

To Smoke's way of thinking, Berto hadn't tried very hard to head off this shooting. Maybe he and Pedro had had trouble in the past. Maybe Berto was just one of those men who stolidly followed orders and never did any more, or less, than what he had been told to do. Or maybe they all knew they were no match for Smoke and Cal when it came to gunplay and simply didn't want to die today.

"Put him back on his horse," Smoke said. "Then take him to Big Rock and tell your boss what happened. *Exactly* what happened. If you try to twist things around, I reckon I'll find out about it sooner or later. But I want Aguilar to know that this wasn't my doing and I didn't want to kill Pedro. He forced it. I don't particularly want to have to kill anybody else, either."

"I will tell him, Señor Jensen. I always tell Don Sebastian the truth."

Berto motioned for a couple of his men to retrieve Pedro's body. He moved his horse next to the fallen gunman's mount and caught hold of the reins. He held the horse steady while the two vaqueros lifted the corpse and draped it over the saddle. They tied Pedro's hands and feet together under the horse's belly so he wouldn't fall off. Then one of the men picked up Pedro's sombrero, which had come off when he collapsed, and handed it to Berto, who hung it from the saddle horn.

"Let us go," he ordered. "We have found out what we came for."

He turned his horse and rode off, leading the animal that carried Pedro's body. The two vaqueros who had loaded the corpse hurriedly mounted up, and they and the others followed Berto.

As Cal watched them ride off, he asked, "What did he mean by that? They found out what they came for?"

"Maybe they wanted to know if I was as fast on the draw as they'd heard."

"Well . . . now they know."

"Yeah," Smoke said. "Now they know." He holstered the gun he was still holding and turned toward the juniper with the ax stuck in its trunk. "Come on. We've still got a Christmas tree to cut down and drag back to the ranch house so Sally can hang baubles on it."

CHAPTER 18
DENVER

Adelaide DuBois was staying in a smaller, less expensive hotel. Preacher offered to get her a room where he was staying, but she declined. They were both old enough not to care too much about appearances anymore, but some things were still beyond the bounds of propriety, Adelaide claimed.

Preacher didn't argue with her, but he did insist on walking her back to her hotel.

"These days, Denver's a mighty civilized place most of the time," he said, "but you got to remember, it ain't been much more'n twenty years since there weren't nothin' around here but a mess of wild, lawless gold camps. Some of that could still be lurkin' under the surface."

She smiled across the table at him and said, "I'm sure I'll be safe with you, Arthur."

"Why don't you call me Preacher? If you keep callin' me Arthur, I'm liable to forget it's me you're talkin' to."

"I'll try," she said, "but I can't make any promises. I always thought you were such a dignified man, and the name Arthur suits you so well."

Preacher frowned and said, "Me? Dignified? Are you sure you're talkin' about the right fella? I'm nothin' but a grizzled ol' mountain man."

"No, you're my friend," Adelaide said, squeezing his hand again.

Preacher cleared his throat. His face felt slightly warm. *What the hell!* he thought. He hadn't blushed in fifty years or more, he told himself, but somehow this woman sitting across the table from him had a way of making him feel like a kid again.

The walk to the hotel where Adelaide was staying took only a few minutes. When they left Preacher's hotel, she took his arm. Neither of them had to suggest that. It just seemed like a natural gesture.

And she had taken his left arm, so he didn't have to ask her to move to the other side so his gun hand would be free. It was a long-standing habit for him to be ready to reach for a gun if he needed to. At the moment, he carried only a two-shot .41 caliber derringer in his pocket. It packed sufficient wallop and was accurate enough for close-range work, and Preacher didn't expect to need anything else here in town.

As they walked, his head turned slowly, unobtrusively, from side to side. His gaze was on the move, always searching for trouble. That was habit, too, but what Adelaide had told him intensified it. If that no-good grandson of hers, or anybody the varmint had hired, made a try for her, he intended to be ready to stop it. Permanently, if he had to.

Adelaide must have sensed some of what he was feeling, because she laughed a little and said, "My goodness, I feel like I'm walking down the street with a mountain lion at my side. The way you stalk along, Arthur . . . I mean, Preacher . . . you remind me of some sort of predator."

"Sorry," he said. "I don't mean to upset you."

"I'm not upset," she assured him. "It's just that most men, by the time they're your age, tend to shuffle a little when they walk. They don't stride along determinedly like you do. It's almost like you're, I don't know, marching into battle."

Preacher said, "I ain't most men. And I've wound up in fights all my life. So far that ain't showed any signs of changin', no matter how old I get."

"I can't tell you how much safer and more

confident that makes me feel. I knew I did the right thing in trying to find you . . . Preacher."

She tightened her grip on his arm. He felt the soft warmth of her pressing against him. *You're too old for this, you varmint,* he told himself. *Way the hell too old!*

But thinking that was one thing, and believing it, in this moment, was another.

Preacher had planned to ride on to Big Rock and the Sugarloaf, but with Adelaide now accompanying him, he couldn't do that. He knew there was a train to Big Rock leaving at ten o'clock the next morning. He was up early, as was also his habit, and before going into the dining room to eat breakfast, he dispatched one of the bellboys who worked at the hotel to the train station to purchase tickets on that train for him and Adelaide. When the youngster got back to the hotel and delivered the tickets to him in the dining room, Preacher tipped the boy generously.

He finished his breakfast, lingering over a second cup of coffee. Then he went up to his room, collected his war bag and his Winchester, and checked out.

"It's been good having you with us, sir," the clerk said. He was a different one than

196

the man who had been on duty at the desk when Preacher checked in. "I hope you'll come back and stay with us again."

"If I live long enough," Preacher said.

His next stop was the livery stable where he had left the rangy gray stallion and the big wolflike cur who traveled with him. He probably could have made arrangements to have both of his trail partners loaded onto a livestock car and shipped to Big Rock with him, but it seemed simpler just to pay the liveryman to look after them until Preacher returned to Denver after the holidays.

As usual, a couple of double eagles smoothed the path. The livery owner pocketed the coins and said, "Those two certainly seem like best friends. I don't expect they'll give me any trouble, although some of my customers were a little wary of that dog of yours. No offense, but he looks sort of like a wild animal. What's his name?"

"Dog."

"Yes, what's the dog's name?"

"No, Dog," Preacher said.

The man frowned in confusion for a moment. Then understanding dawned on him, and he said, "Oh. His name is Dog."

"Yep."

"What's the horse's name?"

"I call him Horse."

The liveryman gave a little shake of his head and said, "Dog and Horse. I see. Well, I suppose you're not likely to forget their names."

"Always seemed to fit," Preacher said.

In truth, he had ridden a number of similar-looking stallions over the years, all named Horse, and there had been even more dogs named Dog. When one of them passed on, as they inevitably did, fate seemed to lead Preacher in fairly short order to another animal who took to him right away, as if they already knew each other.

Many years earlier, Preacher had had an Indian friend, an old Absaroka called White Buffalo, who claimed to be able to converse with animals, and it had been his contention that the spirits of the original Dog and Horse had been reborn many times.

Preacher didn't necessarily accept that notion . . . but he couldn't disprove it, either.

He rubbed Horse's nose and scratched Dog's ears and said his good-byes to them, promising that he would return for them. He'd had to leave them in places like this before, but he had always come back for them, and they seemed to know that he always would.

He left his rifle at the livery stable, too, with the owner promising to look after it, but he took his war bag with him. Inside was a coiled-up shell belt with a pair of holstered Colts attached to it. Preacher wasn't going anywhere without those guns.

He was good with the Colts, good enough that years earlier, in the days soon after the War of Northern Aggression, he had taught young Kirby Jensen how to draw and fire. Of course, Kirby — whom Preacher had later dubbed "Smoke" — had the natural ability to take what Preacher had taught him and elevate his skills until he was quite possibly the fastest on the draw and the deadliest shot of any man who had ever roamed the West. Preacher would have been proud of that, had he not known that it was due almost entirely to Smoke's own ability, not anything Preacher had taught him.

So instead, Preacher was proud of the fact that Smoke had grown into the finest man he had ever known.

Soon, he would see Smoke again, along with Sally and maybe Luke and Matt. Preacher was looking forward to being reunited with those he considered his family.

He hoped they would like Adelaide. But then he told himself, Of course they would like Adelaide. They were the friendliest, best folks he knew.

When he reached the hotel where Adelaide was staying, he went into the lobby. He had left her at the door the night before, so he didn't know her room number and she hadn't told him. The clerk behind the desk in this hotel didn't look displeased to see Preacher, as had happened in the place where he stayed. This hotel was shabbier and needed more business, not less.

"Help you, sir?" the man asked.

"I'm here to pick up Mrs. DuBois," Preacher said.

The clerk looked a little disappointed. He said, "Oh. You're not checking in."

"Not this time, I don't reckon."

"Well, Mrs. DuBois is in room eleven. Is she expecting you?"

"Yep. She's gonna be checkin' out. Why don't you tell me how much she owes, and I'll just take care of that for her."

Preacher didn't know if Adelaide would go along with him paying the bill for her, but if he had already taken care of it before he went upstairs to get her, there wasn't much she could do about it.

The clerk hesitated, then gave Preacher the amount. The old mountain man slid a coin across the desk and said, "I'm obliged to you, son. The extra there is for you."

"Why, thank you, sir. Thank you very much!"

"Room eleven, you said?"

"Yes, sir. Top of the stairs and then along the corridor to the right."

Preacher nodded his thanks and went to the stairs. As he climbed them, he hoped that Adelaide would be packed and ready to go. He had told her the night before that they would take the train this morning. However, he wouldn't be surprised if she wasn't quite ready. He knew enough about women to be prepared for that possibility, even though he had spent many, many years on the frontier, far away from any females.

He reached the top of the stairs and turned right, and as he did, he came to a sudden stop. His muscles tensed at the sight of a man standing in the open doorway of room eleven, talking to someone inside who could only be Adelaide.

The stranger's face was red with anger, and his jaw was clenched tightly even as he spoke. He looked like he was about to step into the room, but then Adelaide appeared in the doorway and put a hand on his chest to try to hold him out. She glanced over the man's shoulder, with fear contorting her face, and when she spotted the mountain man, she screamed, "Preacher! Help!"

201

CHAPTER 19

The years might have slowed Preacher down a little compared to when he was young, but he was still faster and more efficient in his reactions than most men. He moved swiftly along the hall toward Adelaide's room as he shouted, "Leave that lady alone, you rapscallion!"

The man turned to face Preacher. He was around forty years old, beefy, wearing a brown tweed suit and a dark brown bowler. A thick brown mustache flowed out from both sides of his mouth to join bushy side whiskers. His nose appeared to have been broken more than once.

"Back off, old man," he warned Preacher. "This is none of your business."

"I'm makin' it my business," Preacher declared. He yanked the derringer out of his pocket. He was close enough to use the little gun now.

The stranger's eyes widened at the sight

202

of the weapon. He exclaimed, "Son of a —" His hand dived under his suit coat and started clawing at something.

Preacher had no doubt the man was going for a gun. He snapped one of the derringer's triggers. The derringer's vicious bark filled the hallway. The man took a big step back, howled in pain, and clapped his left hand to his left ear. Blood trickled between his fingers.

"You loco old coot!" he yelled. Whatever he had been trying to get out of his coat, he had forgotten it in the pain of being wounded. With a bull-like shake of his head that sent drops of blood splattering on the wallpaper, he turned and plunged toward the far end of the hallway. Preacher saw the entrance to a flight of stairs down there.

He had drawn even with the open door of Adelaide's room now. He started to line the derringer on the fleeing man's back, but before he could pull the trigger, Adelaide came out into the hall, caught hold of his arm, and pulled it down.

"Preacher, no!" she said.

"But the bast— the varmint's gettin' away!"

"I don't want you to kill him."

Preacher understood suddenly, or thought he did.

"That was your grandson?" he asked.

Adelaide shook her head. "No, but George hired him. He was supposed to make me go with him. I'm sure he would have taken me to George."

The man reached the stairs, turned the corner onto them, and started down, with his heavy footsteps echoing in the stairwell.

Preacher said, "Let me go after him. I'll catch the fella and turn him over to the law."

She just held on to him even harder and said, "No, Preacher, please. Don't leave me. George himself could be lurking somewhere nearby. I'm so frightened right now —"

She threw her arms around his neck. Instinctively, Preacher folded his arms around her to comfort her.

"All right, all right," he told her. "I reckon I ain't goin' nowhere. You don't have to worry about that no-good varmint. I'll be right with you and won't let him come anywhere near you, nor anybody else who means you harm."

She pressed her head to his chest and said, "Thank you, Preacher. You don't know how much that means to me."

A little awkwardly, he patted her on the back with the hand that wasn't holding the derringer.

"It's all gonna be all right. If you've got

your things together, we'll head on down to the railroad station, and before too much longer, we'll be on our way to Big Rock and then to the Sugarloaf."

"Your friend's ranch?"

"Yep. Won't nothin' bad happen to you there. I guarantee it."

A little shudder ran through her. She said, "That man may try to follow us."

"I don't reckon he will, the way he took off from here. Anyway, he's got other things to worry about right now." Preacher grinned. "Like the way I just about plumb shot off his ear."

Adelaide straightened some, tipped her head back to look up at him, and said, "You did what?"

"Yeah, it looked like that was where I nicked him. He's lucky the light ain't that good up here in this hall, and I hurried my shot a mite, too."

"He's lucky that you almost shot his ear off?"

"Yep," said Preacher. "I was aimin' between the son of a gun's eyes."

They made it to the train station with time to spare, Preacher having hired a carriage to take them there. Adelaide had only two small bags with her, so in that way, at least,

205

she was different from most of the ladies Preacher had had any dealings with. Most of them, when they traveled, took along enough to outfit a fur-trapping expedition.

This trip wouldn't be a long one. The train would arrive in Big Rock that afternoon, and once they were there, Preacher could rent a buggy or a buckboard at Patterson's Livery to take them the rest of the way to the Sugarloaf. By nightfall, they would be safe in the ranch house and Adelaide could relax. It would take an army to get to her there, and depending on how many Jensens were on hand, Preacher wasn't sure even that would be enough.

As they sat on the comfortable bench seat and the train lurched a little as it pulled out of the station, Adelaide sighed and said, "I can't tell you how much I appreciate everything you've done for me, Arthur. I mean, Preacher."

"That's all right," he told her. "You call me whatever you want."

He was sitting by the window, and Adelaide was next to the aisle. Preacher's right hand rested on his thigh. She took it in both hands and held it tightly. She leaned over to rest her head against his shoulder.

"I don't dare even think about what might have happened if you hadn't come to my rescue," she murmured. "I wish I could have you with me always, to look out for me."

Preacher cleared his throat and said, "There, there. I'm sure everything's gonna be fine."

"I am, too . . . now."

She sighed and snuggled closer against him. Preacher looked straight ahead for the most part, but from time to time, his eyes darted toward the window and the landscape that rolled past as the train began to pick up speed.

The black porter was trying not to stare at the bloody rag tied onto the side of Jed Avery's head, but he wasn't succeeding very well. Avery was aware of the scrutiny, and it irritated the hell out of him.

They were standing in a corner of the train station lobby, out of the ebb and flow of passengers arriving and departing.

"Well?" Avery demanded. "Where are they going?"

The porter didn't answer. Instead, he asked, "What happened to your head, mister?"

Avery bit back an angry curse and said, "Never mind about my damn head. Where did the old man and woman go?" He scowled. "If you didn't find out, I'll be taking back that dollar I gave you, you —"

"Hold on, hold on, mister. Sorry. I done found out what you want to know. That old couple, they's headed to Big Rock. A friend o' mine loaded their bags, and he seen the tags on 'em."

"Big Rock," Avery repeated.

"Yes, sir. It's a town up in Eagle County, north and west o' here. Mighty pretty country, I hear tell."

Avery couldn't give less of a damn about the scenery. He said, "How long will it take them to get there?"

"Should roll in about three o'clock this afternoon. It ain't a long trip. That is, if the train's on schedule, and the engineer on this run, Red Ralston, he's a pure demon for stayin' on schedule. Why, if he gets even a little late, he'll highball it on the straight stretches —"

Avery shut up the man's jabbering by tossing him another half-dollar. "There. You never saw me. Got that?"

The porter had caught the coin deftly and made it disappear into his pocket even more smoothly. He nodded and said, "I never laid eyes on you, mister."

Avery grunted and started to turn away.

The porter added, "I surely do think you need to get that head looked at, though.

Whatever happened to you, it must hurt like blazes."

Avery just growled and kept moving toward the lobby doors. As he pushed out through them into the cold, cloudy day, a buggy pulled up on the brick street in front of the station. The well-dressed man who hurriedly climbed out of it stopped abruptly at the sight of Avery.

"What happened to you?" he asked. He gestured at the makeshift bandage on Avery's head.

"That old bastard shot me."

"What old bastard?"

"The one traveling with your grand-mother. When you hired me to find her, DuBois, you didn't tell me she had taken up with some crazy old mountain man!"

For a moment, George DuBois didn't say anything. He was around thirty-five, clean shaven, with fair hair under his hat. He wore spectacles over cold blue eyes. Finally, he sighed and said, "How badly are you hurt?"

"Well, this ear will never be the same, I can tell you that. I don't know how bad it is. I haven't been to the doctor yet." A note of pride entered Avery's voice as he went on, "I'm a good detective. I figured it was more important to follow them and find out where they were going."

"And did you? Find out where they're going?"

"Some place northwest of here called Big Rock. If you'd been here a little sooner, you could have stopped them, or at least gotten on the same train."

"I got here as soon as I received your message," DuBois said, sounding irritated himself now. "And as long as I know their destination, I can find a way there. I've been on her trail for quite a while now . . ." His words trailed off, and he sighed. "I'll see to it that you get a bonus for your injury. I didn't know about the old man, but I'm not surprised she found someone to take care of her. She's always had a knack for doing that." His voice hardened again. "But it won't matter."

Avery frowned as he asked, "Just what are you gonna do to get what you want?"

"Whatever it takes," George DuBois said.

CHAPTER 20
UTAH

Luke knew good and well that the livery-man and the storekeeper in Amity had gouged him on the prices of his purchases, but he couldn't do anything about that. They had had him over the proverbial barrel. Buying the wagon and team he needed to carry the three Trafford children, plus the supplies that the trip to the Sugarloaf would require, had just about wiped him out.

It was good to leave the settlement's hostility behind, though. He glanced over at Bodie, the oldest of the three youngsters, who rode on the driver's seat beside him while Luke handled the reins. The boy looked out ahead of the wagon with a certain eagerness in his gaze that hadn't been there before, thought Luke. As if Bodie wanted a fresh start for himself and his brother and sister . . .

Hannah and Teddy rode in the wagon bed,

among the crates and bags of supplies. Luke had piled all the blankets he had bought around them to form a nest of sorts, to help keep them warm. They were playing some sort of word game that involved bursting out in laughter now and then. Since they seemed to be satisfied back there, Luke wasn't going to bother them.

He spoke to Bodie, though, in a voice quiet enough that the other two kids wouldn't be able to make it out over the rumble and creak of the wagon wheels.

"I'm mighty sorry about your pa," he said to the boy.

Bodie looked up at him with a slight frown and asked, "Why? Marshal Rowan said he was tryin' to kill you when you shot him. Don't seem like there was anything else you could do."

"I would have rather taken him in alive."

"He never would've stood for that," Bodie replied with a shake of his head. "I reckon he'd think it was better you shot him. Anyway, what would've happened if you took him alive?"

Luke avoided a direct answer to that, saying, "That would have been up to a court somewhere. To a judge and jury."

"I reckon they would've stretched his neck," Bodie said solemnly. "He would've

212

had it comin', too. My ma said he was a bad man. She guessed he always was. She just didn't see it at first."

Luke wasn't sure what to say to that. He wasn't going to lie to the boy. Hank Trafford had been a bad man, all right, no doubt about that. Did any son need to hear that about his father, though?

Instead, he asked, "Have you ever driven a wagon before?"

That question made Bodie perk up even more. He said, "No. Are you gonna let me drive, Mr. Jensen?"

"Not today, but we'll see. It'll take a while to get where we're going. I'll probably need somebody to spell me at the reins now and then."

"I can do that," Bodie said. It was good to see that eagerness in his face and hear it in his voice, thought Luke.

They traveled on toward Fillmore, which, Luke recalled, had been the first capital of Utah Territory, before the seat of government was moved to Salt Lake City. He had been there before, but it had been a number of years since his last visit.

He knew they wouldn't reach the town today, so he kept an eye out for a good place to camp. He wanted to get out of the weather as much as possible. They were traveling through a valley running roughly north and south between two small mountain ranges. The peaks were tall enough to funnel all the cold air right down the valley, into the faces of anybody heading north, as Luke and his three young companions were doing.

When he spotted a rocky outcropping to the left that would block that frigid wind, he angled the wagon toward it with a feeling of relief. At this time of year, darkness came early, and with the thick overcast in the sky, night would fall even more quickly than usual.

Teddy climbed over the wall of stacked-up blankets and leaned on the back of the driver's seat.

"Is that where we're gonna camp?" he asked in his high-pitched voice.

"Yes, it is," Luke answered. "Does the place look all right to you?"

"Sure," Teddy said, sounding surprised that anybody would ask him for his opinion.

Hannah joined him in leaning over the seat and said, "It's cold."

"I know, honey. But we'll be behind those rocks soon, and I'll build a fire. It'll be nice and warm."

Luke knew that more than likely, the camp wouldn't really be all that warm, but it would be considerably better than being out in the open. If he built a good fire and the kids piled plenty of blankets on themselves, they would be all right.

Fifteen years earlier, it might have been worth a man's life to build a big fire out here. The Utes and the Paiutes were still on the warpath then, the Navajo weren't exactly friendly, and there were even some Apaches around these parts who would have been happy to wipe out any white travelers they came across. In those days, a fire drew way too much unwanted attention. It was better to risk freezing to death.

Now the Indians were peaceful for the most part. Some were on reservations, while others had withdrawn deeply into the mountain fastnesses and wanted only to be left alone. Luke was glad to oblige them on that score.

The air felt less chilly as soon as Luke drove the wagon behind the outcropping. He maneuvered into a good place and then pulled back on the reins to bring the four-horse team to a stop. Some small, scrubby trees grew nearby. Luke had a hatchet in his gear that he could use to chop branches off them for the fire.

"Bodie, climb back there and sit with your

brother and sister until I get the camp set up."

"I can help," the boy said.

"No, that's all right. Just do what I said."

Bodie didn't look very happy about that, but he climbed over the seat and settled down in the wagon bed with Hannah and Teddy. Luke told himself to come up with some chores for the boy to do later, to make him feel better about things, more like he was contributing. But right now, Luke didn't know Bodie well enough to say what he could or couldn't be trusted to do.

The first thing was to get the team unhitched. In country like this, a man took care of his horses, because he had to rely on his horses to take care of him. They all worked together to survive and get where they were going.

Luke tied the horses from the team to the trees and then untethered his saddle mount from the back of the wagon and moved him over to join the other animals. He rubbed down the team, gave them water from a bucket, and put nose bags of grain on them.

With that done, he turned his attention to building a fire and soon had an armful of firewood. He arranged it in the lee of some huge rocks, which would protect the fire from the wind and reflect the heat from the flames. Using the bowie knife that was sheathed behind his left-hand Remington, he peeled shavings from one of the branches to use as tinder. When he snapped a lucifer to life with his thumbnail and held the burning match to the thin slivers, they caught fire. Quickly, he added small branches. Soon, flames were jumping up strongly enough that he knew they wouldn't go out.

"All right, you kids," he called to the three youngsters. "Come on over here and warm up some."

Bodie climbed out of the wagon first and helped Hannah and Teddy to the ground. Luke was glad to see the boy giving his brother and sister a hand. Bodie had that solemn expression on his face again. He was older than his years, Luke thought. He'd probably been looking out for the little ones for quite a while. That was sad, in a way — Bodie hadn't had a chance to be just a kid for long enough — but learning how to be responsible at a young age wasn't a bad thing, either.

The children gathered around the fire and extended their hands toward it. Luke had bought gloves and fur hats for them before leaving Amity, but he knew they had to be half frozen, anyway. They soaked up the fire's warmth gratefully.

"We'll have bacon and biscuits for supper tonight," he told them. "I reckon you're too little to drink coffee, aren't you?"

"What's coffee?" asked Teddy. As young as he was, if he'd spent the past several years in the Mormon community, there was a good chance he honestly didn't know.

"You'll find out when you're older," Luke told him.

Hannah said, "That's what grown-ups say about *everything.*"

"I guess you're right about that, honey. It does take time to learn things."

"Do you have any kids, Mr. Jensen?" Bodie asked.

"Me?" The question took Luke by surprise. "Not that I —" He stopped short. He'd almost said, "Not that I know of," but that might have opened the door for more questions he didn't want to answer, so he just said, "No, I sure don't."

"Then how will you know how to take care of us?" asked Hannah.

"Well, I guess I'll, uh, have to figure it out as I go along."

They all gave him dubious looks, as if they didn't have high hopes of that working out well.

Keep 'em fed, keep 'em warm, and keep

'em safe, he told himself. If he did those three things, then everything else probably would turn out all right.

The gray light in the sky faded out fast, so it was completely dark by the time Luke had supper ready for them. He had a pot of coffee boiling, too, and Hannah made a face at the smell.

"I don't think I'd want to drink anything that smelled like that," she said.

"You'll feel different about it when you're older, I promise you," Luke told her as he handed her a tin plate with a biscuit and a couple of pieces of bacon on it.

They sat on rocks around the campfire and ate their supper. Luke sipped on a cup of coffee and relished its heat and its strong, bracing bite. After this long, mostly unpleasant day, he welcomed that. If he had been alone, he might have laced the coffee with a dollop of bourbon from the flask in his saddlebags, but he figured he ought to set a good example.

As good an example as a grizzled old bounty hunter with the blood of countless men on his hands could set, anyway . . .

That thought was percolating in his mind when he suddenly heard a swift rataplan of hoofbeats somewhere not far off. As he lifted his head and listened more intently, he could tell that the fast-moving horse was coming closer.

Out here, a rider in a hurry nearly always meant trouble. He set his cup and plate aside and said, "Kids, get under the wagon."

"Why?" Bodie said. "It's warmer here by the fire."

"Just do what I told you," Luke snapped. He stood up and went over to the wagon. Reaching to the floorboard of the driver's box, he picked up the Winchester he had placed there earlier. Without wasting any time, he worked the rifle's lever and jacked a round into the chamber.

He looked to see that the three children had followed his instructions and had crawled underneath the wagon. Seeing that they had, he walked around the vehicle and stood on the other side, planting himself between them and whoever was galloping toward them through the night.

Whoever the rider was, he needed to be careful. Moving that fast in the dark, he was liable to take a tumble if his horse took a misstep. . . .

Instead, the rider skillfully brought his mount to a rearing, skidding halt as the horse loomed up out of the darkness. In the glow of the firelight, Luke leveled the Winchester at the stranger and said, "Hold it right there, mister! Any closer and I'll blow you out of the saddle!"

CHAPTER 21

What happened next shocked Luke almost as much as a punch in the guts.

"Mr. Jensen!" the rider cried. "Mr. Jensen, is that you?"

It was a woman's voice.

And it sounded vaguely familiar to Luke, although he couldn't place it right away.

The problem was that, under the right circumstances, a woman could be just as dangerous as a man. A bullet didn't care who fired it. So he kept the Winchester leveled and called, "Who are you? What do you want?"

"I'm Ruth. Ruth Backstrom. From the café in Amity."

Luke remembered her now: the tired-looking young blond woman working behind the café's counter. She had tried to get the proddy young man called Eli to leave Luke alone, prior to the fight between them breaking out, and from the conversation between the two of them, Luke knew that Ruth was married to Eli's father. He wasn't familiar enough with the Mormon faith to know if all of a man's wives were considered stepmothers to the children they hadn't given birth to themselves.

"You still haven't told me what you're doing here," Luke said.

Ruth cast a frightened glance over her shoulder and then said, "Where are the children? Oh! There they are, under the wagon."

Luke could tell she was afraid of somebody she believed was chasing her. He said, "Who's after you? Eli? Or your husband?"

"Please, I . . . I came to warn you. Eli is coming after you. He has some of the men from his father's ranch with him. After what you did to him —"

"Defended myself from him, you mean?"

"After you beat him in that fight . . . he couldn't stomach that. He brooded over it all afternoon, and then he got some of the men who were in town and told them to come with him. He plans to catch up to you, and when he does . . ."

She didn't finish, so Luke did it for her. In a flat, hard voice, he said, "Eli intends to kill me."

"That's right. His wounded pride won't

let him do anything else."

The perilous life Luke had led had made him a pretty good judge of character. He believed that Ruth was telling the truth. He lowered the rifle at last and let out a disgusted snort.

"There's nothing much more dangerous in this world than a boy's wounded pride," he said. "Why did you decide to come after us and warn me?"

"I couldn't just stand by and . . . and let him kill you."

"Why not? You don't owe me a thing."

"Well, there are the children to consider. If something happened to you . . ."

Luke's voice hardened as he asked, "Are you saying Eli might kill them, too?"

He hated for the three youngsters to have to hear this conversation, but he needed to know what sort of trouble he was facing.

"No!" Ruth exclaimed. "I don't believe he'd do that. I really don't. But he's capable of just riding away and leaving them to take care of themselves, since, after all, they're . . . well . . ."

"Gentiles," Luke said. "Their father was Mormon. Doesn't that count for anything?"

"It would have," Ruth answered, "if their mother had raised them to follow our faith. But she didn't really want anything to do with us or our ways. She was always an outsider."

This wasn't the time or place for theological discussions, thought Luke. He listened to the night, didn't hear anything except the wind and the quiet crackle of flames from the campfire.

Then his ears caught a hint of distant hoofbeats, so there wasn't really time to argue about anything. That campfire hadn't drawn the unwanted attention of an Indian war party, but it was attracting trouble, anyway.

"Get on around behind the wagon," he told Ruth, "and put your horse with the others. Then keep your head down."

"What are you going to do?"

"Whatever it takes." Luke looked around, spotted an opening between two of the giant slabs of rock that formed the outcropping, and went on, "You kids come out of there. Go with Mrs. Backstrom and hide over there in that crevice."

The three youngsters crawled out from under the wagon. Hannah stared at the dark, narrow crack in the outcropping and said, "I don't want to go in there! There could be monsters!"

If it had been summer, Luke would have worried about rattlesnakes being in the cleft, but at this time of year, they were all denned up. The opening wasn't big enough for a mountain lion or a bear. He said, "Don't worry, honey. There's nothing in there that will hurt you."

"Are you sure?" Hannah asked.

Any monsters were a lot more likely to be out here, he thought. But he said, "I'm sure. You'll be all right. Bodie, watch out for your brother and sister and Mrs. Backstrom."

The boy nodded and said, "All right. Come on, Hannah. Come on, Teddy."

The riders were close now. Luke wished Ruth and the kids would hurry up. Bodie went into the crevice first to prove to the little ones it was safe. Hannah and Teddy disappeared into it warily; then Ruth paused at the opening to look back over her shoulder at Luke.

"Be careful," she said.

"I intend to," he said. He threw some more branches on the fire so the flames blazed up brighter. He might need the light to shoot by.

Then he got behind the wagon and waited.

The hoofbeats were loud now. The riders were almost there. Luke waited until five men on horseback, led by Eli Backstrom, entered the circle of light cast by the fire. Then Luke thrust the Winchester over the wagon's sideboard and fired a shot into the ground a few inches in front of Eli's horse.

At the crack of the shot, the horse stopped short and reared up, spooked not only by the loud noise but also by the spray of dirt the bullet kicked up when it hit the ground. Eli yelled in surprise and had to grab the saddle horn with both hands to keep from falling out of the saddle.

Luke worked the rifle's lever swiftly and fired a second shot, this one whining over the heads of the other men, who were hurriedly reining in their mounts. A couple of them reached for the guns they carried on their hips, but Luke jacked the lever again and shouted, "Don't do it! I'll put a bullet through the first man who touches a gun!"

Eli managed to get his horse under control again and pulled the animal around in a tight circle.

"Don't listen to him!" he yelled to his companions. "He can't kill all of us!"

"Then I'll kill you first!" Luke roared back at him.

That made Eli hesitate. He motioned for the others to stay back, then said, "This is between you and me, Jensen. Nobody else needs to get hurt. You step out here and face me like a man, and I give you my word no harm will come to those kids."

He didn't say anything about Ruth, Luke noted. Maybe that meant he didn't know she had gotten ahead of him and had carried a warning to the man he was after. Luke wasn't going to bring her up, either. What Eli didn't know . . . might not hurt Ruth.

"If I go along with what you want," Luke said, "do you promise to take the children back to Amity?"

"There's no place for them there," Eli said stiffly. "They don't belong in Amity."

"They're just kids," Luke responded, not bothering to keep the note of outrage he felt out of his voice. "They're innocent."

"They're not of our people," Eli said stubbornly. "I won't hurt them, but they'll have to find some other place to live."

"By themselves? In the middle of winter? And Fillmore's the nearest settlement. That's a Mormon town, too. Will things be any different for them there?"

"That's none of my business."

"Well, I've made it *my* business," Luke said. "This is crazy, Eli. Why don't you just go home and let us go on our way? We'll all leave Utah Territory, and you won't have to worry about me or those kids again."

For a second, Luke thought the young man might listen to reason. While Eli hesitated, Luke glanced at the other men. They were hard-faced, cold-eyed hombres, not professional gunmen but plenty tough, and they had the same sort of fanaticism in their faces that Eli did. Plus, they worked for Eli's father. They would back Eli's play, whatever it turned out to be.

The brief moment of uncertainty passed. Angry determination and wounded pride welled up again inside Eli. Luke saw it on his face. Eli leaned forward in the saddle to make himself a smaller target, grabbed for his gun, and yelled, "Get in there and kill him!"

Luke squeezed the Winchester's trigger as soon as Eli moved. Eli was quick, though, and instead of the bullet plowing into his chest, it tore through his left arm, halfway between the elbow and shoulder. Eli screeched in pain, dropped the revolver he had just jerked out of its holster, and grabbed the saddle horn with his right hand.

In the half second that passed after Luke fired, he saw the other four men slapping leather. Any hope that they might decide to stay out of the fight evaporated instantly. Luke crouched slightly behind the wagon as he swung the Winchester from left to right, working the rifle's lever and spraying lead through the group of riders.

Two men cried out and went backward out of their saddles without getting a shot off as Luke's bullets pounded into them. The other two opened fire. Luke bent even lower as slugs chewed splinters from the sideboard near his head. One of the wood slivers stung his right cheek.

The Winchester blasted again. A man's head snapped back as the bullet bored through his forehead. He flung his arms out wide to the sides, swayed for a second, and toppled to the ground.

The fourth man urged his horse forward and fired wildly as he tried to get around the wagon. With bullets whipping past his ears, Luke had to dive to the ground to escape the lead storm.

He dropped the rifle as he fell and palmed out the Remingtons instead. The guns came up as he landed on his belly and raised himself on his elbows. The man on horseback loomed over him, looking gigantic from this angle. Flame gouted from both revolvers and caused the horse to shy away. That gave Luke more of an opening, and when he fired again, the bullet ripped through the man's throat, tunneled through his brain at a sharp angle, and exploded out the back of his head. He died instantly and landed on the ground in a limp heap.

Luke scrambled to his feet. He had killed or mortally wounded four men in about ten seconds, but Eli Backstrom was unaccounted for. Luke looked around for the young man, expecting him to attack again, but realized he didn't see any sign of Eli.

As the echoes of all the gun thunder died away, though, Luke heard hoofbeats receding in the distance. He uttered a heartfelt "Damn!"

Eli had gotten away.

And that meant there was a good chance this trouble wasn't over, after all.

In the now eerie quiet, Ruth called from the crevice in the rocks, "Mr. Jensen, can . . . can we come out now?"

Luke looked at the bloody, sprawled bodies scattered around the camp and said, "No, I know it's probably cold in there, but you and the kids best stay put until I've tended to a little chore out here."

The grim chore of dragging those corpses off into the darkness, where children's eyes wouldn't have to see them . . .

"You could come with us, you know," Luke said as he turned to Ruth. He had just lifted Teddy into the back of the wagon and set him down next to his sister, Hannah. Bodie was on the wagon seat.

Ruth shook her head and said, "Eli never saw me and doesn't know I warned you. He doesn't have any more reason to dislike me than he already did."

"I got the feeling you weren't all that happy being married to his pa," Luke said.

That was true, but he had another motive for telling Ruth she could come along. The idea of having a woman around to look after those kids during the journey to Colorado held some appeal for him. He'd never taken care of youngsters before, and while he was willing to shoulder that responsibility, if fate saw fit to lend him a hand . . .

"No, I'm going back to Amity," Ruth said, dashing that hope. "We can't always run away from the things we don't like in our life."

Luke grunted. Maybe she was talking about him and his drifting ways, and maybe she wasn't. It didn't really matter either way. He wasn't going to try to talk her into doing something she didn't want to do. He had extended the offer, and that was as far as he would go.

"All right," he said. "Good luck to you."

"And to you, as well." She looked at the children. "All of you."

More than likely, they would need it,

thought Luke. It was a long way to the Sugarloaf. . . .

CHAPTER 22
RATON

After their run-in with Clint Starkey and the warning from the Indian boy, Ace and Chance postponed their visit to any of Raton's other saloons and got themselves a room in the Sierra Hotel instead.

While they were checking in, Ace asked the short, well-fed clerk if he knew anything about Starkey.

The man's eyes widened as he said, "You mean Clint Starkey, the gunman?"

"Got a reputation, does he?" Chance said.

The clerk's head bobbed up and down. "And not a good one, either. He's killed three men since he showed up in these parts about six months ago. All in fair fights, you understand, or what the law considers fair fights, anyway. I'm not so sure about that, myself." The clerk suddenly looked nervous. "Please, don't repeat any of what I just said. I wouldn't want it getting back to Starkey."

"You don't have to worry about us saying

anything," Ace assured him. "What else do you know about him? How does he make his living?"

The clerk shook his head and said, "Honestly, I don't know. He always seems to have plenty of money. Sometimes he disappears for four or five or six days at a time, and there are rumors about . . . Well, I don't really like to say . . ."

"You don't have to," Chance said. "Starkey's going off somewhere and holding up a stagecoach or rustling some cattle or pulling some other sort of owlhoot job. Right?"

"You didn't hear it from me," the clerk insisted.

"Nope, we didn't hear a word from you," Ace agreed. "But I reckon it's pretty clear that Clint Starkey's not a good man to cross."

"I think anyone in Raton would go along with that," the clerk said fervently.

With the room rented, the Jensen brothers went to look for a livery stable where they could leave their horses. They found one in the next block, run by a friendly middle-aged man named Gonzalez.

When they asked him about Clint Starkey, he reacted much the same way as the hotel clerk: clear disapproval, but also a wariness and reluctance to say too much, for fear of it getting back to Starkey and causing trouble for him.

With that done, Ace and Chance walked back up the street. Chance's desire to visit one of the other saloons wasn't going to be denied much longer.

Ace said, "From the sound of what everybody tells us, we'd be wise to avoid Starkey as much as possible."

"I don't plan to go looking for him," Chance said. "It'll be just fine with me if we don't run into him again. Besides, we're probably only going to be here one night. What are the odds that we'll wind up in the same place as him?"

Ace shook his head and said, "I don't know. You're the gambler. You figure them out."

"Maybe I will," Chance said with a grin. Then he nodded toward a building ahead of them. "The Red Top Saloon, the sign says. Let's have a look."

Ace nodded and turned his steps in that direction. The saloon was a stone building with a red slate roof, which obviously had inspired its name. When they stepped inside, out of the chilly late afternoon air, the place had a welcoming warmth to it. It wasn't fancy, by any means. Plain tables and chairs; a hardwood bar with no brass footrail;

simple shelves on the wall behind the bar, with bottles of whiskey on them; no gilt-framed mirror or painting with an opulent nude. The customers all looked like working men, and the only female in sight was a heavyset middle-aged woman tending bar.

She grinned at the brothers and said, "Come on in, boys, and close the door behind you! You're lettin' in the cold air."

Ace closed the door and said to Chance, "This looks like a nice place."

"Are you joking?" asked Chance. "There's probably not more than fifty dollars in the whole room! We're not going to find a good poker game here."

"Then how about just some good company?"

"Well, I suppose if that's all you're looking for . . ."

They went up to the bar, where Ace smiled at the woman and said, "Can we get a couple of beers?"

"That's what we're here for," she replied with a smile. "Welcome to the Red Top. My name's Selma. This is my place."

"I'm Ace, and this is my brother Chance."

The woman gave him a skeptical look and said, "Now, I know good and well those can't be your real names."

"No, but that's what we've been called

our whole lives. We were raised by a gambler, you see."

"What was his name?" Selma wanted to know. "I might be acquainted with him. I spent a lot of time in saloons over the years, before I settled down here in Raton."

Chance said, "His name is Ennis Monday. Doc, most people call him."

"Doc Monday!" Selma's pleasantly ugly face became almost as pretty as her smile widened and lit up her features even more. "Oh, shoot, yeah. I knew him back in St. Louis when I was dealing blackjack there. Would've been eighteen fifty-six, fifty-eight, somewhere in there." She laughed and slapped a meaty hand down on the bar. "Lord have mercy, we were all a lot younger then! You boys probably weren't even born yet."

"We were born in eighteen sixty-one," Ace said.

"And old Doc is your father? I never would've guessed he'd settle down."

Chance shook his head and said, "He's not our father, but he was friends with our mother and promised her he'd look after us."

"She passed away when we were born," Ace added.

A solemn expression came over Selma's

238

face. She said, "Oh, now, I'm sorry to hear that. So you never knew her?"

"No, ma'am, we didn't. Doc took good care of us, though," Ace said.

"How *is* the old rapscallion?" she asked. "Is he still alive and kicking?"

Ace smiled and said, "As far as we know. We've been out on our own for a couple of years now. Doc's been in poor health, so he's staying in a sanitarium up north of Denver. We're on our way to see him, in fact, after we spend Christmas at a ranch belonging to some friends of ours."

Selma frowned and said, "Maybe you ought to spend Christmas with Doc, if he's doing poorly. When we get to a certain age, you never know how much longer any of us are going to be around."

"That's sort of true for everybody, isn't it?" Chance said. "There are no guarantees in life."

"Well, sure," Selma replied with a shrug. "But it gets more true the older you get." She brightened again. "Say, I didn't get you boys those beers yet. We got to talking instead. I'll take care of that now."

She drew the beers and set the foaming mugs on the bar in front of Ace and Chance. The brothers picked up the mugs and drank.

"That's good," Ace told Selma.

"Glad to hear it. First one's on the house, boys. That's the rule here at the Red —"

She stopped short and stared over Ace's shoulder at something. He'd heard the door open just now, so he figured she was looking at whoever had come into the saloon — and she wasn't too happy to see them.

"Not him again," Selma muttered.

Somehow, Ace had a hunch who he was going to see when he looked around. Sure enough, Clint Starkey had just entered the Red Top. The gunman heeled the door closed behind them, then started stomping a little snow off his boots. He didn't seem to be paying any attention to who was in the saloon.

That was pretty careless for a man who had a reputation as a shootist. Such a man never knew when he might run into someone who wanted to take that reputation away from him — permanently.

Chance glanced around and saw Starkey, too. He started to turn to face the man, but Ace said under his breath, "Just let it alone, Chance. He might not notice us."

Chance frowned and asked, "Do you really believe that?"

"I don't know, but we might as well let it play out?"

Selma leaned forward over the bar and asked in a half whisper, "You boys know that varmint?"

"We had a little run-in with him earlier," Ace replied.

The woman's eyes got bigger. She said, "Some fellas who were in here were talking about a couple of young strangers who threw down on Starkey. That was you?"

"Guilty as charged," said Chance.

"He was about to beat an Indian boy," added Ace. "We couldn't sit still for that."

"Maybe you should have," Selma said. "Starkey's bad medicine."

"That's what we keep hearing," Chance said.

"You hear right." Selma's eyes cut back and forth nervously. "Is there fixin' to be a shoot-out in here?"

"I hope not," Ace said. "We're not looking for one."

"We're not in the habit of running away from trouble, though," Chance said. "So don't suggest we sneak out the back door."

Selma grunted and said, "Don't have one. Anyway, I can tell by looking, you boys aren't the sneaking sort."

She was right about that. Ace and Chance stood there, calmly sipping their beers, while Starkey finished cleaning off his boots and then tramped toward the bar, spurs ringing and the high heels of his boots coming down hard on the thick, sawdust-littered planks of the floor.

The atmosphere in the saloon hadn't been raucous to start with, but it quieted down even more when Starkey came in. By the time he reached the bar, everyone in the place was silent. A couple of men who had been standing at the bar, drinking, moved over to give him plenty of room. He acted like such deference was his natural due as he slapped a hand on the hardwood and barked, "Rye. And make it quick."

Then he glanced along the bar and stiffened when he saw Ace and Chance.

"Oh, hell no," Starkey said. "Not you two pissants again."

"Take it easy, Starkey," Selma said. "Nobody's gonna start any trouble in here. Not as long as I've got a sawed-off shotgun under this bar."

Starkey sneered and said, "You think I'm scared of some fat old woman? Even if you really do have a gut shredder under there, you'd never get it out in time to bother me. Now, shut your mouth, you old bat. This is between me and these snot-nosed little bastards." He turned so he was facing Ace and Chance directly and hooked his thumbs in the crossed gunbelts. "I told you brats that the next time I saw you, you wouldn't get off so easy. Your luck's run out. You didn't take me by surprise this time." His mouth twisted in a snarl. "Let's get to it."

"Mister, there are two of us," Chance said mildly.

"Yeah, and I got two guns. A bullet for each of you. Now, step out away from that bar so you'll have plenty of room to fall when I plug you."

Ace was the closest to Starkey. He sighed, lifted his beer with his left hand, and took another sip from the mug.

"You claimed earlier that you lost twenty dollars," Ace said. "How about if we pay that back to you? Would that make everything square?"

"Not hardly," Starkey snapped. "It's not about the money, and it hasn't been since the two of you pointed guns at me. Nobody does that and lives to brag about it."

"Nobody's bragging," Chance pointed out.

Starkey ignored that and said, "You're gonna draw, or I'll just shoot you down where you stand. Just like stepping on a couple of bugs. That's all the two of you amount to."

"Let it go," Ace said.

Starkey cocked his head to the side, and an ugly grin split his face. He said, "What's that, boy? Let it go, you said? Are you *beggin'* me, you little bastard? Beggin' me for your life?"

"No," Ace said. "It's just that I kind of like Miss Selma here — she said the first drink was on the house — and I'd hate for her to have to clean blood off the floor."

Starkey's grin turned into a snarling rictus of hate. His hands stabbed toward the guns on his hips. Ace turned smoothly at the bar. Starkey cleared leather a split second ahead of him, but Ace's Colt spouted lead and flame first. Starkey jerked back a step, jolted by the bullet that drove into his chest. He struggled to lift both guns, but judging by the expression on his face, each revolver suddenly weighed a thousand pounds. They went off, and the twin blast was deafening inside the saloon. The bullets thudded into the floor in front of Starkey.

Then his legs buckled, and he dropped to his knees. An instant later, his face hit the floor as he pitched forward.

Chance, with the Smith & Wesson in his hand just in case, circled Ace and approached the fallen gunman at an angle. With his foot, he slid the guns that Starkey had dropped well out of reach, then hooked a boot toe under the man's shoulder and rolled him onto his back. He studied the planks for a second and then nodded in apparent satisfaction.

"Not much blood on the floor, after all," he said. "You did a good job of drilling him through the heart, Ace. Not much blood flows after it stops."

"Any blood spilled uselessly is too much," Ace said as he thumbed a fresh cartridge into his Colt's cylinder to replace the one he'd fired. "I'm sorry about that, Miss Selma."

"Lord!" the woman said as excited chatter burst out from the saloon's customers. "Where'd you learn to draw and shoot like that, son?"

"I reckon it just comes natural," Ace said as he slid the gun back into leather.

"Wait a minute," Denny said. Fully dressed now, with her curly blond hair still damp, she sat on the log with Ace, Chance, and her brother Louis. She lowered her voice and imitated Ace. " 'I reckon it just comes natural.' You can't say things like that and then claim you had no idea you were really Jensens!"

"Do you know how many different bunches of Jensens there are in the world?" Ace said.

"That's not what I mean, and you know it!

245

Sure, your name is Jensen, but you really didn't know then that you're part of *our* bunch of Jensens?"

"The gunfighting branch of the family," Louis put in dryly.

"We didn't know," said Chance. "Honestly."

"But you said you had your suspicions," Denny responded.

"*Suspicion* is a strong word," Ace said. "We were just . . . curious, let's say . . . about Luke being acquainted with a woman who had the same first name as our mother."

"And you didn't think there was anything odd about the way you kept running into him and our father and Uncle Matt? Something like . . . fate, maybe?"

"Looking back on it now, that makes sense if you believe in such things," Ace admitted. "And the way things finally turned out, it does seem a little like fate. But you've got to remember . . . Christmas is the time of year for miracles . . ."

Chapter 23
Denver

Doc Monday had never been given to flights of fancy. He was a practical, hardheaded man. But even he had to admit that it was something of a miracle that he survived on that snowy night, as cold as it was and as poorly dressed as he was.

His feet were so numb, he couldn't feel them at all by the time he reached the little settlement not far from the sanitarium, and the rest of him wasn't in much better shape. Now that he was here, he needed some help, and he needed it quickly.

The problem was, he didn't know anyone who lived here, and he wasn't sure where to turn. Most of the staff members at the sanitarium probably lived in town, but although Doc was friendly with them, that friendship didn't extend beyond the grounds of the sanitarium. He didn't know how to find any of them.

Then he heard singing, and something

about the sound drew him toward it.

As he stumbled through the darkness, hugging himself ineffectually against the cold, he saw a large yellow glow ahead. In the swirling snow, it was just an irregular blob of light, but as he came closer, he began to be able to distinguish more. The light came from several windows, he realized. Tall, narrow windows, not really like what you'd normally find in a house.

A few moments later, he realized why the windows were shaped like that. This was not a regular house he was approaching.

It was a church. A house of worship.

The singing came from inside it. Faint and muffled by the building's walls, the way it was, he never should have been able to hear it, but somehow, he had. The people inside were singing hymns. Christmas hymns, he thought as he recognized the melody, even though he couldn't make out the words.

He couldn't recall the last time he had set foot in a church — but he was going in this one, make no mistake about that. And the congregation would help him. They were good people, good Christian people. They would have charity and compassion, even for a degenerate old gambler. . . .

He was still at least fifty feet from the church's front door when his frozen legs gave out. He fell, crying softly, no longer able to support himself. He landed on his hands and knees in snow that was now a couple of inches deep, but he was so numb, he no longer felt the cold.

He tried to push himself upright, but his muscles simply wouldn't obey his commands. As much trouble as he already sometimes had getting his body to do what he wanted it to, the terrible cold that had him in its grip just made everything worse. A desperate sob came from his mouth as he struggled, knowing that his life depended on what he did next.

If he collapsed and just lay there in the snow, as a part of him wanted to do, when the churchgoers finally came out, they would find his frozen, lifeless body.

Giving up meant death.

Unfortunately, Doc Monday no longer had the strength to do anything else.

With a groan of despair, he slumped to the ground. He felt the snow on his face, in his mouth and nose and eyes. *Stop fighting it,* he told himself. *It's over.*

That thought still echoed in his mind when two strong hands took hold of him and lifted him. The hands were big enough that they went all the way around his slender arms.

"Here now, mister," a high-pitched voice said. "You can't be a-layin' in the snow like that. You'll catch your death." The powerful grip turned Doc around. "Well, Lord have mercy! You sure ain't dressed for weather like this, friend. The way you're shakin', you must be plumb froze!"

Doc's teeth chattered. He said, "I . . . I . . . ," but that was all he could force out.

"No need to talk right now. You just hang on. My wagon's right over here. I got what you need."

In the faint light from the church windows, Doc could see that his unexpected rescuer was a man in a thick, bulky coat and a battered old hat. He was several inches shorter than Doc but appeared to be almost as wide as he was tall. He possessed a great deal of strength, too, which he demonstrated by picking Doc up, cradling him in his arms, and carrying him toward a wagon parked nearby as if he were weightless.

Doc hadn't seen the vehicle until now. It was a freight wagon, piled high with cargo. A team of six mules was hitched to it. The man carried Doc to the seat and lifted him onto it.

"Stay right there," he said in his squeaky voice.

There wasn't anything else Doc could do. He was too weak to go anywhere.

The man went to the back of the wagon, got something from it, and hurried back to the front just in time to catch Doc as the gambler began swaying on the seat. The man climbed up beside him and wrapped a thick blanket around him. He had a pair of socks and some boots, as well, and he worked Doc's numb feet into them.

"We'll stop in a spell, once we get outta town, and I'll build a good fire. That'll thaw you out, you wait and see. In the meantime . . ." The man lifted an unstoppered flask to Doc's mouth. "Your fingers are tremblin' too much to handle this, so let me do it. You just drink."

Doc gulped the whiskey the man spilled into his mouth from the flask. The warmth that burst to life inside him might be temporary, but it was welcome. Doc would have guzzled down more, but the man said, "Hang on. Not too much at a time, now." He lowered the flask, wrapped a second blanket around Doc's scrawny form, and tucked it in securely.

Then he took up the reins and said, "I just thought of somethin'. Do you live around here, mister? Can I take you home?"

Doc managed to form words this time.

He said, "No . . . no home."

He didn't want to go back to the sanitarium. As long as Bill Malkin was there, it would be a death sentence to return.

"Yeah, I kind of had a feelin' it was like that," the man said. "I'm sorta the same way. No real home. It's a good thing for you I was passin' by here tonight, though, heard the singin' from the church, and decided to sit a spell and listen to it. I never would'a seen you if I hadn't."

He flapped the reins and got the mules moving. Doc swayed a little on the seat as the wagon lurched into motion. The blankets felt good to him as he sat wrapped up in them, but he was still chilled to the bone.

"Wh-why didn't you . . . go inside?" he asked.

"Haw! Those folks, they wouldn't want an ol' sinner like me in their church. Shoot, I've done so many black-hearted things in my life, was I to step into the Lord's house, the heavens'd likely split open in outrage." Another laugh boomed out of him, and then he asked, "What's your name, friend?"

"D-Doc. They call me Doc."

"Pleased to make your acquaintance, Doc. Don't you go freezin' to death on me." He flicked the reins again and clucked loudly to the mules to keep them moving through the snowy night, then added, "Oh, yeah. Folks call me Mongo."

Montmorency Weems was the real name of Doc's benefactor, so Doc could understand why the man went by Mongo. As promised, he made camp and built a large fire that gave off plenty of heat. However, he didn't let Doc sit too close to it, insisting that it was better to warm up gradually. He also took the boots and socks off Doc's feet and rubbed them with his huge but gentle hands, coaxing life and feeling back into them. The pins and needles Doc experienced while Mongo was doing that were painful but welcome, because they meant that his feet hadn't frozen solid and would recover.

When Doc felt a little better, Mongo gave him another drink from the flask, then cooked a pot of stew. That helped, as well. After a couple of hours, Doc felt almost human again.

He couldn't stay awake, though. Mongo helped him crawl into the wagon, where he stretched out on some large bags of grain, wrapped up in blankets again, and fell into a deep, dreamless sleep.

The next morning, over a breakfast of coffee and leftover stew, Mongo asked a few probing questions, which Doc skillfully avoided answering.

Doc asked a question of his own, saying, "Where are you headed?"

"Denver," Mongo replied. "I'll deliver these goods there and pick up some more to carry on elsewhere."

Doc's brain was working better this morning. He knew from a letter Ace and Chance had written to him that the boys intended to come to the sanitarium to visit him after they spent Christmas on the ranch belonging to their friend Smoke Jensen. That ranch was located near the town of Big Rock, and Doc was pretty sure the railroad from Denver ran through there. If he could make it to Big Rock, he could find the Sugarloaf and, more importantly, find Ace and Chance.

With the two of them to help him, he felt sure he could deal with the menace of Bill Malkin. . . .

"Can you take me with you, Mongo?" he asked. "I really need to get to Denver. I'm afraid I have no money . . . I mean, you saw the way I'm dressed . . . but I can get hold of some and pay you back later for your trouble —"

"Hellfire, it's no trouble, Doc! I was goin' there, anyway, and there's plenty of room

254

on that wagon seat. I don't mind the company, neither. Them jugheads are the finest team I ever had, but they ain't much on conversalizing. You don't have to pay me nothin'."

"I insist," Doc said. "I'm going to need some clothes, too, but if I can just find a poker game, I can see to it that our acquaintance doesn't cause you to lose money."

Mongo grinned and said, "Cardplayer, are you?"

"I've been known to sit in on a few hands now and then," Doc said with a smile.

"All right. Tell you what I'm gonna do. I'll take you to Denver and stake you to food and clothes and whatever else you need, and then you go to a place called Hood's Saloon and tell 'em Mongo sent you. You'll be able to find a game there." The big freighter squinted at Doc in sudden suspicion. "You play a straight game, don't you? Folks there are friends o' mine, and I don't want to send no tinhorn cheat to take advantage of 'em."

"I've never cheated a day in my life, Mongo. I give you my word on that."

"That's good enough for me," Mongo said with a nod.

"You can come with me and see for yourself."

Mongo shook his head and said, "Nope, I trust you. I'll have to be movin' on as soon as I get another load of freight to deliver. But I'll see to it you're squared away first."

"I really want to pay you back," Doc insisted.

"I'll give you an address where you can send the money, if you want to. It's where my daughter lives, and I'd just as soon the money go to her and her family. My needs are simple enough, I don't need much in the way o' dinero."

"If you're sure . . ."

"Sure as can be," Mongo said. "Now, when you get to Hood's, don't forget to tell 'em that I sent you."

Doc nodded and said, "Mongo sent me. I won't forget."

And he hadn't. The trip to Denver had passed without incident. Mongo had stopped in the first small settlement they'd come to, and had bought Doc a shirt, trousers, and a coat, plain, cheap garments but very welcome. Then in Denver he had given Doc enough money to sit in on a game at Hood's Saloon and try to turn the funds into more. The people at the saloon had welcomed him, as Mongo had promised they would. Not wanting to take advantage of the big man's friends, Doc had won just enough to buy some better clothes and a train ticket to Big Rock.

He was at the depot now, waiting for the train to arrive. Soon he would be at the Sugarloaf Ranch, he told himself. Ace and Chance might not have arrived there yet — it was still several days until Christmas — but Doc thought if he told Smoke Jensen who he was and explained the situation, Jensen would allow him to stay there and wait for the brothers.

Smoke Jensen had quite a reputation, Doc mused. He would be safe there, on the Sugarloaf.

The westbound train rolled in, and Doc boarded. The stop in Denver wasn't a long one, so he was on the way again soon. As the locomotive blew steam from its stack and the cars jolted into motion, Doc glanced over at the station platform as it seemed to move past the window. Quite a few people were still milling around there. From the looks of them, mostly families who had come to meet someone getting off the train.

Doc spotted a man moving quickly through the crowd, though, heading toward the train, which was now gathering speed, as if he were trying to catch it. Doc caught only a glimpse of the man, though, before losing sight of him.

That glimpse was enough to make Doc catch his breath and stiffen on the bench seat. He couldn't be certain, by any means, but the man had reminded him of Bill Malkin.

Could Malkin have trailed him here, all the way from the sanitarium? It seemed unlikely, but Doc couldn't rule it out. Malkin had been desperate to end the threat to his safety, to preserve his masquerade as Bill Williams.

Or maybe his nerves were in such bad shape that he was just imagining things, Doc told himself. He didn't *know* that the man he'd just seen was Malkin.

But there was an uncertainty that was even more troubling: If that man on the platform really *had* been the outlaw . . . had he managed to get on the train before it left the station?

He was going to be very glad to see Ace and Chance again, Doc thought. If he lived that long . . .

Chapter 24
The Sugarloaf

Sally was humming a Christmas song to herself as she adjusted a length of red ribbon she had wrapped around the tree Smoke and Cal had brought in a couple of days earlier. They had set it up in the parlor, in a bucket of dirt that Sally watered to keep it fresh. Since then, she had been decorating it with ribbon, carved ornaments, little bells, and anything else she could think of that would be festive.

The song she was humming caught in her throat a bit as she thought about what had happened when Smoke and Cal went out to cut down that tree. Smoke had told her about the encounter with Don Juan Sebastian Aguilar's men, of course, including the shoot-out with the gunman called Pedro. She and Smoke didn't keep secrets from each other. No more trouble had occurred since then, but the possibility of it still loomed.

Why did some sort of conflict *always* seem to erupt right around Christmastime? This ought to be the happiest, most peaceful season of the year, and yet that never seemed to be the way it worked out for the Jensen family.

Sally had no answer to the question, so she just sighed and shook her head. She would continue trying to make this a good holiday. There was nothing else she could do.

The front door of the house opened, and boots clomped in the foyer, accompanied by the jingling of spurs. Sally turned and saw Pearlie standing in the entrance between the foyer and the parlor, holding his high-crowned black hat in front of him.

"You wanted to see me about somethin', Miss Sally?" the Sugarloaf's foreman asked. Sally had gone out to the bunkhouse earlier, looking for him.

"Yes, I need a few more things for the baking I plan to do," she said. "I was hoping you and Cal could take the buckboard into town to get them for me."

"Why, sure. No need to take Cal, though. I reckon I can handle a trip to the store by myself."

Sally smiled and said, "I know you can, but take him with you, anyway. You know how much he enjoys a trip to town."

"Huh. He enjoys not havin' to work for a while." Pearlie shrugged and went on, "But sure, I reckon he can go along, too."

Sally nodded, glad that Pearlie had agreed with her suggestion. It wasn't all for Cal's benefit, but she didn't tell Pearlie that. With the situation involving Aguilar's claim on the ranch still unresolved, and those gunmen who worked for him possibly lurking in the vicinity, Sally thought it best that Pearlie not take the buckboard to Big Rock by himself. She didn't actually expect him to run into trouble . . . but if he did, it would be better if there were two of them to deal with it.

Sally gave him the list she had written out earlier, and Pearlie tucked it away in his shirt pocket, where he also carried his bag of makin's. He nodded politely and left the house to hunt up Cal and hitch a couple of horses to the buckboard.

Sally went back to rearranging the Christmas tree decorations. She had been doing that off and on and intended to keep it up until she had everything perfect.

Because she was concentrating on that, she didn't know anyone else had arrived at the ranch until a knock sounded on the front door. Frowning in puzzlement, she

261

turned away from the tree. She wasn't expecting visitors.

As she went to the door, she glanced at the loaded Winchester leaning against the wall in a corner. That wasn't the only loaded weapon tucked away in various places around the house, and Sally knew how to use them all. Smoke had made sure of that, and he had instilled a habitual sense of caution in her, as well.

She looked out the narrow window beside the door and saw a buggy parked in front of the house, with a riderless saddle horse standing next to it. A man and a woman sat in the buggy. The man was a stolid, wide-faced Mexican, probably a servant.

The woman was Doña Mariana Aguilar.

Sally didn't think she would need the rifle, since Mariana had come calling and probably wasn't looking for trouble. She opened the door and found the lean, straw-haired gunman from Texas, Travis Hinton, standing on the porch, with his hat in his hand.

"Miz Jensen," he drawled as he gave her a polite nod. "Hope you don't mind some company. Doña Mariana wanted to pay you a visit, and the don sent me along to keep an eye on her."

"Of course," Sally said. "I'm happy to see her. Please, ask her to come in."

"Yes'm." Hinton nodded and turned to walk back to the buggy. He spoke to Mariana, then took the gloved hand she offered to him and helped her climb down from the vehicle. Smiling, she came toward the house. Hinton trailed behind her.

Sally hadn't actually invited the gunman in, but she was too polite to tell him he wasn't welcome in her house. Besides, he'd said that Señor Aguilar had told him to watch out for Mariana, and Hinton might have taken that order literally.

It was too late to do anything about it now. The man was on the porch again, with Mariana this time.

"Sally, it is so good to see you again," she said. She removed her gloves. "I enjoyed our visit in Big Rock the other day."

Sally had enjoyed it, too — at first. Before the friction between their husbands had become obvious.

But even though Sally would stand and fight side by side with Smoke against any attempt to take their home away from them, she wasn't going to be inhospitable to a young woman who apparently had no control over what her husband did. She opened the door wider and said, "Please, come in, Mariana. Welcome to my home."

Mariana paused before coming in and

turned to Hinton. She said, "Señor Hinton, please tell Enrique to take the buggy over to the barn, and then the two of you can wait there." Sally heard the imperious tone in her voice. Mariana looked back at her and added, "I assume that is all right? My man can water the horses and put them inside, out of the cold?"

"Certainly," Sally said.

"Hold on a minute," said Hinton. "The don told me to look out for you. I reckon I ought to come in the house with you."

"Whatever for?" Mariana asked with apparent sincerity. "I am simply going to sit and visit with Señora Jensen. Nothing will happen to me."

"But the don said —"

"And *I* am saying for you to wait in the barn with Enrique. Unless you want me to tell the don that you were quite defiant and rude to me."

Hinton's angular jaw was tight as he said, "No, ma'am. But I'll be close by if you need me."

"I assure you, I won't," Mariana said.

Hinton gave her a curt nod, then turned and stalked off the porch. He went back to the buggy and spoke to the driver. The man turned the vehicle and headed for the barn. Hinton followed, leading his horse, but he cast an angry glance over his shoulder as he did so.

As Sally ushered Mariana into the house, the younger woman said, "My husband hires these men, and sometimes they forget their place. My apologies, Sally."

"None necessary," Sally said. "Up here in the States, we're pretty evenhanded about such things."

"Yes, but we come from two different worlds, in many ways."

"More than you know. I was raised in New England."

"Oh!" A smile lit up Mariana's face. "You must tell me all about it."

"Why don't we go in the parlor," Sally suggested, "and I'll bring us some tea."

"*Gracias,*" Mariana said.

Once the two women were settled in the parlor, drinking tea, they talked about their lives until now. Their childhoods were similar, Sally having lived a pampered existence in New England, and Mariana in Mexico City. But their paths had diverged after that, with Sally going to Idaho to accept a teaching position in a wild frontier town, while Mariana continued living in the lap of luxury.

Without that flight of daring on Sally's part, she never would have met Smoke, so

265

she had never regretted the decision to leave her comfortable life behind.

Still smiling, Mariana asked, "Where is your oh-so-handsome husband today, Sally?"

"He rode into Big Rock early this morning," Sally said. She would have asked him to bring back the supplies she needed for her Christmas baking, but at the time, she hadn't realized that she was running low on a few things. "He had a little business to take care of."

She knew what that business was. He had gotten replies to the wires he'd sent to the lawyers in Denver and San Francisco, and after studying what they had to say, he had written out more messages and was going to the Western Union office to send them today. All the lawyers had been cautiously encouraging about Smoke's chance of prevailing in court over Señor Aguilar's claim, if it ever came to that, but Smoke didn't want it to get that far. He wanted the lawyers to head things off, if possible.

"I am sure he is a very astute businessman," said Mariana, "seeing what a success he has made of this ranch." She added, "With your help, of course, Sally."

"It's been a partnership right from the first," Sally agreed. "I suppose Smoke and I knew we were meant to be together, just as soon as we laid eyes on each other."

"That must be a wonderful feeling," the younger woman murmured.

Sally suddenly felt a little bad about what she'd just said. Mariana's marriage to Aguilar had been an arranged one, she recalled. She would have apologized, even though that would be awkward, too, but Mariana went on, "What sort of business did Señor Jensen have in Big Rock today?"

Sally opened her mouth, closed it again, and shook her head.

"Why, I'm afraid I don't know," she said. "Smoke doesn't talk to me about such things."

"Oh?" Mariana cocked her head a little to the side. "But I thought you just said that you and he are partners."

"We are," Sally said. "He runs the ranch, and I run the home."

"I see." Mariana took another sip of her tea.

Why, the little minx! Sally thought. She was fishing for information about what Smoke was doing to counteract her husband's land grant claim. That was probably the only reason she had come out here today. The question was whether Aguilar had sent her or she had come on her own.

And it didn't matter, because either way she wasn't getting any answers out of Sally.

They chatted about other things for a few minutes. Sally changed the subject to Christmas, and Mariana praised the tree Sally had decorated.

"In Mexico *Las Posadas* has already begun," she said. "That is our Christmas celebration, and it lasts for nine days. It is so beautiful. We have trees like this and many lilies, and candles everywhere! And the children are so happy with their piñatas filled with sweets."

Sally managed to smile again as she said, "I can think of some cowboys who would like it if we had that tradition here. I don't think anybody has a bigger sweet tooth than a young man who works for us named Cal." A genuine laugh came from her. "He'd like it if you filled up a piñata with bear sign and let him bust it."

Mariana shook her head and said, "Bear sign? I do not understand."

"Doughnuts," Sally explained. "Cowboys call them that because they're round and look similar to the tracks that bears leave. I'm going to make a batch for Christmas, along with some pies and cakes."

"I am sure your servant will enjoy them."

Sally almost corrected her. Cal wasn't a

servant, any more than Pearlie or any of the other hands were. Employees, yes, technically, but anybody who rode for the Jensen brand was more than that. They were part of the family.

Sally didn't think Mariana would ever really understand that, and neither would Aguilar. But that was their loss.

Mariana finished her tea and set the cup and saucer on the low table in front of her chair.

"I should be going," she said. "I would not want Sebastian to worry about me."

"He didn't know where you were going?"

"He knew, of course, but anytime I am out of his sight for too long, he becomes concerned. I suppose most older men would, if they were married to a younger woman."

"I suppose," Sally said, although she didn't really know. The gap in ages between her and Smoke was much smaller.

"Thank you so much for your hospitality. I enjoyed our visit."

"I did, too," Sally said. That might have been stretching the truth just a little . . . but Mariana's visit to the Sugarloaf had been educational, at the very least. Her attempt at spying, feeble though it might have been, had taught Sally not to fully trust the young woman.

Hinton must have been watching from the barn. He stepped out, leading his horse, as soon as Sally and Mariana emerged from the house onto the porch. A moment later, Enrique drove the buggy out of the barn. Skillfully, he brought the vehicle to a stop in front of the porch.

Hinton helped Mariana into the buggy. She said, "*Buenos días,* Sally," and waved a gloved hand as Enrique got the team moving.

"Good-bye," Sally called. She stood there while Hinton gave her a sardonic look, swung up into his saddle, and cantered his horse after the buggy.

Sally wasn't sorry to see any of them go.

Especially the gunman.

CHAPTER 25

"God rest ye merry, gennullmunnn! Let nothin' you dismaaay!"

Pearlie looked over at Cal on the buckboard seat and said, "Will you quit that infernal caterwaulin'? You sound like a durn coyote with somebody a-steppin' on its tail!"

"You just don't appreciate a good Christmas song," Cal replied defensively. "I'm full of the Christmas spirit."

"You're full of somethin', all right," Pearlie muttered as he flapped the reins against the back of the two horses pulling the buckboard toward Big Rock.

Cal nudged Pearlie with an elbow and said, "What'd you get me for a Christmas present, Pearlie?"

"I thought maybe I'd give you an extra hour off'a work. That's more'n you deserve."

Cal laughed and said, "Just wait'll you see what I got for you. You're gonna like it."

Pearlie concentrated on his driving. Calvin

Woods was just about his best friend in the world, other than Smoke, but when the boy was in one of his exuberant moods, he could be a sore vexation to a serious man.

"You think Miss Sally's gonna make enough bear sign for everybody?" Cal asked.

"I reckon with all the cookin' and bakin' she's plannin' on doin' between now and Christmas, ain't none of us gonna go hungry," Pearlie said.

"You ever had a Christmas goose?"

Pearlie looked at Cal again and saw the mischievous smile on the young cowboy's face. He gave Cal a stern look and said, "Don't you even think about it, boy. I'll kick you right off this buckboard."

Cal laughed. "Don't worry, Pearlie. I'm not gonna —"

The sharp crack of a gunshot interrupted him, followed instantly by the thud of a bullet hitting the edge of the seat, only inches from Cal's hip. He yelped in alarm as splinters sprayed up from the impact.

Pearlie had been shot at plenty of times in his life. He didn't stop to think. A moving target was harder to hit, so he slapped the horses with the reins again and shouted, *"Hyaaahhh!"* at them. The horses lunged forward so violently that both Pearlie and Cal were thrown back against the seat.

Another shot blasted. This time the slug came so close to Pearlie's ear that he felt as much as heard it whip past him.

There were trees and rocks up ahead on both sides of the trail. Pearlie heard more shots over the thunder of the team's hooves, but he couldn't tell if they were coming from just one side of the trail or if he and Cal were caught in a cross fire.

Either way, if he slowed the horses in an attempt to turn the buckboard around, they would get picked off, he was sure of that. The only way through this ambush was straight ahead, as fast as possible.

"Keep your head down, kid!" he called to Cal. "We're goin' through!"

Cal hunkered lower on the seat, but he wasn't exactly keeping his head down. Instead, he had his Colt in his hand now and blasted away at the trees, triggering twice at the growth to the right and then swinging the gun to the left and blazing two rounds at the trees in that direction. Pearlie didn't know if he had spotted any real targets or was just firing blind.

Cal answered that by shouting, "I saw powder smoke on both sides of the trail!"

Pearlie bit back a groan.

"That's what I was afraid of!" he yelled as he whipped the team again.

The buckboard was going fast enough by now that if the bushwhackers shot the horses, the vehicle would wreck, probably with disastrous results. At the very least, the two cowboys would be thrown off and would be easy targets for the hidden riflemen, if they didn't break their necks when they landed.

So far the horses were running strong and steady. Cal emptied his Colt and reached over to pluck Pearlie's revolver from its holster. He slung more lead on both sides of the trail. Maybe that forced the bushwhackers to keep their heads down and threw off their aim. Pearlie hoped that was the case, anyway.

The buckboard flashed between the clumps of trees. Up ahead, about fifty yards away, the trail curved around a large rock. If they could reach that point, thought Pearlie, they would have some cover from the ambushers and might actually have a chance of getting away.

But then, as the buckboard raced ahead, half a dozen men on horseback rounded that bend and galloped toward Pearlie and Cal, smoke and flame spurting from the guns they triggered at the two cowboys.

"Lord have mercy!" Cal shouted as he saw this new danger.

Pearlie bit back a curse and glanced to the left and right. The ground was too rugged to the right; the buckboard would never be able to negotiate it.

But to the left the terrain was flatter and mostly covered with dead grass, with a few small upthrusts of rock here and there.

Pearlie didn't hesitate. There was only one way he could go.

He swung the buckboard to the left, off the trail, and charged across that open country.

The ground might have *looked* level, but it really wasn't. The buckboard bounced and jolted heavily as Pearlie continued whipping the team. Beside him, Cal was trying to reload the guns, but he kept dropping bullets when he was forced to grab hold of the seat to keep from being thrown off.

Pearlie glanced over his shoulder. The gunmen who had attacked them head-on were now giving chase, and their ranks had been swelled by a couple of other riders. Those were the varmints who had been hidden in the trees, Pearlie decided.

He believed there was a gully up ahead, maybe a quarter of a mile away. The buckboard wouldn't be able to get across it. His eyes searched desperately for some place where he and Cal could make a stand against the men trying to kill them.

The buckboard went over a little hump and suddenly was airborne for a second. When it came down, a sharp crack sounded. Pearlie knew one of the axles had cracked. An instant later, the right front wheel went out from under the buckboard. It tipped, and that corner dug into the ground. Pearlie yelled, "Watch out, Cal!" Both of them went flying wildly into the air.

Pearlie slammed to the ground with bone-jarring, tooth-rattling force. The thin, dead grass provided no cushion. His momentum sent him rolling over and over.

He came to a stop on his belly and raised his head to look around for Cal. The youngster lay a few yards away, shaking his head groggily.

A bullet kicked up dirt between them. Gun thunder still rolled from the approaching riders. Even though he was still a little stunned, Pearlie scrambled to his feet and ran over to Cal. He bent over to grab the young cowboy's arm and haul him upright.

One of the rocky outcroppings was nearby. Pearlie shoved Cal toward it and said, "Get behind those rocks! That's the only cover around here!"

Both of them raced for the scanty protection of the little upthrust. Bullets whined around them. They threw themselves forward and landed on the ground behind the rocks. Slugs began thudding into those rocks.

The two of them were safe, Pearlie thought — but only for a few seconds.

Because after that, the bushwhackers would surround them, and since both of their Colts had gone flying off the buckboard, too, they had no weapons with which to fight off those killers.

Smoke was in a bad mood as he rode toward the Sugarloaf. The snow had stopped, and although the temperature was still cold, a few bits of blue sky were beginning to appear in the gray overcast that had lingered over Colorado for days. Normally, a break in the weather like that would have raised his spirits. Today, though, he was too preoccupied with the problem represented by Don Juan Sebastian Aguilar to think about much of anything else.

He had never been the sort who liked to wait around while trouble was hanging fire. He preferred to battle his foes head-on. So far in this case, the challenge had been a legal one, and so he'd been forced to fight it by legal means.

Sending telegrams wasn't nearly as satisfying as settling things the old-fashioned way, with fists or guns or knives. On the other hand, nobody died from using a telegraph key, so he supposed that was better in the long run.

Anyway, this clash was going to come down to violence again before it was over. Smoke was convinced of that. He could feel it in his bones.

As if to prove his hunch right, the distant crash of gunfire made him lift his head and straighten in the saddle. The shots came from somewhere ahead of him, not too close but not too far away, either.

He was nearing the edge of Sugarloaf range, so he didn't hesitate to heel his mount into a run. Whatever was happening up there, he considered it his business. Even if he hadn't been in such close proximity to the ranch, he would have investigated, anyway. From the sound of the shots, somebody was in trouble, and he wanted to help if he could.

His horse's hoofbeats drummed steadily on the trail. The animal was big and sturdy and had considerable speed and stamina when called upon. Smoke leaned forward in the saddle and reached for the Winchester that rested in a scabbard strapped under the fender. He pulled the rifle free and worked the lever to load a round into the chamber.

The trail twisted back and forth, around and between rocks and clumps of trees. Smoke's horse took those turns in sure-footed fashion, guided by his expert touch on the reins. He rounded one such bend in time to see several riders galloping after a buckboard cutting across open country. Shots blasted from those horsebackers as they fired at the vehicle.

The buckboard was moving so fast that it bounced crazily. Two figures perched on the seat, in constant danger of being thrown off. Smoke's heart slugged in his chest as he recognized not only the two men but also the buckboard itself.

That was Pearlie and Cal, on the Sugar-loaf's buckboard, and they were in deadly danger!

Smoke was in rifle range now, and none of the men seemed to have noticed him. He could have blown several of them out of their saddles before they knew what was going on, but he waited for a second to see if Pearlie and Cal were going to get away.

The next instant he grimaced as he saw the wagon tilt badly and then overturn in a splintering crash. The team pulled loose and kept running, taking the buckboard's broken singletree with them.

Pearlie and Cal flew in the air, thrown clear of the crash, but they landed hard, and the attackers were still charging toward them, firing their guns as they dashed toward their intended victims.

Smoke had seen more than enough. He hauled his mount to a stop, snapped the Winchester to his shoulder, drew a bead, and squeezed the trigger.

The riders might not have noticed the crack of his rifle over the sound of their own horses' hoofbeats and the shots they were firing, but they saw one of their own number suddenly fling his arms out to the sides, topple forward over his mount's neck, and then slide off to the side to land in the path of another horse.

That rider tried to swerve his mount around the fallen man. Instead, the animal's forelegs tangled up, and it plunged forward, headfirst into the ground. The rider flew over the horse's head, then screamed as the horse rolled over him.

Smoke had already worked the rifle's lever and tracked the barrel to the right. He fired again. His horse, like all the horses Smoke rode, was trained to stand still even when guns were going off around it, so he had a steady platform from which to shoot. His second shot caught a rider in the side just as the man was trying to pull his horse around. The bullet caused him to twist in the saddle as it ripped through him, but he managed to grab the saddle horn and hang on instead of falling off.

The others forgot about their pursuit of Pearlie and Cal. With this new threat to deal with, they wheeled their horses around and charged Smoke.

One of them rode right into a bullet, which knocked him backward off his horse. That left four of them, and they must have decided that they didn't want to ride directly into more fire from Smoke's rifle. They veered their horses to Smoke's right and dashed for some timber about fifty yards away. Smoke heard them yelling and saw the muzzle flashes from their handguns, but they were far enough away that the shots weren't any real threat, especially being fired from the backs of galloping horses.

He hurried them on their way with a couple more rounds, but all four fleeing men made it to the trees and disappeared into the growth. Smoke didn't know if they planned to keep going or if they might be regrouping for another attack, but he wanted to check on Pearlie and Cal while he had the chance, so he rode swiftly toward the rocks where his friends had taken cover.

The two cowboys ran out from behind the rocks and scooped up the Colts they must have dropped when the wagon crashed. Pearlie waved Smoke on. The horse thundered up, and as Smoke hauled back on the reins, he called, "Are you two all right?"

"Banged up a mite, but we'll live," Pearlie replied. He was thumbing fresh cartridges from his shell belt into the revolver with practiced efficiency. Cal was busy reloading, too. Pearlie went on, "Did those varmints light a shuck?"

"I don't know," Smoke said. He peered into the trees as he held the Winchester ready for more action. He didn't see any movement, and as he listened intently, he heard the swift rataplan of hoofbeats fading into the distance. "I reckon they decided they'd had enough. You boys be ready to duck back behind those rocks if you need to, though."

"What are you gonna do, Smoke?" asked Cal.

"Check on the ones I ventilated," Smoke said grimly.

He turned his horse and rode back to the scattered motionless bodies. He had glanced at them as he galloped past, to make sure none of them represented an immediate threat. Now, as he took a closer look, he saw that none of them would endanger anyone again.

The horse that had fallen had gotten up and bolted off after the others, but the man it had rolled over was crushed into a shapeless bag of bones. Two of the men Smoke had shot were dead. He had wounded one of the men, who had gotten away, probably pretty badly.

Satisfied, but not pleased by what had happened, he rode back to Pearlie and Cal. The two horses that had been hitched to the buckboard were grazing about a hundred yards away. They hadn't gone very far, dragging the broken singletree.

Smoke said, "I'll go round up those two horses, and you can ride them back to the ranch. We'll deal with the buckboard later."

"Did you recognize any of those sons o' bitches who got left behind, Smoke?" Pearlie asked.

"I did," Smoke said as he nodded. His face was as hard and bleak as stone. "They're some of those gunmen who work for Don Juan Sebastian Aguilar."

CHAPTER 26

It was afternoon before Smoke rode into Big Rock for the second time today. Pearlie was with him on this trip. They went straight to Sheriff Monte Carson's office, swung down from their saddles, and looped their reins around the hitch rail in front of the stone building.

Monte was behind his desk, frowning and licking the lead in a pencil he was using to laboriously write a report for the county commissioners. When the door opened and Smoke and Pearlie strode in, a pleased expression appeared on the lawman's face. He hadn't been expecting Smoke, but they were old friends, and he was always glad to see him.

The same was true of Pearlie. Both he and Monte had worked together as hired guns in the past. In fact, they had been drawing wages from the same man when they first met Smoke. That fateful encounter had changed both their lives much for the better.

When Smoke was in town earlier, he and Monte had had coffee together at Louis Longmont's. Because of that, Monte said, "I didn't figure I'd see you again today, Smoke, but come on in and sit down, both of you. There's coffee on the stove."

"I'm too mad to sit, Monte," Smoke said. The dark, stormy expression on his face confirmed that.

Monte frowned and asked, "What's put a burr under your saddle? Is it that business with Aguilar again?"

As Smoke had suspected, Monte had been out of town on law business the day Aguilar and his entourage had arrived in Big Rock. He'd been called out to one of the smaller spreads in the valley to settle a dispute over a bull. But when he'd gotten back to town, Louis had filled him in on what had happened, and he had discussed the matter with Smoke since then, too.

"You could say that," Smoke replied to the sheriff's question. "Tom Nunnley needs to take his wagon out on the trail to the Sugarloaf. About five miles west of town, in a field just north of the trail, he'll find the bodies of three of Aguilar's hired gunmen."

Tom Nunnley owned the hardware store

in Big Rock and also served as the town's undertaker. Hearing that his services were required in that capacity made Monte take a deep breath and press both hands down on the desk, hard.

"What happened?" he asked. "Is anybody else hurt?"

"Me and Cal are gonna be bruised and sore in the mornin'," Pearlie said. "We were on our way to town in the buckboard, to pick up a few things Miss Sally wanted, when a bunch of those varmints ambushed us. The buckboard wrecked, and the two of us were pinned down behind some rocks. They would've finished us off if Smoke hadn't come along just then, killed three of 'em, and wounded another. The rest of the bunch decided to light out instead of keepin' the fight goin'."

Monte's face had settled into grim lines as he listened to Pearlie's story. When the foreman was finished, Monte stood up and said, "We need to go have a talk with Aguilar. I'm no lawyer and don't know what sort of legal case he has with his claims, but I know good and well he can't send gunwolves out to the Sugarloaf to murder your men, Smoke!"

"You can talk to him," Smoke said, "but I don't expect it to do much good. All Agui-

286

lar has to do is deny knowing anything about what happened, and chances are we won't be able to prove otherwise. But I reckon we ought to at least make the effort."

Monte reached for his hat and nodded, saying, "We sure as hell will."

The three men headed for the Big Rock Hotel. The overcast had continued to break up as the day went on, and the sky had quite a bit of blue in it now. The air still possessed a chilly bite, though, and was cold enough for their breath to fog in front of their faces as they crossed the street and angled toward the hotel.

The hotel lobby was warm, maybe a little too much so. Smoke would have asked the clerk if Aguilar was in, but he didn't have to. The don himself sat in one of the armchairs arranged near the big front window. He had an open newspaper in his lap.

In a chair next to his sat his wife, Mariana, who was doing some sort of needlework; and a little farther away, in a straight chair, was the heavyset Mexican woman who was usually around anytime Mariana was — although Smoke recalled from his conversation with Sally when he returned to the Sugarloaf with Pearlie and Cal that the servant hadn't accompanied Mariana on her visit to the ranch that morning.

Sally had still been irritated that Mariana had come out to the Sugarloaf supposedly on a friendly visit when her real purpose had been to dig for information about Smoke's efforts to contest her husband's claim. She had put that annoyance aside immediately when she heard about Pearlie and Cal being ambushed. She had fussed over the two cowboys, treating their minor injuries and promising treats to make them feel better. That had caused Cal to perk right up.

Smoke had left him at the ranch to keep an eye on things while he took Pearlie with him to Big Rock. He didn't believe Aguilar's men would try anything else so soon, but he wanted Cal on hand at the Sugarloaf just in case of trouble.

A cigar smoldered in an ashtray on the small table next to Aguilar's chair. Not getting in any hurry, he folded the newspaper, dropped it in his lap, picked up the cigar, and took a puff on it before he looked up at Smoke, nodded, and said coolly, "Señor Jensen."

He probably suspected that Smoke was here because of the ambush. He might not be aware yet it had failed, though. That would depend on whether or not any of the gunmen who had fled the scene had brought word to town of what had happened. To the best of Smoke's knowledge, Aguilar had never laid eyes on Pearlie until now, so the foreman's presence wasn't enough to tip him off.

"Don Sebastian," Smoke said in an equally chilly tone. Calling him that was more respect than the man deserved, in Smoke's opinion, but he supposed it wouldn't hurt anything to be civil.

It was quickly getting past the time for civility, though.

"I have some news for you," Smoke went on. "Three of your men are out at the edge of my range, dead."

Mariana gasped and dropped the needlework she was doing. Aguilar sat up straighter. His nostrils flared from the sharp breath he took, and his left hand dropped to the folded newspaper and clutched it hard enough to make the paper crackle. If he wasn't genuinely surprised, he was a good actor.

His lips tight under the narrow mustache, Aguilar said, "You found the bodies, señor?"

"No," Smoke said. "I killed them."

Aguilar's jaw clenched even harder. He looked at Monte and said, "You heard him, Sheriff. He admits to the killings."

"You haven't heard the whole story," Monte snapped.

More in control of himself now, Aguilar gestured with the hand holding the cigar and said, "Then, by all means, continue, Señor Jensen."

Beside him, Mariana looked pale and shaken. She might have been willing to serve as a spy for her husband, but Smoke had a hunch she hadn't known anything about the ambush.

"Two of my men were on their way to town in a buckboard," Smoke said. "They were ambushed by eight of *your* men. I happened along just in the nick of time, when they had my foreman here" — he nodded toward Pearlie — "and another of my hands pinned down and were about to wipe them out. I killed three of them with my rifle and wounded another, and then the wounded man and the rest of the bunch lost their nerve and took off for the tall and uncut."

Aguilar stared at him for a couple of seconds, then demanded, "How do you know they were my men?"

"I recognized them," Smoke replied bluntly. "I saw them with you here in town the day you arrived. They work for you, all right, no doubt about that."

"There is *every* doubt," Aguilar snapped.

"It just so happens that yesterday I discharged three of the men working for me under Señor Hinton's supervision. I decided that their services were no longer required. Those three must be the ones who invaded your ranch and attacked your men."

It was Smoke's turn to stare, only his look was one of disbelief rather than a stall to think up a lie, which obviously was what had just taken place on Aguilar's part. He laughed humorlessly and said, "Do you expect us to believe that, Aguilar?"

Instead of answering the question, Aguilar looked at Monte and said, "Are you going to stand by and allow this persecution, Sheriff?"

"It seems to me that Smoke has reasonable cause to believe you're involved in what happened, Señor Aguilar," Monte said. "After all, the men work for you —"

"*Worked* for me," Aguilar interrupted.

Monte shrugged and went on, "That story about you firing them yesterday seems mighty convenient."

"Then go find Señor Hinton and ask him. He was there when it occurred. I believe you can probably find him at the . . . What is it called? Oh, yes, the Brown Dirt Cowboy Saloon. If he is not there, one of the other men probably will be and can tell you where to locate him." A calculating look appeared in Aguilar's eyes. "Better yet, just ask my wife here. Mariana, darling, you remember how I mentioned to you last night that I had dismissed several of the men?"

Aguilar was quick on his feet mentally, Smoke realized, and evidently, so was Mariana, because she summoned up a weak smile and said, "*Sí,* of course, Sebastian." She looked at Smoke, Monte, and Pearlie and went on, "*Es verdad.* It is the truth. My husband said something to me about this very matter yesterday evening."

Smoke's jaw tightened. Mariana was lying, too, just like Aguilar. He was too much of a gentleman to accuse a lady of something like that, though, at least without proof.

However, Pearlie took exception. He blurted out, "Why, if that ain't the biggest pack of —"

Smoke stopped him with an upraised hand. He said, "I understand you paid a visit to the Sugarloaf this morning, Doña Mariana."

"*Sí,* I did. It was a very pleasant visit with your lovely wife."

"Sally's mighty fond of Pearlie and Cal. She would've been mighty upset if they'd been killed."

"And she would have every right to be."

Her mouth was a thin line now. "But that does not change the truth of what Sebastian has told you."

For whatever reason — avarice, fear, or something else — she was a faithful wife and was going to support her husband's story, thought Smoke. He supposed he shouldn't have expected any other response from her. Aguilar had been certain she would back his play.

Monte asked, "What about the other men who were with the hombres Smoke killed?"

Aguilar shrugged and said, "What about them? I have no idea who they were. They have nothing to do with me. I am certain what happened is that the three I discharged persuaded some other lowlifes to help them ambush Señor Jensen's men. They probably had the misguided idea that if they harmed Señor Jensen in some way, I would take them back into my employ."

"You have an answer for just about every-thing, don't you, mister?" Smoke said.

"It is easy to answer questions when one tells the truth."

Smoke doubted whether Aguilar had more than a nodding acquaintance with the truth. But the man's smug, smoothly constructed wall of lies seemed to be impenetrable . . . except for maybe one small chink.

"I'm going to talk to Hinton."

"Go right ahead. I am certain he will tell you the same thing I have."

Aguilar's confidence seemed genuine. Either they had worked out their story earlier, in case of the ambush's failure — although it had seemed to Smoke that Aguilar was taken by surprise and was coming up with things on the spur of the moment — or else Aguilar knew exactly where Hinton was and intended to get word to him before Smoke and Monte could find him.

Either way, the gunman from Texas would be another dead end, more than likely.

"I try to let my lawyers handle legal matters," Smoke said, "but when friends of mine get bushwhacked and nearly killed, that takes it to a whole different level."

"So what are you saying?" Aguilar shot back. "That you intend to take the law into your own hands?" Again, he looked at Monte. "You heard him threaten me, Sheriff."

"That didn't sound like a threat to me," Monte said.

"Then clearly your friendship with Señor Jensen is blinding you to your duty as a lawman."

That was the wrong thing to say to Monte Carson, whose own shady past as a gunman had made him determined to uphold the law once he pinned on a badge. He stiffened and said, "You'd better rein that in, Señor Aguilar. Nothing blinds me to enforcing the law, and I'm not scared of your money — or your hired guns."

Smoke touched his friend lightly on the arm and said, "We might as well go, Monte. We're not doing any good here."

"No, I reckon not," Monte said heavily.

The three of them left the hotel, with Pearlie casting a couple of angry glances over his shoulder as they did so. Outside, as they paused on the boardwalk, Monte sighed and went on, "I'll hunt up Hinton and talk to him, anyway, but I've got a hunch I'll be wasting my time, Smoke."

"I agree with you. Aguilar's slick, and Hinton will be, too."

"It's just that without any proof, and with them denying everything, there's not much I can do other than sending Tom Nunnley out to bring in those bodies."

"Well, there's that much, anyway. I'd just as soon not have their carcasses polluting my range any longer than necessary."

"If Aguilar sent them after you — and I don't doubt that for a second — they failed. You think he'll make another move against you?"

"I don't doubt *that* for a second," Smoke said.

CHAPTER 27
THE MACMURPHY SANITARIUM

The man who walked into the sanitarium's front entrance was a little above medium height, broad shouldered, and had a darkly tanned face, with a hawk nose above a brown mustache. He stepped into the opening between the foyer and the sitting room and looked around, his deep-set eyes darting back and forth as he studied the patients who were there. Evidently not finding who he was looking for, he approached one of the nurses and took off his hat.

"Excuse me, miss. I'd like to see one of your patients here. Bill Williams is his name."

The young woman's eyebrows rose in surprise under her starched white cap. She repeated, "Bill Williams?"

"That's right," the visitor said with a nod. "Good-sized fella, dark hair —"

"I know who Mr. Williams is," the nurse said. "If you'll come with me, sir, I'll take you to Dr. MacMurphy's office."

The man shook his head. "I don't need to see the doctor. I just want a word with old Bill —"

"Please, sir, follow me."

Frowning in confusion and irritation, the visitor trailed the nurse from the sitting room, along a hallway, to a door with a fancy gilt nameplate on it that read DR. WALTER MACMURPHY. She knocked on the door. A man's voice called brusquely from inside, "What is it?"

"There's a gentleman here I think you should speak with, Doctor," the nurse replied.

The visitor heard some muttered complaining inside the office, then heavy footsteps approaching the door. It opened to reveal a bald, overweight man in a dark suit. His black beard was shot through with gray. He glowered at the nurse for a second; then his gaze switched to the visitor, who stood there with his brown Stetson in his hand.

"He was asking about Mr. Williams, Doctor," the nurse went on.

That made MacMurphy's expression change from annoyance to interest. He said, "Is that right? Well, come in, sir. Come in, please."

When the visitor was inside the office,

where the darkly paneled walls were lined with bookshelves containing hundreds of thick leather-bound volumes on medicine, MacMurphy extended a pudgy hand to him.

"I'm Walter MacMurphy, the owner and chief physician of this sanitarium," he introduced himself.

The visitor took MacMurphy's hand in a hard grip and said, "My name is Thackery."

"You have an interest in our patient Bill Williams?"

"That's right."

"You're . . . a relative? A friend?"

"A friend," Thackery said.

MacMurphy gestured toward a red leather chair in front of the large desk and suggested, "Please, sit down."

Thackery looked a little reluctant to do so. He had an air of impatience about him, which he seemed to be keeping in check. But after a moment, he settled in the chair and rested his hat on his knee. MacMurphy went behind the desk and lowered his considerable bulk into a thickly cushioned swivel chair.

"I'm not sure why you folks are getting so worked up about this," Thackery said. "Aren't people allowed to visit your patients?" His frown suddenly deepened. "Wait a minute. Is Bill dead?"

"I wish I could tell you what his current state of health is, Mr. Thackery," MacMurphy said. "Even more so, perhaps, I wish *you* could tell *me.*"

"What the hell does that mean?"

MacMurphy spread his sausage-like fingers, shook his head, and said, "Mr. Williams disappeared several nights ago."

Thackery leaned back against the red leather, almost as if he had been struck. "Disappeared?" he repeated. "You mean . . ."

"I mean that sometime during the night, Mr. Williams left this establishment without telling anyone where he was going or leaving any clue as to his plans."

"What did he do? Climb out a window and run off?"

"That appears to be exactly what he did," MacMurphy said with a sigh.

"And nobody stopped him?"

"This is not a prison, Mr. Thackery." A harder edge came into MacMurphy's voice. "Our patients are here because they want to be, because they need our help." He shrugged. "True, a few have been admitted at the request of family members or guardians, and we keep a closer eye on those individuals. But Mr. Williams came to us of his own free will and sought medical treatment. We had no reason to suspect that he might take his leave in the middle of the night."

"No, I reckon not," Thackery said. "What sort of medical problems did he have?"

"You're his friend, and you don't know that?"

"He was hale and hearty the last time I saw him," snapped Thackery. "That's why I was surprised when I heard that he was here."

"I'm not sure Mr. Williams would appreciate me sharing his medical condition. I don't usually disclose such information except to close family members."

"I'm the closest thing to family that Bill has."

MacMurphy shrugged again, as if to say that he took no responsibility for what he was about to reveal, and said, "He suffers from palpitations and weakness of the heart."

"Bad ticker, eh? I suppose that can come on a person without much warning."

"There are nearly always symptoms." MacMurphy's voice took on a smug tone as he added, "I suspect that as a layman, you simply never noticed them."

Thackery mulled over what had been said, then asked, "Is he likely to just drop dead?"

"That's always a possibility in such cases, but as long as he receives proper care, Mr. Williams has a reasonable expectation of living for a number of years yet. I hesitate to put an exact number on it . . ."

"That's all right. But since he's not here anymore, he won't be getting that proper care, will he?"

"I'm sure I can't say, since I don't know where he is or what he's doing." MacMurphy blew out a breath and shook his head again. "It was quite cold the night he disappeared. In fact, it was snowing. I don't like to think about him being out there in such extreme conditions. To be honest with you, sir, he was not one of our most amiable patients, but he *was* a patient, and I feel a certain amount of responsibility for his welfare."

A faint smile appeared on Thackery's lips. He said, "Yeah, Bill was never all that friendly to anybody. He had a way of always coming out on top, though, so I think there's a good chance that he's all right, wherever he is."

"I hope so."

"But you can't tell me where to look for him?"

"Honestly, I have no idea, Mr. Thackery. I couldn't even tell you which direction he went. The snow covered up any tracks he might have left."

Thackery started to get up, saying, "I reckon I might as well go, then —"

"Just one more moment, if you will. Do you know a man named Ennis Monday?"

Thackery settled back down on the red leather and frowned. He said, "Why do you ask?"

"Because Mr. Monday, who was also a patient here, disappeared on the same night as Mr. Williams."

Thackery looked utterly baffled. He said, "You're saying they ran off together? Were the two of them friends?"

"No, I'm not saying that they left together. I have no way of knowing that. As for them being friends, they were acquainted, certainly. I've seen them playing cards together on many occasions."

"Bill liked to play poker, all right."

"And Mr. Monday, at one time in his life, was a professional gambler, I understand. I have no reason to believe the two of them were close . . . but I have no reason not to believe it, either."

Thackery sat there in silence for a long moment, then said, "I wish I could help you, Doctor, but I never heard of any Ennis Monday. I don't recall Bill ever mentioning the name, I'm sure of that."

"I was hoping you'd know something about Mr. Monday that might lead us to both him and Mr. Williams. But Mr. Monday was here of his own free will, too, so as things stand now, there's really nothing we can do."

"This fella Monday, what else do you know about him? Does he have any family?"

MacMurphy thought about it and then said, "There are two young men who come here to visit him from time to time, and he receives letters from them. I gather that they move around a lot, though, so I don't have any reliable way to contact them."

"You remember their names?" Thackery asked.

"Jensen," the doctor replied. His upper lip curled a little as he added, "I believe they go by the unlikely names of Ace and Chance."

A short time later, Lane Thackery walked into Tilly's Saloon in the settlement near the sanitarium. Normally, the saloon didn't do much business at this time of day, but this afternoon half a dozen men were sitting at a big table in the back of the room, drinking idly. An empty whiskey bottle sat on the table, in addition to the one they were passing around.

A couple of townsmen stood at the bar, each casting an occasional nervous glance toward the men at the table, all of whom had hard-bitten, dangerous airs about them. Tilly Howard, the plump middle-aged woman who owned the saloon, stood on the other side of the bar and regarded the men at the table with equal wariness, as if a pack of two-legged wolves had strolled in and set themselves down.

That was a pretty good description of the group. There wasn't one of them who wasn't wanted in at least one jurisdiction, mostly for serious crimes. Thackery had gathered them with the promise of a good payoff, after the men he'd been running with before had all drifted away.

The men were getting impatient, though, and Thackery knew that what he had found out at the sanitarium would just make them more so. They had all hoped that the search was finally nearing its conclusion. If he was going to keep the bunch together, he needed something to make them believe they hadn't hit another dead end.

Thackery thought maybe he had an idea that would keep them feeling that way.

The men appeared not to be paying attention as Thackery approached, but he knew that was a sham. Men who lived close to the edge of death, as these did, were aware of everything that went on around them. If they weren't, they didn't survive very long.

One of them, dark, lean Del Bryson, glanced up and asked, "How'd it go at the lunger hospital, Lane? Did you find Malkin and make him talk?"

"It's not just a lunger hospital," Thackery replied as he pulled out an empty chair to sit down. "From the looks of it, they treat all sorts of ailments there. Some of the patients I saw didn't look like there was anything wrong with them except for being too damned old."

One of the other men asked, "Yeah, but what about Malkin?"

"He's not there."

That made all of them drop their casual poses and look sharply at him. Bryson said, "You told us you had a good lead on him this time. We've been traipsin' around for months now, tryin' to find him. It's gettin' a little old, Thackery."

"The lead was good," Thackery replied in a flint-edged tone. He wasn't going to allow Bryson or any of these other men to disrespect him. "Malkin was there, but we just missed him by a few days."

"The hospital let him out? He was cured?" Bryson asked.

Thackery grated a curse and said, "I don't know that he was ever sick. Maybe he was. He seems to have convinced the quack who runs the place, anyway. But I know damn well the real reason Bill went there. He thought it was a good place to hide out."

"He was right," Jack Eberle said. Eberle was the oldest member of the bunch, pushing fifty, but he was nobody's friendly grandpa. In his case, his age just meant he'd had time to get even meaner and more dangerous than when he'd started out on the owlhoot trail. "He hid out there for a long while before we picked up his trail."

"So what happened?" Bryson asked. "Where'd he go?"

Thackery shrugged and said, "The people at the sanitarium don't know. He just up and disappeared a few nights ago. Ran off into the cold and snow, maybe with a gambler named Ennis Monday, who vanished at the same time."

A man named Bud Hawkins said, "Is that Doc Monday? I knew a tinhorn called that, and it seems to me his right name was Ennis. I could be wrong about that, though."

Thackery could only shake his head and

307

say, "I don't know. I never ran across anybody by that name. But there's got to be a reason he and Malkin went missing on the same night."

"Maybe they're planning on pulling some sort of job together," a man suggested.

"Not likely. Bill never worked with anybody but professionals, like me. If Monday's just a tinhorn gambler, I can't think of anything they'd get mixed up in together." Thackery reached for the bottle. "I was pondering on it during the ride back from the sanitarium, and it makes more sense to me that Malkin is after this fella Monday for some reason. Maybe Monday stole something from him, and Malkin wants it back. That would explain why they both disappeared the same night."

"The fifty grand you boys took off that train," said Eberle. He leaned forward with an avaricious look in his eyes.

"Not likely," Thackery said. "I still believe Malkin hid that money somewhere after he double-crossed me and the rest of the gang and took off with it on his own. But this fella Monday *could* have found out somehow where Malkin stashed the loot. He could have gone after it. And Malkin could be trying to catch up and keep him from getting his hands on it."

Thackery had mulled over that theory, and it made sense to him. Now, as the other men thought about it, several of them began to nod slowly, as if they agreed.

"I reckon it's worth checking out, anyway," said Bryson. "But if they vanished into thin air, how are we gonna find them?"

"According to the doc at the sanitarium, Monday has a couple of young friends who visit him and write letters to him now and then. He might try to reach them, so they can help him get the money."

"You know where they are?"

"No, but I know their names," Thackery said. "Ace and Chance Jensen. There's somebody else named Jensen who has a ranch not too awful far from here. If he's related, we might be able to pick up the trail there."

Bryson frowned and asked, "You're not talkin' about *Smoke* Jensen, are you?"

"That's right."

"Smoke Jensen has a reputation for being hell on wheels where trouble is concerned," Eberle said. "You want to get mixed up with him, Thackery?"

"For that fifty thousand dollars Bill Malkin stole from me, I'd charge hell and spit in the Devil's own face," Lane Thackery said.

CHAPTER 28
BIG ROCK

Always on the hunt for news, Phil Clinton, the editor and publisher of the *Big Rock Journal,* made it a habit to be on hand at the railroad station whenever trains rolled into town. It wasn't always possible for him to show up at those times, of course, but he did so as often as he could.

He was at the station today as the westbound from Denver arrived with a squeal of brakes and billows of smoke from the diamond-shaped stack on the Baldwin locomotive. The train lurched and rattled to a halt with the passenger cars lined up alongside the depot platform.

The platform was crowded. People traveled a lot during the holiday season, and quite a few were on hand today because it was only a few days until Christmas. Some were about to board and head off to faraway places, while others were there to welcome family members and other visitors who would soon disembark from the train.

Clinton stood back out of the way, a pad of paper in his left hand and a pencil in his right, in case he needed to make any notes about who he saw coming or going.

He was most interested in those who were arriving in Big Rock. You never could tell when someone newsworthy might show up in town. With the practiced eye of an editor, he cataloged the people who got off the train: families who'd come for a visit with relatives; middle-aged women traveling alone, most likely mothers-in-law here to make life miserable for their sons' wives; single men in shabby suits, who were probably drummers trying to make one last sale before Christmas.

Phil Clinton abruptly straightened from his casual pose where he'd slouched against the wall of the station building. An old man had just gotten off the train and turned back to help an old woman down the steps to the platform. The woman was rather handsome, despite her age. The man had a distinguished air about him and didn't look a day older than he had the first time Clinton had laid eyes on him, several years earlier.

"Preacher!" called the newspaperman as he began making his way through the crowd and across the platform.

The old mountain man linked arms with his female companion. His gaze darted swiftly around the platform before coming to rest on Clinton, who knew that Preacher was checking for the presence of enemies. Preacher always did that, no matter where he was. He didn't want any threats taking him by surprise.

As Clinton came up to the couple, Preacher gave him a friendly nod and said, "Howdy, Phil. Still livin' the life of an ink-stained wretch, I reckon?"

"Always," Clinton replied with a grin. "It's in my blood, I'm afraid. Have you come to visit the Sugarloaf for Christmas? I thought you might."

"That's right."

Preacher didn't offer to introduce the woman, even though Clinton glanced at her and then gave him an expectant look.

"It's good to see you again." The newspaperman chuckled. "You always bring excitement with you, and that sells copies of the *Journal*."

"Not this time," Preacher said. "It's gonna be a nice, quiet holiday."

Clinton didn't believe that for a second, but he didn't argue. "Would you like to make a statement for my readers?"

"Nope," said Preacher. "We're just here to

celebrate Christmas, that's all."

He nodded again and started walking with the woman toward the baggage car. Clinton stared after them and debated whether he should trail along and pester them with more questions.

That probably wouldn't be wise, he decided. Preacher didn't cotton much to pestering, and even though he was getting on in years, he still had the bark on, as the old-timers might say. For now, Clinton would mention in the next edition of the paper that Preacher was in town visiting Mr. and Mrs. Smoke Jensen at the Sugarloaf Ranch for Christmas, and that would be enough to interest his readers.

He turned around and almost bumped into a nondescript middle-aged man who had gotten off the train and was headed for the station's lobby. Clinton didn't spare the gent a second glance.

Doc Monday hurried into the lobby and moved quickly over to one of the windows that looked out on the platform. He watched the crowd intently, hoping that he wouldn't see Bill Malkin's burly form.

On the other hand, if Malkin *had* managed to catch the train, Doc wanted to spot him and be warned.

He stayed where he was until everyone who was leaving Big Rock had boarded the train and the locomotive pulled out with the usual melody of puffs and whistles. Doc hadn't recognized anyone on the platform.

He told himself that he ought to breathe easier because of that, but his nerves were still taut. When he lifted his left hand and looked at it, the tremor was very noticeable. The painful stiffness had returned across his shoulders and the back of his neck. He didn't know if that was from his medical condition or the strain of being on the run from a merciless outlaw who wanted to kill him. Probably some of both . . .

Once the train was gone, Doc went to the ticket window and spoke through the wicket to the clerk.

"Can you tell me how to find the Sugarloaf Ranch?"

The clerk raised his eyebrows and said, "Mister, anybody who's been around these parts for more than five minutes can tell you where the Sugarloaf is. Take the main road out of town to the west for seven miles. You'll already be on Jensen range by the time you go that far, but that's where the trail to the ranch headquarters turns off to the north. You'll see a sign. Follow that trail for about half a mile, and you can't miss it."

"Thanks," Doc said. "One more question. Where can I rent a horse and tack?"

"Patterson's Livery is the best place in town." The clerk gave Doc directions, then asked him curiously, "Why are you looking for the Sugarloaf? Are you friends with Smoke?"

"We have mutual friends," Doc replied.

That didn't appear to satisfy the clerk, but Doc didn't offer any more details. He turned away from the window, still watching warily around him. No one seemed to be paying any attention to him, which was just the way Doc wanted it.

The way he felt now, the idea of riding all the way out to the Jensen ranch was pretty daunting. He didn't have much money left from his poker winnings, though. Enough to rent a horse, but that was about all.

He hoped that Ace and Chance were already at the Sugarloaf, but even if they weren't, he told himself, Smoke Jensen would help him. Smoke had a reputation for sticking up for the underdog, and anyway, Doc had a connection to the Jensen family, which no one suspected, not even Ace and Chance. He would be safe if he could just get there.

With that thought in mind, Doc left the train station and walked toward Patterson's

Livery Stable.

Many of Big Rock's citizens knew Preacher from his previous visits. Dicky Patterson greeted him with a smile when he walked in with Adelaide DuBois on his arm.

"Hello, Preacher," the stableman said. "I heard that you were coming to spend Christmas at the Sugarloaf. Pearlie was in here last week and said something about it."

"Yep, lookin' forward to seein' the whole bunch again," Preacher replied. He hadn't introduced Adelaide to Phil Clinton, because he knew Clinton would put something in the newspaper about her. Having her name in the newspaper like that might make it easier for her grandson to track her down. He knew he could trust Patterson, though, so he went on, "This here is an old friend of mine, Mrs. Adelaide DuBois. I'd be obliged to you, though, if you'd keep that name under your hat, Dicky."

"Sure, Preacher. Be glad to."

Adelaide smiled and said, "When introducing a lady, Preacher, it's probably best to refer to her as a 'friend,' rather than an 'old friend.' "

"Dang it, I should'a thought of that. I've spent too much of my life way out in the high lonesome, a far piece from civilized folks."

"I thought that was the way you liked it," Adelaide said.

"Well, I got to admit, that's where I always felt it was the most like a real home to me. Smoke's ranch runs it a pretty close second, though." Preacher turned back to Patterson and went on, "You got a buggy on hand we can rent?"

"I sure do," the stableman said. "And a couple of good horses to hitch to it. Give me fifteen minutes and I'll have you all ready to go."

Preacher nodded and said, "That'll work out just fine. One of the porters from the train station is bringin' over Mrs. DuBois's bags in a few minutes. He can load 'em in the buggy whilst you're hitchin' up the team."

While Patterson was doing that, another man came into the stable. Preacher thought he looked vaguely familiar, but couldn't place him or recall his name, if indeed he even knew it. The man asked about renting a saddle mount, and Patterson told him he'd tend to that just as soon as he finished getting the buggy ready for Preacher and Adelaide.

Preacher drove the buggy out of the stable

a few minutes later, handling the pair of matched grays pulling it with an expert touch on the reins. He had always preferred a saddle and going horseback, but he had driven buggies before, and once he learned how to do something, he never lost the knack of it. At least, he hadn't so far.

The bags were loaded in the area behind the seat. There had been a thick flannel lap robe back there, but now it was spread over Adelaide's legs. She tried to get Preacher to wrap up in it, too, but he shook his head and said, "Naw, I'm fine. The air's a mite chilly —"

"Chilly?" Adelaide repeated. "It's not far above freezing! Do you see the snow melting?"

That was true — the shallow layer of snow on the ground didn't seem to be going anywhere. It would be a lot deeper than that before the winter was over, though.

"I'm used to it. Spent a lot of winters in the high country, where it gets a lot colder than this. Why, I recollect one time me and ol' Polecat was camped up there, and he built a fire and brewed a pot of coffee. He picked up the pot and started to come around the fire so's he could pour some in my cup, but then he tripped on somethin' and like to fell down, and when he flung his

318

arm up in the air, the lid come off that pot and all that boilin' coffee flew out. I thought it was gonna go all over me, and I sorta flinched, but then I heard this thud, and when I looked, there was this hunk of somethin' black layin' in front of me. It was that coffee! It had done froze solid before it could ever hit me or the ground!" Preacher shook his head. "Now *that's* cold."

Adelaide laughed and said, "I knew exactly how that story was going to end, Preacher, and I don't believe a word of it."

"Well, I can understand how you wouldn't, since you wasn't there to see it with your own eyes. But it happened, sure enough."

"I'll take your word for it. And if you're determined not to wrap up in this robe with me, I'll just have to scoot a little closer to you. You may not need the body warmth, but I do."

"You go right ahead and do that," Preacher told her. He wasn't going to complain at all.

It had been a long time since Doc had ridden very far on horseback. Within a mile of leaving Big Rock, he was beginning to regret his decision to do so today. There was nothing else he could do, though, so he clung to the saddle horn, clamped his aching legs tighter on the horse's body, and kept the animal moving.

This was why he had always traveled by train or stagecoach. He wasn't cut out for this.

The older couple who had left the livery stable in front of him in the buggy were headed in the same direction he was. He spotted them from time to time up ahead of him as the vehicle topped a rise. They didn't seem to be getting in a big hurry, but he wasn't catching up to them.

He wondered idly where they were going. There had been something very companionable about them. Maybe they were an old married couple and had a ranch out here. Maybe they were headed home.

Doc wondered what that would be like. He'd never had anything like that since he was a boy, and even then, his life had been far from blissful with a drunken father and a slatternly mother and older brothers whose chief pleasure had been beating the hell out of him.

As an adult, he had known many women, but he hadn't been involved with any of them for any length of time. The months he had spent with Lettie Margrabe had been the only real relationship he'd had that might have turned into something more. The two of them might have wound up together for the long haul, if she had lived. At least, he liked to think so.

But she hadn't survived giving birth to the twin boys. Before passing on, she had made him promise not to hold that against Ace and Chance, and he had honored that pledge, devoting himself to raising the brothers as best he could, which, Lord knew, wasn't any too well!

Having a drifting gambler for a surrogate father wasn't a good thing, but thankfully, due to the fine natures they had inherited from Lettie and from their real father, they had turned out all right. *Better than all right,* mused Doc. He had never known any better young men than Ace and Chance.

He wasn't a praying man, but if he were, he would have sent up a plea to heaven that they were there at the Sugarloaf, and that soon he would be with them again.

What instinct warned him just then, he never knew, but he stiffened suddenly in the saddle and turned to look back over his shoulder. He could see the road rising and falling over the rolling hills, and there, about half a mile behind him, visible in the wan late afternoon sunlight, was a lone rider coming hard in this direction.

Doc's heart gave a painful leap in his chest. That horseman was too far away for him to make out any details about the man, but he didn't need to be able to see him to know who he was.

Fate had caught up to him, thought Doc. Fate in the deadly person of Bill Malkin. Doc was sure of it.

With his pulse hammering in his head, he jabbed the heels of his shoes into the horse's flanks and urged the animal ahead. The horse broke into a run. Panting, Doc leaned forward and hung on for dear life as shudder after shudder quivered through him.

CHAPTER 29

Preacher sat up straighter in the buggy seat as his still-keen hearing detected the swift rataplan of hoofbeats coming up fast on the road behind them.

Feeling him grow tense beside her, Adelaide asked, "What is it, Preacher?"

"I don't know," he said. He hauled back on the reins and brought the team and buggy to a halt. "Listen."

Adelaide's eyes widened in recognition of the sound. She said, "My, someone is really in a hurry, aren't they?"

"Yeah," Preacher said, "and out here on the frontier, anybody who's in that much of an all-fired hurry is usually carryin' trouble with 'em." He listened intently to the rapid hoofbeats as they came closer. "Just one rider, I think. Reckon it could be that no-good grandson of yours?"

"I . . . I don't know." Adelaide sounded frightened now. "I don't think that George would be likely to ride at such a breakneck pace, but I really can't be sure anymore what he's capable of."

"Well, if it *is* him, he shouldn't have come after us by himself."

"Preacher, you can't fight him. It's too dangerous."

"For me or for him?"

"I'm worried about you, of course. George is in the prime of life. You might get hurt."

The old mountain man snorted and took up the reins. He flapped them and got the horses moving again.

"We'll just see about that," he said as he drove toward a large rock that sat to the left of the road ahead of them. When he circled the buggy behind the rock, he knew the pursuer galloping after them wouldn't be able to see the vehicle until he came even with it.

He stopped the buggy again and told Adelaide, "You stay right here. Don't budge out of this seat, and be ready to hunker down if you need to."

She clutched at his arm and said, "Preacher, what are you going to do?"

"I'm fixin' to see who's followin' us like a bat outta hell."

He pulled loose from her grip, stepped down from the buggy, and pushed his coat back so he could reach underneath it and pull out the Colt he had stuffed under his belt. He had been carrying the gun, being careful not to let Adelaide know about it, ever since they had set out from Denver, just in case the scoundrel George DuBois caught up with them. Preacher's caution might be about to pay off, as it always did, sooner or later.

"Preacher, wait!" Adelaide exclaimed at the sight of the gun. "If . . . if that *is* George following us, you can't kill him. No matter what he's done, he's still my grandson . . . and Pierre's."

Preacher scowled as his hand tightened on the Colt's grips. She was tying his hands with that plea, and he didn't like it. As far as he was concerned, George DuBois had forfeited any rights as family when he tried to have Adelaide killed. But if that was what she wanted, he would try to abide by it.

As long as she didn't expect him to stand by and do nothing while George hurt her. He wasn't capable of that.

He nodded his agreement and motioned for Adelaide to bend down lower on the buggy seat. The way the vehicle was parked, its frame and the back of the seat would provide some protection if any bullets came her way.

He stood there with his thumb looped around the .45's hammer as he held the gun beside his right ear, with the barrel pointed skyward. The hoofbeats thundered closer and closer. Preacher waited until he judged the rider had almost reached the rock; then he stepped out into the open and leveled the revolver.

"Hold it right there, mister!" he called in a loud, commanding voice.

The rider was no more than twenty feet away from where Preacher stood. He jerked back hard on the reins, and the horse didn't take kindly to it. The animal skidded to a halt, reared up, and pawed at the air. Unprepared for such a thing, the rider yelped in alarm and slid backward in the saddle. He grabbed for the saddle horn, but his fingers slid off it.

"Kick you feet outta the stirrups!" Preacher yelled at him. If the man fell with one or both feet hung up and the horse bolted, he would be dragged to death. Preacher still didn't know if this hombre was George DuBois, and Adelaide had begged that her grandson's life be spared.

The rider was saved from falling off when the horse dropped its forelegs back to the ground, but only for a second. Then the horse reared again, and this time the man went out of the saddle. He had gotten his feet loose from the stirrups in time, though. He fell and landed with a thud and a grunt on the hard-packed dirt of the road. The spooked horse danced skittishly around him, putting him in danger of being stepped on.

Preacher saw the man's gray hair and weathered, lined face and knew he couldn't possibly be Adelaide's grandson. He was too old for that. Still holding the gun, Preacher dashed forward and used his left hand to grab hold of the dangling reins. He hauled down on them and brought the horse under control while still keeping the fallen man covered. Just because he wasn't George didn't mean he wasn't a threat.

The man sat up, grimacing. His face was gaunt, haunted. He looked sick.

Preacher aimed the gun in his general direction and said, "Just stay right where you are, old son, until we get this sorted out."

"I . . . I don't think I could do anything else right now." He panted as he struggled to catch the breath the fall had knocked out of him.

"Who are you, and why were you chasin' us?"

"Ch-chasing you?" The man shook his

327

head stiffly, as if it hurt his neck to do so. "I wasn't chasing you. I was trying to get away from the man who's chasing *me*."

Preacher had considered the possibility that the rider didn't have anything to do with him or Adelaide. He knew if that turned out to be the case, he was going to feel plumb foolish. But he wasn't convinced of that yet.

"Is this fella who's after you some sort of holdup man?"

"A holdup man? You could certainly say that. But he doesn't intend to rob me. I don't have anything he wants — except my life."

"You mean he figures on killin' you?" asked Preacher.

"That's right." The man looked back up the trail toward Big Rock, then turned his attention to Preacher again. "You and your wife had better get out of here, my friend. If he finds you with me, he'll kill you, too, to cover his tracks."

Preacher snorted in contempt and said, "He might try. But he'd find it a heap bigger chore than he'd expect. And the lady ain't my wife. She's a friend who's goin' with me to visit another friend who has a ranch near here."

A startled expression appeared on the

man's face. He said, "A ranch? You don't mean Smoke Jensen's ranch, do you? The Sugarloaf?"

The man didn't look any more surprised than Preacher felt just now. The old mountain man said, "That's right. Do you know Smoke?"

"I've never met him, but we have some mutual friends. And it just so happens that's where *I* was headed. I . . . I hoped he would help me."

"You never told me your name."

The man glanced nervously back up the road again, then said, "It's Ennis Monday. But my friends call me —"

"Doc," Preacher finished for him.

Doc Monday stared at him for several seconds, then said, "Good Lord. You're him, aren't you? You're Preacher."

"Guilty as charged, I reckon."

"Ace and Chance have told me about meeting you. And, of course, I've heard of you. You're a legend everywhere west of the Mississippi."

"Those two youngsters have mentioned you, too. You're the fella who raised 'em after their ma died. But I thought you was in some hospital, in bad health."

Doc raised a trembling hand to show Preacher and said, "It was a sanitarium.

And my health isn't good. But it's going to be a lot worse if Bill Malkin catches up to me."

"He's the varmint who's after you?"

"That's right. And he can't be very far behind now."

Preacher's brain worked quickly as he reached a decision. He stuck the Colt back in the waistband of his trousers and extended his right hand to Doc Monday. The man hesitated, but only for a second. His tremor lessened as he tightly clasped Preacher's hand, and Preacher helped him to his feet.

"Climb in the back of the buggy there. It'll be kinda crowded there behind the seat, but I don't reckon you'll mind bein' a little uncomfortable."

Doc nodded and said, "Under the circumstances, I won't mind a bit."

Preacher kept a hand on Doc's arm, but the man made it to the buggy largely under his own power. Adelaide looked at him curiously.

"When I didn't hear any shooting, I knew it must not have been George following us," she said. "Who is this, Preacher?"

"His name's Doc Monday. We ain't been acquainted until now, but him and me both know a couple of fine young fellas who should be on their way to Smoke's ranch, too."

"I'm pleased to meet you, Dr. Monday," Adelaide said, still looking confused but polite, anyway.

"I'm not a doctor. That's just a nickname. But the pleasure is mine, madam," Doc said as he clambered awkwardly into the cramped space behind the seat.

"We got to get movin'," Preacher said briskly. "No time to explain any more. Did you rent that hoss from Dicky Patterson in Big Rock?"

"That's right," said Doc.

"It'll go on back to the stable, then." Preacher swung onto the seat and gathered up the reins. "Hang on, both of you."

He slapped the reins against the horses' backs and called out to them. The team lunged ahead and broke into a run. The buggy bounced a little, but the road was in pretty good shape, so the passengers weren't jolted around too much.

Adelaide held her hat on with her left hand, although, pinned in place as it was, there wasn't much danger of it flying off. She clung to the edge of the seat with her other hand and exclaimed, "My goodness!"

"Any sign of the fella who's chasin' you, Doc?" asked Preacher.

Doc leaned to the side to peer around the black canvas cover over the rear of the buggy. He said, "No, I don't . . . Wait! I do see him now. He's about three hundred yards back."

The horses were running flat out now. They couldn't maintain that pace for very long, Preacher knew. A lone man on horseback could move faster. Malkin would catch up to them sooner or later, if the chase lasted long enough.

But the trail that led to the Sugarloaf's headquarters was less than a mile away. Preacher was sure of that because of the landmarks they had passed. He never forgot things like that.

Not only were they fairly close to their destination, but there was always a chance, too, they would run across some of the cowboys who rode for the Jensen brand. If that happened, most of the members of Smoke's crew would recognize Preacher and come to his aid. Any owlhoot with murder on his mind was liable to regret it if he tackled that salty bunch.

"He's getting closer!" Doc called over the hoofbeats from the team.

"You know how to use a gun?" Preacher asked over his shoulder.

"Some. I'm no gunfighter!"

Preacher held on to the reins with one hand and used the other to pull the gun from his waistband. He turned on the seat enough to pass the Colt back to Doc.

"You don't have to be a gunfighter to slow a varmint down! If he gets close enough to be in handgun range, take a few potshots at him! That'll worry him."

"Maybe I'll get lucky and put a hole in him," Doc said.

"I ain't never opposed to good luck," Preacher said as he continued urging the team on. He could tell that the horses were already getting tired. Another few minutes and they would slow down, whether he wanted them to or not.

The inevitable occurred. The horses began to falter. The pursuit closed in from behind. Doc leaned out again, steadied the Colt with both hands, and fired twice. The loud booms made Adelaide gasp and cry out involuntarily.

"Get him?" Preacher called.

"No! He's still coming!"

Doc took aim and triggered another pair of shots as Preacher spotted the Sugarloaf trail up ahead. The horses were already slowing, so he didn't have to pull back much on the reins. But the turn was going to be a sharp one, so he shouted again, "Hang on!"

The buggy careened to the left as Preacher tugged on the reins and turned the horses to the north. For a second, he thought the vehicle might overturn, but then it righted itself, the wheels coming down with a thump on the trail.

"He's slowing down!" Doc yelled excitedly. "I don't think he wants to follow us onto the ranch!"

"He ain't completely loco, then," Preacher said. "But that means you ain't out of the woods, neither. If that fella wants you dead bad enough, he's liable to make another try."

"I won't be a bit surprised if he does," Doc said. But Preacher heard the man heave a sigh of relief. For now, Doc Monday was probably safe, and once they reached the ranch, Smoke was bound to have some ideas on how to make sure that state of affairs continued.

And Preacher wanted some answers, too. He recalled Ace and Chance telling him about how the man who'd raised them was a drifting gambler, and how they had drifted along with him for most of their lives.

Preacher wanted to know why some outlaw named Bill Malkin suddenly wanted Doc Monday dead.

CHAPTER 30
THE SUGARLOAF

Still angry over the ambush carried out on Pearlie and Cal the day before, Smoke had spent most of the day riding his range. Under the best of circumstances, he wasn't a man given to sitting still. When he had a burr under his saddle like this, he had to be up and moving around, searching for a way to put an end to the trouble.

Since the whole mess was in the hands of his lawyers right now, he couldn't do that, but he could check the higher pastures and make sure all the cattle had been brought down to more hospitable sections before winter set in with a vengeance.

Satisfied that everything had been taken care of properly — which was no surprise since Pearlie was a top-notch foreman — Smoke rode slowly back toward the ranch headquarters. The hours he'd spent in the saddle had eased his tension . . . but only a little.

He sat up straighter and frowned as he thought he heard the faint popping of gunfire in the distance. The shots, if that was what they were, sounded like they might be coming from the road that led west from Big Rock. There were only a few of the sounds, and then, as the echoes faded, silence reigned again. It probably didn't amount to anything, Smoke told himself.

But he nudged his horse into a faster gait, anyway, as he headed for the ranch house.

When he and Pearlie had gone back into town the day before to tell Monte Carson what had happened and confront Don Juan Sebastian Aguilar about the ambush, they had stopped at the store and picked up the last of the supplies Sally needed for her Christmas baking and decorating. Everybody was sticking close to home today . . . except for Smoke himself.

Pearlie and Cal had both suggested that they ride along with him, but Smoke had turned down those offers. He knew he wouldn't be very good company today, and he sure as hell didn't need any babysitters.

Here and there, slanting rays of wan, chilly sunlight darted through openings in the clouds. Smoke was still about two miles from headquarters when one of those pale rays touched the top of a rocky knob a couple of hundred yards farther along the faint trail he was following. Smoke saw the sunlight reflect from something up there.

Honed by years of keeping him alive, his reflexes and instincts took over instantly. Smoke bent forward in the saddle and hauled the horse hard to the right. The crack of a rifle shot and the flat whap of a bullet passing close by his head came to his ears at the same time. He saw powder smoke spurt from the rocks on the knob as he kicked the horse into a run.

He angled to the right, away from the knob, which sat to the left of the trail. More shots came from the rocks. At least two riflemen were hidden up there, thought Smoke. He had no doubt they were Aguilar's men. Obviously, the don's hired guns liked to bushwhack their intended victims.

Smoke didn't plan on being anybody's victim, though. The horse was running flat out and hadn't broken stride. Smoke saw bullets kicking up dust to his left. They were tracking closer, and he knew the would-be killers would have the range in a matter of seconds.

What he did next might strike some people as foolhardy, but he knew it was his best chance. He yanked the horse back to the left, seemingly riding directly into the storm of bullets searching for them. But Smoke's hunch was right, and the next volley sailed past him and struck to the right. He had caused the ambushers to overcorrect in their aim.

A clump of trees loomed ahead of him. He guided the horse into them and weaved back and forth among the trunks. The horse was sure-footed as well as strong and managed well at the quick, sharp turns. Smoke continued bending forward in the saddle so no low-hanging branches would sweep him off the horse's back. He heard bullets whipping through the branches and thudding into tree trunks, but the ambushers were firing blind now, and none of the shots came near him.

When he emerged from the trees, he was even with the knob where the bushwhackers were hidden. It stood about 150 yards to his left. He pulled the horse to a stop and jerked his Winchester from its saddle sheath.

"Steady now, boy," he said calmly to his mount.

All the horses Smoke rode on a regular basis were accustomed to the sound of gunfire. This one didn't shy as Smoke cranked five rounds from the rifle as fast as he could work the lever, spraying the bullets among the rocks where he had seen powder smoke earlier. He had no way of knowing if he hit any of the bushwhackers, but he figured he had them diving for cover once those slugs started bouncing around up there.

Without waiting to see what happened, he turned and rode quickly back into the trees. This time he swung down from the saddle and let the horse go, knowing that it wouldn't wander far with trailing reins. He leaned against one of the pines, felt the trunk's rough bark through his coat, and peered around it at the knob. He held the Winchester at his shoulder, ready to squeeze off another round if he caught even a glimpse of one of the bushwhackers.

When that glimpse came, it was accompanied by drumming hoofbeats. A rider emerged from behind the knob, galloping directly away from it. He was too far away for Smoke to recognize him or make out any details.

He drew a bead on the horseman and fired twice, but the horse kept going and didn't break stride. The man was crouched low in the saddle and didn't show any signs of being hit, either. Smoke was one of the best rifle shots on the frontier, in addition to being blindingly fast and deadly accurate with a Colt, but hitting a running target at that range, one moving away at an angle, was almost impossible. Smoke didn't waste another bullet as the rider dwindled from sight.

As he lowered the Winchester, he heard more hoofbeats. These came from a different direction and were even fainter. That would be the second bushwhacker, he thought. They had split up and fled, probably realizing that their ambush had failed once Smoke reached the shelter of the trees. They weren't going to be able to root him out of there, and although they could have sat up there and poured lead into the pines all day, any shot that found its target would be pure luck.

And all that racket would have drawn the attention of the Sugarloaf's crew, as well, probably sooner rather than later. The bushwhackers didn't want to deal with a bunch of angry, fast-shooting cowboys, so they had cut their losses and gotten out of there.

Smoke hadn't liked Don Juan Sebastian Aguilar to start with. The fact that the men working for the don preferred ambushing their targets just made him even less fond of Aguilar, if that was possible. Attempted bushwhackings two days in a row were just too damned much to stomach.

Filled with fury, he was about to swing back up into the saddle when he realized he could be falling for a trick. There could have been *three* would-be killers hidden on that knob. It was possible two of them had lit a shuck in order to try to draw him out so the third man could take potshots at him. Smoke mounted his horse, but instead of riding out into the open, he moved slowly and carefully back through the trees. He wanted to come out at a different spot from where they might be expecting him.

He had the Winchester ready as he nudged the horse out of the trees. Keen eyes scanned the top of the knob and then checked the area around it. Nothing moved anywhere. Smoke kept the horse moving and guided it with his knees. He didn't relax, even though no shots rang out and he didn't see anything to warn him of another bushwhack attempt.

Taking several minutes to do it, he circled the knob. He knew every foot of ground on the Sugarloaf and was aware that the knob's slope on the other side was gentler. Horses would have a hard time getting up it, but a man could climb it with no problem. For that reason, he figured the ambushers had left their mounts tied at the knob's base on that side.

Sure enough, Smoke had no trouble finding the large area of snow that the horses had disturbed while they were waiting for their riders. The numerous tracks were muddled enough that he couldn't be completely sure only two horses had been tied here, but he believed that to be the case. He also saw the marks in the snow on the back side of the knob where the bushwhackers had slid down in a hurry.

That wasn't all. Smoke saw bright red splashes here and there, standing out in sharp contrast to the white snow. That was blood, he knew, and it meant that at least one of the slugs he had flung up there among the rocks had found its target. It was impossible to say just how badly the man had been hurt, but judging by the amount of blood Smoke saw, the wound had to be more than just a scratch.

He dismounted, let the reins dangle again, and started up the slope, with the rifle held at a slant across his chest. The knob wasn't very tall. It took him about a minute to climb to the top. When he got there, he was able to look down among the boulders just below the crest on the trail side. More blood had splattered here. He saw brass cartridge casings littering the ground, too.

But no dead gun-wolf. Regardless of how bad the ambusher had been hit, he'd been able to get back down to the horses and ride off.

It would be interesting to find out if any of Aguilar's men were nursing a wound back in town, Smoke mused. But it probably wouldn't do any good to try. Aguilar and Hinton would just lie about it.

He searched the ground behind the rocks where the men had been hidden but didn't find anything that would help him identify them. The cartridge casings were like thousands of others. He saw the butts of a couple of quirlies, but again, there was nothing distinctive about them.

Knowing that he had reached a dead end here, Smoke went back down to his horse and resumed his ride toward the ranch headquarters.

He still had that little matter of the other gunshots he had heard to investigate.

When he was a half mile from the ranch house, he saw two riders coming toward him and recognized them as Pearlie and Cal. As they came up to Smoke and reined in, Pearlie said, "One of the boys came a-foggin' in and told us he'd heard shots from this direction. I knew you should've taken me and Cal with you, Smoke!"

"I'm here and not sporting any bullet holes, aren't I?" Smoke wanted to know.

"Well, yeah, but are you tryin' to claim you didn't get mixed up in some sort of fracas?"

Smoke chuckled and replied, "No, I wouldn't say that." He was actually in a better mood now, even though he was still angry at being bushwhacked. But the swift action had burned off some of the tension that had gripped him in such annoying fashion earlier in the day. "Aguilar's men made another bushwhack try, but I was their target this time."

"Dadgum it!" A few stronger oaths followed Pearlie's exclamation.

Cal asked, "Did you get any of them, Smoke?"

"Not this time. I wounded one of them, from the looks of the blood he left behind, but there were only two of them, and they both got away." Quickly, he sketched in the details of the attack for his friends, then went on, "There's no doubt in my mind that it was a couple of Aguilar's men throwing lead at me."

"How much longer?" asked Pearlie. "How much longer are we gonna wait before we ride into Big Rock and have a showdown with that varmint? I reckon it's the only thing he's ever gonna understand!"

"I feel the same way," Smoke said, nodding slowly, "but I've promised Sally that I'll try to handle things according to the law."

"When Tilden Franklin was makin' life miserable for folks around here, the only law worth a hill o' beans was what you and me and a bunch of other good hombres carried in our holsters!"

"I don't deny that, and Aguilar's pushed me as far as I'm going to be pushed." Smoke crossed his hands on the saddle horn and leaned forward, easing his muscles, if not his thoughts. "Christmas is only a few days away. I reckon that's slowed everything down, legal-wise. I don't want a war breaking out right when Sally has her heart set on a nice family celebration, but once Christmas is over, it'll be time to settle things with Don Sebastian."

"Can't come too soon to suit me," grumbled Pearlie.

"Although I *am* looking forward to all the good eating we'll be doing over the next few days," Cal added.

Pearlie just gave him a disgusted look.

Smoke said, "Just before those varmints started shooting at me, I thought I heard

some other guns going off, over toward the
road to Big Rock. Do you know anything
about that?"

"Oh, yeah," Pearlie said. "I got so mad
when I heard about that ambush, I plumb
forgot about the other business. You were
right, Smoke. There was some shootin'
earlier, but nobody got hurt. We'd best get
on back to the house, though, since visitors
have showed up."

"Visitors?" Smoke repeated. "What visitors?"

Pearlie turned his horse and said, "I
promised I wouldn't tell, although it ain't
gonna be that much of a surprise."

"Well, I didn't promise anything —" Cal
began, but he fell silent at the look Pearlie
gave him.

"You two will drive a man loco," Smoke
muttered as they rode toward the ranch
house. However, he was relieved to know
that no one had been injured in the shooting he had heard earlier.

They came in sight of the ranch headquarters a few minutes later. Smoke spotted a
buggy parked in front of the house. He
didn't recognize it, but since most buggies
looked alike, especially at a distance, that
wasn't surprising.

As they came closer, he thought maybe it

was one of the buggies Dicky Patterson rented out. That would indicate that whoever had driven it out here had arrived in Big Rock on the train.

Smoke and Sally were expecting guests for Christmas, but Preacher, Luke, Ace, and Chance would all show up on horseback, more than likely. There were no guarantees of that, however, Smoke reminded himself.

Then he decided to stop pondering the question, because in a few more minutes, he would know.

As the three of them rode up to the barn, Pearlie said, "You go on in the house, Smoke. Cal and me will tend to your horse."

"I can take care of my own horse."

"We know you can, but I told Miss Sally that if we ran into you, I'd tell you to head right on in, and I don't plan on breakin' a promise to Miss Sally."

"Well, in that case . . ."

Smoke handed over the reins and strode toward the house, the little bit of snow that was on the ground crunching under his boots.

A mixture of warmth and wonderful smells washed over him as he went inside and closed the front door behind him. Something that smelled delicious was baking in the oven, and blended with it were

347

the scents of pine from the decorated tree in the parlor and the spices that Sally had been using in her cooking for the past several days. Normally, Smoke would have paused to take a deep breath and appreciate all the fine aromas, but today he was eager to find out who the visitors were and what was going on here.

He hung his hat on a hook, then stepped into the opening between the foyer and the parlor and stopped short when he saw the older couple sitting on a sofa opposite Sally. Another older man sat in a chair near the fireplace, holding a cup in both hands but unable to keep it from trembling a little.

Smoke instantly recognized the man sitting on the sofa. He said, "Preacher!" and strode forward to greet his oldest friend in the world — other than his brother Luke, whom Smoke had believed to be dead for many years. Smoke and the old mountain man embraced, slapping each other on the back. Preacher seemed to be as hale and hearty as ever, despite his advanced age.

That certainly wasn't true of the other man, who was gray and gaunt, obviously either in poor health or under a lot of strain, or both.

"Preacher, it's good to see you again!" Smoke said. "I didn't expect you to show up in a buggy, though. I reckon that's because you have other company with you."

"That's right," Preacher said. He took advantage of that opening to continue, "Smoke, I want you to meet an old friend of mine . . . Mrs. Adelaide DuBois. You've heard me speak of ol' Polecat DuBois, from the fur-trappin' years. Adelaide's his widow."

"I'm pleased to meet you, Mrs. DuBois," Smoke said. Sally had stood up and come alongside him. He put his arm around her shoulders and went on, "Welcome to our home."

"Thank you, Mr. Jensen," Adelaide said. She had a cup, too, and Smoke could tell now that it had spiced apple cider in it. He could smell it. "I'm very glad to be here."

"And you've heard this fella's name before, too," Preacher continued as he turned toward the other man, who set his cup on a table with a slight rattle and then stood up to step forward and extend his hand. "He's Ennis Monday, better known as Doc."

"Doc Monday?" Smoke said as he clasped the man's thin, shaking hand. "Why, you're —"

"Ace and Chance's friend," Doc said.

"More than that. You raised those boys!"

Doc shrugged a little and said, "They

349

probably raised me just as much. I had to grow up some when I took responsibility for them."

"Well, you're mighty welcome here at the Sugarloaf. Ace and Chance may be showing up —"

Sally said, "I already told Mr. Monday that I wrote to them and asked them to come for Christmas."

"And they wrote and told me about the invitation," Doc said with a smile. "They were supposed to come and see me after they were here, but . . . I'm afraid I couldn't wait."

That didn't sound good, thought Smoke. He looked back and forth between Adelaide DuBois and Doc Monday and asked, "Just what is it that brings you folks to the Sugarloaf? Other than Preacher, that is, since I figure you must have come out with him in that buggy."

"That's right, Smoke," the old mountain man said, "and I reckon it ain't gonna surprise you one bit when you hear that both of these fine folks have trouble trailin' 'em!"

The intervals of sunshine during the day had been welcome, even though they hadn't brought much actual warmth with them. However, as the afternoon wore on, the overcast began to thicken again, and gray clouds completely covered the sky by late in the day. The wind from the mountains picked up, as well. Night would come early, and it would be a cold one. At least no fresh snow was falling . . . yet.

"Should we push on to the Sugarloaf or stop in Big Rock for the night?" Ace asked Chance as they rode past the railroad station and along the main street into the settlement's business district.

"It wouldn't take that much longer to make it to the ranch," said Chance, "but Smoke and Sally aren't expecting us at any particular time. Sally's letter just said for us to try to make it by Christmas, if we could."

"So you're saying there's no hurry."

351

"I'm saying I'm pretty cold already, and it'll just get colder on the way out there. Whereas —"

"Whereas?" Ace interrupted. "You've been giving this some thought, haven't you?"

"Whereas," continued Chance, as if his brother hadn't broken in on what he was saying, "I'll bet it's nice and warm in Longmont's, and Louis *does* have the best whiskey and some of the best food to be found in Big Rock."

"And card games and pretty girls working for him."

"You brought those things up, not me," Chance said, but he had to follow it with a laugh. "You do know me well, brother."

"I ought to. I've been around you long enough." Ace turned his horse toward the boardwalk. "All right, we'll stop at Longmont's for a spell and then get a room at the hotel. I don't want to leave the horses out in this weather, though. Let's go ahead and put them up at the livery stable."

"Sounds like a good idea to me," Chance agreed.

They followed the street, close to the boardwalk on the north side now because the buildings helped block the wind a little as they aimed for the barnlike structure up ahead. Because of the early dusk, lights already glowed in the windows of Goldstein's Mercantile when they drew even with it.

"Hold on a minute," Chance said as he reined in abruptly in front of the store.

Ace brought his mount to a stop, as well, and saw that his brother was peering intently through Goldstein's big front window. Ace asked, "Something you want in there?"

"You could say that," Chance replied.

Ace moved his horse over next to Chance's and joined him in looking through the glass. He saw immediately what had fascinated Chance — or rather, *who* had fascinated him.

A young woman stood talking to Goldstein, who was behind one of the side counters. She wore a long dark skirt and a lightweight dark jacket. Her black hair was piled on top of her head in an elaborate arrangement. The colorful shawl she had worn outside as protection from the cold was draped around her shoulders while she was inside.

From out here, they could see only her profile, but that was enough. It took only one glance for Ace to know that she was beautiful. If he was aware of that, then Chance certainly was, since he had even more of an eye for a pretty girl than Ace did. Ace wasn't surprised that his brother had spotted her through the store window, even on a cold, blustery late afternoon like this.

"I don't remember her from when we were in Big Rock before," Chance said without taking his eyes off the young woman.

"We haven't been here all that often," Ace pointed out, "and we didn't meet everybody who lives here."

"No, but I'd remember her if we had met her." Chance sighed. "I think I'll remember her for the rest of my life."

Ace didn't remind him that he said much the same thing about every good-looking woman he met and then promptly forgot about when the restless urges overcame them and it was time to drift on to whatever adventure was in store for them next. Chance was sincere in his infatuations; they just didn't last for very long.

Inside the store, the young woman turned away from the counter where Goldstein stood and started toward the door. Chance quickly began to dismount.

"Wait a minute," said Ace. "I thought we were going to put the horses up at Patterson's place."

"They'll be all right for a little while. I

want to say hello."

It would take less time and trouble not to argue with him, Ace knew. He tugged down his hat, turned up the collar of his sheepskin coat, and said, "All right, but don't linger. The lady's not really dressed for the cold. She won't want to stand around outside, and I don't, either."

"I'll just say hello," Chance said again.

He tied his horse at the hitchrack, which was empty since Goldstein didn't appear to have any other customers at the moment. More than likely, the merchant would start getting ready to close up as soon as the attractive young woman was out the door.

Chance reached the door and opened it just as the woman approached it on the other side. He held the door with one hand while he swept the hat off his head with the other.

"Come right ahead, miss," he greeted her, not actually bowing but coming close. "Or should I say . . . señorita?"

Ace had nudged his horse over next to Chance's but was still in the saddle. As his brother asked that question, he took a better look at the young woman in the light that spilled out from the store, and saw that she did indeed appear to come from south of the border.

She smiled at Chance and said in slightly accented but excellent English, "You may address me as señora, señor."

Ace managed not to chuckle when he saw the eager hopes drop from Chance's face. Chance said, "You're married?"

"*Sí.* But I still very much appreciate you holding the door for me, señor . . . ?"

Chance realized she was asking for his name and said quickly, "They call me Chance." As an afterthought, he jerked his head toward his still-mounted twin and said, "That's my brother, Ace."

"Doña Mariana Aguilar," the young woman replied, introducing herself. She moved aside a little, and a thickset older woman dressed in black followed her out of the store. This woman had several large, awkward-looking packages in her arms.

"Are those yours?" asked Chance as he nodded toward the packages, which were wrapped in brown paper and tied with twine.

"They are. This is my servant Estellita."

Ace noticed that Señora Aguilar had made no effort to carry any of the paper-wrapped packages herself. The air of aristocracy about her made it clear that she was accustomed to having others do such things for her.

Ace wondered what in the Sam Hill a lady like her was doing in Big Rock.

Chance said, "There's no need for your servant to struggle like that. My brother and I can carry those packages for you. Come on, Ace. Lend a hand here."

With Chance volunteering their services like that, there really wasn't any way Ace could refuse gracefully. And his natural inclination was to lend folks a hand whenever he could, so he didn't actually mind. He dismounted and tied his horse next to Chance's, then stepped up onto the boardwalk.

Chance took two of the packages. Ace lifted the other two out of Estellita's arms. He said, "I reckon you're staying at the hotel, Señora Aguilar?"

"That's right," she said. "How did you know that?"

"Well, I didn't figure you and your husband were permanent residents, otherwise you'd be better prepared for the cold here in Colorado at this time of year. That jacket you're wearing is mighty pretty, but it won't do a very good job of keeping out the chill."

Mariana smiled, draped the shawl over her head, and tightened it around her shoulders.

"You are right about that, Señor Ace," she said as she turned toward the Big Rock

Hotel. "We left Mexico rather quickly. The winters there can be quite cool, but not like this. Still, you are incorrect about one thing. My husband and I intend to be permanent residents of this valley. At the moment we are waiting only for some legal questions to be settled regarding the ranch he owns."

"Is that so?" Chance said. "I'm mighty glad to hear that you're going to be staying around here. Big Rock can always use such a charming citizen as yourself."

"Which ranch?" asked Ace. "We're not really from around here, but we know some of the folks who live in the valley."

Before Mariana could answer that question, several men emerged from the hotel, which was just a few doors ahead of them, and started along the boardwalk toward them.

"There you are, Señora Aguilar," the man in the lead said. "It's getting late enough that Don Sebastian was getting a mite worried about you."

"There was no need for him to worry, Señor Hinton," Mariana replied coolly. "It merely took me a bit longer than I expected to decide on everything I wanted at the store."

The two groups had stopped now and faced each other across twenty feet of boardwalk. As Ace looked at the men, it suddenly bothered him that his arms were full of packages. If he needed to reach for a gun in a hurry, that was going to slow him down.

Of course, he had no reason to think he was going to need to slap leather, but the man called Hinton and his four companions put Ace's nerves on edge. All of them had that indefinable air of gun-wolves about them. Ace had seen enough just like them to recognize the breed.

And the name Hinton was familiar, although Ace couldn't place it right away. He knew he had heard *something* about somebody named Hinton, though, and it hadn't been anything good.

Ace glanced over at his brother and saw that Chance was tense, too. Chance's instincts were also warning him to be careful, thought Ace.

Hinton seemed to be feeling the same edgy reaction to this encounter. He nodded toward Ace and Chance and asked, "Who are these two hombres?"

"These young gentlemen very kindly volunteered to assist Estellita in carrying my purchases," Mariana said. "This is Señor Ace and Señor Chance."

One of the other gunmen let out a sneer-

359

ing laugh and said, "What kind of names are those?"

"We like them," Chance said. "You boys need to step aside now so Señora Aguilar can go on in the hotel and get out of this cold weather."

The sneering gunman stiffened and demanded, "Who are you callin' *boys*, kid?"

"Forget it, Cort," snapped Hinton. "The don's anxious to see his wife, so get out of the way like . . . Chance, was it? Like Chance said."

All four men glared as they moved aside on the boardwalk. Ace still didn't like the fact that he and Chance had their hands full, but they couldn't do anything other than carry the packages on to the hotel. He watched the men warily as he and Chance moved past, following Mariana.

When they had gone by, Hinton and the others were *behind* them, and Ace didn't like that, either.

Nothing happened, though. The servant, Estellita, went ahead and opened the hotel's double doors. Mariana swept through them as if she owned the place. Ace and Chance followed.

A stolid-looking, thickset Mexican man was sitting in one of the chairs in the lobby. He got up hurriedly and moved to meet them. Without being told to do so, he took the packages from Chance, while Estellita reclaimed the ones Ace was carrying.

"My servants will take the packages on up to our suite," Mariana said to the brothers. "*Muchas gracias* for your help. I wish everyone in Big Rock was as friendly and helpful as the two of you."

"Give them a chance," Ace said. "There are plenty of good folks around here."

Chance and Ace had replaced the hats on their heads when they took the packages to carry. Now Chance took his off, did that almost bow again, and said, "Just so you'll feel more at home here, Doña Mariana . . ."

Before she could stop him, he took hold of her hand, bent lower, and pressed his lips to the back of it. A delighted smile appeared on her face, but she said, "Señor Chance, you must not! You are too bold."

"Beauty inspires boldness," he told her. "It always has, all the way back to Helen of Troy."

"Seems to me some fellas fought a war over her," muttered Ace.

Chance either didn't hear him or pretended not to. Instead, he said to Mariana, "I hope we'll see you again. There's usually a Christmas Eve church service for the whole town. Maybe we'll all be there."

"If fate wishes it so," she said. He was still holding her hand. She slipped her fingers from his, gave him another smile, and turned toward the staircase at the side of the lobby. The male servant had already disappeared up the stairs, but the woman, Estellita, still stood there, expressionless, as she waited for her mistress.

Ace and Chance watched Mariana climb the stairs to the second floor. She cast a couple of coquettish glances over her shoulder at them as she ascended.

Once she had crossed the landing and was out of sight, Ace said quietly to his brother, "That's a married woman, you know. I shouldn't have to remind you of that."

"I behaved myself."

"You kissed her hand!"

"I was just being polite," Chance insisted.

"Well, gallant, if you want to be precise."

Ace rolled his eyes, shook his head, and said, "Come on. Let's get the horses put up. I'm sure they're ready for a warm stall and some oats."

Chance didn't argue. Now that Doña Mariana Aguilar had gone up to her and her husband's suite, there was no reason for the brothers to linger at the hotel. They went out, untied their horses from the hitch rail, and led them toward the livery stable.

Fifteen minutes later, after arranging for Patterson to take care of their mounts and exchanging some friendly conversation with the stableman, Ace and Chance left the stable. Patterson had told them about Preacher arriving in Big Rock earlier in the day and renting a buggy for himself and his female companion.

"Who do you think that woman was with Preacher?" Ace asked as they turned toward Louis Longmont's restaurant and saloon. "You don't think he's going to get married and settle down, do you?"

"At his age?" Chance sounded like that was the most ridiculous idea he'd ever heard. "I guess we'll find out when we ride out to the Sugarloaf tomorrow . . . unless the lady was bound for somewhere else and Preacher was just making sure she got there all right before he goes to Smoke's himself."

"I suppose that could be it, all right," Ace said.

Chance rubbed his hands together in anticipation and went on, "I'm not going to worry about it. I want a drink and then a nice thick steak, and then I'm going to see if Louis has a card game going tonight —"

His brisk stride and his words both stopped short. Ace halted just as abruptly beside him. The overcast dusk was so thick, it was almost full night, but the shadows that had gathered didn't completely conceal the three men who stepped out from an alley mouth ahead of them to block their path.

"Uh-oh," Chance said. "Looks like trouble."

Ace heard a stealthy footstep behind them and glanced back to see more men closing in on them from that direction. Trouble was right, he thought.

The luck of the Jensen boys was holding — all bad.

CHAPTER 32

One of the three men blocking the board-walk in front of Ace and Chance hooked his thumbs in his gunbelt, which was visible because his coat was pushed back on both sides. He drawled, "You young fellas are out kind of late. Isn't it past your bedtime?"

The shadows prevented Ace from being able to make out the man's face that clearly, but his voice was familiar. It belonged to the hombre called Hinton, whom they had encountered earlier.

Chance said, "You're mistaken, mister. Our evening's just getting started."

"No, *you're* wrong," Hinton replied with a shake of his head. "It's over."

With that, he stepped back, and the other four men rushed Ace and Chance, two in front, two from behind.

The brothers didn't have to talk about what they were going to do. Each seemed to know what the other's actions would be.

365

Ace whirled to meet the attack from behind, while Chance stepped forward to engage the two hard cases in front.

One man coming at Ace had gotten a little ahead of the other. He swung a looping punch at Ace's head, but the blow, although undoubtedly packing plenty of power behind it, wasn't very fast. Ace ducked under it easily and hooked a hard right to the man's ribs that jolted him to the side.

That involuntary step took him into the path of his companion, who bumped heavily into him. Their feet tangled, and the man Ace had punched fell to the boardwalk.

While the second man was off balance, Ace stepped in and whipped a left jab to his nose. The man's head rocked back. Ace followed with a right to the jaw that spun the man around and bent him over the railing along the boardwalk's edge.

The first man may have been down, but he wasn't out of the fight. He pushed himself to hands and knees, threw himself forward, and tackled Ace around the knees. Ace went over backward as the man jerked his legs out from under him.

Ace landed hard but managed to keep his head from banging against the planks. If it had, he would have been stunned, and that probably would have been the end of the battle for him.

Instead, he was ready when his opponent tried to scramble on top of him and pin him down. He lifted a knee hard into the man's midsection that made him gasp and gag. Ace clubbed his hands together and smashed them against the side of the man's head, driving him toward the edge of the boardwalk. He rolled under the railing and dropped into the snowy street.

The second man had pushed himself up from the rail and came at Ace again, stomping and kicking this time. Ace rolled away from a swiftly descending bootheel that might have broken his head open if it had landed. Before he could get up, a kick caught him on the left shoulder and sent pain shooting through him for a second before that arm and shoulder went numb. Without it to support him, he sprawled awkwardly on his back.

The man tried again to stomp on his face in. Ace got his right hand up in time to block the boot. He heaved up on it, and although that effort didn't topple the man, it made him stagger backward wildly for a couple of seconds.

That respite was long enough for Ace to get his knees under him and then scramble to his feet. He ducked his head as the man charged in. Ace took a couple of blows on his hunched shoulders, then rammed his right shoulder into the man's chest and drove him backward against the rail. This time it cracked under the impact and broke apart, dumping both of them into the street.

The thin layer of snow scattered around them as they landed. Ace was on top, and both his knees drove deep into the man's stomach. The feeling was seeping back into his left arm, but it still wasn't working correctly. There was nothing wrong with his right, though, so he slugged away with that fist, smashing three hard, fast punches into the man's face, which left him senseless.

Meanwhile, a few yards farther along the boardwalk, Chance had met the attack of the other two men with equal speed and skill. Chance dressed well and had the look of a dandy, but he could handle himself just fine in a fight.

Unfortunately for him, his opponents had better timing than the men Ace was battling. They came at Chance together and threw their punches at the same time, and he couldn't avoid both fists. He blocked one punch, but the other caught him on the chin and made him reel back a step.

One man caught hold of Chance's left arm and swung him hard against the building. Chance's hat flew off his head. He caught a glimpse of a fist shooting toward his face and jerked his head to the side. The fist scraped his ear as it went by, but the force of the blow went into the wall. The man who had thrown the punch yelled from the pain that exploded through his knuckles as they struck the wood.

Chance lifted a left uppercut that levered the man's head back. His opponents had actually done him a favor by slamming him against the wall. They were both in front of him and couldn't get behind him or even flank him. It was almost like fighting back-to-back with his brother, which he had done many times in their adventurous lives.

For a long moment, a flurry of punches flew back and forth there on the boardwalk as the two men bored in on Chance. He blocked as many of the blows as he could, but inevitably, some of them landed. He tasted blood in his mouth.

But Chance's pugilistic skills allowed him to deal out as much punishment as he was enduring, which was amazing considering the two against one odds. The same keenly honed reflexes and coordination that allowed him to deal cards with such speed and deftness sent his fists snapping out to land with stinging power on his opponents.

369

His hands already ached, and he knew he might not be much good for card playing for a few days, while they recovered, but caught up in the heat of battle as he was, he didn't care.

A solid right slewed one hard case's head to the side. His knees buckled. As he went down, Chance hit him with a left that stretched him on the boardwalk.

While Chance was throwing that punch, his remaining opponent took advantage of the opening and crowded in. He grabbed Chance by the throat with both hands and rammed him back against the wall again. The man's thumbs pressed hard against Chance's windpipe. Chance hammered punches at him, but at such close range, he wasn't able to get much strength behind them.

Red rockets exploded behind Chance's eyes and left glittering trails of sparks behind them. He caught hold of the man's wrists and tried to dislodge the death grip, but he didn't have enough strength to do it. Chance knew he was on the brink of passing out, and if that happened, there was a very good chance he would never wake up again. . . .

A resounding thud sounded, followed by instant relief as the choking hands fell away from Chance's neck. His vision wasn't good, because the world had started swimming around him as he was deprived of breath, but it cleared quickly, and he saw his brother standing there over the man, who had just collapsed in a senseless heap at Chance's feet. Ace's Colt was in his hand, reversed so that he had been able to use the butt to knock out the man who'd been about to choke the life out of Chance.

"You all right?" Ace asked.

"Y-yeah," Chance rasped. It hurt his throat to talk. "You?"

"Just banged up a mite." Ace looked around. "What happened to the other fella?"

It had occurred to him that when this fracas started, there had been five men on the boardwalk around them, not four. The fifth man had stepped back and let the others do the fighting.

Now Ace tensed as he caught sight of a figure looming up from the shadows, with a gun thrust out in front of him.

"I know what you're thinking, son," the man said. "You're going to try to turn that gun around and use it. I can tell you right now, you won't make it."

"Let's both holster our irons and see what happens then," Ace snapped.

The man chuckled and said, "Why would

I do that? I've got the drop on both of you, and I'd be a fool to give it up."

"Maybe so," Chance said, forcing the words out through his sore throat, "but you can't kill us both at the same time, and the one still standing is going to kill *you.*"

"Actually, that would be a pretty good challenge," said Hinton, "but it's not necessary. I think you boys have learned your lesson. Steer clear of Doña Mariana."

"That's what this is about?" Ace asked in amazement. "You jumped us because we were polite to a lady?"

"Well . . . that's not all of it. But it's part of my job to look out for that lady, and you — especially *you,* Fancy Dan — were being too forward with her. You were pretty damned disrespectful to me and my friends, too. You showed us up in front of her, and I don't like that."

"Isn't it her husband's job to look out for her?" Ace said.

Hinton's shoulders rose and fell as he replied, "Don Sebastian's got me and my associates to handle chores like that . . . and others, besides."

Ace had a strong hunch those other chores involved gun work. He didn't know exactly what had brought the Aguilars to Big Rock. Doña Mariana had said that she and her husband were moving here, or at least onto a ranch in the vicinity. Ace didn't think the situation was quite that simple, though.

Right now, it didn't matter. He said, "You can't just gun us down. That would be cold-blooded murder. The sheriff here wouldn't stand for it."

"Monte Carson doesn't worry me, but nobody's paying me to kill you . . . yet. I'll be fine with it if you'll just avoid the lady in the future. Now, pouch that iron you're holding, kid. Be mighty careful, though, when you're turning it around to holster it."

Slowly, Ace slipped the Colt back into leather. By now, the men he and Chance had battled with were starting to regain their senses, moaning and moving around a little where they lay on the boardwalk and in the street. Ace thought bleakly that he and Chance might have to fight this battle all over again — and it likely wouldn't turn out the same way the next time.

Instead, Hinton said, "Go on, get out of here before they wake up good."

"This isn't over," Chance blustered.

"This part of it is," Hinton said calmly. "And if there *is* a next time . . . maybe I'll just kill the both of you and be done with it."

CHAPTER 33
THE SUGARLOAF

Smoke was eager to hear about the trouble that had brought Preacher's companions here to the ranch, but since it was already late in the afternoon and was growing dark outside, Sally said there would be time for that after supper.

"I'm sure Mrs. DuBois and Mr. Monday are tired after traveling," she said. "They can rest for a bit, and then we'll eat."

"That sounds wonderful, Mrs. Jensen, but you might as well call me Doc," the man said. "Not many people call a tinhorn gambler like me 'mister.' "

"You're more than a tinhorn gambler, Doc," Smoke said. "You took on the job of raising those two boys when you didn't have to, and that tells me a lot about you."

"They're special youngsters," Doc said with a smile. Something about the expression struck Smoke as being slightly mysterious, as if Doc knew more than he was saying.

"That they are," agreed Smoke. "We've run into them enough times, and they've helped us out often enough, that we've come to think of them as honorary members of the family."

Doc nodded and said, "I can understand that. I'm no blood relation to them, but I feel about them almost like they were my own sons."

Adelaide DuBois spoke up, saying, "I can't thank the two of you enough for your hospitality. I don't know what I'd do without people like you and friends like Arthur here." She smiled. "I mean, like Preacher."

"We know his real name," Sally said, returning the smile, "but it *did* take some prying to get it out of him."

"Yeah, like pulling a tooth," added Smoke.

The old mountain man said, "It's just that I been called Preacher so long, I don't hardly know how to answer to my borned name. All my family and most of the folks who ever knowed me by that moniker are long gone now."

Adelaide squeezed his arm and said, "You're the last of your line? I didn't know that."

"Well . . . I am and I ain't." Preacher

grinned at Smoke. "I reckon I'm one of those — what'd you call 'em? — honorary Jensens."

"No doubt about it," Smoke agreed.

Sally said, "Why don't the two of you come with me? I'll take you up to the rooms you'll be using, so you can rest a bit, and then I need to get back to my kitchen."

"If there's anything I can do to help, dear . . . ," Adelaide began.

"Not at all. You're a guest. Although with a lot of company in the house, I'll probably need a hand now and then before Christmas is over!"

She ushered the two visitors out of the parlor, leaving Smoke and Preacher there. They listened to the footsteps going up the stairs; then Smoke said quietly, "How bad is the trouble?"

"Bad enough I figured it'd be a good idea to get Adelaide here, where she'd be safe. But I ought to let her explain it. The whole thing's a mite personal."

"What about Doc Monday?"

Preacher shook his head and said, "Now that, I don't reckon I can tell you, because I plumb don't know much. We run into Doc on the way out here from town. He was ridin' one of those saddle horses Dicky Patterson rents out, and a fella name of Bill

Malkin was chasin' him. From the sound of what Doc said, this Malkin is an owlhoot of some sort and wants him dead, but I don't know the details. I gave Doc my hogleg to hold him off whilst we was outrunnin' him to the ranch."

"I heard those shots, I think."

"Wouldn't be surprised," Preacher said. "Malkin give up the chase when we reached the turnoff from the main road, but Doc seems convinced he'll be back. He's hopin' that by comin' here, he can find those Jensen boys, Ace and Chance, and they'll give him a hand dealin' with Malkin."

"Ace and Chance may well be here," Smoke said, nodding, "but if Doc needs help, I'll be glad to pitch in."

"I figured as much. That's why I told him to pile on into the buggy and I'd bring him here."

Smoke clapped a hand on his old friend's shoulder and said, "You did the right thing. Sally and I will always lend a hand to someone who needs it. And I know that you feel the same way, which is good, because we've got some pretty bad trouble of our own brewing."

Preacher's eyes narrowed. He said, "I had a feelin' that somethin' was goin' on here at the Sugarloaf, and it wasn't nothin' good.

But Sally was a-fussin' over Adelaide and ol' Doc, so I didn't push her for answers. But you can tell me all about it, Smoke." A gleam appeared in the old mountain man's eyes. "Just who is it we're gonna need to shoot?"

Dinner was a big pot of savory beef stew, along with beans and corn bread, greens, and apple pie. Sally had invited Pearlie and Cal to join the rest of them for dinner, so the big table in the dining room, while not full, had enough people around it to create a festive mood.

At least under normal circumstances it would have. Tonight, with the weariness and strain that were visible on the faces of both Adelaide DuBois and Doc Monday, the atmosphere was more subdued. Pearlie and Cal tried to lighten the mood with some of their usual banter, but when the japes fell flat, they abandoned the effort and concentrated on eating.

"This is all mighty good, Miss Sally, just like always," Pearlie said.

"Can't wait to try that apple pie," added Cal.

After the meal was finished — and Cal had declared the apple pie to be as delicious as ever — Sally stood up and said,

"Mrs. DuBois . . . Adelaide . . . if you wouldn't mind giving me a hand in the kitchen . . . ?"

"Of course, dear," the older woman responded as she got to her feet, as well. "After you've welcomed me into your home like this, especially at this time of year, it's the least I can do."

The five men had gotten up when Sally did. She waved them back into their chairs and told them, "Go ahead and enjoy your coffee."

Earlier, during a brief conversation between Smoke, Sally, and Preacher, they had agreed that Adelaide would tell her story to Sally, all of them thinking that she might be more comfortable giving the painful details of her problem to another woman. While that was going on, and while Smoke and the others lingered over cups of coffee, they would get Doc Monday's story.

Smoke turned his chair so he could extend his legs in front of him and cross them at the ankles. He looked along the table to where the gambler was sitting, and said bluntly, "I understand you've got trouble on your trail, Doc. Tell us about it, and we'll figure out what to do."

"I don't want to impose that much on you . . . ," Doc began.

"It's not imposing," Smoke said. "You're a friend — more than a friend — to Ace and Chance, which means the rest of us are your friends, too. Blood relations or not, Jensens stick together."

"About that —" Doc stopped short and shook his head. "Never mind. If you're sure you want to know, I can tell you about Bill Malkin . . . and why he wants me dead."

"Go ahead," said Preacher.

For the next few minutes, Doc explained about his stay in the MacMurphy Sanitarium and how the surly patient Bill Williams had turned out to be notorious train robber and outlaw Bill Malkin.

"He came close to killing me the same day I found out," Doc went on. "It was a narrow escape indeed. I knew I couldn't risk letting him catch me again."

"You didn't tell anyone at the sanitarium about this?" Smoke asked with a frown.

"What proof did I have? By the time anyone could check, Malkin would have disposed of everything that could identify him or even cast any doubt on his true identity. And then I would have been left in there with him, while he waited like a hungry tiger for an opportunity to pounce." Doc shook his head. "Maybe I panicked a little, but it just seemed to me like the only

380

safe thing to do was run." His mouth twisted. "And as we've seen, even that wasn't safe, because Malkin left the sanitarium, too, and came after me."

Preacher said, "It ain't likely he'll be able to get to you here on the Sugarloaf. With me and Smoke around, not to mention Pearlie and Cal and the rest of the crew, he'd be bitin' off a hunk that's a heap too big for him to chew."

"And that's before Ace and Chance even get here," Smoke added. "You're safe, Doc."

"But for how long?" Doc shook his head. "I appreciate your hospitality, Smoke, but we both know I can't stay here on the Sugarloaf from now on."

Smoke shrugged and said, "You can if that's what you want to do."

"What I want is not to have to spend the rest of my life looking over my shoulder."

Preacher said, "That varmint Malkin's gonna kick the bucket sooner or later. You said that he was hidin' out at the sanitarium, but that his health was actually poor, too."

"That's the way it seemed to me. But say he dies in a few years. How would I ever know? How could I be sure?"

"There's one way," Smoke said. "Deal with him now. Capture him and turn him over to the law."

"You're talking about —"

Smoke nodded, having reached a decision.

"That's right. We're going to set a trap for him."

Adelaide DuBois sat at the kitchen table, using a cloth Sally had given her to dab at the tear streaks on her weathered cheeks.

"You don't know how much it means to me to be able to talk to you about this, Sally," she said. "I've kept it all inside for so long, just living with the worry and the outright fear. I know I told Arthur about it, but it's different somehow, sitting and pouring out my heart to another woman."

Sally reached across the table and rested her hand on Adelaide's.

"I know," she said. "Although Preacher is one of the finest men I've ever met, and he definitely does seem to have a soft spot for you."

Adelaide smiled wanly and said, "It's just because we're such old friends. Of course, he and I were never really that close, but he and my Pierre . . . the one he calls Polecat . . . were partners on several fur-trapping expeditions, and after Pierre gave that up, Preacher came to see us several times in St. Louis. Really, I suppose he's the only one I know who even still remembers those days.

So many years have gone by. So much has changed . . ."

"Life has a habit of doing that," Sally said in a gentle voice.

"Of course it does." Adelaide's voice took on a plaintive tone as she added, "But couldn't it slow down just a little bit every once in a while?"

Both of them laughed at that, and then Adelaide grew serious again and went on, "I just don't know what to do about George."

"Why not let Preacher and Smoke worry about that?" Sally suggested. "You're safe here, and you can stay as long as you like."

"I wouldn't want to be a burden . . ."

"It's no burden at all," Sally assured her. "In fact, it'll be good having another woman around the place for a while." She laughed again. "Goodness knows, neither of Smoke's brothers has shown any signs of getting married and settling down. I don't have any prospects for sisters-in-law. And as for Preacher . . . !"

"You don't believe Preacher will ever get married?" asked Adelaide.

"Well, I don't suppose it can be ruled out, but at his age, I don't think it's very likely."

"It's just difficult to remember that he's as old as he is. He still seems to have such vitality. Why, anyone who didn't know him would think he was a young man of sixty!"

Sally nodded and said, "That's true. He's changed hardly at all in the time I've known him. Even so, I'm not sure he would make a very good husband. If anyone was ever set in his ways, as the old saying goes, it's Preacher."

"Perhaps, but he might discover that he likes being married." Adelaide heaved a sigh. "I suppose we'll never know."

Sally tried not to frown. It almost sounded like Adelaide had set her cap for Preacher. She wondered if she ought to warn the old mountain man. She was fairly confident that he didn't have similar feelings for Adelaide. He had offered to help her purely out of friendship for her and her late husband.

At least, that was what Sally had believed at first. But she didn't know what was in Preacher's heart, she reminded herself. He had always been capable of surprising those around him. Maybe she was wrong about how he felt. Maybe something real was growing up between him and Adelaide, and their advancing years didn't make it any less genuine.

She reminded herself of something else: It was none of her business. She had offered her help, and Smoke's, to Adelaide in dealing with the problem of the grandson who seemed to want her dead. Anything beyond that was meddling.

"The men have probably had time to hash out whatever it is they wanted to talk about," Sally said. "Why don't we go on back out and see what they're doing?"

"I do hope that poor man, Mr. Monday, is able to find a solution to his problems. He seemed quite upset and frightened when we met him."

"One thing you can count on," Sally told her. "Smoke will find a way to deal with all the trouble. He's been doing it for a long time now."

Even though this Christmas, trouble seemed to be coming at them from several different directions at once . . .

CHAPTER 34
BIG ROCK

Thick gray clouds promised more snow the next morning, but so far it had held off. The air was cold but nothing was falling from the sky as Ace and Chance left the hotel and headed for the livery stable where their mounts had spent the night. They were carrying their rifles and saddlebags, which they had kept in the hotel room with them during the night. "I was sure hoping we might see Doña Mariana in the dining room this morning," Chance commented.

"Folks like that probably have their breakfast sent up to their suite. It takes 'em a while to get going in the morning, more than likely."

"I know the feeling. I've never cared for getting up early, either."

Ace laughed and told his brother, "That's because we grew up living with a gambler who spent all those late nights in saloons, playing cards."

386

"So you see, I come by it honestly."

"I guess you could say that," Ace allowed. "You pick up things from the folks who raise you, whether you're actually related to them or not. Like that bluff you ran during the game at Longmont's last night. You learned how to do that from watching Doc."

"It worked, didn't it?" Chance asked with a grin. "I won enough money for us to get a room at the hotel without having to worry about how to pay for it. That was nice, for a change."

"Yeah, it was."

Chance shook his head and said again, "I sure hoped we'd run into Doña Mariana, though."

"Aren't you already stiff and sore enough from that trouble last night? And you know good and well she's married and isn't ever going to give you a second look. The most she'd ever do with you is flirt a little."

"Well," said Chance, "that's enjoyable, too, isn't it?"

Ace didn't bother responding. There was no point in arguing with his brother when it came to pretty girls.

As they walked along the street, Ace kept his eyes open for the hard case called Hinton or any of the other men they had clashed with the previous night. They must have been sleeping late, too, because Ace didn't see any sign of them.

That was just fine with him, not because he was afraid of more trouble but because he didn't see any point in looking for a fight when one would come to them sooner or later, anyway. In their relatively short but eventful lives, ruckuses had seemed to have an inevitable way of seeking out the Jensen brothers.

They reclaimed their horses from the stable, and as they were saddling up, Patterson asked them, "Are you boys headed on out to Smoke's this morning?"

"That's right," Ace said.

"We just wanted to have a night in town first," Chance added.

Something seemed to be bothering the stocky, red-bearded liveryman. He said, "Could I ask you fellas to keep your eyes open while you're riding out to the Sugarloaf?"

"Sure," said Ace, "but keep them open for what?"

"More like who. I told you about renting a buggy to Preacher and his lady friend yesterday."

Chance said, "Yeah, and the idea of Preacher taking up with a woman at his age is still pretty puzzling."

388

"As long as a man can remember what it was like being young, he's not going to forget about women," the liveryman said. "But that's not what I'm talking about. After Preacher left with the lady and the buggy, I rented a horse to another fella who said something about riding out to the Sugarloaf. I thought that was kind of odd, him coming along like that right after Preacher did, but I just figured it was somebody who had business with Smoke. But then, late yesterday afternoon — and this is the part that's got me worried — the horse I rented to him came drifting back in by itself, still saddled but with no sign of the man."

Ace frowned and asked, "Any blood on the saddle or on the horse?"

"Nope," Patterson replied with a shake of his head. "What I'm wondering is if the fella dismounted for some reason, and then the horse ran off and he couldn't catch it."

"Could be. But if that happened, wouldn't he just walk the rest of the way to the Sugarloaf? He probably would have been mighty cold and tired by the time he got there, but a man could make it on foot."

"Yeah, I suppose. But then I got to thinking, What if the horse threw him, and he was hurt? He could have laid out there all

389

night, not able to move or get any help."

"Now, that could be pretty bad, all right," Ace admitted. "I don't think it was cold enough last night for a man to freeze to death, but he might be in a bad way this morning."

Chance asked, "Is the horse you rented him the sort that's liable to throw a rider?"

"Not at all," Patterson said. "It's that gray gelding of mine, a pretty easy ride for anybody. But it's always possible for a horse to spook at something, and even a good rider can be taken by surprise."

"So you want us to look for this fellow," Ace said.

"Well, don't go out of your way. Like I said, if you could just keep your eyes open while you're riding out there, I'd appreciate it."

Chance nodded and said, "Sure, we can do that. What does he look like?"

"He's not young. I'd say he's in his fifties. Gray hair, medium height, on the slender side. He didn't look like he was in very good health, either, which is another reason I'm concerned. His face was kind of gaunt, and his eyes were sunk a little in his head."

Ace frowned, glanced over at Chance, and saw that his brother had the same reaction.

"If he's somewhere between here and the

Sugarloaf, we'll find him," Ace said.

"Now, I don't want you going to any trouble —"

"It's no trouble," Chance assured the liveryman.

They swung up into their saddles, lifted hands in farewell, and rode out of the livery stable. As they turned west on the main road leading out of Big Rock, Chance asked, "Did you have the same thought I did when Mr. Patterson was describing that fella?"

"I'm sure there are hundreds of men in Colorado who match that description," Ace said.

"Yeah, but I can tell you think it sounded like Doc, too."

"What in the world would Doc be doing down here in Big Rock? He's in that sanitarium up north of here."

"He was the last time we heard from him," Chance said. "Lots of things could have happened since then."

"I suppose. But it just doesn't make sense to me that he'd be down here." Ace paused. "I'd sure like to know it *wasn't* him who rented that horse, though."

"Me too. What say we go try to find out?"

They heeled their mounts into a faster pace as they rode out of Big Rock.

■ ■ ■

The Sugarloaf

Smoke was up early, as was his habit, but not early enough to beat Preacher and Sally into the kitchen. The old mountain man was sitting at the table with a cup of coffee, while Sally was at the stove, preparing breakfast.

"Good morning," she greeted Smoke, who stepped up behind her, rested his hands on her shoulders for a moment, and kissed her on the neck. "I was just telling Preacher about my conversation with Mrs. DuBois last evening."

"I know about her problems with her grandson," Smoke said. "Preacher told me. I hope she realizes we'll do everything in our power to keep him from bothering her."

"Well, here's something I don't think either of you are aware of. I believe Adelaide intends to marry you, Preacher."

Smoke's eyes widened in surprise, but Preacher just sat there and sipped his coffee. That calm reaction made both Smoke and Sally stare at him.

After a couple of seconds, Preacher said, "Yeah, I sort of figured that out. She's been droppin' hints now and then ever since she showed up in Denver and told me about the problems with ol' George." He lifted the cup to his mouth for another sip of the hot black brew. "What the two of you don't know is that I'm thinkin' about it."

"Thinking about getting married?" Smoke said in amazement.

"Yep."

"After all this time?"

"It ain't like I never been married before," Preacher pointed out. "Maybe not legally, but back in the old days, there was more'n one Injun gal who figured her and me was hitched. In the eyes of the tribes, we were." He shrugged. "None of 'em really lasted, but even so, at the time it was sorta the same thing."

"It wasn't anywhere near the same thing," Sally responded with a touch of heat in her voice. "If you stand up in front of God and everyone and promise to be with that woman from now on, it means more. You can't just wander on when the next fur-trapping season rolls around."

Preacher squinted at her and asked, "Are you sayin' that what the Absaroka and the Shoshone and all the other tribes believe in don't matter as much as what so-called civilized folks believe?"

"I'm not . . . I don't . . ." Sally was starting to sound exasperated now. "I don't know what I'm trying to say, but, Preacher, you can't agree to marry Adelaide unless you really *mean* it."

"If that day comes, I'll mean it," Preacher said, slowly nodding. "You can bet a hat on that. But don't get a burr under your saddle just yet. I'm just thinkin' about it, that's all. Besides, if me and Adelaide was to get hitched, that might make George back off on tryin' to hurt her."

Smoke said, "Or it might make him even more determined to kill her before she has a chance to change her will, if that's what you're talking about."

"Now, hold on a second! I never said nothin' about her changin' her will. I don't need any inheritance from her —"

"But George won't know that."

Preacher set his cup down and frowned.

"You've given me more to think about, that's for durned sure," he said. "I don't want to do the wrong thing and make it worse for her."

"Just take your time," Sally told him. "Enjoy the holiday. You don't have to make up your mind about anything right away."

"I reckon that's true. Anyway, we got another problem to deal with, don't we, Smoke?"

"You're talking about Doc Monday?" Smoke said. "That's right. It's funny that two strangers showed up here at the same time with trouble on their trail."

"That's because Jensens attract trouble like a lodestone," Sally said as she turned back to her cooking. Smoke couldn't argue with that statement. She went on, "In fact, I'll bet you've already come up with a plan to help Doc."

Smoke poured himself a cup of coffee and sat down at the table with Preacher. He said, "I don't think that outlaw Malkin is likely to venture onto the Sugarloaf to look for Doc, but I'll bet he's not far off, watching the road and hoping to get another chance at him. So we're going to give him that chance."

Sally looked over her shoulder and raised an eyebrow. "You're going to use Doc as the bait in a trap?"

"He's not only willing, but once we started talking about it, he actually suggested that very thing. He's going to borrow a horse and ride back to Big Rock today."

"Alone?"

"Preacher and I will be close by, and so will Pearlie and Cal."

"But what if Malkin shoots Doc from hiding, and you don't have time to stop him?"

Sally asked. "You know there are plenty of places along the road where he could set up an ambush."

Smoke said, "I don't think he's going to do that. He doesn't just want Doc dead. He wants to make sure his trail is covered. In order to accomplish that, he's going to have to talk to Doc and make sure he didn't tell anyone else who Malkin really is."

Sally thought about that, then said, "So you think he'll try to capture Doc, question him, and *then* kill him."

"That's the way it seems to me," said Smoke, nodding.

"But you're betting Doc's life on that, and so is he."

"That's why they call it gamblin'," Preacher said. "And if there's one thing in this life that ol' Doc Monday is . . . it's a gambler."

CHAPTER 35

His hands were remarkably steady as they held the reins of the sturdy brown horse underneath him, Doc thought as he rode slowly toward Big Rock. Often, stress seemed to make the trembling worse, but sometimes it had the opposite effect.

Maybe his nerves and muscles and whatever else it was that went wrong inside him finally realized that he was at the end of his rope. Everything depended on what happened today. One way or another, it would dramatically affect the rest of his life.

Of course, if things went wrong, the rest of his life might be very short indeed. But Doc wouldn't have it any other way. Better that than living in fear from now on.

And he didn't want Bill Malkin to get away with everything he had done, either. That played a big part in Doc's determination to go through with this.

The looming clouds promised more snow,

but so far all they had done was threaten. A blustery wind whipped through the valley now and then but didn't bring any real changes with it. But it was gusting, moaning through the trees, and that was enough to mask the sounds of a horse coming up behind him until it was too late.

Doc heard the harsh voice quite clearly, though, as it called out, "Hold it right there, Monday!"

He pulled back on the reins and brought the horse to a stop.

"Don't try anything!" Malkin went on. "Have you got a gun?"

"I'm unarmed, Bill," Doc said without turning around.

"Put your hands up, anyway. Make any funny moves and I'll blow a hole through you!"

Slowly, Doc raised both hands, still holding the reins in the right one. He made sure to lift them high enough that Malkin could see them clearly and know that he didn't represent any sort of threat. Now he needed to keep Malkin talking until Smoke and the others showed up and stepped in.

"I guess the folks at that ranch didn't help you, after all," Malkin said with a smirk in his voice. "I asked around in town. It belongs to some big shot named Jensen.

What made you think you could hide out there?"

"I didn't." Doc had searched his memory, and as far as he could recall, he had never mentioned Ace and Chance to Malkin back in the sanitarium, or Smoke Jensen, either. "My horse got away from me, and then those folks in that buggy came along and offered me a ride. That was where they were going. It scared the hell out of them when you chased us, and I started shooting at you."

He had worked out that lie to keep Malkin from getting suspicious and rushing to kill him. Doc knew he needed to stall as much as possible.

Malkin snorted and said, "They would have been a lot more scared if I had caught up to you. I didn't need to leave any witnesses behind."

The callous way he talked about murdering two strangers just because it would have been convenient made Doc feel hollow inside.

"You really don't have to do this, you know," he said. "Your secret is safe with me. I told you that before. I give you my word on it."

Malkin snorted contemptuously as he nudged his horse up alongside Doc's. He had the same revolver in his hand that Doc had seen in the drawer back at the sanitarium. Doc felt a chill go through him that had nothing to do with the weather as he saw the gun pointing at him, ready to deal out death.

"Your word doesn't mean a damn thing to me," Malkin said. "The only thing that I *know* will keep my secret safe is you being dead. But before I take care of that, I want to know who else you've told about me."

"No one. I swear it."

"And I'm supposed to just believe that?" Malkin shook his head. "No, Doc, you and I are gonna go someplace quiet and private and have ourselves a nice long talk. There's only one way you're going to convince me you're telling the truth."

He meant torture, thought Doc. Malkin meant to torture him until there was no possibility that he was lying — and then kill him once he'd found out what he needed to know.

And Doc *would* tell him the truth. Doc knew he wasn't strong enough, physically or mentally, to withstand such an ordeal. He would spill everything . . . if it came to that.

But maybe it wouldn't. Everything depended on Smoke now.

Smoke was riding about three hundred yards to the right of the road. Preacher's position had him the same distance to the left, and Pearlie and Cal were half a mile back on the road itself. They would come rushing forward if they heard any shots, and they would be ready to stop Malkin if he fled in their direction.

Smoke's route took him through thick growths of trees, areas of abundant brush, and stretches of huge, jumbled boulders. That gave him plenty of cover, so that he wasn't likely to be spotted. At the same time, there were enough gaps for him to keep track of Doc Monday as the gambler rode toward Big Rock. A lot depended on Smoke's ability to read the situation correctly, but as Preacher had pointed out to Sally, Doc was willing to run the risk.

Smoke wouldn't have wanted to live the rest of his life with such a threat hanging over his head. Of course, he had ways of dealing with such threats that Doc Monday didn't. Doc was no gunfighter, and he was physically frail. He couldn't fight a man like Malkin head-on and survive.

The thought of being plagued by the sort

401

of illness that had befallen Doc *was* frightening to Smoke. He couldn't imagine having his own body betray him like that and refuse to do what he wanted it to do. Thinking about it made him realize how blessed he had been to have such good health all his life. He had worked to live up to the potential of his strength and abilities, no doubt about that, and he wasn't going to apologize for things over which he'd had no control. But he was humbly thankful for what he'd been able to accomplish and hoped he always would be.

Smoke weaved his mount through some boulders and then up a gentle slope onto a small ridge topped by pines. From there he could look down onto the road Doc Monday was following, and so he had a good view when Bill Malkin emerged from some brush and came up behind Doc.

From where he was, Smoke could have pulled out his Winchester and put a round through Malkin before the outlaw ever knew what hit him. But Doc had told him about Malkin hiding the loot from that railroad holdup, and Smoke knew the authorities would like to recover that money. They never would if Malkin was dead. Because of that, Smoke intended to capture the man, if possible.

But if he had to kill Malkin to save Doc's life, he would do it without hesitation.

Smoke drew the rifle from its saddle sheath and started his horse toward the road, not rushing, because that could make too much racket and warn Malkin. If Preacher had spotted the confrontation, he would be closing in from the other side. Malkin was trapped; he just didn't know it yet.

As Smoke approached, he saw Doc and Malkin talking, saw the outlaw brandishing a gun toward the gambler. When he was close enough, Smoke dismounted and slipped forward on foot through the brush, making as little sound as he could.

Malkin jabbed the gun toward Doc and, in a loud, harsh voice, ordered him to get moving. Doc lifted his reins and started to turn his horse. That took him, just for a second, out of the direct line of fire from Malkin's gun.

As Doc did that, Smoke stepped out into the open, fifty yards away now, and called, "Drop that gun, Malkin! You're covered!"

Malkin cursed and tried to swing the pistol toward the unexpected threat. Smoke already had the Winchester's butt socketed against his shoulder. He stroked the trigger. The rifle's sharp crack filled the air and echoed from the thick clouds that were oppressively low overhead.

Malkin jerked as the bullet cut through the fleshy part of his upper right arm. Somehow he held on to the gun, although the arm sagged, so he couldn't aim it.

Malkin snatched the pistol with his other hand, though, and started to lift it again, this time toward Doc. A shot came from the other side of the road, jolting Malkin. That would be Preacher opening fire, Smoke knew. Preacher was aware they were trying to take Malkin alive, but he might have figured the threat to Doc's life was too pressing to worry about that.

Malkin managed to jerk the trigger, but the shot went wide. He spurred his horse ahead, nearly ramming Doc's mount. Smoke fired again, but Malkin didn't stop. Bending low in the saddle, he galloped hard toward Big Rock.

Smoke ran toward the road and called, "Doc! Are you all right?"

Doc nodded shakily and said, "I'm fine. Go after Malkin!"

Smoke whistled for his horse, and as the animal pounded up to him, he swung into the saddle with such lithe agility that the horse never came to a full stop. Smoke raced after Malkin, who had disappeared around a bend in the trail up ahead.

Ace and Chance heard the rifle shots somewhere up ahead and looked at each other as
Chance exclaimed, "What the hell!"

"Somebody doing some hunting, maybe,"
Ace said. "There were only a few shots."

"Only a few so far. Let's go see!"

Chance urged his horse into a run. That
was just like him, charging blindly into
trouble, without waiting to see what was
going on, thought Ace.

But Ace galloped right behind him, anyway.

They thundered around the curves in the
road, past rocks and ridges and trees, and
then, as they entered a stretch that ran
straight for a couple of hundred yards, they
saw a man on horseback pounding toward
them. He was bent forward in the saddle,
maybe hurt, maybe just trying to get his
mount to go faster.

Ace and Chance hauled back on their
reins.

"Do we try to stop him?" Chance asked.

"We don't know who he is or why he's
riding so hard," Ace answered.

"Yeah, but anybody riding like a bat out
of hell away from the scene of a shooting
has to be up to no good!"

"Either that or an innocent man with trouble after him," Ace said.

Chance nodded in acknowledgment of that point. They would need to make up their minds quickly, because the gap between them and the other man was closing in a hurry.

But then the man turned his horse so sharply that the animal almost lost its footing and went down. The horse recovered just in time and surged ahead, moving now away from the road, across some open ground, toward a heavily wooded area. Ace and Chance had been in these parts before but didn't know the region all that well. Neither had any idea what was over there beyond the trees.

"He must have seen us and didn't want us stopping him," Chance said. "Do we go after him? I know it's none of our business, but —"

Ace held up a hand to stop him and said, "Somebody else is coming."

It was true. Drumming hoofbeats sounded from the west. Another hard-charging rider came into view, obviously giving chase to the first man the brothers had seen. Ace looked closely, and a shock of recognition went through him.

"That's Smoke!" he said.

■ ■ ■ ■

Bill Malkin wasn't sure what hurt worse:
the wounds in his arm and side, the fury
that filled his soul, or the terrible pounding
pain in his chest.

He should have killed Doc Monday as
soon as he had the son of a bitch in his
sights. He knew that now, but he'd been
trying to make sure he didn't face any other
threats because of the gambler. Instead, his
hesitation might have cost him everything.
He didn't know who those bastards were
who'd interfered and gunned him, but even
though their bullets might not kill him, the
shock of being shot just might.

Malkin fought to stay in the saddle. He
rode through the trees and came out in a
rugged area of gullies and ridges. The terrain was rough enough that he should be
able to use it to give the slip to any pursuers . . . provided that he could stay mounted
and conscious.

He turned his horse into one of the gullies, following a barely visible game trail
through the thick brush. Branches clawed
and pulled at him. The horse shied away,
but Malkin forced it on. He came to a slope,
climbed it, dropped down into more brush

on the other side.

His chest tightened and hurt even more. His jaw clenched hard against the pain. He told himself that he was going to get away. It would take an expert tracker to follow his trail through this thicket. Doc Monday would never be able to do that . . . but he didn't know who Doc's friends were, Malkin reminded himself.

He came to a small clearing ringed by trees. The horse started across it but had taken only a couple of steps when the worst pain so far struck Malkin in the chest like a sledgehammer. And like the impact of a sledgehammer, it drove him out of the saddle. He swayed far to the left, lost his grip, and thudded to the ground.

Spooked by that, the horse danced away skittishly, so Malkin couldn't even reach up and grab hold of the stirrup to help him back to his feet. He crawled and scooted instead until he made it to one of the trees and fought his way into a sitting position with his back braced against the rough-barked trunk. He stayed there, breathing hard, head and shoulders hunched forward because of the ball of agony in his chest.

He couldn't hear the footsteps approaching, because of the thundering pulse inside his head, and his eyesight was blurry, so he didn't recognize the boots standing in front of him at first. Then he realized somebody was there, and struggled to lift his head and see who had found him.

The man helped by hunkering down on his heels, so his head was roughly on the same level as Malkin's. Malkin blinked at the rugged face. He knew it, but he couldn't come up with the name right away. Then, in a raspy whisper, he said, "Th-Thackery?"

"That's right, Bill," the man said. "It's your old partner, Lane Thackery. I've been on your trail for a long time, and I've finally caught up to you. And not a minute too soon, by the looks of you." Thackery's lips pulled back from his teeth in a hate-filled grimace as he grabbed Malkin's wounded arm and squeezed. "Where'd you hide the money, Bill? Where's that damn loot?"

Under normal circumstances, the pain in Malkin's arm might have made him scream. But it was nothing compared to what he was already experiencing. He heard a grotesque sound and realized that he was laughing.

"By God, you'd better tell me," Thackery said. "You're not wounded that bad, but both of those bullet holes are leaking quite a bit. I'll leave you right here to bleed to death if you don't talk. Is that what you want?"

"You're not gonna . . . let me live." Malkin forced the words out. "Not after I . . . double-crossed you . . . the way I did. If I tell you . . . where the loot is . . . you'll put a bullet . . . in my brain."

Thackery didn't realize what was really going on here, thought Malkin. He had no idea that the man he had sought for so long was going to be dead in a matter of minutes, if not sooner. Malkin knew nobody could hurt the way he did right now and survive. All he wanted to do now was to go ahead and die, so that Thackery would be frustrated and would never find that money.

"Damn you —" Thackery began.

"W-wait," Malkin gasped out as another thought occurred to him. Again, the ugly laugh bubbled from his throat. "I . . . I told . . . a friend of mine . . . He knows where . . . the loot is . . . His name . . . is Doc Monday."

Thackery leaned back in surprise. He said, "Monday? The man you ran away from that sanitarium with?"

"Y-yeah. Doc and I . . . were gonna . . . get that fifty grand . . ."

That'll teach you, Doc, Malkin thought. The world was bobbing crazily around him now. *That's what you get . . . for ruining all my plans. . . .*

"Malkin! What the hell! You're not hurt that bad. Listen to me, damn it. Tell me where to find . . ."

Thackery's voice faded away. Maybe he was still talking — Malkin didn't know — but it didn't matter. Nothing mattered now. The pain was gone suddenly, and Malkin laughed.

He kept laughing, all the way to hell.

CHAPTER 36

Smoke wasn't surprised to see Ace and Chance. He had known that they might be showing up any day now to help celebrate Christmas on the Sugarloaf.

Running into them here on the road to Big Rock while he was pursuing Bill Malkin was a little unexpected, though.

"Smoke!" Ace called as he lifted a hand in greeting. "What —"

"A man on horseback!" Smoke said as he reined his mount to a temporary halt. "Did you see him?"

Chance leveled a finger toward some trees and said, "He headed that way, riding hell-for-leather!"

Smoke knew the Jensen boys would join him in the pursuit if he asked them to, but it might be better if they didn't. He waved back up the road in the direction he'd come from and said, "Doc Monday is that way. You'd best go see about him."

"Doc!" Ace and Chance exclaimed together.

Preacher was with Doc, Smoke knew, and Pearlie and Cal would have joined them by now, so Doc was perfectly safe and had said that he wasn't hurt. But Smoke didn't want to delay the reunion between the brothers and the man who had raised them.

Besides, if they went after Malkin with him, there was a chance they might get hurt, and he didn't want that. Malkin was wounded, and a wounded animal was the most dangerous creature of all.

"Doc can explain the whole thing," Smoke went on. "I'll go after that varmint!"

Ace and Chance looked reluctant to leave Smoke to the chase, but at the same time, Smoke knew they were anxious to see Doc and make sure he was all right. After a second, Ace nodded.

Smoke turned his horse and started toward the trees. Malkin could be holed up in there, waiting to ambush anybody who came after him, so Smoke guided his mount with his knees and held the Winchester ready for instant use. Behind him, hooves clattered on the road as Ace and Chance rode off toward the Sugarloaf.

No shots rang out as Smoke approached the trees. He threaded his way through the growth, then spotted the tracks of Malkin's horse on the other side. The trail led into an area of rugged wilderness that sprawled on the edge of the Sugarloaf's range.

Smoke had learned how to read sign from Preacher, one of the best trackers who ever lived. He was able to stay on Malkin's trail through dense thickets and across stretches of rock. Malkin had used an almost invisible game trail to get through the worst of the obstacles.

Smoke paused and lifted his head. He thought he heard a horse moving somewhere ahead of him. Malkin's mount . . . or someone else's? There was no way of knowing, so Smoke forged ahead.

He stiffened in the saddle as he entered a clearing and spotted the man sitting with his back against a tree trunk on the other side. Even though he hadn't gotten a close look at Bill Malkin, he recognized the outlaw from his clothes and from the bloodstains on the man's arm and side, where he had been wounded.

Malkin wasn't moving. As Smoke edged his horse closer and kept the rifle trained on the motionless figure, he saw why. Malkin's face was twisted in lines of agony, frozen permanently that way. His open eyes stared sightlessly. Smoke had no doubt that

Malkin was dead, but he held the rifle ready, anyway, as he swung a leg over the saddle and slid down to the ground.

In a way, Malkin's death was a blasted shame, thought Smoke. There was a very good chance he was the only person who knew where the loot from the train robbery was stashed. Now it would never be recovered, unless someone happened upon it purely by chance.

Smoke started to approach the outlaw's body but stopped short. A frown creased his forehead as he looked closely at the ground in front of Malkin. He saw two indentions there. Those marks, he realized, had been left by bootheels.

Someone else had been here.

But who? Not Ace or Chance, or Preacher, Pearlie, or Cal. They were all back on the road. Smoke thought about the hoofbeats he had heard. Malkin's horse was here, standing at the edge of the trees, looking spooked. Smoke looked around, but there were too many hoofprints on the ground for him to determine if another horse had been here. That seemed highly likely, though.

Somebody riding along who had happened to find Malkin's body? That was possible, Smoke supposed, but he couldn't think of a good reason for anyone to be traveling through this rugged area. Legally, it fell within the bounds of the Sugarloaf, but it wasn't good range, and he hadn't ever used it for anything except some occasional hunting.

Smoke didn't have any answers, but he was curious about something else. He could tell that his bullet had passed through the fleshy part of Malkin's upper arm. It wasn't, or shouldn't have been, a fatal wound. He knelt in front of the outlaw, pushed Malkin's coat back, pulled up his shirt, and looked at the wound in Malkin's side from Preacher's shot. The injury was a deep graze, messy but not serious, and again, it shouldn't have been fatal.

Yet judging by Malkin's expression, he had died in great pain. What had caused that? Smoke thought back to Doc Monday's story. Malkin had been a patient at that sanitarium, too, and Doc believed he'd had a genuine heart condition. Could the shock of being shot, along with everything else that had happened today, have caused Malkin's ticker to stop working?

Smoke had a hunch that was the case, but he sighed as he rose to his feet. It didn't really matter. Malkin was dead, and that fifty thousand dollars was lost. But Doc

416

Monday was safe and had been reunited with Ace and Chance by now, and Smoke was going to accept that victory with satisfaction.

Ace and Chance saw a small group of men on horseback in the road up ahead. It was easy to pick out Doc among them. He was the only one who looked awkward and uncomfortable in the saddle.

That didn't stop him from breaking away from the others and riding quickly toward the brothers.

"Ace! Chance!" he called.

They reined in and swung down from their saddles. As Doc brought his mount to a clumsy halt, he all but fell off. Ace and Chance were there to help him, though, and the three of them pounded each other on the back as they hugged roughly.

"We ran into Smoke back down the road," said Ace. "He told us you were all right. Is that true?"

Doc nodded. "I'm fine now that you boys are here," he declared as he stepped back to look them over from head to foot. "You haven't changed a bit."

"You have, Doc," Chance said. "You look worn out."

Doc sighed and said, "It's been a rough

417

few months, and the past week or so got even worse."

"What are you doing here on the Sugarloaf?" Ace asked.

"It's the proverbial long story. A man named Bill Malkin is after me. An outlaw who wants me dead. I . . . I knew you were planning to come here for Christmas, so I thought I might find you."

"We saw a fellow riding hell-for-leather away from here," Chance said. "Was that the outlaw you're talking about?"

"That's right. Did he get away?"

"Don't know. Smoke went after him."

Preacher spoke up, saying, "We'd best go see if he needs a hand, now that you boys are here to keep an eye on Doc. Pearlie, Cal, you fellas come with me. It's good to see you boys again, by the way."

"You, too, Preacher," said Ace. "And Pearlie and Cal."

The two cowboys nodded. Pearlie said, "Howdy, boys. Keep your smokepoles handy. Can't never tell when hell's gonna go to poppin' around here."

The three of them galloped up the road in the same direction Smoke had gone. Ace took Pearlie's warning seriously and studied the landscape all around them, looking for any sign of a threat. He didn't see any, but

418

that didn't make him relax too much.

Chance frowned and said, "Doc, your hands are shaking more than they used to, aren't they?"

"Yes, that's been part of the problem. Some of the time, my muscles just don't work like they should." Doc smiled. "I don't care about any of that right now, though. I'm just so glad to see you boys."

"And we're glad to see you, too, Doc," Ace said, "but you're going to have to tell us about Malkin and why he was after you."

"Of course. It can wait, though. Right now, just let me look at you again. And tell me all about what *you've* been up to since the last time I saw you."

"Oh, all kinds of hell-raising," Chance said with a grin.

Doc said, "I don't doubt it! You boys come by it honestly."

"What does that mean?" Ace asked quickly.

Doc shook his head and said, "Never mind. Just tell me what you've been doing."

Doc dodged any further questions as they got caught up over the next fifteen minutes. Then Ace said, "We shouldn't be standing out here in the cold. Look at the way you're trembling, Doc."

"Not all of that is because of the weather,

but I'll admit there's a chill in the air." Doc held out a hand, which shook a little. "And something else, too. Look. It's starting to snow."

He was right. Tiny flakes swirled down here and there. It was about as light a snowfall as one could find, but from the ominous way the clouds looked, this was just a precursor of something more significant.

The sound of horses made them look around. A good-sized group of riders came toward them, with Smoke in front, leading another horse with a body draped over the saddle. Preacher, Pearlie, and Cal followed close behind.

Doc's eyes widened. He said, "Is that . . . ?"

"It could be," Chance said. "I didn't hear any more shots, though."

"Malkin was wounded when he rode away from here," Doc explained. "I didn't know how badly, but maybe it was bad enough."

The three of them didn't mount up but waited for Smoke and the others to reach them instead. As Smoke reined in, he said, "I found Malkin a ways off the trail. Looked like he tried to get away but fell off his horse and then died while he was sitting with his back against a tree."

420

"Died from being shot?" Doc asked.

Smoke shook his head. "I don't think so. You said he had a bad heart, Doc. I think it played out on him."

Doc sighed as he looked at the bulky figure tied onto the horse's back.

"That seems likely, all right, if he wasn't wounded bad enough for that to have killed him. He had some sort of attack from it that night at the sanitarium when he tried to murder me. If it hadn't happened then, I probably never would have gotten away from him." Doc shook his head and murmured, "Now it appears to have ended his threat once and for all." He lifted his head and added, "At least he doesn't have to worry about his secret coming out anymore."

"No, but I reckon he's taking another secret to the grave with him," Smoke said.

"The whereabouts of the money from that train robbery." Doc's words were a statement, not a question.

"Yep." Smoke turned in the saddle. "Pearlie, Cal, how about the two of you take Malkin's body into town and turn it over to Tom Nunnley? And let Monte know what happened, too, will you?"

"Sure, Smoke," Pearlie replied as he took

the reins from Smoke to lead Malkin's horse.

"Just be careful. We don't know whether Aguilar's hard cases might have another ambush in mind."

Cal said, "They've tried twice and failed both times. Even gun-wolves ought to have enough sense not to try again."

"Yeah, but you know how it is in that newfangled baseball game folks are playin'," said Pearlie. "It takes three strikes to be out."

Cal just snorted in disgust and turned his horse toward Big Rock. He and Pearlie rode off to deliver the body to the town's undertaker.

Ace said, "Hold on a minute, Smoke. Who's this fella Aguilar, and why does he have hard cases working for him?"

"I'll tell you about it on the way to the ranch." Smoke smiled. "Sally's going to be happy to see you two boys. It's too bad you may just be riding into more trouble."

"Well," said Chance as the snow began to fall harder, "there's nothing new about that, is there?"

CHAPTER 37
THE WESTERN RANGE OF THE SUGARLOAF

"It's snowin' again," Teddy announced from his perch on the wagon seat next to Luke.

"Yeah, I can see that," Luke replied. "Why don't you get in the back and crawl under the blankets with your brother and sister?"

"No, I want to see where we're goin'." Teddy reached up with both hands and pulled his hat down tighter on his head. "I'll be all right. I don't mind bein' cold."

Luke smiled. The little boy's voice held a certain amount of bravado, but Luke knew Teddy really *was* cold. All of them were. Bodie and Hannah were huddled in the wagon bed, under several blankets, where a layer of snow was beginning to collect. The flakes swirled and danced and already were falling thickly enough to make it difficult to see the trail in front of them. Luke's experience and instincts told him it was going to get worse before it got better.

It had been snowing, off and on, all during the journey from Amity. Luke had worried that they would run into an actual blizzard. If that happened, they would need to find shelter somewhere, either in a settlement or, if there weren't any towns close by, a cave or some other refuge in the mountains.

But fortune had smiled on them, and they had been able to keep moving steadily. Luke had a pretty strong hunch that they were already on Sugarloaf range, and he expected to reach the ranch headquarters sometime today. It would be mighty nice for these kids to have somewhere warm and comfortable to stay for a while, and to be honest, he wouldn't mind that himself.

The snow fell heavier and heavier, whipped around by the gusting wind. There was enough on the ground now that even Luke's keen eyes had trouble seeing the trail. They weren't in a good place to stop, though, so he had no choice except to keep the wagon moving.

"Mr. Jensen!" Teddy suddenly exclaimed. "Look! There's a dog!"

The boy pointed a finger excitedly, and as Luke's gaze followed that indication, he caught his breath. The shaggy shape loping through the trees to their right might look like a dog at first glance, but Luke knew it wasn't.

That was a wolf pacing them, and where there was one of the cunning predators, there was likely to be another — or more.

Luke's head swiveled to the left. He thought he caught a glimpse of a second ghostly shape through the twisting, writhing clouds of snow. With an urgent note in his voice, he said, "Teddy, you need to get in the back now, under the blankets, and tell Bodie to come up here."

"I don't want to! I want to ride with you, Mr. Jensen. I want to see that dog!"

Teddy didn't know it, but that "dog" was just about the last thing he wanted to see right now. And it might well *be* the last thing the boy saw if the pack that was trailing them was too large. Winter brought on desperation in the creatures. It might have been a while since they'd come across any prey. Luke knew that Smoke and his crew had hunted down many of the wolves that had once roamed this area, and had driven out others, but it was impossible to account for all of them.

"Damn it, Teddy, just do what I told you!"

Teddy stared up at him, bottom lip beginning to quiver. He said, "You . . . you used a bad word!"

Luke wasn't going to waste time apologizing for his language or for the harsh tone of his voice. He said, "Get back there, Teddy, and tell Bodie I need him."

Finally, Teddy scrambled over the back of the seat and dropped into the wagon bed. As Luke turned his head to the right to check on the wolf pacing them on that flank, from the corner of his eye, he saw Teddy clambering among what was left of their dwindling supplies. The boy lifted the snow-covered layer of blankets spread over an open space between several crates and ducked into the little fortlike area.

The wind was blowing harder now, driving the snowflakes against Luke's grizzled cheeks and into his eyes and nose. It made a howling sound. . . . Or was that something else? Luke didn't know, but his mouth was a grim line under his mustache.

Bodie threw a leg over the seat back and climbed down beside Luke. He said, "What is it, Mr. Jensen? Teddy said you were mad at him. He's crying."

"No, I'm not mad at anybody," Luke told him. "I'll explain it to him later. But right now I need your help, Bodie. You're going to handle the team."

He pressed the reins into the surprised youngster's hands.

A few times during the trip from Utah, Luke had allowed Bodie to drive the wagon. Bodie had done a good job of guiding the horses, but the conditions hadn't been as extreme as this, nor the situation as dangerous.

"Mr. Jensen, I . . . I don't know if I can. There's so much snow . . ."

"Just keep them moving," Luke said as he reached down to the floorboards for the rifle at his feet. "If I tell you to, whip them and yell and make them run. The trail's hard to see, but I know you can do it."

"I . . . I'll try. But what are you gonna be doing?"

"Keeping us all alive, I hope," Luke muttered.

He worked the Winchester's lever to jack a round into the chamber and lifted the rifle, but he didn't place the butt against his shoulder yet. Instead, he stood up on the driver's box and looked around.

His jaw tightened as he realized he couldn't see any of the wolves anymore. That *could* mean that the pack had decided to abandon its stalking. Luke didn't believe that for a second, though. Those beasts had a hankering for horsemeat, and they wouldn't turn their noses up at a taste of human flesh, either.

"Mr. Jensen, the team's acting up!" Bodie cried.

Luke glanced at the horses, saw the way they were tossing their heads and jerking against the harness. They smelled the wolves and were panicking. That meant the wolves had to be close. . . .

A dark shape darted out of the snowy wasteland and leaped toward the right-hand leader. With blinding speed, Luke raised the rifle to his shoulder and fired. He didn't have time to aim. It was pure reflex and instinct that guided his aim.

The wolf yelped, twisted in midair, and dropped to the ground to writhe in pain from the bullet that had torn through it. Luke called to the youngster beside him, "Go, Bodie! Whip 'em up!"

"Hyaaahhh!" Bodie cried as he slashed at the wheelers' rumps with the lines. The horses lunged forward. The leaders took their cue from the wheelers and pulled harder, too.

Luke knew that wolves attacked in numbers, rather than alone, so he was already turning back to the left. He spotted the one charging in on that side and fired just as the animal gathered itself to spring. The bullet took it in the chest and knocked it spinning.

The skin on the back of his neck prickled.

He turned on the driver's box and saw a pair of wolves charging in from behind. The wagon bucked and swayed as it picked up speed on the rough trail, and the floorboards under Luke's booted feet pitched like the deck of a ship at sea during a storm. He braced himself and fired over the wagon bed and saw one of the wolves go rolling through the snow, leaving red splashes of blood on the white.

The other wolf sailed through the air and struck the wagon's tailgate. Clawed rear feet scratched at the closed gate and powered the wolf up and over.

Hannah and Teddy might not know what was going on, but they had heard the shots, and both screamed in fright. The wolf was about to leap on the pile of blankets when Luke palmed out one of his Remingtons. For close work like this, the revolver was better than the Winchester.

The gun roared and bucked a couple of times in his hand. The bullets struck the wolf and drove it back against the tailgate. It flopped and shrieked madly, adding to the children's terror. Luke fired again. This time the slug crashed into the wolf's brain, stilling it forever.

Luke twisted from side to side, searching for more threats. He didn't see anything except the swirling snow. A glance at Bodie showed him the boy's pale, strained face. Bodie was handling the team with grit and determination, though.

Luke holstered the Remington and sat down beside Bodie again. He lowered the Winchester to the floorboards and took back the reins.

"You did a fine job, son," Luke said. "You helped me save your brother's and sister's lives, and probably our own, too."

Bodie twisted around on the seat and stared in horror at the wolf's carcass lying just in front of the tailgate.

"Were . . . were those wolves?" he asked.

"They sure were."

"Teddy said they were dogs!"

"Maybe they were related a long, long time ago, but those varmints were nobody's pets."

"They would have killed us!"

"And eaten us," Luke said. Bodie gulped, and Luke thought maybe he shouldn't have been so blunt about it. But on the other hand, it wouldn't hurt anything for Bodie to learn that the world was a harsh, merciless place at times, even during a holiday season like this one.

Actually, mused Luke, since Bodie was the son of a no-good outlaw like Hank Trafford, he probably already had a pretty good idea how rotten the world could be.

"Climb back there and see if you can get Hannah and Teddy to settle down," Luke went on.

"Wh-what about that wolf?"

"He's dead. He can't hurt you or anybody else anymore."

"But he's *right there.*"

Bodie had a point. Luke handed him the reins again, stepped over the seat, moved around the blanket-covered shelter, and bent to grasp a couple of the wolf's legs. With a grunt of effort, he lifted the carcass and heaved it out. It landed in the snow and soon disappeared behind them.

Luke returned to the driver's box and took back the reins.

"Go on back in there with your brother and sister," he told Bodie. "We should be where we're going pretty soon."

"Everything's gonna be all right now?"

Luke hated to make that broad of a statement. It was a lie, because in all the history of the world, there had never been a time when *everything* was all right.

But he was dealing with youngsters, he reminded himself, and adults always had to walk a fine line between protecting them from the truth and making sure they understood how the world really worked.

It was probably a good thing he'd never had any kids of his own, he told himself. He didn't think he would have made a very good parent. Too likely to lay the facts out there, unpleasant though they might be.

Right now, though, he made himself nod and say, "Yeah, everything's going to be all right."

And considering they would soon be at the Sugarloaf headquarters, maybe this time that far-fetched notion was true.

It took longer to reach the ranch house than Luke expected. As the late afternoon darkened until it was almost like night, he began worrying that he had lost his way somehow. He had visited Smoke and Sally a number of times and had even approached from this direction more than once, but that had been in better weather, in broad daylight, and while riding horseback instead of driving a wagon. The kids were cold and hungry, and Luke was, too. They probably believed he was lost.

Luke Jensen wasn't the sort of man to allow despair to take hold of him, though, or one to sit still and feel sorry for himself. He liked to keep moving, so that was what he did.

Hannah stuck her head out from under the blankets and asked, "Mr. Jensen, when are we gonna get there?"

"Soon, honey, soon," he told her.

"I need to pee!" Teddy announced. Luke didn't want to stop, but the note of desperation in the boy's voice made him decide that it was advisable.

He said, "All right," and hauled back on the reins. Teddy scrambled out of the "fort" as the wagon came to a stop.

Luke went on, "Just hop down right beside the wheel, though. Don't wander off. Either of you other two need to go?"

Bodie and Hannah told him they didn't. Luke stood up on the driver's box and held the Winchester ready as his eyes tried to penetrate the stubborn gathering darkness around them.

"Mr. Jensen?"

It took Luke a second to realize that Hannah was talking to him. He looked down at her and asked, "What is it? You decide you need to go, after all?"

The little girl shook her head. She said, "No. I hear somebody singing."

Luke frowned. The wind was still making quite a bit of racket as it whipped through the trees. He was sure that this was what Hannah heard and that she had mistaken it

433

for singing —

"Herald angels —"

"Newborn king —"

Luke lifted his head. Danged if the wind didn't sound like words there and there.

"Peace on —"

"You hear it?" asked Hannah, excited now. "It's 'Hark! the Herald Angels Sing.' "

Luke surprised himself by feeling his spirits lift as he said, "You know, sweetheart, I believe you're right. Teddy, are you done? Climb back in the wagon. All you kids crowd up here on the seat with me. You're going to help me listen while we follow that song."

Luke took up the reins and started the wagon rolling through the gloom again, on the trail of that beloved Christmas carol.

CHAPTER 38
THE SUGARLOAF RANCH HOUSE

Platters of food filled the dining room table this evening, and seven of the chairs around it were occupied. Smoke sat at the head of the table, of course, with Sally to his right and Preacher to his left. Adelaide was next to Preacher. Ace, Chance, and Doc sat on the other side, with Sally. Smoke had just asked the blessing, and now everyone was digging into the meal Sally had prepared.

Thick slices of ham, sweet potatoes, corn on the cob, greens, and huge, fluffy biscuits were piled on plates. The music of silver and china counterpointed the conversation and laughter.

Earlier, Preacher had introduced Ace and Chance to Adelaide DuBois and explained that she was an old friend of his, but he hadn't gone into any detail about the problem with her grandson. Smoke knew that was because the old mountain man didn't want to embarrass her.

435

According to what Preacher had told him, Smoke also knew Adelaide was still worried about George showing up and causing trouble. He didn't think that was likely, with so many fighting men now surrounding her. George would have to recruit an army of hired guns to reach her, and he didn't have the money to do that. In the long run, he and Preacher might have to look up George DuBois and have a nice long talk with him, Smoke mused, but that could wait until after Christmas. For now, Adelaide was safe.

And so was Doc Monday, at least apparently. The fact that somebody else had been in the clearing where Bill Malkin died continued to nag at Smoke's brain. Was it possible Malkin had had a confederate in his pursuit of Doc? According to Doc, Malkin hadn't had any friends at the MacMurphy Sanitarium, but the outlaw could have teamed up with a member of his old gang after running off from the sanitarium. Smoke couldn't rule it out.

That meant Doc might still be in danger . . . but now that Ace and Chance were on hand, Smoke was confident the brothers could look after him.

Doc's health was worrisome, too. Smoke wasn't a doctor and had no idea what the long-term outlook was for somebody with

Doc's affliction, but he didn't see how it could be good.

As Smoke glanced over and caught Sally smiling at him, he told himself to stop worrying so dang much. He was surrounded by friends and family, and in a couple more days, it would be Christmas. This was a time for joyous celebration, not brooding. He smiled back at Sally.

Preacher paused with his fork part of the way to his mouth and said, "You folks hear somethin'?"

Smoke cocked his head to the side and listened. The others at the table assumed attentive attitudes, as well.

"Come to think of it, I believe I do," Smoke said. "It sounds like . . . singing." He stood up. "I'd best go see what it's all about."

"I'll come with you," Preacher said as he pushed his chair back.

"So will we," added Ace.

Sally said, "You're all ready for trouble, aren't you? But it's *singing*. I hardly think that's a threat."

"You don't ever know," Smoke said.

"Could be a trick o' some sort," Preacher said.

The four men moved toward the foyer and the front door. Sally frowned after them for a second, then stood up and followed them. Smoke motioned her back, but she ignored him, strode past the men, and went to the front door. When she opened it, the deep-voiced strains of a Christmas carol filled the foyer.

"Hark! the herald angels sing
Glory to the newborn King!
Peace on earth and mercy mild,
God and sinner reconciled!"

Smoke looked over Sally's shoulder and grinned when he saw Pearlie, Cal, and the other members of the crew standing in the snow in front of the porch, hats in hand, as they sang. Sally stepped out onto the porch. Smoke and Preacher followed her, as well as Ace and Chance, and then Doc and Adelaide joined them, too.

"Reckon we're bein' serenaded," Preacher said as the cowboys continued to sing. They finished "Hark! the Herald Angels Sing" and launched into "God Rest Ye Merry, Gentlemen." On the porch, Adelaide clapped her hands in delight. Preacher slipped an arm around her shoulders as they listened.

Smoke put his hands on Sally's shoulders as he stood behind her. She leaned back against him and sighed in contentment. He put his mouth close to her ear and said, "I'll bet this was Cal's idea."

"Or Pearlie's. He has a very sentimental nature, you know."

That was true. Pearlie had lived a hard life, spending years as a hired gun and almost an outlaw before meeting Smoke and settling down on the Sugarloaf. But often even hard cases like that had a soft interior, if anybody could ever get through all the tough bark outside.

Whoever had come up with the idea of singing Christmas carols, Smoke was grateful to them. Sally looked positively radiant with happiness.

Then movement out at the edge of the light that came from the house caught Smoke's eye, and he stiffened. It would be just like some sort of threat to show up at a really nice moment such as this.

Instead, a team of horses moved forward into the soft yellow light, pulling a wagon behind them. Smoke raised his eyes to the driver's box and saw a man dressed all in black sitting there, handling the reins, with three much smaller figures beside him. The man's head was down, so the brim of his black hat shielded his face for a moment, but then he looked up, as if realizing that he and his companions had arrived somewhere. Smoke saw the mustache and the familiar craggy features and exclaimed, "Luke!"

The caroling cowboys fell silent at that and turned toward the newcomers. On the wagon, Luke hauled back on the reins and brought the vehicle to a stop. Sally had seen him, too, and she cried, "Luke!" as she went down the steps and hurried through the snow toward him.

Smoke was right behind her. Luke looped the team's reins around the brake lever, put a hand on the seat beside him, and jumped to the ground in time for Sally to throw her arms around him in a big hug.

"It's so good to see you," she said. "I hoped you'd get here before Christmas!"

When Sally stepped back, Smoke clasped his older brother's hand and pumped it, then drew Luke into a backslapping hug. Luke grinned as they broke apart. He thumbed his hat back and said, "Looks like you've got a full house. Hope you can find room for a few more."

"Of course we can," Sally assured him. She looked at the three small figures still huddled on the seat. "Who in the world is this you have with you?"

"That's Teddy, Hannah, and Bodie," Luke said, pointing to each of the children in turn. Their pale, big-eyed faces looked a little apprehensive as they gazed at Smoke and Sally, who were strangers to them.

Luke took care of that by continuing, "You kids, this big galoot is my little brother Smoke, and the pretty lady with him is his wife, Sally. Mr. and Mrs. Jensen. This is their place."

"And you're all very welcome here," Sally told them with a welcoming smile. She glanced at Luke. "Brothers and a sister?"

"Yep. Their last name is Trafford. They traveled over here with me from Utah."

Smoke had a hunch there was a lot more to the story than that, but whatever it was, it could wait. He said, "If you came all the way from Utah at this time of year, you must be plumb frozen by now. Come on inside and start warming up." He looked toward the members of the crew, who had been singing a few minutes earlier. "Pearlie, have a couple of men take care of this team and wagon."

"Sure thing, Smoke," the foreman replied. "Cal and me will do it ourselves, won't we, Cal?"

"I suppose," the young cowboy answered with a notable lack of enthusiasm.

"Come on," said Pearlie. "Christmas is more than singin' carols. It's helpin' folks out, too. Ain't you got the Christmas spirit, Cal? You was the one tellin' me about that just a few days ago, remember?"

Cal grinned and said, "Yeah, sure. Don't worry, Luke. We'll take care of things."

"I'm obliged to you, boys," Luke said. He lifted Teddy down from the seat, then Hannah. Bodie scrambled off by himself. Sally took charge of the children and started herding them toward the house. With the light shining from it and the promise of warmth, it was like a beacon in the snowy night.

Luke extended his hand to the old mountain man and said, "Preacher, good to see you again, as always."

"You still bounty huntin'?" Preacher asked as they shook.

"That's all I know how to do." Luke turned to Ace and Chance and went on, "Hello, boys. I figured you'd be here."

"I just hope we're not intruding, since we're not blood relations," Ace said as he shook hands.

Smoke clapped a hand on his shoulder and said, "We've told you about that. We're all family here, and all are welcome." He looked at Luke. "That goes for those three youngsters, too . . . although I *do* want to hear about how you came to be traveling with them."

"That's a story for later. It's not very . . .

442

festive, let's say."

Smoke nodded and said, "I thought it might be something like that." He leaned a head toward the house. "Well, come on inside. We have a lot of catching up to do."

Adelaide had gone inside with Sally and the children, but Doc still stood on the porch, holding on to the railing. As the others approached, Luke asked, "Who's that?"

"Doc Monday," Chance said.

"Your pa?"

"Not actually our father," said Ace. "The man who raised us, though."

"Yeah, I remember now. I thought he was in some hospital."

"Sanitarium," Chance said.

"Then what's he doing here?"

"That's another one of those stories that's not very festive," Ace said.

Luke nodded and said, "Then we'll just leave it all for later." He went up the steps and held out his hand to Doc. "I'm Luke Jensen. Heard a lot about you, Doc. It's nice to finally meet you."

"And I've heard —" Doc began, but then he stopped short and just clasped Luke's hand. "Good to meet you, too."

Smoke noticed Doc's hesitation but didn't know what to make of it. Nor did it seem overly important at the moment. He ushered everyone inside, saying, "Luke, you and those youngsters got here just in time. We're having supper, and there's plenty to go around."

"We interrupted your Christmas concert, though," Luke said. "We heard the singing from a ways off and followed it in. Having something to guide us was mighty handy on a snowy night like this."

"I'll be sure to tell Pearlie and Cal and the other fellas about that," Smoke said as he rested a hand on his brother's shoulder. "They'll be pleased that they helped you find your way home."

Luke nodded and said with a touch of wistfulness in his voice, "I reckon the Sugarloaf is as close as I'll ever come to having one of those."

CHAPTER 39

Smoke and Luke stayed up late that night, talking. Smoke told his brother about Don Juan Sebastian Aguilar and his so-called land grant claim to the Sugarloaf, and Luke explained how he had come to be responsible for three children under the age of ten.

"Never had any kids of my own," Luke concluded gruffly, "but I reckon this is like having grandkids, in a way. I'm damn sure too old for them to be mine!"

"You thought maybe Sally could help find families willing to take them in, I suppose," Smoke said.

Luke shook his head and said emphatically, "No, not families. *A* family. For too much of their lives, those three young'uns have been all each of them really had. From what I heard, their ma wasn't too bad, but they've grown up relying on each other. They shouldn't be split up now."

"I agree with you," Smoke said with a

nod. "And I'm sure Sally will, too, when we talk to her about it. If there's anybody around here who can find a good home for them, she's the one."

"You know, it's about time you and her started thinking about a family of your own," Luke said.

Smoke chuckled. "We've talked about it. And I reckon that day is going to come, sooner rather than later."

"First, though, you've got to deal with that fella Aguilar. I know better than to think you're going to let him steal the Sugarloaf out from under you."

"Preacher was ready to go to war a couple of days ago, after those ambushes. So were Pearlie and Cal and the other boys. The only reason we haven't ridden into Big Rock for a showdown with Aguilar and his hired guns is that Sally has her heart set on a peaceful family Christmas for a change. I'm doing the best I can to give that to her. But once the holiday is over . . ."

"Then you'll settle things with Aguilar," Luke finished for him.

"Whatever it takes," Smoke said.

"You know you can count on my help."

"I never doubted that."

"And I reckon those two Jensen boys, Ace and Chance, will back whatever play you make, too," Luke said. "They're pretty much members of the family now."

"That's what we've told them." Smoke put his hands on his knees and pushed himself up from the comfortable chair in the parlor where he had been sitting. The lamp was turned low, casting a soft light that didn't quite fill the corners of the room. "I guess we'd better turn in. You must be tired after that long trip from Utah."

"It was a mite wearisome," Luke admitted. "I'll see you in the morning."

Smoke nodded and left the room to head upstairs. Luke started to follow, but before he could climb the stairs, a figure stepped out of the shadows that now filled the dining room.

"Luke," Doc Monday said quietly, "could I have a word with you?"

Luke frowned a little, surprised that Doc hadn't already gone up to bed. Doc was frail, the sort of fellow who needed a lot of rest. Also, Luke couldn't think of anything Doc would have to talk to him about, let alone in a somewhat secretive manner like this.

There was an easy way to clear it up, though. Luke said, "Sure, Doc, if you want. Is this about that outlaw, Bill Malkin? Smoke told me about the trouble you had with him. I recognize the name, but he and I never crossed trails, and I never set out to collect the bounty on him —"

Doc held up a hand to stop him. The gambler shook his head and said, "No, this isn't about outlaws or bounties or anything like that. Can we step out onto the front porch?"

"It's cold out there," Luke warned. "Well below freezing by now, I'd say."

"I know. But I want this conversation to be just between the two of us, for now, anyway."

That was puzzling, too, thought Luke. He said, "Get your coat. Whatever you want is fine with me, Doc."

They put their coats on but left their hats in the house as they stepped outside. Their breath fogged in the cold air, creating substantial clouds in front of their faces, as they buried hands in pockets and stood there looking out at the snow, which was still falling heavily.

"What's this about, Doc?" Luke asked bluntly. "I've heard the boys talk about you before, but you and I just met a few hours ago. I can't see that we'd have anything to talk about requiring this much secrecy."

Doc said, "We may have just met, but there's a connection between us that goes back a long time, Luke. More than twenty years, in fact."

Luke shook his head and said, "I don't have a clue what you're talking about."

"Those boys you just mentioned. Ace and Chance."

"What about them?"

"I knew their mother, back in Denver. A mutual friend of ours suggested that she look me up, and when she did, the two of us hit it off right away."

"The boys' mother, was she a gambler, too, or a —"

Again, Doc held up a hand to stop him. The gesture was curt this time, almost angry.

"If you're about to ask if she was a whore, don't," Doc said. "You'll understand why in a minute. In fact, back in Missouri, where she came from, she had been a school-teacher. Her name was Lettie. Lettie Margrabe."

Luke's heart thudded hard. His nostrils flared as he took a deep breath. He couldn't have been any more shocked if Doc had hauled off and punched him. He couldn't find any words to say.

"You know the name, don't you?" Doc asked softly. "You can probably guess what I'm about to say. She told me about a young man she was in love with in Missouri. He went off to war, and only after he was gone did she realize that the two of them had made a son together. Well, two sons —"

Luke's hands shot out and closed around Doc's slender arms. He jerked the gambler toward him and said through clenched teeth, "Ace and Chance?"

"William and Benjamin Jensen," said Doc. "Lettie insisted on those names. I was the one who called them Ace and Chance, and the names stuck." He paused to draw in a breath. "They're your sons, Luke. There's no doubt in my mind. I figured it out a while back, after Ace mentioned that you had known a woman named Lettie before the war. It's uncommon enough that it puzzled him —"

"Does he know? Does Chance?"

Doc shook his head. "No. I could have told them . . . but I didn't think it was my place. I . . . I wasn't sure if I should tell *you,* but then I overheard you talking to Smoke, and you mentioned never having any kids . . . and I thought you had a *right* to know . . . Luke, I'm sorry, but . . . you're hurting me."

Luke realized he was still squeezing Doc's arms. He let go of them abruptly and took a step back.

"Sorry," he muttered. "You just took me by surprise."

Doc straightened his coat and said, "I know. Believe me, I thought an awful lot about what I ought to do."

"But the boys don't know?"

"No. Ace might suspect, but I think he's mostly forgotten about it. And any time he brought it up, Chance just laughed it off." Doc smiled. "You see, when they first met Smoke, Ace got it in his head that *he* might be their father, since they have the same last name. Chance has made a joke of it ever since. But neither of them ever dreamed that Smoke is actually their uncle."

Luke scrubbed a hand over his face as he struggled to come to grips with what Doc had just told him. He recalled Lettie Margrabe, of course. She had always been vivid in his memory. He had been in love with her, and he'd hoped to marry her when he got back from the war. They had been together only once, the night before he left to join up, their mutual passion getting the best of them. . . .

And that union had resulted in twin boys, unknown to Luke until now. In a way, he supposed it had been responsible for Lettie's death, too, since she had died giving birth to Ace and Chance. He felt a surge of anger at that thought, but it faded quickly. No one could predict what was going to happen in life, least of all two young people facing a desperate future.

His pulse still hammered in his head. He stepped over to the railing and leaned on it for a moment as he took several deep breaths. Then he turned to face Doc again and asked, "What are you going to do?"

Doc shook his head and said, "No, my friend, the question is, What are *you* going to do?"

"You're not going to tell them?"

"I think they have a right to know," said Doc, "but if anyone is going to tell them, it should be you, don't you think?"

"Not now," Luke snapped. "I've got to sort through all of this. A man can't just go from being childless all his life to having two grown sons in the blink of an eye."

"No, I suppose not. But there's one thing to be thankful for. They turned out to be fine young men, didn't they?"

Luke nodded slowly and said, "That's all your doing, though, Doc, not mine. I didn't have a damned thing to do with it."

Doc smiled.

"I'm not so sure about that. This particular strand of Jensen blood is very powerful, and it runs through their veins. If nothing

452

else, that gave them something of an advantage starting out. They have keen minds and quick reflexes and strong bodies." Doc added dryly, "None of which came from me. Of that you can be certain."

"Don't underestimate yourself," Luke said. "Anyway, I'm not sure it would be a good idea to tell them. They probably wouldn't want a scruffy old bounty hunter for a father. Hell, Doc, I'll never *be* their father in anything but blood. They've already got somebody who's their pa in every other way."

"Now you're the one who shouldn't underestimate yourself. But take some time and think about it. Just not for too long, all right?"

"Why not? What's the hurry?"

"The way trouble follows you Jensens around, you never know how much time any of you have left! If you have something to say, it's probably wise to go ahead and say it."

Doc had a point there, Luke thought. Maybe those Jensen boys were going to get a brand-new pa for Christmas, whether they wanted one or not!

CHAPTER 40

The next day was Christmas Eve. Sally was up even earlier than usual to finish all the last-minute preparations, getting everything ready except for the wild turkey Smoke had brought in. He and Preacher had gone hunting the day before, and the turkey was plucked and hanging in the smokehouse. Sally would roast it the next morning so it would be ready for Christmas dinner.

When Adelaide got up, Sally put her to work in the parlor, stringing a few more strands of red berries to go on the Christmas tree. She fed breakfast to the men and then shooed all of them out of the house, prompting a grinning comment from Smoke.

"I reckon Sally doesn't want us underfoot today, boys. That's all right. There's a nice warm bunkhouse out there, where we'll be welcome."

Doc took a deck of cards from a coat pocket and asked, "Do any of your men like to play poker, Smoke?"

That drew laughter from his companions, except for Luke, who smiled briefly but otherwise kept a solemn expression on his face, as if he were in deep thought about something.

"Just don't clean them out, Doc," Smoke said. "That wouldn't be a very nice thing to do on the day before Christmas."

The snow had stopped falling, although the clouds remained. About eight inches of the white stuff had piled up overnight. The air was cold enough to keep the snow from melting, but it lacked the bitter edge it sometimes had here in the high country.

Late in the morning, Monte Carson rode in. Smoke was glad to see the sheriff but was somewhat puzzled by his visit.

"What brings you out here on a day like this, Monte?" Smoke asked as he ushered the lawman into the parlor. Sally had relented enough to allow them to enter her domain. Adelaide sat quietly on one side of the room, still stringing berries for decorations.

"A couple of telegrams came for you, and I volunteered to deliver 'em," Monte replied as he opened his coat. "Brought out a pile of mail from the post office for you, too." He smiled. "I reckon mainly, though, those

455

were just excuses to ride out here and wish you folks a Merry Christmas."

He took a handful of envelopes from inside his coat and gave them to Smoke, who dropped the regular mail on a small table and opened the Western Union envelope containing two telegraph flimsies. He read the messages and nodded.

"Good news? Bad news? Not that it's any of my business either way, I reckon," Monte said.

"From my lawyers," said Smoke. "A hearing's been scheduled in Denver for the first week of January. The court is going to take up Aguilar's claim that he really owns the Sugarloaf and most of the rest of the valley."

"There's no chance he's actually going to win, is there?"

Smoke shook his head and said, "Not much of one. If there was, he wouldn't have resorted to those bushwhack attempts. I don't know if I'm going to wait that long to settle this, though."

Monte frowned and said, "Hold on a minute, Smoke. You're not talking about taking the law into your own hands, are you? Because I can't allow that any more than I can when Aguilar tries it."

"We're not going to ride in shooting, if

that's what you mean. But I think there's a good chance Hinton and those other gun-wolves will start the ball when they see that their string has played out."

Monte shook his head. "I wish it hadn't come to this," he said.

"So do I. But you know I'm not going to let anybody steal my home from me."

"Yeah. And I can't say as I really blame you."

Sally came into the room and greeted the lawman with a hug and a kiss on the cheek.

"I thought I heard your voice, Monte," she said. "I hope you're not here on official business."

"Well, not really. Just dropping off the mail and some telegrams for Smoke."

"Being a deliveryman isn't part of the sheriff's job now, is it?"

Monte chuckled and said, "No, but you notice I timed my visit to when dinner might be ready soon."

Sally laughed, too, and told him, "You're invited to stay, of course. In fact . . . why don't you have dinner with us today and then come back and help us celebrate Christmas tomorrow?"

"You already have a lot of company —"

"So one more won't matter," Sally said. "Please say you'll join us."

"I don't see how I can say no," Monte told her. "Thanks, Sally. I appreciate this more than you know."

She hugged him again. Smoke had a pretty good idea why she had insisted on the invitation. Monte's wife had passed away a while back, and Sally didn't want him to be alone on Christmas. She would have taken in every stray and orphan in the world if it was possible, Smoke knew.

He put a hand on Monte's shoulder and said, "Until dinner's ready, why don't you come on out to the bunkhouse with me? There's a big poker game going on, and we can spectate."

They went out, and Sally returned to the kitchen. Adelaide stayed where she was, working on the string of berries, for a couple of minutes.

Then she put the berries aside, stood up, and moved over to the little table where Smoke had dropped the mail. In apparent idle curiosity, she picked up the stack of envelopes and began looking through them. She grew tense at the sight of one of them, set the others down, and stared at the envelope in her hand for a long moment.

Then she folded it so it would be smaller, stuck it inside her dress, and returned to the chair where she had been sitting. She picked up the string of berries again, and after a minute or so she began humming a Christmas carol under her breath.

All the churches in Big Rock got together for the annual Christmas Eve service, putting aside denominational and doctrinal differences for this holy evening. The service was held in a different church each year. This year, the citizens of the town and the surrounding valley would be gathering in the Ranney Street Baptist Church. Before that, there would be a Christmas social held in the town hall.

Everyone at the Sugarloaf began getting ready in the middle of the afternoon, in both the ranch house and the bunkhouse. The cowboys would be decked out in their Sunday best, even though it wasn't actually Sunday. Sally would be breathtakingly lovely, Smoke knew, because she always was.

Preacher would clean up, too, although that sometimes went against his nature. Smoke recalled that the first time he had ever laid eyes on the mountain man, Preacher had reminded him of Santa Claus . . . although an exceedingly grimy Saint Nick.

Sally had some nice children's clothes on hand from the various times she had provided temporary homes for orphans in the past. She did some fast sewing to adapt them to fit Bodie, Hannah, and Teddy.

Ace and Chance, as well as Luke, had only their usual clothes, but they shaved and donned fresh garb and looked respectable, especially Chance, who was always something of a dandy. He loaned a clean suit to Doc, as well, even though the coat and trousers were too big on the gambler.

All in all, they made a pretty respectable-looking bunch, thought Smoke as they mounted up and climbed into buggies and started into Big Rock late on the afternoon of Christmas Eve, leaving only a few of the hands on the ranch to keep an eye on the place. The men had drawn lots to see to whom that chore would fall.

When they reached the settlement, the main street was already crowded with horses, wagons, buggies, and carriages. People thronged on the boardwalks. They had come from miles around to worship together.

The group from the Sugarloaf was going first to Louis Longmont's, where the usual drinking and gambling activities had been curtailed for the day. Louis had served a good dinner to those in town who needed it and couldn't afford it. He did this every year, one way that he tried to pay back the community for welcoming him.

As they passed the hotel, with Smoke at the reins of the buggy carrying him and Sally, he glanced over and saw Don Juan Sebastian Aguilar and Doña Mariana emerging from the building. They looked resplendent in their best clothes. Mariana saw them and waved and smiled as she called, *"Hola,* Sally*! Feliz Navidad!"*

"You have to stop, Smoke," Sally told him quietly.

"Yeah, I reckon so," he said, but his jaw was tight as he made the reply. He pulled back on the reins and brought the buggy horse to a stop.

Mariana hurried over to the buggy and reached up to clasp Sally's gloved hands with her own.

"It is good to see you again," she said. "Are you attending the Christmas Eve service later?"

"Of course," Sally said. "We always do when we're in town at this time of year."

"And Sebastian and I will, as well, since we, too, are now citizens of this valley."

Smoke wanted to say something, but he caught the warning glance that Sally threw his way and kept his mouth shut. He even managed to force a semblance of a smile onto his face.

Aguilar remained on the boardwalk, regarding Smoke with an impassive expression as he clenched a cigarillo between his teeth. As his eyes met Smoke's, he nodded curtly, a gesture that Smoke returned.

"We will see you later," Mariana told Sally. "Merry Christmas."

"And *Feliz Navidad* to you and your husband," Sally replied.

Travis Hinton had ambled out of the hotel behind the Aguilars. The Texas gunman stood on the boardwalk, with one shoulder leaned against an awning post. He smiled lazily at Smoke. The tension between the two men was thick. Smoke knew that sooner or later, Hinton would have to test his speed against him. To such a man, being the fastest draw wasn't just everything. It was the only thing.

Farther back in the procession, Luke drove the wagon he had brought from Utah. Beside him on the seat, with their faces scrubbed and shining, were the three youngsters. They were chattering happily, even the normally solemn Bodie. Luke had made a quick trip into Big Rock that morning to buy a present for each of them. Toy soldiers for the boys and a doll for Hannah, all purchased at Goldstein's Mercantile. He didn't know if they had ever gotten Christmas presents in the past, but they were going to this year.

Luke's mind was full of something else, though: the shocking news that Doc Monday had broken to him the previous night. He glanced ahead of him at Ace and Chance, who were riding on a buckboard with Doc. His sons, thought Luke. The words just sounded wrong to him . . . but yet, when he looked at them now, he saw traces of Lettie in their faces. He even spotted the resemblance to the face he saw in the mirror every morning. If Doc hadn't told him the truth, he might not have ever noticed those things, but now they were inescapable.

And he still didn't know what he was going to do about any of it. The simplest thing, he knew, would be to just celebrate Christmas, keep his mouth shut, and ride away when the festivities were over. Ace and Chance had lived their own lives up until now. He didn't have any right to intrude on that, did he?

But if it was a question of rights . . . they had a right to know their real father. And he had a right to acknowledge his sons. . . .

"What's wrong, Mr. Jensen?"

The question from Bodie broke into

Luke's reverie. He gave a little shake of his head and said, "What do you mean? Nothing's wrong."

"Well, you were frowning like you were worried about something."

"Not really," Luke assured him. "I reckon some fellas just get in the habit of worrying all the time, and that's not a good way to be. You don't want to do that."

Hannah piped up. "Ever since we got here, I haven't been worried about a thing."

"That's good, darlin'," Luke told her. "You just keep on feeling that way."

And he would keep on trying to figure out what he should do about Ace and Chance, but he had a hunch there weren't going to be any good answers coming to him.

CHAPTER 41

Although the Christmas Eve service was a serious occasion, there was still plenty of the joyousness of the season to be found in Big Rock today. Everyone looked forward to the Christmas social held in the town hall before the service that evening, with music and singing, punch and apple cider, cookies and cakes, and good fellowship for all. The crowd for that began gathering late in the afternoon.

Preacher's arm was linked with Adelaide's as he escorted her into the town hall. He said, "It's been a while since I been to one of these whoop-de-dos, but as I recall, they're pretty nice."

"I'm sure it will be, Arthur. I mean, Preacher."

"I've told you, I don't care what you call me."

"I was thinking," she said, "that this might be a good opportunity to make an announcement, since everyone you care about is here. If you had anything to announce, that is."

Preacher's forehead furrowed. He said, "I sorta been thinkin' about the same thing. Ain't quite ever'body here . . . Smoke said ol' Matt, him and Luke's brother, ain't gonna be able to make it this year . . . but this is a big bunch of Jensens in one place, all right."

Adelaide squeezed his arm.

"Whatever you think is best, Arthur. I know you'll do the right thing."

In another part of the hall, Ace, Chance, and Doc were paying a visit to the punch bowl. Doc's hand shook a little as he lifted a cup of the sweet concoction to his mouth, but he managed not to spill any of it as he drank.

"I'm sorry you had to go through so much trouble to get here, Doc," Ace told him, "but I have to say, I'm glad it gave us an opportunity to spend Christmas together again."

Chance said, "We should have come up to the sanitarium first, instead of here to Big Rock."

"Well, as it turned out, I wouldn't have been there," Doc replied with a shake of his head. "Anyway, this is where you boys really

466

belong, with all these other Jensens."

"The same last name doesn't mean we're family, no matter what Sally and Smoke keep saying," Ace said.

"You should listen to them," Doc said firmly. "I understand that Smoke and Luke's other brother, Matt, is adopted, and yet they consider him every bit as much a member of the family as any of the rest of them. So you and Chance should certainly —" Doc stopped and shook his head. "Nope, I've said all I have to say."

That puzzled Ace, but Doc wouldn't do anything else except chat about Christmas and the brothers' plans for the coming year, which, as usual, were pretty vague. When you spent your days drifting from adventure to adventure, worrying too much about the future didn't really make sense.

Smoke and Sally were talking to Monte Carson and several other of Big Rock's leading citizens when the buzz of happy conversation in the hall suddenly fell off. Smoke looked around and saw that Aguilar and Mariana had just entered the hall, followed by Hinton and several more hard-bitten men who were part of Aguilar's gun crew.

"You reckon he's looking to make trouble?" asked Monte under his breath.

"More than likely, Doña Mariana insisted

that they come," Smoke said. "She's been trying mighty hard to see to it that they fit in here."

"She has," Sally agreed. "I'm a little sorry that it's not going to come to anything for her. She can't help it that her husband is going to lose out on that phony claim of his."

Smoke chuckled and said, "You sound pretty sure of that."

"I am," Sally declared. "Nobody's getting their hands on the Sugarloaf."

That determination didn't surprise Smoke one bit. It was one of the reasons he had fallen in love with Sally in the first place.

The noise level in the room went up again as the reaction to the Aguilars' arrival wore off. Most of the cowboys were gathered around the table where bowls of apple cider had been placed. It wasn't hard cider, and it wasn't supposed to be spiked, but a few dollops of Who-Hit-John always found their way into the mix from flasks that the punchers smuggled in, and Monte Carson always looked the other way about that. Not so the good women of the town, so the cowboys had to be careful and not let themselves get caught sweetening the cider, or else they'd get a tongue-lashing and maybe wind up kicked out of the social. They were willing to run the risk, though.

Smoke had noticed a number of unfamiliar faces in the crowd this year. Some of them might be Aguilar's men, he supposed, but others were simply newcomers to the valley. Ranch hands came and went, and so did others who moved in to try farming in the area, although it was more suited to raising cattle. Few people in the world were more stubbornly determined than farmers. Smoke knew that from being raised on a farm himself, back in the Missouri Ozarks.

As he thought about that, he missed his father, Emmett, long dead now, murdered by evil men, who had had justice delivered to them by Smoke, in the form of hot lead. Although the pain of the loss had eased over time, it had never gone away entirely and likely never would. Smoke hoped his father was looking down on them now, pleased with what the Jensen family had become.

Chairs were lined up along the walls, and after a while, Doc Monday went over to one of them and sat down. He got tired easily these days, and the stiffness and pain in his neck and shoulders were worse when he stood up for too long. He leaned back in the chair and rested the back of his head against the wall, grateful for its support.

He smiled as he watched Ace and Chance talking to a couple of young women from Big Rock. Chance was flirting shamelessly, of course; the youngster really had an eye for the ladies. Ace was more reserved, but he seemed to be enjoying the conversation, too.

A man sat down on the chair next to Doc, who glanced over at him and saw only a stranger carrying his coat over his arm. The man was middle aged, with a rugged face that showed the deep tan of someone who had spent much of his life outdoors. He still had his hat on, but it was pushed back to reveal gray hair.

"Howdy," the man said. "You're the one they call Doc Monday, aren't you?"

"That's right," replied Doc. He supposed the man was just trying to be friendly.

His next words seemed to confirm that, as the man said, "My name's Thackery. Lane Thackery. That mean anything to you?"

The question surprised Doc, who said, "No, I don't believe so. Should it?"

"I thought maybe your pard Bill Malkin might have mentioned it."

As if that statement wasn't surprising enough, Doc felt a sudden pressure against his side. Thackery had just jabbed a hard, round object against his ribs. Doc caught his breath.

"Yeah, that's a gun barrel," Thackery said quietly, with an apparently friendly half-smile still on his face. "Nobody can see it with my coat draped over my arm like this. If you don't want it to go off, you won't raise a ruckus."

Doc's pulse pounded hard. After a moment, he got control of his shock and was able to say, "I don't know what you want, but you're all wrong about Bill Malkin being my friend."

"That's not what he said, and he was just about to die, so I don't reckon he'd lie about a thing like that. That son of a bitch and I were partners for a long time, and I don't appreciate being double-crossed."

"You were part of his gang," Doc breathed. "I remember seeing your name now, in that newspaper article. You're one of the men who held up that train . . ."

"And stole fifty thousand dollars, which we never got our share of. Well, it's all mine now, because you're going to tell me where it is."

Doc thought about that, and as he did, he began to laugh.

"What's so damned funny?" Thackery grated.

"You think I know where Malkin hid that

loot? You're wrong about everything! He wanted to kill me so I couldn't tell anybody who he really was. He never would have shared that secret with me."

Thackery didn't look convinced, but some doubt had entered his eyes. He said, "You're lying because you want all that money for yourself."

"Money's not all that important to me anymore, Thackery," Doc said. "And to tell you the truth, that gun doesn't scare me much, either. A man gets to be my age, with his health the way mine is, he doesn't give a damn about such things."

Thackery hesitated but then said, "I don't believe a word of it. You'll talk, once we get you out of here. I'll see to that. I know ways of making anybody talk."

Malkin had threatened him with torture, too. Doc knew now, as he had known then, that he couldn't withstand much of it. But he wasn't going to allow things to go that far.

"You might as well put the gun away and get out of here," he said, "because I'm about to stand up and call my friends for help —"

"If you do that, those two boys you care so much about will be dead a second later," Thackery cut in. At Doc's surprised glance, he went on, "Yeah, I know about those

Jensen boys. I asked around about you when my men and I drifted into town earlier, and I found out how you raised them like your own sons. I've got men watching them right now. All I have to do is give the signal, and they'll put bullets in those kids' brains before they ever know what's happening. Is that what you want, Doc?"

Doc felt his whole body trembling now, from a combination of his physical condition and the fear for Ace's and Chance's safety that welled up inside him.

"Leave them out of it," he said. "They don't know anything about Bill Malkin's money."

"*My* money," Thackery said. "Nothing has to happen to those kids. All you have to do is come with me and tell me what I want to know."

He could do only the first part of that, Doc realized. He couldn't tell Thackery where the loot was hidden, because he honestly had no idea. But if he made the outlaw believe that he had such knowledge . . . if he cooperated now . . . Ace and Chance would be safe.

"All right," he said. "If you'll promise that Ace and Chance won't be hurt —"

"You have my word on that. I don't have any interest in those two."

473

Doc put his hands on his knees and said, "I'll come with you, then."

Thackery was bound to be disappointed, and Doc felt certain he would die before the night was over, but none of that mattered. Only the boys . . .

The gun went away from his side. Thackery stood up at the same time Doc did. The outlaw said, "Don't get any ideas, just because I'm not holding a gun on you anymore. I can still snuff out those two little bastards' lives with a nod if you force my hand."

"Don't worry. That's not going to happen."

"Come on, then." Thackery started toward a side door that led out of the town hall. He had a hand on Doc's arm, guiding him.

As Doc moved toward the door, he wondered if Thackery was lying about the men with orders to kill Ace and Chance. It could all be a bluff. Thackery might be the only enemy here.

But he couldn't afford to risk that, Doc decided. He'd been a gambler all his life, but he wasn't going to gamble with the lives that meant more to him than anything else in the world. Those stakes were just too high.

Thackery opened the door, and the two of

them slipped outside, into the shadows. The night of Christmas Eve had fallen over Big Rock.

CHAPTER 42

Whenever Chance started sweet-talking some local girl, Ace was always wary of the possibility that she might have a beau who would take offense and they would all wind up in a brawl. He didn't want to abuse Smoke and Sally's hospitality by having that happen, and for sure not on Christmas Eve!

However, the two young ladies from Big Rock they were talking to had volunteered the information that they didn't have sweethearts at the moment, so Ace supposed they were safe. And he had to admit, the one who seemed to be the most interested in him, whose name was Mary Lou, was sure pretty. . . .

But why in blazes was Doc sneaking out of the town hall with some hombre Ace had never seen before?

The first thing Ace thought of was that Doc was going to play in a poker game somewhere. The lure of the pasteboards had always been difficult for Doc to resist.

However, Doc's face didn't have any of the usual enthusiasm for the cards that it would normally possess in such circumstances. In fact, Doc looked strained and upset about something, Ace realized, and he couldn't let that pass without trying to find out what was wrong.

He touched Chance's coat sleeve and said, "I'll be back in a minute."

"Where are you going?" Chance wanted to know. "We're having a good time here."

"Yeah, I know. I won't be gone long."

Chance looked annoyed, and the two girls appeared puzzled, but Ace didn't linger to offer any explanations. He made his way through the crowd and out of the hall by the same door Doc and the stranger had used a minute earlier.

The town hall was next to a vacant lot, and a grove of trees grew behind that open ground. Ace heard horses moving around and looked toward the trees. His keen eyes picked out large, dark shapes against the pale background of snow. Saddle leather creaked as men mounted up over there.

"Doc?" Ace called. "Doc, where are you going?"

"Ace, don't —"

The urgent cry, cut off so abruptly, made

Ace stiffen in alarm. His hand darted toward the place where his gun was usually holstered, but too late, he remembered that everyone had taken off their gunbelts as they entered the hall for the social and had left the weapons on several shelves built just inside the doors for that purpose.

He might be unarmed, but that didn't mean Ace was going to stand by and do nothing while Doc was in obvious trouble. He paused only long enough to kick open the door he had just closed behind him. Then he yelled, "Chance!" and charged toward the trees.

"Ace, no!" Doc cried, but it was too late. Several men leaped from the shadows under the trees and surrounded Ace. Hard fists swung at the young man.

Ace's momentum bowled over a couple of his attackers, and his own rocklike fists lashed out. A few of his punches went wild in the bad light, but most landed solidly.

"Bryson! Eberle!" a man yelled harshly. "Get that damn kid!"

Ace's swift blows had cleared an area around him. He heard the scuff of a footstep behind him and started to turn, but before he was halfway around, from the corner of his eye he saw a gun barrel swinging toward his head. He tried to jerk out of the way but was too late. The gun crashed against his skull. His knees buckled, and he felt them hit the ground.

He didn't feel it when he landed face-first in the snow, though. He was already unconscious.

Chance loved the smiles on the girls' faces, and the sound of their laughter when he said something witty was music to his ears. But Ace's shout from outside made all that disappear. Chance knew from the sound of the cry that something was wrong. He turned and broke into a run toward the side door that had just flown open, the two young ladies totally forgotten behind him.

He burst out into the night and spotted a number of men on horseback milling around under the trees behind the vacant lot beside the town hall. It was too dark for him to be able to tell anything about them, but since nothing else seemed to be going on out here, those riders had to be the reason for Ace's shout of alarm.

"Ace!" Chance yelled as he started toward the men and horses.

"We only need one of them!" a man barked. Instantly, Colt flame bloomed in the darkness like crimson flowers. Chance dived forward as bullets whipped over him.

He wished he had his Smith & Wesson, but he'd left it inside the hall, just like everybody else attending this Christmas Eve social.

He couldn't open fire, anyway, he realized, because he didn't know where Ace was and couldn't risk any shots. Those men, whoever they were, must have taken Ace prisoner.

Hooves pounded the ground as the riders wheeled their mounts and galloped away, still throwing lead behind them. The shouts, followed by the burst of gunfire, had attracted plenty of attention, and others were spilling out of the town hall now, calling questions. Chance heard Smoke shout, "Ace! Chance! Where are you?"

Chance scrambled to his feet and yelled, "Smoke, get everybody back insi—"

Something slammed into his left arm and knocked him spinning. He wound up on his belly in the snow again. His arm was numb, which told him one of those parting shots had struck him. The numbness wouldn't last long, and then his arm would hurt like blazes.

Smoke dropped to a knee beside him, gun in hand. Chance supposed Smoke had grabbed the weapon before he hurried out here. Smoke thrust the Colt toward the riders, who were no longer visible, even though the hoofbeats of their horses could be heard.

Chance managed to get his right hand up and closed it around the gun barrel.

"Don't . . . shoot," he gasped. "I think they've got . . . Ace!"

"How bad are you hit?" asked Smoke as he lowered the revolver.

"Just nicked . . . my arm. I'll be all right. You'd better . . . get after them."

"Why would somebody kidnap Ace?"

"Dunno . . . but he came out here . . . like something was wrong . . . and then I . . . heard him yell . . ."

Luke had joined Smoke, and he was armed, too. He put a hand on Chance's uninjured shoulder and said, "Take it easy, son. We won't let anything happen to your brother. Are you *sure* you're all right?"

The level of concern in Luke's voice surprised Chance a little, even under the circumstances. He said, "Yeah, I'll be . . . fine. Just go after them!"

Then Smoke and Luke were gone, and Sally and some of the townspeople had taken their place. Chance felt hands on him, lifting him and helping him back into the town hall. He caught glimpses of Smoke, Luke, Preacher, and Monte Carson, all of them grim faced as they buckled on gun-belts.

But there was no sign of Doc Monday

anywhere in the hall, and Chance's spirits sank as he wondered if the kidnappers had taken Doc, too.

Doc couldn't stop shaking. Lane Thackery demanded, "What the hell's wrong with you?" The outlaw had Doc on the back of the horse with him, left arm clamped painfully taut around him to hold him in place.

"If . . . if you hurt those boys, I'll —"

Thackery hit him on the side of the head with an open hand. The blow rocked Doc, but he couldn't fall off the horse with Thackery holding him so tightly.

"You won't do a damned thing," the outlaw said. "But if you don't want to listen to the one you called Ace screaming in agony, you'll tell me where to find that damned money!"

Doc's head sagged forward. After a moment, he said, "I . . . I'm sick. I'm going to pass out —"

"You'd better not, and you'd better not up and die on us, either. Because if you're dead, there's no reason in hell to keep that boy alive."

Doc knew Thackery meant it. Thackery's ridiculous assumption that Doc knew where the loot was hidden was the only thing keeping either of them alive.

The group of riders, half a dozen or so, galloped through the night, with snow flying up from their horses' hooves. Doc had no idea where they were going, other than away from Big Rock. Thackery was probably looking for a place where he could stop and carry out the torture he'd been threatening.

That might not be easy, though. One of the other men raised his voice above the hoofbeats and said, "All that shooting's liable to bring a posse after us, Lane! We need to hole up somewhere and get ready for a fight."

Another man added, "They'll be able to follow our trail through the snow, even in the dark."

Thackery cursed bitterly and said, "Don't you think I know that? We just need a few minutes . . ."

A few minutes to force him to talk, thought Doc. That was what Thackery meant.

"Up there on that hill," Thackery exclaimed suddenly. He veered the horse carrying him and Doc toward the left. They came to a slope and began ascending it. The climb was steep enough that the horses had to struggle, especially the two mounts carrying double.

When they reached the top, Doc saw a number of boulders bulking up in the snow. Thackery reined in and told his men, "The rest of you can hold off anybody who comes after us while I find out what we need to know."

An older outlaw rubbed his mouth and asked, "What'll we do then? Fight our way out? Some of us are liable to get killed."

"Fifty thousand dollars is worth running a few risks," snapped Thackery. "A couple of you grab this bastard and hang on to him."

Strong hands closed on Doc and lifted him down from the horse's back. He didn't try to get away from the outlaws, since he knew it would be futile. He wasn't strong enough to break their grips.

"He's shakin' like a leaf," one of them said. "He must be so scared he's pissin' his pants."

"He'll be doin' more than that by the time Thackery's through with him. And if Thackery can't get him to talk, I'll bet Bryson can. I've heard that he learned a few things from the Apaches."

Meanwhile, Thackery had dismounted and was telling two more of his men to place Ace on the ground. Doc watched in dismay as the young man was stretched out next to one of the boulders. Ace groaned and moved around a little as he started to come to.

Thackery came over and took hold of Doc's arm, telling the other men, "Get behind those rocks and be ready to fight if you have to. Del, you have your knife?"

"Of course I do," a lean, wolfish owlhoot replied. "And I don't mind usin' it."

"Get to work on the kid, then. He's waking up. I want him wide awake and screaming." Thackery drew his gun and jabbed the barrel into Doc's ribs again. "You're gonna watch the whole thing, mister. But the sooner you tell me what I want to know, the sooner the boy won't be hurting anymore."

Doc gasped from horror and the pain in his side and said, "That's because . . . because you'll kill both of us!"

"I promise you, being dead is better than what Del's going to do to him. So what's it gonna be, Doc? Tell me where to find that money . . . or listen to him scream?"

CHAPTER 43
BIG ROCK

Smoke, Luke, and Preacher hadn't brought saddle mounts to town, but all the Sugarloaf hands had ridden in, so the three of them borrowed horses for the pursuit.

While they were quickly getting ready to go, Pearlie and Cal approached, and the foreman declared, "We're comin' with you, Smoke."

"No, only one of you," Smoke said. "You figure out which, but do it fast. The one who stays behind is responsible for seeing that Sally and Mrs. DuBois and the Trafford kids get back to the ranch safely after the Christmas Eve service."

Monte Carson came up in time to hear that and said, "I don't know if they're going to have the service, Smoke. With a gunfight and a couple of men kidnapped and another wounded, folks are mighty upset."

"Then it's a good time for them to get together and pray for good things to happen, as well as giving thanks for the birth of the Lord," Smoke said. "Pass the word about that, Monte."

"I'll tell somebody else to do it. I'm coming with you, too."

By this time, Pearlie had laid down the law to Cal, pulling rank as foreman to order the young cowboy to stay here and keep an eye on things in town, then see to it that the ladies and the children got back to the Sugarloaf if Smoke and the others hadn't returned by then. Cal wasn't happy about it, but he wasn't going to argue too much with Pearlie.

Smoke walked over to where Chance sat on one of the chairs against the wall. The young man's coat was off, and his shirtsleeve had been cut away to reveal the hole that a bullet had punched through the upper part of his arm. The local medico had cleaned and bandaged the wound, and as Smoke approached, Chance started to get to his feet.

Smoke waved him back into the chair and said, "I know what you're thinking, Chance, but you're hurt. You need to stay here."

"I can sit a saddle just fine," argued Chance, "and it's not my gun arm that's wounded."

"The doctor says you lost quite a bit of

blood, though, and it's best you take it easy. But don't worry. We're going to bring back Ace and Doc."

Chance shook his head and said, "I just can't figure out who might have done this. That fellow Malkin is dead."

"He may have had a partner, though." Smoke didn't want to take the time to explain about the other prints he had seen in the clearing where Malkin died. "Whoever it is, we'll take care of them. You've got my word on that."

Chance nodded and sat back with a weary sigh. He winced as a fresh twinge of pain shot through his injured arm.

Smoke gestured to the men who were going with him, and stalked out of the town hall. Some of the Sugarloaf hands were holding horses for them right outside. The delay while everyone was getting ready had seemed gratingly long to Smoke, but in actuality, only a few minutes had passed since the shooting died away. The men swung up into saddles and rode around the hall to pick up the trail, which was clearly visible in the snow, leading away from the settlement toward the northwest.

Inside the hall, Chance heard the swift rataplan of hoofbeats and wished once again that he was going with them. Knowing that

Ace and Doc were out there somewhere in the night, in danger, gnawed at his guts. Several of the local young ladies gathered around to fuss over him, but for once, the attention of some pretty girls didn't mean a blasted thing to Chance.

After a while, Sally came over, shooed the girls away, and asked, "Is there anything I can get you, Chance? Some punch or cider?"

"No, I'm not thirsty, but thanks, anyway, Mrs. Jensen."

"You know by now that you can call me Sally," she chided him gently, smiling to take any sting out of the words.

"Yeah, I know. That business about being a member of the family —"

"Matt!" exclaimed Sally.

"Yeah, like Matt being Smoke's adopted brother —"

"No, I mean it's Matt. He's here!"

Chance looked up and saw Matt Jensen striding through the crowd toward them. Tall, broad shouldered, fair haired, he was a bit of a drifter like Ace and Chance and had held down many exciting jobs over the years: army scout, shotgun guard, trouble-shooter for the railroad, and more.

Smiling, he embraced Sally and then extended his hand to Chance. They had met before, during another eventful Christmas season.

"Good to see you again, Chance," Matt said. "I understand that I got here a little too late and missed all the excitement."

"Not too late at all," Chance said as he got to his feet and clasped Matt's hand. "I was just resting up a mite, but now I'm ready to go after Smoke and the others, and you can come with me."

Sally said, "Chance, that's not what you're supposed to be doing at all!"

"It's my brother who's in danger. Matt, would you stay behind if Smoke or Luke was in trouble?"

"Not hardly," Matt admitted. "If Smoke told you to stay here, though —"

Fresh determination welled up inside Chance. He picked up his bloodstained coat and said, "I'm going after them, one way or the other. You can come with me or stay behind, whatever you want."

"Stay behind?" Matt repeated. "You don't know me very well, do you? Jensens don't stay behind."

"Damn right," said Chance.

Doña Mariana Aguilar was standing with her husband when she saw him stiffen and glare across the room.

"What is it, Sebastian?" she asked.

He didn't answer her. Instead, he turned and beckoned to Travis Hinton, who was leaning against the wall not far away. The gunman straightened and drifted over to Aguilar, who said tensely, "We must make our move tonight."

"What's wrong, Don Sebastian?"

"Things have changed," snapped Aguilar. "There is no longer any time for delay."

Hinton shrugged and said, "That's all right with me, boss. I never did like the idea of sitting around and letting a bunch of lawyers handle things, anyway. Especially when we knew how that was going to turn out."

"Gather the men and be ready," Aguilar responded with a curt nod.

As Hinton moved away to do the don's bidding, Mariana grasped her husband's arm and said, "Sebastian, whatever is going on here, I do not like it."

He turned to her with a savage scowl on his hawklike face.

"The time for worrying about what you like or do not like is past," he told her. "Now you will do as I say. And tonight what we came for . . . will be ours!"

As the man with the knife in his hand knelt

beside Ace and reached out toward him, Doc said abruptly, "Wait!"

"You're going to talk before Del even gets started?" asked Thackery. He chuckled. "He's going to be disappointed."

"Look, I don't know where Malkin hid that loot —"

Thackery said, "Start carving, Del."

"No! I don't know," Doc insisted, "but I can tell you how to find out. Malkin told me that he wrote down the location and sent it in a letter to someone . . . a woman . . . and he had the letters she wrote back to him, there at the sanitarium. You can go back there and get those letters, and they'll tell you where to find her. Then *she* can tell you where the money is."

Doc had made up that tale on the spur of the moment, taking bits and pieces of what he knew about Malkin and putting them together with pure conjecture. It all added up to a lie, but if it was a convincing enough lie, it might send Thackery back to the sanitarium.

Of course, if the outlaws believed what Doc had just said, they had no reason to keep him and Ace alive, but all Doc was trying to do right now was muddle Thackery's mind and keep the man with the knife from torturing Ace. Maybe, as Thackery had

492

said, a quick death was better. . . .

"You're lying," Thackery said. "You don't expect me to believe that, do you?"

"It's the truth. My God, at this point, what good is a lie going to do me?"

The man with the knife said, "He sounds pretty convincin', Lane. But why don't you let me cut on this boy a little, anyway, just to be sure?"

"Yeah, that's a good idea —" Thackery began, but before he could finish, one of the outlaws hidden behind the boulders called, "Riders comin', Thackery! Looks like a bunch from town on our trail!"

Thackery turned his head and said, "We're ready for 'em. They won't know we're up here, so let them get closer and then blow them out of their saddles!"

The odds were good that an ambush would work, thought Doc. And it was possible that Chance was among the pursuers! If that was the case, when the outlaws opened fire and bullets scythed down on the approaching riders, Chance might be killed. Doc couldn't allow that, any more than he could stand by and watch Ace be tortured.

He was out of time now. Out of options. Lying and delaying were no good. The only thing he could do was warn the others somehow, and to accomplish that, he would have to rely on his body. His damned weak, treacherous body . . .

When Thackery had turned slightly to order his men to ready the ambush, the barrel of his gun had left Doc's side. Doc saw it in the faint light that reflected from the snow surrounding them. He drew in a deep breath and willed his hands to stop shaking. That had never worked before . . . but he had never been faced with such a desperate dilemma, either.

A couple of seconds ticked past. Doc's hands stilled.

And then he moved, lunging at the gun, grasping the barrel with his left hand, and forcing it up while his right closed around the cylinder and he searched frantically for the trigger guard. Thackery yelled in surprise and tried to wrench the gun away from him, but Doc clung to it with all his strength. He found Thackery's finger on the trigger and shoved his finger in with it, then pressed back. . . .

The gun boomed, the report rolling down the snow-covered hill to the pursuers who were closing in.

A few feet away, Ace wasn't quite as groggy as he was pretending to be. His head still throbbed from being knocked out, but he thought he could move if he needed to. The question was how quickly he could react. He had been waiting for an opening to turn the tables on their captors.

Doc's unexpected action gave him that opening. The outlaw called Del took his eyes off Ace when the gun went off. Ace's hands shot up to grab Del's wrist. He twisted and shoved as he jacknifed up from the ground. Del gasped as the blade he still held drove deep into his belly, with all of Ace's strength behind it.

Ace rammed his shoulder into Del's chest and knocked him over backward. Del's hands fell away from the knife's handle, allowing Ace to rip it free, opening a larger wound in the process. Ace made it to his knees and started to his feet, but as he came up, he saw Thackery backhand Doc and knock him loose from the gun. Doc staggered back a couple of steps.

Ace was about to rush Thackery, even though gun against knife made for bad odds. Before he could move, though, Thackery jerked the Colt toward him and fired.

At that same instant, Doc recovered and threw himself forward again. Ace heard the slug thud into Doc's frail form. He yelled, "No!" as Doc collapsed. Doc fell against

Thackery's legs, throwing him off-balance for a second.

That was long enough for Ace to flash across the intervening distance and ram the blade into Thackery's chest. The impact drove Thackery back a step. Ace grabbed the wrist of Thackery's gun hand and shoved the weapon aside, then yanked the knife out and stabbed the outlaw again. In and out the blade drove a third time, then a fourth, piercing Thackery's heart more than once. His mouth opened, but nothing came out but a strangled gasp. The gun slipped from nerveless fingers and fell to the ground. Thackery went down, and Ace let him go. Blind rage filled Ace, but the small part of his brain that was still working told him that Thackery was dead.

The other outlaws were still alive, though, and gun thunder filled the night, the darkness split by orange muzzle flashes. Ace had left the knife buried in Thackery's chest on the last thrust, but the gun the outlaw had dropped was a dark shape in the snow. Ace dived for it, scooped it up. He wanted to see about Doc, but a couple of the gang had turned from their concealment among the rocks and started throwing lead in his direction. Ace tilted the gun up and triggered it, spraying bullets among the rocks.

Some ricocheted with high-pitched whines, but others found their targets and drove outlaws back against the boulders.

Then hoofbeats pounded, and men on horseback were among the boulders, firing down at the remaining members of the gang, wiping them out or at least knocking them out of the fight.

"Ace! Doc! Where are you?"

That was Luke Jensen's voice, Ace realized. He cried, "Here!" and dropped the empty gun. He turned and scrambled over to Doc's sprawled form. Ace got his arms around the slender figure and lifted him, pushed with his feet until his back was against one of the boulders and Doc was lying across his lap, his head supported by the crook of Ace's right arm.

"Doc!" Ace said urgently. "Doc, how bad are you hurt?"

For a moment, Ace thought he was too late, that Doc was dead. Judging by the size of the dark bloodstain on his shirtfront, that might be the case. But then Doc coughed a little, and his eyelids flickered open.

"A-Ace . . . ? You're . . . all right?"

Ace could barely make out the husky whisper that came from Doc's lips. Blood trickled from a corner of the gambler's mouth. Ace leaned over him, cradling him as gently as possible, and said, "Yeah, I . . . I'm fine, Doc. Fine as can be. Not hurt at all."

"Ch-Chance?"

Ace was about to say that he didn't know, but before he could, one of the men who had charged up the hill to do battle with the outlaws dropped to his knees beside Doc and said, "I'm right here. I'm all right, too, Doc. Don't you worry. Looks like I caught up just in time."

Ace lifted his eyes to his brother. He wasn't surprised to see Chance among the men who had ridden to the rescue.

He was a little surprised, though, when Luke Jensen knelt beside them, as well, and reached out to grasp one of Doc's hands. Luke and Doc had just met the day before.

"How bad are you hit, Doc?" the bounty hunter asked.

Doc coughed again and said, "Bad enough . . . I think. This is . . . the last hand I'll play."

"Damn it, Doc," moaned Chance. "Don't say that."

"It's . . . true. You boys . . . both know that."

"We'll get you back to town —" Ace began.

Weakly, Doc shook his head. "Don't

waste . . . your time. Just . . . prop me up . . . a little. I need to . . . talk to Luke."

Confusion mixed with the grief that filled Ace's heart. He didn't know what Luke had to do with any of this, but clearly, it meant a lot to Doc, so carefully, he raised the slender figure in his arms.

"You know . . . what you need to do . . . Luke." Doc was fighting hard to get the words out now. "I was going to . . . give you the time . . . to make up your own mind . . . but now there's . . . no more time. And they deserve . . . deserve to know . . . the truth."

Luke's voice was more twisted with emotion than Ace had ever heard it as he said, "I know, Doc. I know you're right. I just don't know if *I* deserve to be . . . I mean, I never even —"

"You didn't know." Somewhere inside him, Doc found a little more strength. Ace saw him squeeze's Luke's hand. "Now you do. Now you know, and it's a good thing. I've . . . done my best. Now it . . . it's up to you . . ."

A long sigh came from Doc, and again, Ace thought he was gone. But the gambler had one more thing to say, and he wasn't cashing in his chips until he said it.

"I love you . . . boys . . ."

■ ■ ■ ■

It was a toss-up for Luke which had been the bigger surprise when the two riders caught up with the posse: the fact that Matt had shown up unexpectedly or that Chance had disregarded Smoke's orders and had followed them, anyway. Come to think of it, Chance being stubborn really wasn't that much of a shock.

He was a Jensen, after all.

Now, as Luke gently let go of Doc's hand, he drew in a deep, ragged breath. He had lived a hard life and generally kept his emotions well in check, unless he was mad as hell at some outlaw he was going after. What he was feeling now, though, was something he hadn't experienced in . . . well, ever!

He rose to his feet and looked down at Ace and Chance as they sat with Doc's body. Smoke came up and rested a hand on Luke's shoulder.

"You all right?" he asked.

"Yeah," Luke rasped. "All those varmints accounted for?"

"They are. I'm not sure what they were after, but I reckon Ace can explain all that . . . later."

Matt moved up on Luke's other side, as if

500

sensing that his brother might need him right now, and asked quietly, "What was that fella talking about, Luke? It sounded like you and him maybe knew something that nobody else does."

Slowly, Luke nodded. "That's true," he said. "We were the only two people in the world who *did* know. And now there's just me."

That was right, he realized. He *was* the only one who knew the truth. He could make up some lie, and if he did, he could still ride away. He could turn his back on the responsibilities he'd never known he had. It wasn't his fault, after all. Lettie had never told him. Hell, even *she* hadn't known when he rode off to war. But she'd known later, and she could have written to him before the boys were born. She hadn't, and even though they were good young men, he didn't owe them a damned thing. . . .

But even as those thoughts went through his head, he knew better. The bond was there, and it could never be broken. He should have figured it out before now, he told himself. He should have *sensed* it.

So there was only one thing left to do. As they looked up at him, he said, "Ace . . . Chance . . . I'm your father."

CHAPTER 44
BIG ROCK

Sally Jensen was annoyed. It seemed like *every* Christmas, something happened to ruin everyone's plans for a joyous holiday.

More than just being annoyed, though, she was downright mad. Mad that somebody would shoot Chance and kidnap Ace and Doc. Even though she knew it was better that she hadn't gone along with the men who had pursued the kidnappers, a part of her wished she could buckle on a gunbelt and throw her leg over a saddle like Smoke, Luke, and the others. She had fought evildoers side by side with Smoke in the past and was always willing to do so again.

Then Matt had shown up, and of course, he and Chance had charged off to join the chase. That was frustrating, too.

By mutual agreement, the social was cut short, and everyone who was left in town adjourned to the Baptist church for the Christmas Eve service. With the town in a state of uproar, that didn't last long, either. Several of the local ministers each gave a short message, the combined congregations sang a hymn, and then the benediction dismissed everyone into the night.

One thing Sally noticed about the service surprised her. Sebastian and Mariana Aguilar weren't there, and Mariana had specifically stated that they would be in attendance. Clearly, the events of the evening had changed their minds.

As they left the church and went back into the chilly night, Cal came up to Sally and asked, "Should we wait here in town for the others to get back or head for the Sugarloaf, Miss Sally?"

"Do you think Smoke will come straight back here?" she asked.

"Hard to say. The trail those varmints left led northwest out of town. There's no way of knowing how long it'll take the fellas to catch up to those no-good skunks, whoever they were. When it's all said and done, it might be closer and quicker for 'em to head back to the ranch instead. They'd do that for sure if —" Cal stopped short.

Sally asked the young cowboy, "If what, Cal? If someone was hurt and needed medical attention?"

"Yes, ma'am, that's what I was thinking,

503

all right. Smoke would go there if somebody needed patchin' up, and then would send a rider to town to fetch the doc."

"Then we'll go back to the Sugarloaf," Sally said. "We can't know for sure, but I believe the odds are that's where Smoke will go."

"I'll get everybody rounded up, then," Cal replied with a nod.

Sally had left Adelaide to watch the three children while she talked to Cal. When she rejoined them, Bodie looked up at her and said, "We're going to wait here for Mr. Jensen, aren't we? Mr. Luke Jensen, I mean."

"No, we're going back to the ranch," Sally told him. "Cal and I believe there's a better chance Luke and Smoke and the others will return there instead of coming here to town."

Hannah said, "But if we're not here, won't they get lost?"

Sally smiled and said, "No, dear. Don't ever worry about those men getting lost. I don't think it's possible. If they do come here and don't find us, they'll just ride on out to the ranch. We'll all be together again soon, I promise you that."

"Good," Hannah said firmly. "Everybody who loves each other should be together on

Christmas."

Sally looked at Adelaide and said quietly, "Out of the mouths of babes . . ."

Adelaide nodded solemnly.

The group left Big Rock a short time later. Sally drove the buggy that she and Smoke had brought into town, and Adelaide rode with her. The three youngsters were on the buckboard with Cal, and another of the Sugarloaf hands drove the buggy Preacher and Adelaide had used, with his mount tied on behind. The other cowboys were on horseback.

No more snow had fallen on Christmas Eve, but the temperature had never risen above freezing, so the world was white and peaceful around them. As long as Smoke and the others brought Ace and Doc back with them and settled whatever trouble had caused the fight at the town hall, the holiday could still be salvaged, Sally told herself. There was still Christmas Day, and as Hannah had said, if they were all together . . .

The ranch headquarters came into view. Sally couldn't see any lights up ahead, but she knew where they were by the way the mountains loomed darkly against the sky on both sides of the valley. This was her home, and while she might not know every foot of the range the way Smoke did, she would never be lost here. Skillfully, she brought the buggy to a stop in front of the house.

She was about to step down from the vehicle when the front door opened and a man stepped out. Sally frowned in surprise and puzzlement. The few cowboys who had been left to watch the ranch should have been in the bunkhouse. It wasn't as if the ranch house was forbidden to them or anything like that, but they shouldn't have had any reason to go in there tonight.

"What's wrong?" she called to the man. She still held the buggy's reins.

He moved closer to the edge of the porch and the steps leading up to it, out from under the shadows of the porch roof, and Sally caught her breath as she recognized the slender, deceptively casual figure.

"Not a damn thing wrong, Miz Jensen," drawled Travis Hinton as he tilted up the gun in his hand.

More men, who had been lurking in the gloom along the porch, stepped forward. The sound of gun hammers being pulled back filled the cold, quiet air. Some of the hands exclaimed in surprise. Sally knew they were probably reaching for their guns.

Winchester levers grated behind the riders. More gunmen emerged from the barn

506

and leveled rifles at the punchers on horse-back.

Hinton said, "You'd best order your men to take out their guns nice and easy and throw 'em on the ground, or those young'uns are gonna see some things they hadn't ought to see, ma'am. And with all the lead that's gonna be flyin' around, there's no telling where some of it might land."

Sally's voice was colder than the snow on the ground as she said, "You'd threaten innocent children?"

"No. That's why I said you'd better be reasonable."

"Miss Sally." Cal's voice was low and angry. "You know what Smoke'd want you to do."

"I certainly do," Sally said. Her left hand still gripped the reins attached to the buggy horse. Her right slid down into the seat cushions and closed around the butt of the little pistol hidden there. She was an expert shot, and she believed she could lift the gun and fire before Travis Hinton realized what she was doing. The gun was a small caliber, but big enough so a head shot would put him down. As soon as she pulled the trigger, she would whip the horse and make it lunge ahead, away from the pitched battle that was sure to erupt behind her. She knew that Cal would protect the children to the best of his ability, even if it meant throwing himself over them and protecting them with his own body. . . .

But before any of that violence could break out, another figure stepped through the doorway onto the porch, and Mariana Aguilar said in an urgent voice, "Please, Sally, do as Señor Hinton asks. If you do, I promise that no one will be hurt. Not Señora DuBois, not those three poor children, and not you or your friends. *Por favor,* Sally, just let us have what is ours."

"It's not yours," Sally replied through clenched teeth. "The Sugarloaf is mine and Smoke's! It always will be, as long as we live."

"Then, I am very sorry to say . . . you will not live. My husband will not be denied."

"He's a thief! Let him come out here and make his demands himself!"

Aguilar's knife-edged voice said, "I am already here, Señora Jensen." He stepped up beside Mariana and aimed the gun in his hand at Adelaide's head. "And unless you want that old lady's brains splattered all over you, you will do as you are told."

"You're not an aristocrat," Sally said. "You're nothing but a bandit!"

Aguilar shrugged and said, "Either way, I get what I want." He clicked back the gun's hammer. "Now choose."

She couldn't risk it, Sally realized. Too many innocent lives were at stake. Adelaide. Bodie, Hannah, and Teddy. And Cal and the other cowboys, those rough-edged but loyal, courageous, honorable young men.

She took a deep breath, blew it out, and said, "Cal, tell the men to throw down their guns."

"But, Miss Sally —"

"Just do it, Cal. This isn't over yet."

She knew he would understand what she meant. Aguilar and his gun-wolves might have the upper hand right now.

But Smoke, Luke, Matt, Preacher, Chance, and hopefully Ace and Doc were still out there somewhere, as were Pearlie and Monte Carson.

No, Christmas Eve was far from over. . . .

It was a solemn group that rode through the night toward the Sugarloaf. Doc's body was draped over the back of a horse led by Ace. Chance rode to his brother's right, and Luke was to the left. They didn't say much. Ace and Chance were still too stunned by everything that had happened tonight, from the raid on the town social to Doc's tragic death to the revelation that Luke was their father.

Smoke, Matt, and Preacher were in the lead of the little procession. Smoke thought enough time had passed that Sally and the others would have returned to the Sugarloaf by now, so he was heading for the ranch headquarters rather than Big Rock. Monte Carson was the only one who had angled back toward the settlement.

Ace had explained who the outlaws were and why they had kidnapped him and Doc. He had overheard enough of the conversation between Doc and Thackery while he was still pretending to be unconscious that he had a pretty good understanding of the situation. As happened all too often, greed had brought death and destruction to what should have been a festive occasion.

The bodies of the outlaws had been left where they fell. Monte Carson and Tom Nunnley would bring Nunnley's wagon back in the morning to recover them — although at this time of year, there was a chance that wolves would have been at them by then. Nobody was going to be too upset if such a grisly fate befell a gang of outlaws and killers.

Preacher said quietly, "You reckon ol' Doc was tellin' the truth about Luke bein' those

510

boys' pa?" They were far enough ahead of Ace and Chance that it was unlikely the brothers would overhear.

"I can't think of any reason he'd lie about it," Smoke replied. "I remember Lettie Margrabe teaching school there in Missouri, where we grew up. I was just a kid, but I know that she and Luke were fond of each other. I guess it was more serious than I was aware of at the time."

Matt said, "So you've run into those boys several times in the past, knew their last name was Jensen, but had no idea they were actually related?"

"You met them, too, and didn't suspect," said Smoke. "There are a lot of Jensens in the world. The whole thing is a mite far-fetched, maybe . . . but life is far-fetched a lot of the time."

"Well, I can't argue about that. If fate hadn't taken a hand, *I* never would have wound up being a Jensen." Matt shrugged. "So now there are two more of us. Can't ever have too many Jensens, I reckon."

They rode on, and as they approached the ranch headquarters, Pearlie urged his horse up alongside Smoke's and said, "I'm gonna ride on ahead and let folks know we're comin' in. Cal and the other boys are probably a mite on edge after what happened in

511

town tonight. They ain't trigger-happy sorts, mind you, but it never hurts to be careful."

"I was about to suggest the same thing," Smoke told the foreman.

"You want me to tell Miss Sally about Doc?"

Smoke shook his head and said, "No, I'll do that when we get there. But you could let her know that we don't have any wounded men who'll need tending to."

"You bet." Pearlie trotted off into the darkness, ahead of the others.

Luke moved up to join Smoke, Matt, and Preacher. He said, "I don't know if those two boys are ever going to come around. Both of them act like they're mad at me."

"They're young," Smoke said. "Give them some time to get used to what they found out tonight."

"Yeah, I know," Luke said with a sigh. "But I don't suppose I can blame them for being upset that they didn't know the truth."

"Well, you couldn't have told them, be-cause *you* didn't know, either," Smoke said. "I imagine they just don't know what to think right —"

He stopped short as gunfire roared in the night, somewhere not far away.

CHAPTER 45

Smoke knew instantly that the shots came from the vicinity of the ranch headquarters. The blasts stopped abruptly, and that was even more ominous.

"What the hell!" Preacher exclaimed.

Smoke reined up and turned in the saddle to call to Ace and Chance, "You boys stay here with Doc."

"We can't do that, Smoke," Ace said.

"That's right," said Chance. "We're Jensens. If there's trouble, we're coming along to help."

"Listen, you two —" Luke began.

"You can stop right there," Ace said. "You may be our father — Doc wouldn't have lied about something like that — but that doesn't mean you can give us orders."

"Yeah, we're all a little past that," Chance added.

Luke glared at them for a second, then

jerked his head to indicate that they should follow.

"Come on, then," he said. "Let's find out what that shooting was about."

The six of them galloped through the darkness, Smoke leading the way because he knew the terrain better than any of the rest of them and didn't need daylight to know where he was going. Ace still held the reins of the horse carrying Doc's body. They weren't about to leave him behind for the wolves.

As they came closer, Smoke slowed and finally stopped. The others did likewise. Preacher said, "You're thinkin' we'd best not go a-chargin' in there without knowin' what's goin' on, ain't you?"

"I think that occurred to all of us," Smoke said. "The rest of you, split up and close in quietly. I'm going to ride in, right out in the open."

Matt said, "You'll be putting a big target on yourself if you do that, Smoke."

"Maybe, but that's the quickest way to find out what's going on. And I'll wait a few minutes to give the rest of you time to get into position. Boys, if there's no one around the smokehouse, you can put Doc's body there. It'll be safe from any animals."

Luke said, "Smoke, you sound like you

514

have a hunch what that shooting was all about."

"I do. I think Aguilar's decided not to wait and let the lawyers hash it out. He probably figured with all of us chasing after those owlhoots, now was the best time to move in with Hinton and the rest of that gun crew and take over the ranch."

"Wait a minute," Matt said. "Aguilar?"

"Yeah, with everything else that's been happening, there hasn't been time to tell you about that. Some Mexican aristocrat, Don Juan Sebastian Aguilar, says an old Spanish land grant gives him ownership of the whole valley."

"Sebastian Aguilar!" Matt spit out the name almost like it was a curse. "He's not any sort of aristocrat, Smoke. He's nothing but a damn bandit. The *Rurales* ran him out of Mexico, and then lately I was helping the Texas Rangers track him down in the Rio Grande valley. He and his gang hit some banks down there and grabbed considerable loot, but then the Rangers caught up to them and wiped out the rest of the bandidos. Aguilar got away with the money, though, along with some señorita he picked up in a border cantina."

Smoke's jaw clenched. He asked, "Did you and Aguilar ever come face-to-face?"

"We sure did. We got a good look at each other — over gunsights and through clouds of powder smoke!"

"Then that's what happened," said Smoke with a curt nod. "Aguilar saw you come into the town hall tonight, recognized you, and slipped out before *you* spotted *him.* He knew he couldn't keep up that masquerade as Don Sebastian anymore, so he got his men and rode out to take over the ranch and fort up." Smoke's heart twisted a little in his chest. "He's liable to have Sally as a hostage."

"And Adelaide," Preacher said.

"And those kids," added Luke.

"And maybe Pearlie, since he probably rode right in on them," Smoke said. "That would explain the shots we heard." His voice hardened. "Do like I said and be ready to move when the time comes. We're going to root out those rats." He looked over at Ace and Chance. "Are you two sure you want to be in on this?"

"Just try and keep us out," Chance said.

The Sugarloaf ranch house
Sally knelt next to the sofa in the parlor and knotted a bloody rag around Pearlie's right thigh. The bleeding where a bullet had gone straight through his leg had slowed down

516

but didn't appear to have completely stopped yet. One of Aguilar's men stood guard in the corner, with a rifle in his hands.

"I'm sure sorry, Miss Sally," the foreman said, his voice taut from the pain of his wound. "As soon as I figured out them fellas were some of Aguilar's hired guns, I should'a turned my horse around and lit a shuck outta here, instead of tryin' to fight it out with 'em. That way I could'a warned Smoke and the others."

"You just followed your instincts, Pearlie," she told him. "No one can fault you for that." She paused as she finished the rough job of bandaging his wound. "Anyway, you got several shots off. That was probably enough to let Smoke know that something is wrong."

"Yeah, more'n likely." Pearlie grimaced. "And more'n likely, Aguilar's gonna be damned sorry he ever tried to pull off this slick job." He glanced across the room to another sofa, where Adelaide DuBois sat with the three children huddled around her. "Pardon my language, ma'am."

"Don't worry about that, Mr. Fontaine," Adelaide said. "Right now, I feel the same way."

Mariana Aguilar came into the parlor and nodded toward Pearlie. She said to Sally,

"Your man, he is not badly hurt?"

"Bad enough," Sally said. "And totally unjustified. Your husband has no right to do any of this."

Mariana shook her head and said, "I wish no one would be hurt, but Sebastian, he must have what is his."

"But it's not —" Sally stopped. She was tired of the argument. She didn't know if Mariana was totally deluded or just filled with the same sort of greed that possessed her husband.

Travis Hinton stepped into the parlor and said to Mariana, "Don Sebastian sent me to find you. He says you need to go on upstairs and stay there."

"There is about to be more fighting?" she asked.

"Bound to be. That fella" — Hinton nodded toward Pearlie — "tried to claim Jensen and the rest were nowhere around when he rode in, but Don Sebastian doesn't believe that, and neither do I. Jensen will be showing up soon. I reckon we can count on that."

The gunman's fingers caressed the butt of his Colt in anticipation. The gesture made a little shudder go through Sally.

Mariana said, "I want Señora Jensen, Señora DuBois, and the children to come with me, so they will be safe."

"The boss didn't say anything about that," Hinton replied with a frown.

"Then he did not forbid it, did he?"

"All right. But that cowboy's going, too, and, Carpenter, you'll keep an eye on him." Hinton chuckled. "We found a pistol hidden in the seat of that buggy. You were about to try to blast me, weren't you, Miz Jensen?"

"Maybe," Sally said.

"That's why I don't trust you, and I'm not gonna let you have a chance to get your hands on another gun. You watch *her,* too, Carpenter. She's probably more dangerous right now than this ranch hand is."

"I wouldn't bet your life on that, you low-down skunk," Pearlie said.

"I don't bet my life on anything except my own gun hand," Hinton snapped. "Get up."

With the hard case called Carpenter covering them, Sally helped Pearlie onto his feet. He hobbled across the parlor to the stairs and climbed them slowly, again with Sally's assistance. Carpenter followed them; then Mariana ushered Adelaide, Bodie, Hannah, and Teddy up the stairs in front of her. The children were clearly terrified, but so far they had kept their fear under control, except for a few muffled sobs from the two younger ones. Bodie was obviously struggling to keep a look of resolute courage on his face.

Hinton blew out the lamp in the parlor and stepped outside again. As Sally heard him close the front door behind him, she thought about Smoke. Earlier, Pearlie had whispered to her that Smoke was indeed close by, along with Luke, Matt, Preacher, Ace, and Chance. He had told her that Ace had been rescued safely but that Doc hadn't made it. Smoke had wanted to break that news to her, according to Pearlie, but under the circumstances, he thought it best that she know.

"Don't you worry," Pearlie said to her now as they climbed the stairs. "This'll all be over soon. Smoke'll see to that."

"I hope so, but Aguilar has more than twenty men."

"Yeah, and there are five Jensens, plus Preacher, out there. Those varmints don't know it, but they're plumb outnumbered."

The ranch house was dark and quiet as Smoke rode slowly toward it. With snow all around on the ground, on the roof, and in the branches of the trees, everything appeared as peaceful as could be, almost like one of those Christmas scenes in a Currier and Ives lithograph.

Smoke knew how deceptive that was, though. Death lurked behind all that apparent tranquility.

Smoke didn't take his horse to the barn, as he normally would have. He rode directly to the house and swung down from the saddle in front of the porch. Before he could move toward the steps, someone warned from the shadows, "Stop right there, Jensen."

"Hinton," Smoke said, recognizing the gunman's voice.

"You don't sound surprised."

"I'm not."

Hinton eased forward into view with another man beside him. That man spoke up, saying, "Let us not waste time, Señor Jensen. I have a deed here. You will sign it, giving me title to the ranch known as the Sugarloaf." A coal glowed orange as Aguilar drew in on the cigar clenched between his teeth. "Once this ranch is mine, I will deal with the rest of the valley."

"You're loco, mister," Smoke said. "I'm not signing that deed or anything else. You can't steal this ranch from me."

"I am not stealing anything. We are making a fair trade, you and I. Your ranch . . . for the lives of your wife, the old woman, the children, and all your men."

"You'd threaten innocent women and children?"

"I do what I must," said Aguilar.

For a moment, Smoke didn't say anything. He was calculating where Luke and the others would be. They'd had time to move in on the ranch on foot. Nobody was better at moving stealthily and spotting enemies than Preacher, and the others were almost as good. By now they would be ready to strike at Aguilar's men in swift and deadly fashion.

"You may have crossed the border and put on a bunch of airs," said Smoke, "but you're still the same cheap Mexican bandido you always were, Aguilar."

That gibe pushed Aguilar over the edge. He threw down the deed in his left hand, jerked up the gun in his right, and the cigar fell from his mouth as he shouted, "Kill him, Hinton! Kill the gringo bastard!"

CHAPTER 46

Hinton's hand flashed toward the gun on his hip at the same time Smoke made his draw. The two Colts cleared leather at the exact same instant.

But Smoke had to worry about Aguilar, too, since the bandit's gun was already out and spouting flame at him. Smoke shifted a hair to his left, and that movement slowed him down just enough for Hinton to get off the first shot. Aguilar's bullet fanned Smoke's cheek.

Hinton's ripped through his coat, missing him by less than an inch.

The .45 roared and bucked in Smoke's fist. He saw Hinton take a step back and knew the shot had found its mark. Hinton gasped, "You son of a —" and fired again. This time the slug whined past Smoke's ear.

Smoke snapped a shot at Aguilar, but the man was already ducking back through the door after firing once. The bullet chewed splinters from the jamb.

Hinton stumbled forward on the porch. Smoke was about to shoot him again when the Texan lost his grip on his gun. It slipped through his fumbling fingers and fell. Hinton came after it, plunging headlong to land with his arms and legs sprawled across the steps and his face buried in the snow at their foot. He didn't move.

Smoke bounded over him and leaped across the porch into the doorway. As he did so, a muzzle flash from the other side of the foyer split the shadows. Smoke didn't know where the bullet went, but it missed him. He returned the fire and then through the echoes heard rapid footsteps headed toward the back of the house. With his top gunman dead, Aguilar was fleeing, rather than standing and fighting.

Smoke went after the man who had tried to steal the Sugarloaf.

Luke and Matt were positioned at either end of the bunkhouse, watching Smoke's confrontation with Aguilar and Hinton. When the shots began to thunder, several of Aguilar's gun-wolves ran out of the building to gun Smoke down from behind.

That was their intention, anyway, but Luke and Matt didn't give them time to do that. They stepped into the open, and Luke shouted, "Hey!" causing the gunmen to stop short and try to swing around. Luke and Matt opened fire, and for a long moment, the area in front of the bunkhouse was a storm of lead sweeping back and forth. Gun flame stabbed through clouds of powder smoke that rolled across the scene. Both Jensens felt bullets slap through the air near them but remained unhit as their slugs plowed down Aguilar's hard cases.

Yelling and more gunfire broke out inside the bunkhouse. Luke turned toward the door and lifted both Remingtons, but he held his fire when he recognized the young cowboy who burst into the open and brandished a gun.

"Hold your fire, Cal!" Luke called. "I think they're all down out here."

"Luke!" Cal exclaimed. "Matt! We jumped the ones who were still inside —"

"Figured as much, kid," said Luke. "Anybody hurt?"

"Yeah, a couple of us were hit. I don't know how bad." Cal looked around. "Where's Smoke?"

"Last I saw of him, he was headed into the house after Aguilar," said Matt.

"Then come on!" Cal cried, breaking into

a run in that direction. "What are we waiting for?"

Ace and Chance were at the back door of the barn. A few minutes earlier, after scouting the smokehouse and not finding any of Aguilar's men lurking around it, they had carried Doc's body into the little building and placed it carefully and respectfully on the ground. They hated to leave Doc there, but at least his body would be safe for a while.

Smoke had told them to wait until the shooting started to make their move, and so far that delay had drawn their nerves taut . . . nerves that were already under a strain because of Doc's death and the life-changing declaration that had followed it.

Both of them believed what Luke had told them, but they weren't sure what to do about it. Or whether they should do *anything* about it. The revelation that Luke was their father didn't have to alter their normal course of action. It wasn't like all of them were going to settle down together. Ace and Chance didn't believe that was possible for Luke, any more than it was for themselves.

Then shots rang out, and the future had to take a backseat to the present. With a grunt of effort, Ace hauled the heavy door open, and Chance charged into the barn, with his brother right on his heels.

Ace had brought a gun taken from one of the fallen members of Lane Thackery's gang back where that battle had been fought. As the group of Aguilar's gunmen posted in the barn started to boil out to open fire on Smoke, Ace and Chance took them from behind, slashing bullets through their ranks. Killers fell without knowing what had hit them, but some of them managed to stay on their feet, swing around, and throw lead at the Jensen boys. A bullet cut Ace's right calf just above the top of his boot and dropped him to one knee, but he steadied himself with his left hand on the ground and drilled the gun-wolf who had just wounded him. A few feet away, Chance's Smith & Wesson barked again and again.

Then, as the last of the hired guns fell, a bullet kicked up dirt between them, causing Chance to jerk a look over his shoulder.

"Ace! Up in the hayloft!"

Ace rolled one way and Chance dived the other as more slugs sizzled between them. Both of their guns blasted at once, and the man who'd been hidden in the loft, cutting down on them with a Winchester, went up on his toes as their bullets ripped through him at an angle. He dropped the rifle and then followed it down, turning over once in the air before landing on his back in a lifeless sprawl.

Ace struggled to his feet. Chance saw the blood on his trouser leg and said, "You're winged!"

"Not too bad," Ace assured him. "There's still shooting going on out there. We need to be right in the middle of it."

"Where else would Jensens be?" Chance responded with a grin.

When he was a young man, during the fur-trapping era, Preacher had waged a long, bloody war against the Blackfoot tribe in the Rocky Mountains. In those days, he had been able to slip unseen and unheard into a village full of his enemies at night, slit the throats of half a dozen sleeping warriors, and slip back out without anyone knowing he had been there . . . until the next morning, when his grim work was discovered. This had prompted the Blackfeet to dub him the Ghost Killer, and Blackfoot mothers had used the threat of that deadly phantom to frighten their children into behaving.

Old or not, Preacher was still damn near as stealthy as he had been back then. Because of that, no one saw him approach the Sugarloaf ranch house. He was just one more shadow in the night. No one heard him raise a window and climb in, and his feet on the rear staircase as he crept up it made no sound.

Smoke would be starting the ball soon, Preacher was sure of that. But before that happened, he wanted to locate Sally, Adelaide, those young'uns, and any other hostages Aguilar might have in here. As he paused in the upstairs hallway, he saw a faint line of light under a doorway farther along the hallway. He slipped up to it silently and put his ear against the door to listen.

"Bound to wind up with a bullet in your gizzard," someone was saying inside the room. "I've seen it happen over and over again to hombres just like you who were dumb enough to go up against Smoke Jensen."

That was Pearlie's voice, thought Preacher as a grim smile tugged at his mouth. He was glad to know that the foreman was still alive. Still full of piss and vinegar, too, from the sound of him.

"Shut your mouth, mister," a man responded harshly. "Jensen would need a small army to take on our bunch."

"That's where you're wrong. When I left

him, he had everybody he needed to win this war. And that ain't even countin' Cal and the rest of the boys. You may have disarmed 'em, but that don't mean they won't fight back as soon as they get the chance."

"You're wasting your breath arguing with him, Pearlie." That was Sally, and another surge of relief went through Preacher at the knowledge that *she* sounded all right, too. "He's going to have to find out for himself . . . to his everlasting regret."

Preacher wished that Adelaide would speak up, too, so he could stop worrying about her. Instead, one of the kids said, "I don't like this. I wish all these men would leave. It's going to be *Christmas* tomorrow!"

"You're right, sweetheart," Sally said. "This is no time for such terrible things to be happening. Sometimes we don't have any choice but to deal with them, though."

Preacher had a Colt in his right hand. With his left, he reached down and took hold of the doorknob. Moving so slowly that it wouldn't be noticed, he tried to turn the knob. It didn't budge. *Locked on the inside,* he thought. That made things more difficult, but it wasn't going to stop him. He backed off a little, sensing that the showdown was going to come soon.

His instincts didn't fail him. Only a few more seconds had ticked by when guns suddenly roared from the front of the house.

Preacher reared back, lifted his foot, and kicked the door. Wood splintered and gave, and the panel flew open. He was through the door in less than a heartbeat, his eyes going to the roughly dressed, bearded hard case who was trying to bring a rifle to bear on him. Preacher pressed the Colt's trigger. The gun boomed, and Aguilar's man flew back against the wall behind him as if slapped by a giant hand. He didn't fall or drop the rifle, though, so Preacher shot him again, the bullet drilling a neat hole an inch above the man's right eyebrow.

That was the end of it. The Winchester and the dead gun-wolf both clattered to the floor.

All three kids were screaming in terror from the gunfire. Sally and Adelaide tried to comfort and quiet them. Preacher heaved a great sigh when he saw that Adelaide appeared to be unharmed.

Pearlie, with a bloody bandage around his thigh, shuffled forward and picked up the rifle. More shooting came from outside, and then some blasts that sounded like they were somewhere in the house.

"Reckon our side needs some help,

Preacher?" asked Pearlie.

"Let's go find out," the old mountain man said.

Sally's heart still pounded wildly, but as Preacher and Pearlie hurried out of the room, she took a deep breath and turned to Adelaide.

"You're all right, aren't you?"

"I'm fine, dear," the older woman assured her. The three children were still crying, but they had stopped screaming.

"Can you watch these little ones?"

Adelaide glanced at the dead man's bloody, crumpled body and said, "They might calm down better if we weren't in here."

"That's a good idea. There's another bedroom right across the hall. Why don't you take them in there and stay with them until I come back to get you?"

"Of course, but . . . where are you going?"

Sally stepped over to the dead gunman, reached down, and took hold of the revolver holstered on his hip. She pulled the iron out of leather and straightened.

"I have to go find Smoke and make sure he's all right."

"Oh. Oh, dear." Adelaide was a little wild-eyed but in control of herself. "Well, do whatever you think best, dear. I'll see to the children."

Sally nodded and stepped out of the room into the hallway, holding the gun in front of her with both hands. Her thumb was looped over the hammer, ready to pull it back if she needed to. She heard shouting and shooting outside, but the battle sounded like it was dying down. She was confident that Smoke and his family and friends had emerged triumphant.

But she wanted to see her husband with her own eyes and know that he was all right.

She had just reached the top of the stairs when a faint whisper of sound came from behind her. She started to turn but froze at the touch of cold, sharp steel at her neck.

"Throw the gun down the stairs, Sally," Mariana Aguilar said. "Otherwise I will have to kill you, and I have no wish to do that."

"Mariana," Sally said. "You don't have to do this. Just because your husband has caused all this trouble —"

"Truly, you think Sebastian came up with the plan to take this valley as our own?" Mariana laughed softly. "He is a bandit, nothing more. Crude and vicious, but he has his uses. He took me from the cantina that was my prison and brought me with him. He might have been content to waste the money he had with him on easy living, but I found a better use for it. A sanctuary where no one — *no one!* — would ever be able to force me to go back to the life I once led."

"Then everything you told me before . . . about the two of you . . . was a lie?"

"We each make our own truths, do we not?" The knife at Sally's throat pressed harder. She felt the sting of the blade, the warm trickle as a drop or two of blood slid down her neck. "Throw the gun down. I will not tell you again."

Sally tossed the gun down the stairs. It thudded and bounced and came to a stop.

"Now we go," said Mariana. "I have to find Sebastian."

A gun blasted as Smoke started out the rear door. He ducked back as splinters stung his face. Aguilar fired again, then ran toward a group of saddled horses milling around, the mounts belonging to some of his men. If he managed to grab one of them, he might still get away.

That had to be his hope, anyway. Smoke darted out of the house and snapped a shot after him. Aguilar cried out and staggered just as he reached the horses. They shied away from him, but as he twisted around, he managed to catch hold of a stirrup and steady himself. The gun in his hand sagged, but he didn't drop it as he stumbled back a step toward Smoke.

Smoke strode toward him, Colt held easily at his waist. He called, "It's over, Aguilar. I know who you really are, and I know that whole land grant business was a sham. I reckon we'll be sending you back to Texas. I figure the Rangers will be mighty happy to get their hands on you."

"I will not . . . go back," Aguilar grated. "I will never go back. This is . . . my land now."

"Maybe you've fooled yourself into thinking that, but you've got no chance of ever making it come true."

"If I can . . . kill you . . ."

From Smoke's right came Luke's voice, saying, "It'll be the last thing you do, mister."

"Because you'll be full of lead half a second later." That was Ace, to Smoke's left.

"You took on the wrong family, Aguilar," Matt said as he strode forward to join Luke. "You should've stayed in Texas."

"Overplayed your hand and lost the bet," added Chance.

From behind Smoke, Preacher said, "Me and Pearlie are backin' your play, too, Smoke."

"And Cal and the rest of the boys would love to get in on this," Pearlie put in.

Smoke never took his eyes off Aguilar, but he could *feel* the strength of the force arrayed behind him. He said, "So you see, Aguilar, you don't have any chance at all."

"No, Sebastian! Do not give up!"

A shrill cry of pain came from the back door of the house. Smoke recognized his wife's voice and jerked around. Mariana emerged, forcing Sally ahead of her. The knife she held at Sally's throat glittered. A part of Smoke's brain realized that it wouldn't be doing that unless light from the moon and stars was shining on the blade. The overcast had finally broken.

The other men split apart, forced by the threat to Sally's life to create a lane, through which the two women advanced slowly. Smoke stayed where he was, between Mariana and Aguilar.

"Step aside, Señor Jensen," Mariana hissed. "Sebastian and I are leaving this place, and no one will follow us, because Señora Jensen is coming with us."

"Don't do it, Smoke," Sally said. "Don't let them get away."

Smoke said, "I don't intend to."

"You have no choice," said Mariana. "Do as I say, or I put this knife all the way in

Sally's throat."

"You do that, you and your husband will both die."

"But it will not bring her back to life, will —"

Sally suddenly twisted in Mariana's grasp and lashed out with an elbow at the other woman's face. The knife must have bitten into her neck, but she kept moving and cried, "Smoke, behind you!" as she dived to the ground.

Smoke whirled and saw that the wounded Aguilar had summoned up the strength to lift his gun. He had been about to shoot Smoke in the back when Sally made her move. It would have been a futile gesture — the others would have filled him with a pound of lead in the blink of an eye — but his hatred had forced his hand up with the gun in it.

Smoke fired at the same time Aguilar did. The bandit's bullet whipped past Smoke. The slug from Smoke's gun smashed into Aguilar's chest and knocked him back. He dropped his revolver, reeled from side to side in an effort to hold himself up, but crumpled inevitably to the ground, to lie in the snow as a dark, motionless heap.

Smoke heard gasping and turned, saw Mariana stumbling toward him. She still had the knife in her right hand, but her left was pressed to her belly, a dark stain spreading around it. Smoke knew then where Aguilar's bullet had gone.

Mariana lifted the knife, driven on by her own dying hate, to try to bury it in Smoke's flesh, but she was still ten feet away when she collapsed facedown in the snow and didn't move again.

Smoke looked at Luke and Matt and said, "The rest of Aguilar's men?"

"Most of them are dead," Matt replied. "The few who aren't are tied up good and tight in the bunkhouse, with men guarding them."

Smoke pouched his iron and hurried to Sally, who had gotten up from where she had fallen. She was using her right hand to brush snow off her dress while she held her left to her neck. Smoke took her in his arms and asked, "How bad is it?"

"Just a cut, Smoke, that's all. I'll be fine, I promise."

He hugged her and let relief wash through him. Then he said, "Come on, everybody. Let's go back around front."

He wanted to leave Aguilar and Mariana back here together. And he would see to it they were buried together in Big Rock. Maybe they deserved that much.

Whether or not they were together in hell . . . well, there wasn't much he could do about that.

When the group reached the front porch, they found Adelaide and the three children waiting for them. The older woman said, "Some of your cowboys said it would be all right for us to come out here, Mr. Jensen. They said the fight was over."

"It is over," Smoke said as he put an arm around Sally's shoulders. "And look up there. You can see the stars again. The clouds are gone."

"I reckon it's after midnight by now," said Preacher. "That means it's Christmas Day."

Smoke might have said, "Merry Christmas," but he was just too blasted tired.

CHAPTER 47
THE SUGARLOAF, CHRISTMAS
MORNING

Maybe Luke was right, Smoke thought as he listened to the happy sounds of the three youngsters playing with the toys Luke had given them as presents. Maybe it was time he and Sally started thinking about having some little ones of their own. There was plenty of room in the house. They had built it with that in mind, in fact, expanding from the log cabin Smoke had built when they first came to the valley, back when he was pretending that the notorious outlaw and gunfighter Smoke Jensen was dead.

Sally sat next to him on one of the sofas in the parlor, snuggled against him, with his arm around her shoulders. The cut on her neck she had suffered the night before had a bandage on it, but that was the only sign of the trouble. Inside and out, the bodies had been carried away and the blood had been cleaned up. Out in the bunkhouse, the two hands who had been wounded in the fighting were patched up and resting, expected to recover fully from their injuries.

Luke sat in an armchair, with his legs stretched out in front of him and crossed at the ankles. He was smoking one of his infrequent pipes. The rich, pleasant smell of the tobacco blended with the delicious aroma of the turkey roasting in the oven, as well as that of baking bread. Luke smiled as he watched the children playing in front of the fireplace, where flames danced merrily.

Then his eyes lifted to Ace and Chance, who sat on the other side of the room, and his expression grew more solemn. Ace's right trouser leg showed the bulge where his wounded calf was bandaged. The same was true for the dressing on the wound on Chance's upper left arm.

"Boys, we need to have a talk," Luke began.

Ace shook his head and said, "Not now."

"Not on Christmas Day," Chance added. "Time enough for that later."

"Yeah, it's already been more than twenty years, hasn't it?" Ace said.

Luke regarded them intently for a moment, then nodded and said, "All right. If that's the way you want it."

Matt came into the room, holding a doughnut in one hand and a cup of coffee in the other. He smiled and said, "I hope you don't mind me stealing one of these early, Sally. I promise it won't ruin my dinner."

She laughed and told him, "Just don't let Cal see you with it. He'd be mortally offended if he knew somebody else got into the bear sign first!"

Matt sat down to enjoy his midmorning snack. A warm, peaceful feeling filled the room. It might have been any happy home on Christmas morning, with the family members gathered around the tree, enjoying being together.

Preacher and Adelaide strolled in, as well, arm in arm, and Preacher cleared his throat before announcing, "Folks, I reckon I got somethin' to say —"

A sharp, urgent knock on the front door interrupted him.

Sally looked up and said, "Maybe that's Monte. He's still coming out to have dinner with us, isn't he, Smoke?"

"As far as I know," Smoke replied, "but that didn't sound like Monte's knock."

The other men in the room seemed to share that feeling. All of them sat up straighter, as if worried that trouble had come calling on the Jensens once again.

Smoke stood up and left the parlor to

answer the summons. He wasn't wearing a gun, but a loaded Winchester leaned in the corner beside the door, within easy reach.

The caller didn't appear threatening, at least not when Smoke swung the door open. He was in his thirties, fair haired, well dressed, and wore spectacles and held his hat in his hand.

"Mr. Jensen?" he said.

"That's right."

"My name is George DuBois —"

That was all Preacher had to hear. He stalked angrily into the foyer and exclaimed, "Watch out, Smoke! That's the varmint who's been tryin' to kill Adelaide."

It was a good thing Preacher didn't have a gun, Smoke realized. If the old mountain man had been armed, he might have been dusting the visitor's britches with lead by now.

George DuBois looked horrified by the accusation. He said, "That's not true! I'd never harm my grandmother. I'm here to keep her from . . . to prevent any more . . ."

As he struggled to find the words for what he was trying to say, Adelaide came into the foyer and gave him a stern look.

"You shouldn't be here, George," she told him. "You can just turn around and ride away, and there won't be any harm done."

543

"Grandmother," George said. "I'm so glad to see that you're all right. You haven't . . . I mean, the old gentleman isn't —"

"The *old gentleman* is right here," Preacher snapped, "and you ain't wanted in these parts, sonny. Fact is, if you ever try to hurt your grandma again, I'll plumb wring your neck and turn your carcass inside out!"

George paled at that threat and even took a step back, but he stopped and visibly gathered his courage. After drawing a deep breath, he said, "I see that I'm going to have to be blunt, painful though it may be for all of us. I'm not here to harm my grandmother in any way, sir. I came to prevent her from killing *you.*"

That brought shocked stares from Smoke, Preacher, and Sally, who had followed Adelaide into the foyer. After a couple of seconds went by, Preacher said, "Of all the loco —"

"I would never hurt Arthur," Adelaide said calmly. "We're going to be married."

George shook his head and said, "No, Grandmother. You know you can't do that."

"I don't see why not."

George looked at Smoke and Preacher. "Please, gentlemen. I have proof of what I'm saying. Perhaps if you'd step outside, I could show you . . ."

"All right," Smoke said as he picked up the Winchester. "But this had better not be some sort of trick."

"No trick, I assure you."

Preacher said, "Smoke, you don't mean you believe this varmint —"

"I'm willing to hear him out," Smoke said. "That's all I mean. And then, when he's said his piece, if I need to run him off the Sugarloaf, I will."

"That's fair enough," said George.

"Sally, why don't you take Adelaide back into the parlor?" Smoke suggested.

"All right, Smoke," she said. She looked upset and confused, but she took Adelaide's arm and steered the older woman back into the parlor.

As Smoke and Preacher stepped out onto the porch with George DuBois and Smoke closed the door behind them, Adelaide was saying, "This is all unnecessary . . ."

The sun was shining brightly today, glittering on the snow, but the temperature was still cold enough to make the men's breath fog in front of their faces. The rented saddle horse George DuBois had ridden out here from Big Rock was tied to the porch railing. He reached inside his coat and brought out several pieces of paper. They were clippings from newspapers, Smoke saw as George held them out to him.

"Those are obituaries," George said. "As you can see, they come from several different cities."

Smoke scanned the printed names and read them aloud: "Charlie Repp. Homer Olmsted. John Nafziger."

"Wait just a damn minute!" said Preacher. "I know all those fellas. Been on fur-trappin' expeditions with all of 'em, back in the old days. And they was friends with . . ."

"That's right," George said as Preacher's voice trailed off. "They were friends of my grandfather, too, just like you, sir."

Smoke read the death notices more closely and said, "Each of these says the fella was survived by a widow named . . . Adelaide."

"Yes, I'm afraid so. My grandmother was married to each of them. And although the obituaries say that each man died after a short illness, if you talk to the authorities in the towns where they lived, you'll find that in each case, the law suspected that the men had been poisoned. There just wasn't any proof of it."

Preacher looked flabbergasted. He said, "This is just . . . I can't believe . . ."

It was unusual for the old mountain man to be thrown for a loop, but clearly, he was.

George went on, "Ever since I realized

546

what was happening, I've been trying to find my grandmother before she could . . . well, before she could do it again."

Smoke held up the newspaper clippings and said, "These don't prove she's done anything wrong."

"No, sir, they don't," George said. "But you have to admit, the circumstances are very suspicious." He looked at Preacher. "Suspicious enough that when I found out she had come west with another old friend of my grandfather's, I thought I ought to warn you."

"I don't believe she'd ever hurt me," Preacher declared. "In fact, I was gonna ask her to marry me just now in there, with the whole bunch gathered around."

"I really wish you wouldn't, sir. I want to take her home with me."

"So you can get rid of her and inherit all her money?"

"No. Because of this."

George reached inside his coat again and took out an envelope this time. He handed it to Preacher, who removed a sheet of paper and read it. When he was finished, he looked even more shaken than he had been before.

"This is true?" he asked George.

"You can see it for yourself." George

looked at Smoke and explained, "It's a letter from my grandmother's doctor back in St. Louis. She may look fairly healthy, but she's actually very ill. A few more months . . ."

George spread his hands helplessly.

Preacher sighed, folded the letter, and returned it to the envelope. He said to Smoke, "Lemme see them obituaries."

Smoke handed over the clippings. Preacher read them all closely, then gave them back to George.

"Only one thing to do," he muttered. He turned and went back in the house.

George looked at Smoke, who shrugged and said, "Come on. I've known him for years, and I don't have any idea what he's going to do, either."

In the parlor, Adelaide had sat down on the sofa with Sally. Preacher went to her and held out his hands. She smiled and took them, and he helped her to her feet.

"Adelaide," he said, "your grandson, George, is gonna spend Christmas with us, and then you and him are goin' back home so he can take care of you. That'll be nice, won't it?"

"Why, Arthur, I thought I would just stay here with you!"

"But I'm not stayin' here," Preacher said.

"The high lonesome's callin' me. I got to go back to the mountains. You know how it is. Us old-timers just can't stay away."

"Are you going fur trapping?"

"I durned sure am. There's a whole heap of beaver pelts just a-waitin' for me out yonder."

"I could come with you —"

Preacher shook his head and said, "No, the high lonesome ain't no place for a woman. You go on back with George, and when I get done with trappin', I'll come see you there. I give you my word."

She smiled and nodded, said, "All right, Arthur. If that's the way you want it."

He hugged her, patted her on the back. George DuBois had moved over to where Preacher could see him as he looked over Adelaide's shoulder. The man mouthed the words *thank you.*

Preacher nodded slowly and held on to Adelaide, clearly not wanting to let go.

The Sugarloaf, 1902
Denny leaned over and punched her cousin Ace hard on the arm.

"That's terrible!" she said. "What a horrible way to end a Christmas story!"

"Not really," Ace said. "Everyone was together, and even though Adelaide and

549

Preacher didn't get married, they were able to spend a little more time together before she went back East with her grandson."

Louis asked, "Did she really kill all those other men she was married to?"

"There was never any proof one way or the other . . . but later, Sally found a letter hidden in the room Adelaide had been using. It was from another of Preacher's old friends, telling him about the deaths of those men and warning him to be on the lookout for Adelaide. She must have intercepted it somehow, and the fact that she kept it from him seems to indicate that she might have felt guilty."

"Did she . . . pass away?" asked Denny.

Ace nodded and said, "Less than three months later. And Preacher went back to visit her grave, just like he'd promised."

Denny frowned and muttered, "I still think it's terrible."

"Life's always a mixture of good and bad," Ace said. "The trick is trying to keep the scales tipped to the good side."

Louis said, "I'm curious about something else. Did anyone ever find the money from that train robbery? The loot that Bill Malkin hid?"

Chance laughed.

"That wild yarn Doc spun was closer to

550

the truth than anybody guessed at the time," he said. "Tom Nunnley, who was the undertaker in Big Rock then, actually did find some letters in Malkin's saddlebags. They were addressed to a woman who had been married to Malkin. He was trying to win her back, and he'd told her where the loot was cached. She didn't want any part of it and gave it up to the law. If Thackery had just listened to Doc —"

"I'd be dead," Ace pointed out.

"Well, yeah, there's that to consider."

Denny said, "It sounded like the two of you didn't get along very well with Luke. I thought everything was fine with all of you."

"It is," Ace said.

"It just took a while to get there," added Chance. "You've grown up knowing who your father is. We had to get used to it."

"I suppose that makes sense."

The sound of a horse's hooves came from nearby. The four of them looked around as Smoke reined up on the creek bank a few yards away. He rested his hands on the saddle horn and said, "Denny, I thought you rode out here on the range to work, and instead, I find you lollygagging around with your brother and your cousins." Then he grinned to show that he wasn't actually scolding her.

Denny stood up, brushed off the seat of her trousers, and said, "I'll have you know you'd have one less calf now if I hadn't pulled it out of a mudhole at considerable risk to life and limb."

"And even more risk to her dignity," said Louis. "You should have seen her, Father, covered in mud from head to foot."

"Wouldn't be the first time," Smoke said as his grin widened.

"Ace and Chance were just telling us about the Christmas when they found out that Uncle Luke is their father," Louis went on.

Smoke thumbed back his hat and nodded.

"That was a pretty eventful holiday, all right," he said. "Lots of things happened, good and bad."

Louis asked, "Are there ever any Christmases in the Jensen family when all hell *doesn't* break loose?"

Smoke chuckled as he turned his horse and lifted a hand in farewell — for now.

"It's a family tradition," he said. "See you back at the house!"

ABOUT THE AUTHORS

William W. Johnstone has written nearly three hundred novels of western adventure, military action, chilling suspense, and survival. His bestselling books include *The Family Jensen; The Mountain Man; Flintlock; MacCallister; Savage Texas; Luke Jensen, Bounty Hunter;* and the thrillers *Black Friday, The Doomsday Bunker,* and *Trigger Warning.*

J. A. Johnstone learned to write from the master himself, Uncle William W. Johnstone, with whom J.A. has co-written numerous bestselling series including The Mountain Man; Those Jensen Boys; and Preacher, The First Mountain Man.